BEYOND THE LIVING:
reconciliation

TJ. NGUYEN

This book is a work of fiction. Any references to real-world events, real people, or real places are used fictitiously. Other names, characters, places, and events are products of the author's imagination, and any resemblance to actual events or persons, living or dead, is entirely coincidental.

Copyright © 2024 by TJ. Nguyen

TO THE REASONS WHY I DON'T RECONCILE
AND TO THE ONES WHO REFUSED WHEN I BEGGED THEM TO

AUTHOR'S NOTE

Everyone knows a good reader visualizes.

I'm not sure if this is just me, but whenever I read cliché romance novels, I always envision *myself* as the main character. I like to play it out like a movie; watch myself live a different life and decide whether I'd like it or not. Sometimes I'd get mad at the actions I see myself making, cringe at dialogue I hear myself say, and close the book due to secondhand embarrassment.

But this isn't a cliché romance novel.

This book is about a teenage girl surviving a modern dystopia.

What I'm asking you is, don't envision Mj as You.

Think of her as someone you don't want to be.

To make the series more enjoyable, reading *298 DAYS* before reading *RECONCILIATION* is extremely recommended.

"You got yourself into this."
I never denied that.
"You went out of your way to ignore the advice you were given—and now you're hurt because you caught *feelings.*"
I didn't catch feelings.
"We all warned you, Mj. We all told you to stay away from Klein."
He is not a good person when it comes to things like this.

PROLOGUE

Every high school freshman drastically matures going into their sophomore year. That's what they sure hope. But things are different now, we *all* had to grow in a way.

It was hard for me at first. I was stuck in my own head, convinced this was just a chance for me to live out my fictional fantasies. Those fun times playing pretend stopped once I realized those last days with my friends were really *my last days with them*, and the choices I made meant *everything*.

I think about the past a lot, and I know I'm hard on myself sometimes. Throughout these years, I've convinced myself I'm unsociable and mean, but I say that then get confused when I find people naturally luring towards me. I guard myself up, Jake was right about that.

I expect the worst.

If they're older, they're preying on me. If they're my age, they're nothing but a bad influence or a bitch I don't feel like talking to.

When they're younger... I guess when they're younger, I go easy on them. I don't like babies unless they're calm. I don't like toddlers unless they're quiet.

It's the pre-teens; the twelve-to-thirteen-year-old girls that for some reason loved me.

It's weird knowing they looked at me the same way I looked at Maxwell, Bailey, and Conti. When I told Sgt Rogers about it, he strongly agreed and told me that was what I was meant to be. I was *their* Aaron Scheuch.

It was hard to process.

The more I think about it, I don't believe him, regardless of how many times those girls could call me and ask me to do their makeup and borrow my clothes, and tell me I was the sister they never had.

The meaningless things those girls would talk about; the things they were convinced were so important, I would do nothing but stand there and listen with that warm feeling in my heart. I would look at them and smile, giving them the advice I wish I could've told *me*.

I don't ever feel the annoyance, nor do I shudder at the fact I used to be just as ignorant as them. Instead, I look at them and sympathize—know they don't know any better. I look at them and remind myself it's all they know, and even though the advice I give won't register immediately, I know they'll take it as they will.

I do that because that's all I want people to do for me.

I once said I'd much rather them think I was upset over him than anyone else. I take that back. I take it all back.

I don't want to write this from start to finish. I don't see any point in telling you the beginning to the end so *you* can picture yourself in my situation and feel the way I felt. I don't need you to do that. I don't need you to pity me.

I just want you to *understand*, understand *WHY*.

I *know* I was just fifteen-sixteen years old. I *know*. But instead of scoffing and thinking *I'm too young—I don't know anything—I don't have any idea*, look at me, and remember how it was when *you* were fifteen. Look at me, and understand that *it was all I knew*.

It was everything until it wasn't.

I understand I'm not innocent. I had the opportunity to leave and I ignorantly chose to stay. That's all you need to know.

You don't need to know about the times he would say stupid shit like: *I'm the J to your M,* or how good my ass looked in jeans, or when I asked him for a drink, he thought it meant booze and not water, or the countless times he'd tell me he was sorry for the way he treated me and blamed it on his sadism because that would be absolutely, incredibly, astronomically *disgusting*.

You already *know* how the story would end, and you'd be sitting or standing or listening to me here thinking, *don't do it, Mj.*

And for the record, I don't care if you're a sadist. I don't care how sadistic you are. I don't need to know why you became sadistic. Stop *telling* me you're sadistic!

People ask why, and I'll say I don't know why. I say I don't know a lot of things from that time of my life, but there was one thing I knew,

I knew how the story would end too.

I don't deserve the reconciliation.

RECONCILIATION

<u>Stop pretending that conversation was real.</u>
<u>Stop pretending that conversation was real.</u>
<u>Stop pretending that conversation was real.</u>
<u>Stop pretending that conversation was real.</u>
<u>Stop pretending that conversation was real.</u>
<u>Stop pretending that conversation was real.</u>

PART 2

reconciliation

I don't want to be a good person anymore.

This part involves potentially sensitive topics including depression, pedophilia/grooming, abuse, addiction, domestic violence, death, gore, abduction, vulgar language, substances, underage drinking, racism, and *possibly* more ...

READER'S DISCRETION IS ADVISED.

section 1

~~DAY 351 / THE NIGHT WE SCATTERED~~
stop pretending that conversation was real.

This part is separated into two sections.
This section will focus on what happened in the year and seven months between CHAPTER 19 and the EPILOGUE of BEYOND THE LIVING: 298 DAYS.
Chapter 1 starts in September 2022, the hour leading up to the epilogue before jumping back and forth between the journal entries Mj Bui wrote prior and chapters that reveal what each cadet was going through after Chapter 19, in early 2021.

1 cheer up, guys, it's labor day

~~MICHELLE MJ~~ CADET BUI

There was something bloodcurdling about the air. It itched me in parts I couldn't reach.

Sully went and sat upon the stone steps of her porch, setting her palms on her lap worriedly. She tilted her chin and shut her eyes, gulping under the faint moonlight and battery-powered lantern above her.

Scheuch was snapping his fingers, looking down at his worn-out sneakers as he passed by on the sidewalk. Once he looked to his left and saw what Sully was doing, he took a second before deciding to join her.

He sighed before sitting down beside her discreetly, resting his elbows on his knees. He fidgeted a bit—wiped his nose then rubbed his neck. Sully opened a single brown eye to take a look at him.

He noticed and gulped briefly. "I don't remember the last time I prayed."

She smiled faintly, seeing the nervousness seep through the honesty in his eyes. "It's been a while since I've prayed too," she replied softly before shutting her eyes again, adjusting herself back to the sky.

He did the same but it seemed hopeless for the both of them—knowing what they went through. They sat there in silence for what seemed like forever, and no matter how hard they tried, even from the deepest depths of their hearts, they couldn't find anything to say to Him.

"Hey, Aaron?" she asked softly.

"Hm?" he replied gently.

"When was the last time you talked to Bui?"

He turned his head, replying vaguely, "I don't know."

Watching her sigh, she opened her eyes. "*Have* you been talking to her at all recently?" she asked, lowering her eyebrows.

It took a second for him to calculate his answer. He was now faced forward, shaking his head as she sat there waiting anxiously.

He replied. "No."

She then scoffed, stood up, and patted down her denim jeans stressfully. "C'mon, we're gonna be late. It's almost curfew."

She began hopping down the porch steps before turning back around, looking at him softly; watching him yawn and take off his glasses to clean them.

"Aaron."

He looked up quickly, raising his eyebrows. "Wassup?"

She took a deep breath. "Remember to tell her happy birthday, okay?"

Sgt. Rogers has been organizing weekly get-togethers in hopes of helping us connect and repair our relationships with one another. He wishes it would be under nicer circumstances, but we are way past the *'getting to know each other'* stage by now. We've been through far too much together.

We've been having these meetings for a few weeks now, but it'll never be the same without Conti and Johnson with us and he knows that. That's mostly the reason why they've all been so miserable these past few months anyway.

Has it been months? No, no, it's been a year now.

I was sitting next to Sully as the group listened to Candreva and Yanes' cheerful jokes over Klein's guitar playing.

We circled around a fire, leaning against logs, tree trunks, and the walls of the RV. I can't remember the last time I said much other than giving simple orders on behalf of Sergeant or Scheuch. I just sit observing as usual. Sometimes I get so silent it starts to feel as if they forget I was there.

It's not like I *want* them to notice me. I never want them to. It was always easier that way.

It's my birthday.

~~Stop pretending that conversation was real.~~

It's my birthday, and I'm still seventeen. I don't feel any different, but I know I did change to an extent. I want to say I'm not as dependent on their validation anymore, but that wouldn't be true.

I never needed their approval, and it wasn't like I needed to prove anything to myself either. I just needed to stop creating unrealistic versions of them in my head and look at them for who they really are—*the worst in them.*

I sat in silence listening to Yanes tease me lightheartedly about my haircut. I looked over at Kim as soon as he mentioned it, looking at the way she nervously had her arms over her knees—but I made sure to not stare for too long before she'd start crying.

My. Hair.

"Hey, why *did* you cut your hair?" Candreva asked.

I replied through gritted teeth. "I didn't."

Every year I cry on my birthday, whether it'd be over a breakup or a fight between my parents and I. Now that I am without a boyfriend and parents this year, I was looking forward to getting away with it.

I was *really* looking forward to a peaceful eighteenth birthday, but Kim didn't like that I was—quote-on-quote—*talking shit* on her again and decided short, collarbone-length hair just—*suited me more.*

I don't know why she won't quit the bullshit yet.

She's nineteen years old.

I can't prove it was her, and even if I could, it wouldn't change anything. What am I going to say? She came into my room and cut my hair in my sleep? What am I going to *do?* Give her a good beating? My hair won't grow back any faster than it'd take for her bruises to heal, so I'll choose to say nothing. I know I'd definitely feel better knocking a couple teeth out, but I don't know. My knuckles need a break too.

I'll choose to say nothing.

I'm still furious about it, though, but I'll choose to say nothing. The last time I cut it was when I let Tyson do it, but I'll choose to say nothing.

Everywhere I go, I lose more pieces of him.

~~Stop pretending that conversation was real.~~

Klein's back to being high and righteous, but the act's transparent. People are starting to see through him the same way as I do, and as much as I'm glad he has no fucking friends and no fucking nobody,

I don't have anybody either.

I don't feel any less lonely picking on him.

He has no one else and it's nothing but a damn shame. But at the end of the day, he put that on himself—*just* as much as I put this on *me*.

I guess I can see why people would think it was my fault he ended up this way.

But issss thaaaat myyyy problemmmm? Doooo I caaarreee?

Nah.

I know I haven't been the most mature about this situation either, but does it look like I have any interest in changing my behavior any time soon?

No!

He turned eighteen
before I could even be old enough
to get my learner's permit.
I am now the age he was when he met me.

"Aw, guys, this is so nice," Sully sighed beside me. "I'm so happy right now." I turned to her, narrowing my eyes. "I don't know," she shrugged, "I like when we do this. It all feels like we're one big family!"

I nodded sarcastically. "Aw, *yeah!* I'm about to *cry!*"

She looked at me. I looked back at her with a straight face.

"Oh-" she replied awkwardly. "What's wrong?" she asked.

"What do you mean?"

"You've been really quiet."

I shrugged. "I don't know. I guess I just zone out a lot."

She stared at me for a moment, quiet as per usual.

I looked back at her. "*What?*"

She took a deep breath and rubbed the back of her neck. "I—I don't know, are you *sure?*" she asked quietly. "You've been quiet for a *while*."

"Yeah, I know," I replied, stretching my shoulders. "Nothing's left, Mary," I shrugged. "We've barely managed with the way our crops have been doing. Autumn's going to pass, then winter will be coming soon and we barely managed the last one."

Nothing came after a year of waiting. No cure. No direction. García was never found. Jade Street was raided another couple times, so every day was the same. A group goes out for supplies, a group stays back and finishes simpler tasks, and a group rebuilds or repairs the barriers. We've only been surviving with what we've got, and what that was, wasn't much.

"Yeah," she sighed, shrugging slowly. "I guess the best thing we can do is just stick together. There's *always* a solution to something."

I sighed. "We're all going to die anyway."

It was weird. The more I spoke, the more her smile grew. I found it in me to admire that about her—the fact there was nothing left for us and yet she still had the strength to find the good.

"Then nothing's really changed," she replied.

I looked over at her.

"I mean ... if you really *think* about it," she shrugged again, waiting for a reply.

I remained silent.

She sighed, lifting her left hand and rubbing my shoulder. "I don't think it's good to be alone in a world like this, so I was wondering if you wanted to hang out with *me!*"

Now Sgt. Rogers sent a lot of the command staff my way after I distanced myself from the group. After a while, I figured he just gave up and let me be—which is what I *wanted*—but I feel like what got my attention this time was that it was *Sully* trying to make an effort with me. He never gets her involved in things, and she and I were never that close, ~~not since I started pushing her away.~~

Now she's allowing me to be.

I guess I shouldn't be as surprised. It was easier to talk to Sully regardless of how shy she was since she was a girl. Maybe I do deserve at least somebody.

We've all been lonelier than we've ever been since they died.

We call that night, the night we scattered.

Conti was the heart of our group—friends with everyone, selfless, patient, gentle, and caring. Even in the worst of times, she could still push through and make the best of it.

And Johnson... I didn't realize how much I'd miss him until he was gone—even with the grudge I held against him for being so aggravating. The others loved him. They always desperately tried to convince him to see how much value he had. I would *occasionally* enjoy his presence, but sometimes it would feel like he was only here to suck up everyone else's negativity—and I know in a way it's true because the second he left us, we all collapsed.

Bailey made it out alive, though. It would've been my last straw if he died on me that night too. He was sitting across from Sully and I, next to Candreva and Yanes, who were still quietly snickering at something that only made sense to them. He sat quietly, picking at the dirt from underneath his nails.

"Maxwell, is that our last jar of pickles?" He broke the silence.

Maxwell was sitting diagonally from him, eating quietly. "Yeah," she replied mid-chew, "gotta eat 'em now or they'll go bad. Want some?"

"Mmm," he narrowed his eyes. "Nah."

"You sure?"

"Mmm," he thought again, "yeah, sure."

He reached over as Yanes finished his little joke, but none of them were really in the mood to laugh. I could just tell by looking at their faces.

I looked around, seeing Scheuch and Klein. I looked and observed, watching the both of them sit silently with dried blood still splattered across their faces from the supply run earlier that morning. Klein wiped his nose before stretching his fingers over his guitar, playing a few tunes to keep himself busy. It wasn't like he had much to say to us.

Scheuch was silent, but only for different reasons. I was actually surprised he was still there. He disliked these types of things.

"I do not thrive during social events," he would say.

I looked away with a disgustingly sour look on my face before I accidentally made eye contact with Bailey. I watched as he observed my face before scoffing, looking around before reaching into his backpack. Once he bent back up it didn't take me long to realize what it was.

He leaned forward, slamming a large bottle of liquor onto the ground. "Cheer up guys," he smiled faintly. "It's *fuckin'* Labor Day!"

Maxwell glanced up. "It's Labor Day?"

He nodded, watching me basically lunge for the bottle since no one else seemed to want it. I figured he would be the type of person to say something like that due to how he was such a workaholic before the outbreak started.

And now, I wasn't sure if he had a drinking problem, but that didn't matter to me. I out of all people should be able to understand why you would want to drink during times like these.

I opened the cap and helped myself as the others watched, mortified.

"Hey—*Hey!* Easy!" Sgt. Rogers lowered his eyebrows.

"Where did you even *get* that?!" Maxwell asked worriedly.

Bailey smiled wide before yanking it from my hand, taking a large gulp himself before hissing, "Found it. Want some? Trade a sip for another pickle."

She hesitated for a moment. "Maybe later."

"What even *is* Labor Day?" Kim asked in her spot. "I always mix it up with Memorial Day."

"How do you mix that up with Memorial Day...?" Yanes murmured.

Candreva joined in, with the same tone. "I would understand mixing Memorial Day with Veteran's Day but-"

"You don't know what Labor Day is?" Sgt. Rogers turned over to her, surprised.

"No," she shook her head shyly, leaning forward and dramatically asking, "*Aaron...?* What is Labor Day?"

"Labor Day is celebrated annually for the social and economic achievements of American workers," he replied in his spot, speaking as he picked at the large scab on his knee.

Watkins leaned over and narrowed his eyes. "What happened to your knee?"

"Fell."

Kim remained in her spot, nodding as I felt her eyes move from his blank face to mine. "Thanks!" she smiled widely.

Sgt. Rogers took that as an opportunity. "Wa-Wait, wait, who can tell me the difference between Memorial Day and Veterans Day?" He looked at all of us with a smile.

"Memorial Day is for—"

"Except Scheuch," he quickly interrupted as a few of them chuckled. He looked over at me. "Do *you* know?"

My face remained still. "Memorial Day is for the dead ones."

Sgt. Rogers nodded with his hands on his lap. "Yes," he sighed with a wide smile. *Is this because I finally spoke or because I got it right?* "Veteran's Day is for *all* of the militaries, Memorial day is for the ones who didn't *duck* in time!"

Okay, not gonna lie, that was funny. Still didn't smile.

"Oh *c'mon*, Mj. You know that was funny," he teased.

Nope. Still didn't smile.

Candreva was sitting cross-legged on the dried grass, staring into the fire as he chuckled. He glanced up at Sergeant, "Is that this week's topic?"

He scoffed. "No, I was hoping one of you guys would come up with something."

Candreva nodded, looking through the fire and over at Sully and I, "You two, what are some of your *biggest* accomplishments?"

Sully looked up to the dull sky to think. "Hmmm, does it have to be *recenttt* ... or?"

"Doesn't matter," he smiled back at her.

I hope she realizes how lucky she is to have someone talk to her like that.

I watched her brown eyes move to mine. "I don't know," she replied cheerfully. "Bui, what's your biggest accomplishment?"

"I'll get back to you on that," I replied automatically, forcing them to move on to another person.

I sat in silence, trying to listen to the others communicate, ignoring the murmurs from my left implying that there was something wrong with me and that I had officially lost my mind.

I think they're a bit late.

But what got to me this time was the fact Kim actually had a point. I *am* losing my mind, and by the looks of it, the other cadets were only talking to me to see if I'd snap or to try to prevent me *from* snapping. She thinks I'm a danger to the group. She thinks my behavior will weaken them.

I. Don't. Belong.

I sat and heard Watkins say something about being sober for a while. I sat and listened to Maxwell say something firefighter-related and Scheuch mention something about—*cheese steak*. I swear he loves those.

The group didn't start *really* laughing until it was Klein's turn to speak. He lifted his chin with a grin on his face, "I'm good in bed."

"WOOOAAAH!!" They collectively reacted. "*KLEIN.*"

Only a few of us remained silent. I was too busy judging how hard Kim had to fake her *flustered, high-pitched, dainty* laugh.

It really wasn't that funny. I swear, maybe she's right about something being wrong with me.

I only chuckled *a bit* when I heard Scheuch mumble as he rubbed his forehead, "That was uncalled for," but then I remembered how I felt about him too.

"C'mon Bui, tell us *your* biggest accomplishment," Maxwell asked me quickly, forcing an uncomfortable smile.

My *true* biggest accomplishment was that I managed to go years without laying a hand on someone, but I couldn't say that.

I gulped. "I've been better at being patient."

My voice sounds as dead as I look.

"*That's* a shocker!" Candreva teased me before shaking his head. "Just kidding, Mj."

He smiled widely, drinking from Bailey's bottle and pointing at Sully. "*My* biggest accomplishment is that she hasn't broken up with me yet."

The group giggled as he nodded his head vigorously. She and I didn't though, we looked at each other confusedly.

"I'm *serious!* I have *no* clue how I managed to pull this off!" he chuckled. "Mary, tell 'em 'bout that one time we went to the mall!" he said as she awkwardly smiled.

She explained and we listened. After a while, this whole group get-together thing didn't seem so bad.

"I miss being able to do those things, y'know?" she explained cheerfully, turning to me. "What about you, don't *you* miss the old times?"

"A little," I replied.

"Oh *c'mon*," she rocked me back and forth gently, "tell me you don't miss being able to swim without *one* piece of trash clinging onto you!"

"That's nobody's fault but our own."

"True," she replied. "What *do* you miss then?"

"Yeah!" Kim joined in. I guess she couldn't stand the fact that I was smiling. "What *do* you miss, *Michelle?*" she asked curiously.

BEYOND THE LIVING

"Your family? Your friends?" She paused, then suddenly slouched, making a pouty-face. "Oh wait…"

Silence. Just silence.

I watched as all of them turned to her resentfully, knowing we all finally had it in us to have an engaging conversation for the first time in a while, and now it was ruined.

She cannot go one day without starting something.

I thought pulling a gun on her was enough.

"Sure," I could've replied nonchalantly to deescalate the situation. "Okay, Eliza."

But I didn't. I let the others attempt to clear the air after processing what was said.

"No, *no*, we are *not* doing this right now!" Sgt. Rogers ordered firmly, which honestly frightened me a bit. "Not after everything we've been through! You two just need to move the hell on at this point!"

"What did *I* do?" I asked defensively.

"What *didn't* you do?" I heard Kim mutter.

My head snapped over. "Are you *asking* me to punch you at this point?"

"*Bui—*" I immediately heard the others groan.

Sgt Rogers was firm, shaking his head. Scheuch was informative, quickly explaining how incredibly unnecessary that was, and watched it seem to upset her more.

I felt my smile fade. I felt my back warm. I looked around realizing nobody was here to baby her anymore, meaning nobody was here to knock sense into me either.

"What the *fuck* is your problem?" I asked.

"*Bui—*" I immediately heard Scheuch.

"No, seriously," Kim began her act—breaking her voice, quivering her lips, tearing up her eyes, trembling her hands—realizing none of them were going to go up, rub her shoulders and tell her, *"It's okay, just ignore her, she's just like that,"* and that the most they were going to do was only shake their head and ignore her comments—exactly how they were going to ignore mine. "I don't understand how any of you guys could still *trust* her!" she began whimpering. "She's putting us in danger!"

Fun Fact: the last time she cried in front of me over the things I've *"done"* to her, I straight up laughed in her face and told her to get a hobby.

"Why would you think she's a danger to our group?" Candreva asked, half-chuckling. "She doesn't even *talk!*"

"*Look* at her, Brody!" she snapped—her voice almost breaking character. "I don't understand how someone could be comfortable with just sitting next to her!"

I leaned closer to Sully, muttering as she and Candreva bitched back and forth, "Do you guys really think that low of me?"

"No," she replied softly, "At least *I* don't." She sighed, "Mj, I don't think anyone here will listen to her, trust me."

"Have you *heard* the things she's said?" I asked.

"I've heard her tell me you had a thing for Brody a few months ago?"

My jaw dropped. "Are you *serious?*"

"But it's *ok—*"

"It's *not,* Mary!" I scoffed. "What if you believed her? Imagine how many *problems* that would've caused!"

"I *didn't* because she told *Brody* the same thing," she reassured, "just about *Scheuch.*"

BEYOND THE LIVING

Suddenly I felt my back tense, my jaw clench, and my lungs cave in. "She—She said I had a thing for *Scheuch?*" I asked as the way her soft smile grew. "What kind of narrative is that?" I scoffed, amused. "A scenario where I ask him to fix my tangled necklaces, stare at him wit' googly eyes for a bit, then go ham?" She laughed along with me as I said, "Like what the fuck's wrong with her?!"

"The tattoos at sixteen...? The scars on her knuckles...?" I heard Kim's voice continuing. "She may be different *now,* but people like that don't change. She's nothing but ... a *trashy hoodrat!*"

"That's *your* opinion," Scheuch replied nonchalantly, eyeing Bailey's liquor thinking he might need a bit of that too.

"Really, Scheuch? *Really?*" she stammered as I gave everything not to crack a smile seeing the snot that just flew out of her nose. "How many times has she dragged you guys down out there?" she argued. "How many times have you had to *help* her?"

"Let me ask you something, Kim," he sighed. "How many times have we brought *you* out for a supply run?"

ZERO!!!! .

"Kim, can you go one day without being so *fucking* desperate for attention?" I asked aggressively. "Can't you tell all the *pouting* you do only makes people wanna stay the *fuck* away from you? You don't even make any sense half the time. *I thought I was a spoiled bitch from the suburbs,* now I'm a *trashy hoodrat*? That's crazy. Stirrin' up a shit-show for *what?*" I leaned closer to her, laughing through my teeth, "cause I know even after all that ramblin', you still ain't got *shit* on me!"

I leaned back and snatched the bottle from Scheuch and chugged down the rest of it. I hissed as I felt my body loosen up, but unfortunately so did my tongue.

"You don't know *anything* about me, Kim, but you're right about one thing, I may be a vile... *vicious*... cunt," I spat, my voice returning back to normal as I absorbed the mortified look on her face, "but you're a *Godless* sack of miserable *shit!* Every time I look at you, Kim, I don't *feel*... anything... until you open that *fucking* mouth of yours and show me that by *some* miracle, after everything I've done to get you to stay the *fuck* away from me, you can *still* manage to stoop down lower than *I* can!"

"Oh my God, Mj." One of them mumbled.

"I think you're a big waste of space," I spoke over them. "So the next time you pout to one of the boys that you're *so* depressed, come to *me*."

I'll *help* you kill yourself.

The loud silence. The quick snickers from Bailey and Maxwell followed the shock on everyone's faces and Kim's ugly crying. My vision began to blur and suddenly I couldn't hear anything but the fire crackling in front of me. I turned, hiding the amused smile hidden behind my hand. I wish I could say I regretted saying something, but I didn't. I couldn't find it in me to.

This was Satan's way of punishing me. Her constant reminders were here to let me know that no matter what I do, I'll never be able to be good enough for redemption. My past will always haunt me, and the choices I made will forever affect the way people treat me.

I've tried to come to terms with it, but it makes me angry.

How could someone judge me without walking *any* distance in my shoes? How could someone judge something they'd never be able to understand?

In moments like these, I look over at Bailey, who knows exactly what happened to me that makes me so angry. I assume that was the reason why he never bothered to try and fix me.

He would just ignore the amount of anger and grief in my veins and pat my head, telling me, "Be good, kid."

I don't think he understands how much I love it when he calls me that.

It wasn't like I buried my guilts and hid them—walked around with my head high like I was better than everyone else, but I wasn't walking around feeling unworthy either. I knew where I was. I assumed people like them knew where they were too. I was wrong.

I had my wrongs written down on a page in my journal so I wouldn't forget. They were all the things I've done, or the things I've done and knew were wrong.

November 18. 2020.
[untitled]

1. aiding and abetting
   - carjacking
   - fraud
   - identity theft
   - stalking
   - trespassing
2. alcohol abuse
3. assault
   - broke a boy's jaw
   - broke a boy's nose
   - knocked a girl's front tooth out
   - gave a girl a concussion
4. breaking and entering
5. drug dealing
6. extortion
   - blackmailed a boy with his own explicit photos
   - blackmailed a boy with his family's history
   - blackmailed a girl with her own incriminating videos

RECONCILIATION

7. forgery
   - screenshots
   - signatures
8. incrimination
9. shoplifting
   - jewelry
   - paint and paint brushes
10. theft
    - stolen watches and pawned it
    - stolen opiates and sold it
    - stolen money and cards out of wallets
11. vandalism
    - keyed a couple cars
    - slashed a couple tires
    - spray painted doorsteps

When I told Bailey, all he did was chuckle. "Rookie."

I paused, looking back at the way he was looking at me. His gestures and tone never changed. "You—don't think?"

"I think most of this shit's *light work,*" he said. "Come back to me when you rob a bank." He paused as I laughed. "I—ehhh—*nevermind,* this program really did a number on you, kiddo."

Kim wiped her tears. "That... *hurt,*" she whimpered.

"Kim, *enough,*" Sgt. Rogers said. "I'm tired of this bullshit." He turned to me, "and *you,* you need to *calm your ass down.*"

I fired up again. *"She's* being fuckin' stup-"

"Mj, you took it *too far!*" He shut me up.

Kim was crying. I wasn't. I guess you can see how that could look from a third party. She looked like the victim and I looked like a horrible person.

I rolled my eyes, my voice frighteningly calm. "I swear Kim, you just be sayin' shit just to say it," I scoffed, turning over to her. She was slouched over her knees lookin' stupid, looking up at me through her eyebrows lookin' stupid, pouting her lips lookin' stupid.

"*Bui!*"

"Do you *EVER* stop to *think* there could be a *reason* for the things I do?" I asked.

"You always make excuses," she shook her head.

My jaw began to fall as I glanced at everyone's faces, knowing exactly what they were thinking, thinking of *me*.

I turned back to her. "Yeah, lemme just go around and start shit I can't finish," I said. "Yeah, lemme just go 'round breakin' people's jaws just for shits and giggles." I took a deep breath, yelling. "ARE YOU *FUCKING* DUMB?"

"Bui, volume," Sully said softly.

"I understand they were treating you horribly—" Kim cried. *You don't understand jack shit.* "But it doesn't matter! *You* should've been the bigger person!"

"Fuck this shit, bro," I scoffed, getting up from my spot. "Fuckin' ignorant bitch!"

2 AUGUST. 2021.

2 August. 2022.
[untitled]

    I think I just might choke the next person that asks me why I'm so quiet.
    I understand people will always talk shit. I've always known that.
    I don't need somebody to enlighten me with a motivational speech about it.
    I genuinely don't care about Kim. No part of me wants to be involved with her.
    At first, the things she came up with were funny. Usually I wouldn't sit and waste my time writing about something I genuinely don't care about, but it's getting to the point where it's not fucking funny anymore. It's getting annoying.
    It's annoying that I feel like I have to bend over backward to accommodate how she's feeling. "She's uncomfortable with me being here." "She's bothered by me." Okay? Go cry me a river.
    I'd understand if it was because of past history or whatever, but we aren't friends. We've never been friends. I've never done jack shit to her. I didn't do any of the bullshit she says I've done in the past either. I swear these bitches be actin' like I fucking murdered somebody.
    I was just fucking troubled. End of story.

Cameron Watkins is one of the only people I can speak to unfiltered. I'm not sure how I feel about that. All I've been doing since Conti dying is making sure he's okay. It was rough watching Aaron break the news to him during that time. We never thought a guy like him could cry like that.

    Sometimes when I'm hanging out with him, I can still hear him sobbing with Aaron telling him that drinking himself to sleep isn't going to make her come back.

    It baffles me that Aaron thinks he's not good with grief. I watched him make Cameron stay occupied with tasks so that he wouldn't think about her. It didn't work.

    Their room was a decent size—looked like any other shared bedroom among siblings; except they *weren't* siblings. No one ever expected Cameron Watkins and Aaron Scheuch to get along.

    The room was split down the middle, almost like how María and I structured ours. Watkins had the left, Scheuch had the right, and walking in, I could just tell whose side was whose.

Scheuch's bed was neatly made. He even had a desk with a lantern, a pencil cup, and a shit ton of textbooks.

"Damn," I chuckled to myself, pointing to them.

"What?"

I bent down to look, "I like how the world has basically ended and yet he still finds time for physics."

Watkins scoffed. "Yeah, he spends at least an hour going through that every night——tried explaining it to me once."

I turned to look at him. "Did you get it?"

"A little."

I tried not to look through his stuff, but my curiosity took over me.

Advanced Physics Textbook. Atomic Structure Textbook. Advanced Calculus Textbook. More math. More science. Blah blah.

I turned around. "Has he been tryna—"

"Yeah," he replied, rubbing his eyes. "Don't tell the others though—"

"OK," I replied, "anyway—do you think I have a right to be upset?"

"Of course you do," he nodded, "but I think you shouldn't let her get to you."

Every day has been the same. I sit on the other side of the room on Scheuch's made bed to face him, and he faces the door with a cigar or joint or blunt or whatever he calls it between his fingers.

"It's a blunt," he chuckled. "Joints are ass."

I still don't know the difference.

"She's not," I replied stubbornly. "I just think it's stupid she's making herself out to be the victim in a situation she created. I swear she's fuckin' lucky I'm not like that anymore 'cause she'd have her teeth knocked out by now."

"Understandable," he replied. "So wait, is this the reason why you're so mad at the group? 'Cause they take her side?"

"Part of the reason, yes. They don't necessarily take her side, though," I replied. "Just—sometimes I get angry at the way they deal with it."

She can call me a spoiled brat, but if I were to say something, I'd be the immature one. I'm not a ran-through slut, but if I were to say something, I'd be told to be the bigger person.

"Like if they're gonna stick their noses into the situation, at least try to deescalate it and not just fuckin' *tell* me to," I scoffed.

"Mhm," he shook his head.

"I mean, it'd make more sense if she called me spiteful or somethin' but the way she does describe me makes me sound like some entitled, cunty bitch and what?" I rambled. "I'm just supposed to stay silent, pretend everything's okay when people around me start lookin' at me like I'm somethin' I'm not?"

Oh, let me guess ... the talk is expected.

There's always gonna be that bitter bitch.

I'm gonna have to be in places where people don't like me.

I gotta suck it up and deal with it,

but since I'm considered 'upset' for even just mentioning it,

I supposedly, 'can't handle it'.

Right?

Is that what they think now?

I can't handle it?

When the group was in shambles for the first few months after waking up from this shithole and Scheuch, Bailey, Sgt.

Rogers, Maxwell, and I were the only ones who kept their shit together,

I. Couldn't. Handle. It.

We flinched as we heard Scheuch walk in. He was covered in blood and filth, even his glasses were crooked.

"Hey Aaron," Watkins smiled.

Scheuch rolled his eyes, smelling the smell of smoke in the air. He dropped his bags and walked over to the window, cracking it.

"I'm too tired to kick you out right now," he mumbled.

I lowered my eyebrows, realizing he was talking to me, but before I could say anything he plopped onto the bed behind me, passing out.

"Oh," I giggled a bit, looking back over at Watkins. "Anyways, they gotta be fuckin' joking, dude," I rubbed my hands down my face, "I'm so done."

"I know," he replied, looking past me and at Aaron, snoring softly behind me. "Just try your best to stay away from her."

"I literally can't," I replied. "This has been an ongoing thing—shit goes way back, long before the outbreak even started! Yet even with the world ending, she still can't leave me the hell alone! Y'know, if I could actually bring myself to, I would go back to the way I used to be and cut contact wit' all of 'em but for once, Cameron, for once I actually value the relationships I have in this group. What she says changes everything!"

"Didn't you just say you were mad at them?"

"No—I meant—" I rubbed my forehead, "—the people I actually give a shit about. Like you, Bailey—and—*Aaron*—" I said his name as he snored.

"So go tell Aaron," he said. "I bet you he has way better advice to give than I do."

I turned around, expecting to smile and lay a blanket over him, not wanting to wake him up, but instead I was horrified at the sight of him. The way he had recklessly fallen had caused his dark gray t-shirt to lift up, revealing mouth-shaped scars along his torso. They were indents, *deep*, indents that have once punctured the skin and now have healed.

He opened his eyes. We stared at each other silently.

"Is he still asleep?" Watkins asked behind me as I stammered.

"I—I—no, he's asleep," I replied as he tugged his shirt, groaning and turning around, facing the wall.

"Oh, alright, just tell him about it tomorrow, then."

That thought horrified me.

Like seriously horrified me.

"Yeah, fuck that."

2 stereotypical
CADET STERLING

I walked into high school preparing to throw every stereotype out the window. I do admit I did have high expectations. I psyched myself out a little too much thinking the upperclassmen were just mature as they portrayed themselves. At the end of the day, they're only a few years in front of me, growing up alongside me. (In some cases, not at the same rate.)

But in NJROTC, specifically *our* high school program, stereotypes meant everything.

Suddenly, I was pushed around and left out, but it was fine since I was a 'freshie' and there were drastic maturity differences among the grade levels. Suddenly all the seniors were entitled and mean, but it was okay because they were seniors and I had to just let it go because they were all gonna graduate soon.

Suddenly the list of "types of people" I made up in my head were real. They were all so real yet it felt weird to describe them out loud.

Carter Sterling: the patriotic redneck from Texas that goes to school in brown leather boots, red and blue flannels, and a cowboy hat who spends most of his time playing hockey or hanging at the firehouse. To my surprise, he's not racist at all. He just chuckled when I told him I would've got a silver Lexus for my sixteenth birthday. (I still don't get it.)

Aaron Scheuch: the female-repellent bookworm—always in the same clothes, running miles for fun, and eating flower stems. I'm talkin' West Point summer camp and Christian youth groups. If he somehow didn't end up shooting up a high school, I bet you twenty bucks in fifteen years, he'd be wrapped up in one of the most notorious unsolved murder cases, landing in the top ten most-wanted serial killers in American history. I weirdly find him cool, though, but it's all fun and games until I find a collection of dissected animals in his freezer.

Kiara Maxwell: the eighteen-year-old millennial. She doesn't dress like one in my opinion. I've only seen her in skinny jeans, silver "crystal-healing" jewelry, and earthy-colored hoodies. I liked how friendly and charismatic she was, even when I sometimes cringe at the things she says. Talking to her felt like gossiping with a 'chill mom'. She used to take a long time to answer texts and would sometimes even forget how to send one. We weren't kidding when it would seem like she was old. The only times I would see her on her phone is when she would fixate on match 3 puzzle games.

She was on Level 5014 in Candy Crush.

Ari Jacob Klein: the guitar-playing, incense-lighting, hopeless romantic, spending his time swooning for a chance to fall in love, to *really* fall in love. He knows he won't be good at that, whether he gets a fair chance at it or not. Every girl knows he's not a good person when it comes to things like this, so if by some miracle you do want to get to know him, you can find him by a bonfire smoking weed or at a college party snorting cocaine off the bathroom counter.

You won't ever catch him drinking tequila again though. The boy does not handle alcohol well.

Cameron Watkins: the car-obsessed, football-playing stoner. Unlike Jake with his blue jeans and bass guitar, Cameron was debatably an even *heavier* party animal than he was. He never talked about it around me though, knowing it sometimes made me uncomfortable. But despite spending most of his time listening to his favorite (deceased) rappers and burning through paychecks within days on drugs and booze, compared to the other bums out on the streets, he was actually doing well. Most twenty year olds would've dropped out after failing twice. He would've been the first in his family to graduate high school. He frightens everyone at first, but he never blames them. Even with the tattoos on both arms, silver weed leaf earrings, and split dyed hair—he's nothing but a sweet, gentle teddy bear; an older brother—until you piss him off. 10/10 don't recommend it.

Mary Sullivan: ... marching band *blah blah blah* the church girl who would never hurt a fly *blah blah blah* had a pet pig and at least 3 dogs *blah blah blah* I've never even heard her say "hell" *blah blah blah* she used to try to convince me to switch from soccer to cross country *blah blah blah* her convincing was by far better than Aaron's way though ...

ME: I would, but Marí and Jada don't want to do it with me.
A-A-RON: Call them fatasses.

Brody Candreva: Eighteen going on twenty-eight *blah blah blah* horror fanatic *blah blah blah* has 'cool uncle energy' and would imitate how NPCs would walk and speak with me *blah blah blah* punctures my knuckles every time we would do our handshake (it's not me!!!) *blah blah blah* used to turn anything into remixes and design posters.

Mickey Yanes: ...

███ Bailey: ...

Elizabeth Kim: ...

And so on.

The point is, everyone was unique in their own special way, yet they all bound together like threads of yarn. It had me wondering who I was and what I had that was special about me. All I have ever done in my life was let people pick pieces of me apart to please them. That's all Michelle did. Mj would tell them to go eat their toe lint and spend the rest of her life angry for letting people make her angry.

I understand Sterling leaving was partially my fault.

I should've understood how it would've felt to be in his shoes. All he's ever wanted was to be included too. But I also realize some people get shut out for a reason, whether they deserve it or not.

His lack of awareness on social queues and failure to handle situations properly sabotaged him, but wasn't that just like any other high school boy? That doesn't mean he was incapable of being a nice person?

Apparently that didn't matter to our NJROTC.

But no matter how high his community service hours were, no matter how many times he showed up to drill, people were still told, *"Yeah ... don't talk to him."*

There *had* to be a reason.

People don't get treated like that just *'cause.*

I know *I* had reasons for people to hate me.

So I hung out with him until I could figure it out in hopes of fixing him, and at that time I didn't care what the others would've thought of me if I did.

"Oh, *she's friends with Carter? That's a red flag.*"

Go choke yourself with a pool stick.

You shouldn't be alone in a world like this.

Sometimes it felt like people disliked him just because everyone else seemed to—as if it was abnormal if you didn't. No one ever gave *Jonah* Adkins shit for it, which I assume was because they considered it lucky he brought himself to socialize with anyone other than his brother, Jackson.

So why would they give *me* a hard time?

I felt bad. I *really,* really felt bad.

I felt bad for him because no matter how mean someone could be to me, I would never allow myself to get used to it. I would never water myself down to satisfy someone's thirst. I would never allow myself to take that disrespect, but he does because he's used to it.

I watch him get along with Klein, Scheuch, Sully, Candreva, and Yanes. I watch him smile and say Hi to them every day. I watch him tell them hockey stories and laugh at his own jokes.

Then I listen to the way they talk about him when he's not there, and fear they do the same to me.

~~Please like me.~~

But after a while, I began to understand. After a while, it was harder to make excuses for him.

"Do you guys have a THOROUGH understanding of this?" Sgt. Rogers asked firmly. "I'm tired of having to answer stupid questions."

Sterling raised his hand swiftly. "I have a question!"

"Oh, dear God," Scheuch put his face in his hands.

But then again, I wasn't there to make excuses, I was there to fix.

He was good at what he did. He contributed to the firehouse. Maxwell wasn't lying when she told me he used to follow her around like a lost puppy. He was one of the best players on his hockey team, which made him come off as cocky whenever he mentioned something about the sport. On the bright side, it's better than being terrible at it and pretending you aren't. Imagine how embarrassing that would be.

He would talk about the same things, and he would talk about them *a lot*——but one thing I noticed ... was how he never talked about his family.

I could just tell he missed being home in Texas.

That's exactly where he headed that night after he took off. He spent nights on the road, silent as he watched hungry roamers trail past his truck before he fell asleep. He traveled down south with the same logic we had. He experienced a winter with us. He's seen what climate change has done to the ecosystems.

We don't know if the roamers can adapt to the cold.

All we can do is *hope*.

The blocked highways and unexpected herds slowed down his process. When he barely reached the border between Pennsylvania and Maryland, he crashed his truck into a tree and cut his left leg pretty badly. Spent nights smearing himself in roamer's blood to ensure himself he'd be safe enough to sleep alone in the forests, but who knew what else could've been out there?

Who knew *who* else could have been out there?

It was hard, but he knew it was better to be alone like this than to feel alone with a group like that. It wasn't like he was useless, and it really did seem like he tried to make up for what happened with Elliott ... and *Benny*. He *was* a nice person. It just wasn't enough. He was always going to be 'annoying'.

He sure did annoy me sometimes.

I was annoyed at how he cared about things he shouldn't have to care about. I got annoyed at how he always tried to talk to me in the mornings—but to be fair, I never told him I'm not much of a morning person. I was annoyed at how quick it was for him to develop feelings for me, which made me feel unrealistically likable. It had me asking if he was just desperate or am I just that pretty?

And oh, did it annoy me.

At first it was cute. It was just a crush. He'll get over it.

"I saw this friendship in a brother-sister way," I told him.

He sighed, shrugging. "Yeah, I guess I just like you a little more than just a sister, y'know?"

I froze. I was already bad enough at handling guys, flirting with guys, anything with guys—so you guessed it. I'm bad at rejecting them too.

"I thought you said you were from Texas, not Alabama," I awkwardly chuckled, attempting to loosen up the room.

He didn't get it. "I *am* from Texas, not Alabama."

I sighed.

It started to repeat to the point where I was too uncomfortable to say anything, but I knew how it felt to be in his position.

He asked me to be his girlfriend.

I answered, "I don't date inside the program."

I don't date inside the program.

I. Don't. Date. Inside. The. Program.

He understood, but then about a few weeks later, he asked if we could give it a try and if I wasn't happy with it, we could stop.

I didn't give him a response. I was grieving Tyson.

He left me alone until I was ready to talk to other people than just Aaron Scheuch and María Colón, but this was when I realized he was hopeless. The more I was nice to him, the more material I gave him to daydream.

And then he would ask the question, chasing after me, and I would just leave him confused. I would let him go and date other girls.

When Yanes asked me if I was into him, I had to restrain myself from saying, "No, I know better." It was blunt, maybe a little harsh, but it was true. I knew better the second I once saw the shattered look on his girlfriend's face after he gave her a lousy, cheap flower and gifted me a stuffed plush at the same time for Valentine's Day back when we were in school. He turned with a wide, proud smile saying, "See I can be a good boyfriend *and* best friend!"

I smacked him on the arm seconds after she walked away crying. "Are you serious? Go after her!"

I don't know what's wrong with me. Why can't I just explain to him no? Why can't I just explain to him *why*? Why is it so impossible?

But it obviously didn't matter anymore because he took off and left me behind, and after spending about two months stranded in the middle of nowhere with no vehicle and barely any water or food, the impossible happened.

With a body incredibly sore and a bad, potentially infected cut running down his left leg, Sterling staggered through the foggy woods in hopes of finding *anything*—a shed or a cabin. Anything that would help fill the worn down bag he carried on his back.

"*Carter?*" a muffled voice spoke.

Sterling turned, seeing a tall brunette speak to him through a respirator gas mask. His eyes widened as he took a couple steps back.

"It's *me*," he said. "It's *Rodney*."

Sterling's eyebrows furrowed as his breathing grew steadier. "D-Daffodil?"

Rodney Daffodil.

Well I'll be damned.

Sterling dropped his things and quickly wrapped his arms around him. "Oh my God," his voice muffled into Rodney's black jacket. "I thought you were away at bootcamp. Why are you back? Were you discharged? Or?"

"I'd rather not talk about that," he nodded hesitatingly, patting him on the head.

Sterling let go, narrowing his eyes to try to make out his face through the glass.

"Why aren't you wearing a mask?" he asked, quickly shaking his head. "H—*How* aren't you wearing a mask?"

Sterling gulped as he stepped back. "Why *would* I be wearing one?"

2 ½ i think i fixed him
CADET STERLING

"Found him roamin' the woods alone," Rodney explained, leaning against the cold, concrete wall. He looked down to his feet, rubbing his hand down his pale face, not knowing what his buddy would say. "*No* bite marks. *No* scratches but that nasty cut down his leg—said he got it from fallin'-"

"But ain't that good?" his buddy, James replied.

Rodney looked up at James through his eyebrows, gulping. "He wasn't wearing a mask."

A sudden puzzled look then grew on James' face. His eyes began to fill with worry, possibly even fear. "T-That can't be possible."

Rodney then took a swift step into the lantern-lit room, finding Sterling sitting on the edge of the mattress bent over with his elbows resting on his knees. He cleared his throat.

"How?" he demanded.

"How *what?*" Sterling replied.

James followed him in, crossing his arms above his chest. "How are you able to withstand the environment?"

Sterling narrowed his eyes, smiling anxiously. He does that a lot. He does this thing with his eyes and smiles until his cheeks turn pink when he's nervous. "I-I don't underst—"

Rodney and James took a quick look at each other.

"How long have you been on your own?" Rodney asked.

Sterling shrugged hesitantly. "I don't know?"

"Make an estimate," James eyed him, tensing his jaw.

"Like—" he shook his head, bouncing his right leg beneath him. "Maybe ... nine—ten months? Maybe a year? What month is it?"

Rodney widened his eyes cautiously, ignoring his question. "Who were you with before that? A group?"

"The cadets."

"*No* kiddin'—" Rodney smiled wide, looking over at James before squatting down, resting his arms on his knees. "*All* of them?"

"I-I can't say," Sterling rubbed the stubble on his face. "It's been so long."

"*Scheuch?*" He scoffed, suddenly lowering the pitch of his voice to mock him, "Mister, *I can't call commands right?*"

"Rodney, what are you talking about?" Sterling furrowed his brows. "Aaron called commands just fin—"

"Maxwell alive?" he interrupted.

Sterling nodded.

"*Klein?*"

He nodded.

"*Sully*, the pretty one."

He nodded again.

"*Olsen?*"

He shook his head.

"Damn," Rodney pushed up his glasses, "what a shame."

Olsen was only a year older than me, making her a *freshman* when Rodney, who was a *senior*, met her.

Rodney grew an infectious grin on his face before leaning over to grab James' wrist, gripping it tightly, shaking it side to side. "You know what this means, James?"

"What?"

"You know what this means?" His voice pitched higher. "*People,* man. There's other *people* out there! There's still hope after all!"

James narrowed his eyes, letting go of Rodney's grip. He crossed his arms over his chest. "Why were you alone?" he asked. "Did something happen to them?"

"No," Sterling replied. "I left."

"*Why?*"

Sterling did it again. He just glanced back and forth between the two with a cheesy grin. "You guys ask a lot of questions!"

"Because you're bad at answering them," he replied, *"why?"*

The smile on his face faded. "Because they were assholes."

"Back to the real question," James repeated, *"how* are you able to survive out there?"

Rodney gulped, looking at Sterling's clueless face. "You know about the power plants being programmed to run on their own, right?"

Sterling nodded.

"Time's up," he explained. "They're not programmed to maintain the nuclear waste anymore. The air quality out there is so bad that if one of us comes out without a mask, we'd be just as dead as the geeks out there."

Sterling looked down to the concrete floor, running his hands down his light brown hair, "Then I guess I'm just immune."

"To the *radiation?*" James asked. "Is that how you haven't—"

Sterling remained silent, which left Rodney and James wondering more. He watched as the two murmured to each other before he began to smile a bit, attempting to loosen up the tension in the room. "You guys call them geeks?" he asked curiously.

"Yeah," Rodney sighed. "You can stay in this room until we figure out what to do," he explained. "Our leader doesn't really like taking in new people, so we aren't sure if he's going to accept you right away."

"Okay."

"Bathroom's down the hallway to your left," James explained, "but don't be leavin' this room for anything more than that. We'll get you the food and anything else you might need."

"Okay."

James sighed, "Look, we got a way of doing things around here. If you're not ready for runs—"

"I'm ready," he immediately said.

James uncrossed his arms, looking at the wall Sterling built over his blue eyes. "Are you sure?"

"I know what I'm doing out there."

"Alright kid, let's get you some new clothes and something to eat first," Rodney stood up, putting a hand on Sterling's shoulder as he looked over at James. "I guess he wouldn't need a mask an' everything, would he?"

To his surprise, Rodney wasn't in charge of the group of people he and James were staying with. The space they were settled in was far more advanced than Jade Street. They had double, possibly triple the amount of people we had and ran on a functioning system. These guys were ten times more experienced too—stuck together like glue.

"I guess not," James replied. "I'll go grab Jayden and we'll head our way out. Martha wants us to scavenge for canned goods. We're running low on food."

"Jayden..." Sterling stood up, grabbing the cowboy hat from beside him, "that name sounds really familiar."

"Jayden García," James said. "He's just like you—immune."

It had been months since Sterling was welcomed into Rodney's group—months with their leader still not aware about him. Sterling was satisfied with where he ended up. For once he felt he was where he belonged.

About three weeks in, he met Karlee, who treated him better than I ever could. Karlee was fun. Karlee once worked at a firehouse as well. Karlee was short and had light brown hair.

He doesn't deserve a person that pushes him away every time he would annoy them. He doesn't deserve a person that gives him false hope, even if they didn't try to. I should've been more clear.

Instead of barely responding, awkwardly hiding behind walls and doors, being irritated every time he'd lurk up to me to tell me something I'd forget in three minutes—I should've just sucked it up and told him that I hated talking in the mornings. I should've just told him I needed some time for myself.

I don't want to be mean. I don't want to be rude.

He deserves a person that would at least give an effort to have a bit of *compassion,* a hell of a lot more patience than I did.

I just want to fix him. Maybe this could teach him how to take hints.

That's all bullshit. I can sit here and say I pushed him away because I was trying to be distant in hopes it'd resolve on its own. I can sit here and say I was really just trying to be as polite as I could and that it wasn't his fault I was going through things.

We're *all* going through things.

But no.

I pushed him away because I was afraid he'd fall in love with me, considering how he'd absorb the advice I'd give him. I felt like he needed to learn it. He needed to learn the value of having a special bond with someone since he was so used to having them easily slip away. He needed to learn how to not be impulsive with the words he said and the choices he chose.

He *needed* to lose me.

"Hey Four-Eyes," Sterling heard James's voice coming from his doorframe. "Follow me."

He looked down and smiled as he let Karlee out of his arms. Karlee stretched and smiled back, leaning forward kissing him on the cheek. "I gotta get back to work anyway," she whispered.

"Okay," he smiled, for the first time in a long time.

"Meet you back here before seven, okay?"

"Yeah," he replied as he slid off the bed, exiting the room.

James looked over his shoulder, seeing how pink his cheeks had grown. "You two have been hittin' it off, huh?" he muttered, looking down at his watch as he led him down the dark, narrow hallway.

"Yeah," Sterling replied excitedly, biting his lip to control how big his smile was growing. He looked back up again. "Where are we going?"

"To meet the highest on our chain of command," he explained, passing a couple flickering lanterns dangling from the ceilings. "Our leader."

"Okay."

James turned to him. "Do you ask dumb questions?"

"I-I don't know."

"Hm," James murmured as they both abruptly stopped, seeing a short, blonde-haired girl walk out of a room and into the room across from it.

"Sorry," she awkwardly apologized, revealing her youthful smile as she giggled away.

James narrowed his eyes before looking into the room she came from. Seeing that it was Rodney's, no muscle in his face moved.

Sterling also peeked over James's shoulder, seeing Rodney roll over in his bed, smiling widely at the both of them.

"Need anything, boys?" he grinned.

"How *old* is she?"

James slowly turned to Sterling, eyebrows furrowed. "Okay. Work on that."

"Work on what?"

"Asking dumb-ass questions, kid," he said before he began walking again.

Sterling awkwardly followed along until they came to a stop. He analyzed James's face carefully, knowing full well they both knew that girl wasn't a day past sixteen.

James sighed as he opened the door in front of them, "Sir?"

The man turned around in his seat. His hazel eyes shot at the two of them coldly.

"Sir, this is the new asset to Rodney and I's crew," James said. He exhaled shakily. "His name is Carter Sterling."

"Can he be trusted?"

James turned to Sterling with anxious eyes. "Y-Yes, sir."

"And how could you possibly know that for sure?"

"Rodney used to go to school with him," James explained, "and Jayden knew him too." He wiped his nose as he glanced back at Sterling again. "Carter, this is our leader, *Gideon.*"

"So... both he and Jayden are immune?"

"Yeah."

"And they were both from the same group before coming here to us?"

"Yeah."

... "You know what this means?"

"You tell me, Rodney."

"They know something we don't."

"I hope she's not lonely in a world like this."

"I'm sure she's not," Sterling told her. "She has people."

"Are you sure? Like who?"

Sterling shook his head, recalling back to the names he forced himself to forget about.
"Avery? Kiara?" he guessed. "They're her friends."
He sighed.
"I think she definitely has Aaron by her side too."

No.
I *don't* have Aaron.

11 AUGUST. 2021.

11 August. 2021.
[untitled]

When Klein told me being with me felt like being with a child, I had to restrain the urge to say, "Well no fucking shit."
What could you possibly expect out of a fifteen year old...
But I know what he's talking about. He's talking about the softness I show once I feel steady with someone; the way the awkwardness fades and how I don't have to force myself to be so quiet anymore.
If you *really* talk to me, you see that I'm "pretty mature for a fifteen year old" but realize I went through things way too complicated for one. You'll see I have the heart of a child but I have the mind of a woman ten years older than me. You'll see I'm "well put-together and presentable" until you see I have the temper of an angry father and I cry like a little girl that just needs one.

When I sit or stand in silence, I can't stay still. I still swing my feet below me and rock people's hands back and forth when I hold them.
Michelle used to sit in silence and smile innocently at everything. She would curiously glance around her surroundings and acknowledge the little things that bring the *softness* out of her.
Now I sit in silence, and even in the hottest temperatures I still remain cold, scanning my surroundings because everything and everyone brings out the *survival* in me.
Klein never got that side out of me again. He only had it when we first met because a little part of me thought I was finally being saved by my knight in shining armor, but I'm no princess that *needs* to be saved.

I finally feel like I can breathe again, counting how many weeks it has been since he's talked to me. As dramatic as this sounds, I know no one will ever be able to comprehend the amount of relief I felt after hearing my gut tell me, "There it is. Something feels different now. He's about to leave."
So I bring him up to emphasize how that part of me is starting to come back. The person who'd force herself to find happiness in little things so she won't lose her will to live—meaning, maybe some good came out of this after all. That should be good, right? All I've literally been doing is running away from something that will end up consuming me if I don't, so why not have some damn fun with it?

RECONCILIATION

23 AUGUST. 2021.

August 23, 2021.
[untitled]

> I have an irrational fear of being socially unaware in fear of how stupid I'd look.
> I've been trying to stay content with things, not giving excuses but rather explanations as to why a person could act a certain way. I can't say it's exactly been easy.

Scheuch told the others it was necessary for me to come along on the supply run this month, and what Scheuch says, goes.

It was just a quick, simple supply run, but at this point, I'll take what I can get. ~~I just want to feel included.~~

I was ready to go until Yanes wanted me to stay back and let Maxwell go out for me instead. I want to say I didn't throw a fit over something that small, but I'm going to be mature for a moment just to have the courage to admit it. Yes, I did get upset. Yes, I did get irritated.

Why am I the one that stays back every time? There are little-to-no tasks for me here. I'm a good shot. I can shoot. I'm a fast runner. I can scavenge.

Why am I not out there?

"Bui, you don't have to take everything so personally," he joked. "You know we just want the O.G. group together right?" He asked as Candreva followed up.

"Why can't we both go?" I asked.

He shrugged. "Not enough seats."

"Scheuch wasn't with you guys in the city either?" I responded confusedly.

"This is your hint to shut up, Mj!"

Scheuch's head snapped over. "Don't tell her to *shut up*?"

I flinched looking up at him, seeing the look of disgust on his face, immediately covering my mouth to hide the smile I had. He said that as if he was completely baffled—like he hadn't believed me every time I complained about how these people talk to me, but a little part of me can't help but love it every time he sticks up for me.

Like yeah, what he said.

Luckily, Candreva and I are cool (I think) and he was just joking (I hope).

"She's coming," Scheuch said. "Sergeant said he wants her included in this too, so she's *coming*," he explained. "We need all the hands we can get. We're running low on almost everything."

We came back around noon. I went straight upstairs to their room and banged on the doorframe.

"Cameron?" I asked. "You in there?"

"Yeah, what's up?"

I stormed in.

Snide remark after snide remark.

I don't know how I stayed calm and just ignored them. ~~Scheuch was there, and I didn't want him to lose respect for me.~~

"I'm guessin' that supply run didn't go well, huh?" he sighed.

"Nah," I replied. "I don't know how many times I need to tell them I don't need to hear another *I told you so!*"

"They still botherin' you 'bout Klein?"

"*Yes,* bro," I groaned. "How many fuckin' times do I need to show them that this is, in fact, *NOT* another opportunity to try to prove they were right——*ALWAYS* walkin' up to me like, *ooh, I told you he'd do that,*" I looked at him as a mocked them. "Like *nooooo wayyyyy* dude——*no way!*"

> Sergeant says it's all about perspective. They're forming opinions on what they see. I understand that.
> What I don't understand is why it's so fucking hard to mind your own fucking business????????? Like why do you care...?
> I've been told I take things too far. I won't deny it. I don't stoop to the same level as people, I stoop lower. But of course I always calm down after the two weeks are up and I'm no longer pissed off at how they made me feel.
> I tell myself I should be able to understand.

"They only tried to warn me about it because they were worried," I ranted. "I get it, I would be worried too——but maybe they should understand how *I* feel when I see the *same* girls who tell me—*you deserve better*——*he's such a dickhead*—go lurk around him with fuckin' heart eyes." I watched him listen, shaking his head. "I get that you're worried, but I know *why* you're worried."

"Yeah, at this point it's not worth being friends with them anymore," he replied.

"Damn right," I scoffed.

> I didn't like their intentions behind getting involved and trying to "talk me out of it." I'm not stupid, okay? I can *tell* when a girl genuinely wants to help me or not. Kiara would never be this persistent with me. Yes, she's talked to me about him every once and a while, but I can tell she wanted to leave it alone because this was something I needed to learn for myself. She's made it clear she doesn't want to associate with him anymore, and he knows that.
> It's been an ongoing thing—feeling a sense of aggression from the others due to him. Why does it have to be your business? Why do you have to let it affect your opinion on me? Who I choose to talk to or come back to are decisions no one can make but *me*.

"You seem to be—handling the situation pretty well—though," he replied, lifting his head. "Sorry, I'm like—high as hell right now."

My smile faded and I sighed, "Wait—when you're high, can you still comprehend—anything I'm saying?"

"Yeah," he replied, laying back into his pillow. "I just won't remember it that well."

"So, you're *present* but *not completely present*," I frowned.

Watkins and I truly get along.

It's just hard sometimes because he reminds me of so many things and it's not his fault that they do.

We're basically the same in a sense. We have things in common, but we have so many things that make us different. We both have tattoos. We both have gotten into fights. We both have similar home lives (in a sense). We have the same sense of humor. We both aren't fond of Klein.

We both play sports. I remember him coming to my soccer games every Tuesday and Thursdays and I came to his football games on Fridays. We both generally listen to the same music, only he prefers a different rapper than I do. We used to lift a lot, only he lifted heavier weights of course, and all I wanted to do was get toned.

Now see, the things we have in common make our friendship difficult to value. I try not to view relationships like this, but after María it's hard not to. *What am I getting out of this other than a good laugh or two?* ~~Will I fall back into the hole that took everything in me to climb out of?~~

And I don't know, I guess something about it just made me sad. I came there to talk to *him*, but I knew his mind was somewhere else when he was replying back to me.

"Hey Aaron," he said as I looked up at the door.

"Hello."

"Hi A-A-ron," I yawned. "I thought you were heading out?"

"We just got back," he answered, looking over at me. We stared at each other. <u>He knows I saw them.</u> "Bui, I need you downstairs in a bit."

I paused, "Okay," choosing to ignore it, *ignore it all.*

After frustration after frustration, I finally found myself going to the one person I knew wouldn't try to tell me who I am as a person and why I do the things I do. ~~He wouldn't because he already knows.~~
Because when it comes to people like Aaron Scheuch, I like to think wouldn't care enough to form an opinion on something that wouldn't concern them.
But like I've felt since the day I met him, the idea of going to him about my internal struggles terrified me. Seeing me talk to Scheuch without getting nervous is like seeing Maria show up to class sober. I'd have to absolutely hate his guts to be anything but giddy around him.
So I didn't know where to start.

We were in the kitchen downstairs unloading all the medicine we've retrieved from the supply run.

Since our group was so large, Sgt. Rogers required two supply runs a month—and we had assigned groups due to the... *drama.* I practically begged him to put me in a group with Sully and Scheuch, but I also understand it can't always go my way.

<u>I am perfectly capable of remaining mature and focusing on what my job and tasks are.</u>

Why can't they understand that?

I stopped unpacking all the travel-size shampoo and conditioner I collected, hesitating a bit. "Aaron?"

"Hm?" He stopped what he was doing. I tried not to giggle at the way he was balancing his bag on his upper leg.

"Remember when we drove back from Tyson's and sped down that street?" I asked nervously.

He looked away and resumed back to organizing the vitamins and supplements into a group—antibiotics into another and—I don't know. I don't remember.

I was too busy thinking about what was under his shirt.

"With you out of the sunroof?" he rubbed his forehead, turning around. "There's more stuff outside."

"Okay—" I chuckled softly as I followed him. "—when I almost fell over like twelve times."

"Well, here's a good idea!" He stopped and put his hands on his hips, smiling down at me. "How about you *hold on* next time!"

"Dude—" I covered my face in embarrassment, "—and that one time I fell out of the truc——*oh shit!!!*"

I scurried around him squealing, hiding behind him. He looked over his shoulder and lowered his eyebrows.

"A fat bee was chasing me," I explained.

He raised them. "You mean a *bumblebee?*" He chuckled softly at me. "You do realize they don't sting, right?"

I immediately let go of his arms. "Oh."

He narrowed his eyes at me, making me smile nervously. "What's going on with you?" he sneered.

~~I know you got bit but you haven't turned.~~

I tilted my head. "How—do you—"

"Well, for one," he readjusted himself on the stone porch under the radiant sunlight, hands in his pockets, "I could hear you shouting from all the way downstairs. You're angry."

I nodded. "Um—I'm just not that—um—"

I wasn't sure what he was going to say. I was *scared* of what he was going to say, but ~~he just gave me this reassuring look that told me I was free to express my concerns with him.~~ he just stared at me. He stared at me as I told him everything calmly. I don't know what it is about him that brings the softness back out of me.

He stared until I was done talking, and it took him a few seconds before responding, "Do you want—me to try and *attempt*—to do anything about this—or—do you just need someone to listen?"

I felt my heartbeat immediately steady, yet I still hesitated.

~~He's bit and he has been hiding it from all of us.~~

~~He's bit and he's still standing in front of me. Alive.~~

~~What else has he been hiding from us?~~

I took a deep breath. "For right now, I just want you to listen."

He held a thumbs up.

3 invasive

CADET MAXWELL

Every now and then, my mind returns to that street where we watched Conti and Johnson get ripped to shreds—and every now and then I remember the month and a half we spent trying to find each other again.

Physically, not figuratively.

The roamers weren't going to stop with them, and more were coming.

We all remember this day as, "Day 351."

The night we scattered.

"Scheuch! Keys!" Candreva called out as ~~Aaron~~ Scheuch turned and tossed them to him. He was on his knee now, urging Klein away from Conti's body.

"Klein, get *up!*" He pulled him away as Klein sobbed, wiping his nose. "C'MON!"

My back tensed as I realized how fast they were coming and how many directions they were coming *from*. I didn't get time to think anything through. I needed to move.

"Mary! Let's go!" Candreva turned on the engine as she let go of me, running to the passenger side.

"MJ! C'MON!" she yelled through the commotion.

~~I was looking at Scheuch.~~

"Shit!" I mumbled as they came, now looking over at Sergeant.

"Okay, you guys know the drill," he quickly said. "Get in formation. No gunfire. I'll get the second car going."

We were too surrounded to make it back to the car safely. Sgt. Rogers had to fight his way through, having Yanes covering him.

I was quickly stranded, being pushed out further and further away from the cars.

"MJ!" Sully's voice worried.

Scheuch dragged Klein back, elbowing the nearest roamer behind him away by reflex. He turned around and began making his way through quietly, quick enough that it was almost impossible for a roamer to even touch him.

I looked at the forests as I stumbled backwards. "Bailey, where are you?" I muttered.

Bailey, where are you? Bailey, where are you?

Bailey, please don't be dead.

"GUYSSSS!!!" Candreva began panicking, watching the roamers cling onto each side of the vehicle, clawing against the glass. "I'm about to get *stuck!*"

"We can't just l-leave her," Klein argued with Scheuch, shoving away the roamers around her.

"They'll consume her first," he replied. "That buys us time."

"She's not just a *fucking* meal!"

"But she slows us down!" Scheuch whacked the roamer lunging from his right. "Klein, this is not the time to debate right now—" he glanced at me, jaw tightening, "Bui, get in the car."

"No—" I shook my head, "—I gotta go find Bailey!"

He snapped his head towards me, making me jump. *"Bailey? Jesus—"* He rubbed his forehead, wiping blood all over his face, taking in a breath. "No," he shook his head, stepping away, "you can't."

"What?!" I panicked. *"What?! Why?!"* He sighed as I grabbed his arm, pulling him back. "Aaron, *please!*"

He looked over at Klein, who could see the situation clearly now. I swear, it was like we were all taking turns freaking out.

He exhaled sharply. "Alright, I'll go."

I narrowed my eyes in confusion, begging my body to allow me to think straight. "What?" The questions flooded my head.

"I'll go and find him," he said, glancing up at Klein. "Sounds good?"

Klein nodded as I smiled, quickly wiping away the one tear down my cheek. "Really?"

Scheuch glared at me. *"Go!"*

Klein led me through a couple more groups, barely making it to Candreva and Sully, but as I watched Scheuch disappear into the woods, it was almost like nothing was ever going to make me step into that car.

"We'll meet back at Jade Street!" Scheuch's voice yelled.

"Alright!" Klein yelled back, looking back at me. "C'mon, Mj. Let's go."

That was the last thing I heard before things went blurry. I only remember my hand leaving Klein's before sprinting off after Scheuch. I ran with backpack straps slipping down my shoulders and feet stomping the highway streets below me; and I heard the others yell for me, but I didn't turn. I ran around cars and swerved roamers lunging from left and right, but not once did I turn back.

I ran until I began to lose vision and balance.

And suddenly I was on the ground.

— — —

"OOOHHHH—*FUCK*——*MY*——*LIFE!*" Maxwell ran from the RV to the other side of the street, getting Kim from her room. "ELIZA!"

"Leave me alone!" she yelled back.

Maxwell squinted, attempting to look through the covered-up windows. She couldn't hear with the commotion approaching.

"ELIZA!" she called again.

"*Ssstooopp!!!*" Kim whined.

"*ELIZA!*"

"WHAT?!"

Maxwell swung her body around, finding Watkins through the crowd, tossing the pre-packed emergency bags the group had put together (It was my idea.) into the trunk. "CAM, WHERE'S STERLING?!"

"HE'S NOT HERE!"

"WHAT DO YOU MEAN HE'S NOT HERE?!"

"I WENT TO HIS ROOM AND ALL HIS STUFF'S GONE!" He yelled back before scurrying back into the pizzeria.

Kim stuck her body out the window, widening her eyes at the sight. "What do you want, Kiara?"

"Roamers broke through the barriers!" she said, hand on her sheath, ready.

Kim groaned. "Just let them pass!"

"There's too many!" she replied. "We *need* to get out of here!"

Sometimes I regret how Kiara and I first met.

Klein had a lot of impact on how I viewed her, but I should've been stronger at building my own opinions on other people, not just perceiving people how others perceive them.

If people perceived me how others did, they wouldn't like me.

Kiara Maxwell was always *annoying*. She was *nosey*. She talked with *authority and it made her sound ridiculous*. She was *uptight* and *bitchy*. But Kiara to me was nothing but a warm hug.

Those phrases came from somebody that was trying to convince themselves of those things.

"Let's keep things on the down low for now, okay?" he told me on homecoming night. "Don't—tell the others in the program about us yet. *Especially* Kiara. She's very nosey and will ask you about it."

WEE-WOO! WEE-WOO! WEE-WOO!

I'm not stupid.

Tyson had to tell his new girls to stay away from me too.

At the time I didn't know it, but he also wanted to keep it from the program due to the fact

it was definitely

not allowed.

He was on the command staff, and I wasn't yet. We were fraternizing.

There was an extreme difference between the way she acted and the way the others did when the shit-show with Klein and I first began. I would be sitting next to her, staring at the wall. She would look over at me and ask me when Jake would be getting his shit together. I would ask her what she meant by that.

~~He's not over Conti and he's using me as a distraction.~~

~~I'm not over Tyson and I'm using Klein to make him jealous.~~

She'd pause from the puzzle game on her phone, wipe her nose and reply, *I don't want you to get hurt.* I would scoff and reply back, *trust me, there's no way that could happen.*

~~I sometimes wish it would've just worked out.~~

But instead of really listening to her, I panicked.

I wasn't used to being the center of a clique's daily gossip. I didn't like that I couldn't have a conversation with them without one of us bringing him up—and I really hate that when I do force myself not to be so "boy-obsessed" and surrounded by the whole thing, they don't talk to me.

I'm alone again.

But Kiara didn't mean to come off that way. I realized that after pulling out my phone to text him.

ME: Kiara just pulled me aside and asked me a bunch of questions. I don't know what you want me to tell her.

KLEIN: Oh my God.

Two minutes later, Kiara nudges me on the shoulder. "Did you tell Jake I asked you questions?" *Uh oh...!* She gave me the phone. "Here, look!"

KLEIN: Kiara can you back off? Quit being so nosey.

MAXWELL: What are you talking about?

KLEIN: I know you're terrorizing her with your stupid questions. She's not going to believe you. And since you want to know so bad then, yes, we are dating. Happy?

"Nah, run that back," I began laughing, hitting her shoulder lightly. "Run—that——oh hi A-A-Ron—"

"Wassup."

I turned back to Kiara, looking at her phone screen. "HAAA—NAH—run——that—fuckin'—back!"

"He's such an ass!" she scoffed, shaking her head.

"He's a fuckin' idiot, *that's* what he is!" I cackled. "What the hell's wrong with him?!"

"You guys are dating?" She lowered her eyebrows.

"*No!*" I scoffed. "He never said *anything* to me 'bout that!"

Kiara was the only person I went to after Klein cut ties with me in October. She was also the only person he specifically told me not to converse with.

He thinks I don't know why.

But all his remarks about her translate to, "I miss her."

"Why'd you tell Kiara we were dating?"

"Well, I thought that since we've been talking for a while now—"

Two weeks. It was two weeks.

"I thought I might as well just call it."

...

"That's the weirdest way to ask someone to be your girlfriend."

"Where are we going?" Kim asked in the backseat of the car, arms folded across her chest.

"I don't know," Maxwell rubbed her forehead. "I don't know, Kim. I *don't* know."

"Geez... I was just asking."

"No, I *know*," she replied, taking a deep breath. "I *know*, Kim."

"Kim, she's just stressed," Watkins turned around in the passenger seat.

"Yeah, yeah," she picked up a water bottle from her side. "Yeah, Kim, you really don't have to take everything as a personal attack on you."

Maxwell and Watkins have been friends longer since I can remember. They began splitting apart a little when she realized alcohol and weed messed with her meds. She only vaped occasionally to help with her anxiety apparently. Nobody has seen her do anything like that in a long time. Except me.

I was the one she asked to find cigarettes for her.

I feel extra guilty for letting Klein's words influence me knowing what she did for me before I even knew who she was.

When I met Cameron in person for the first time, I was nervous—and like I said, it took him a bit to realize it was me. And when I said he's always known me as his little brother's ex, I mean he specifically knows how bad the relationship was, the same relationship that cause grown adults to look at me with softened eyes and shake their heads, telling me, "I feel like I'm talking to a college student right now."

When I finally told Cameron why we broke up, he was infuriated. "Again, I am *so* sorry you had to go through that," he said. "He learned that from our older brother."

I replied, "It's fine."

He told me he'd take care of it, but before he did he sent me a voice memo asking, "Hey, I'm—about to——hang with—my friend Kiara right now—" he said—the sound of leaves rustled over his voice, "—is it okay if I take a couple screenshots and——show these to her?"

I replied, "OK."

Minutes later, he sent one again, only this time it sounded like they were in a car.

"Hey, I'm with—Kiara right now—and Kay's with his friend hanging out at a graveyard——we're gonna go beat his ass."

"There's absolutely *no* possible thing that can excuse that behavior. Nothing!" I heard her ranting in the background. "*Nobody* deserves to be treated that way!"

Her reaction to seeing me in person for the first time stood out too, but at the time I thought she was just trying to be nice. She was walking into the ROTC room with her uniform, freshly dry cleaned. Her eyes shot wide open after hearing Cameron say, "Hey Kiara, this is Mj."

She did a double take. "*THAT'S* Mj?"

I froze in my seat as she stepped closer to me.

"You're telling me, *Kay* did that to *her?!*"

I looked over at Cameron slowly.

"She's *Kiara*—" he said, "the girl I was with when I talked to him."

"Oooh," I nodded. "Hi!"

"Girl, you are *so* gorgeous," she touched my hair. "The hell was he *thinking?*"

He thought getting attention from twelve-year-old girls was better than having me as a girlfriend, but didn't think it was a big deal when he'd let my friends flirt with him. He thought I was obsessive and crazy, but he didn't think I was telling the truth when I said nothing was going on between me and his friends. He thought I was annoying and that I walked around with too much self-entitlement when the only thing I knew how to do was give. I gave and gave and gave—and he was nothing but a fucking idiot who only knew how to take.

I don't like to admit he's part of the reason why it's so hard for me to see how much value I have, so I blame it on my adolescence and say, "I'm still trying to figure myself out."

But till this day, I don't know who I am.

Till this day, I separate myself in three to talk to myself—remind me that what happened, happened, and I can't just sit around pretending it didn't. I have to get up and grow from it.

Kiara Maxwell was so easy to go to because she always gave me a proper explanation to why things happened the way they happened without invalidating my feelings in any way—and in some ways it felt like actually having an older sister. She'd give me advice then if I don't bring up anything new, she'd go on about her sex life or something to keep us entertained.

But just like all older sisters, they seem to grow more distant the more you reach out further to them.

"The group's gonna come back and find us gone," Kim realized. "How are they going to know where to look?"

Watkins gulped in his seat, turning towards her. "I left a bunch of notes. If any of them make it back, they'll know we made it out alive."

"*If?!*"

Maxwell shook her head. "Kim, we don't know if they even made it through the night. If that herd migrated from out west, it would've come right towards them."

"So you're saying Avery and Mary and Brody——they're all *dead?!*" Kim began panicking.

The car went silent, passing burned-down forests and piles upon piles of litter.

Maxwell looked from Watkins' expression to the street ahead of her, sighing, "Let's not worry about things we don't have any confirmation on."

"That's all we do!"

"*Kim—*" I'm pretty sure Maxwell's the only other one who doesn't hide the fact she can't stand her. "Just let me think."

"Yeah, 'cause you make all the calls 'round here," she mumbled.

"I *do* actually," Maxwell replied, keeping her composure. "I am in a position higher than both of you. What I say, goes."

"Those *positions* are part of a bullshit high school program!" Kim argued. "Look around! It's pointless how we still listen to what Scheuch tells us to do and call each other by our last names!"

"You complain that we do, but Scheuch has done more for all of us than any of you cowards would *ever* consider doing!"

I want to be dramatic and say he's risked his life to make sure we have food for the week. I want to be dramatic and say he's sacrificed so much to ensure we're all safe, even when it never feels that way anymore, but even he's too strategic to put himself into situations like that. He does risky things—*stupid* things, but he does them in a way it works out for him every damn time.

At this point, the roamers are scared he'll eat *them*.

"Guys—" Watkins sighed.

Kim sat in the backseat, huddling herself into a ball, and quiet. "So what are we going to do? We only have food that'll last us a month—two if we make it stretch."

"I don't eat much."

"Yeah, we know," Kim rolled her eyes. "But we can't stay in this car forever. It's *too* small and I'm *claustrophobic!*"

"I—kinda guessed that."

"She's not wrong, though," Maxwell looked out the window. "We cannot handle staying confined like this—especially with the arguing."

"So what, then? We just go out and find the others?"

"Exactly."

Kim widened her eyes. "But you just said we don't know if they're still out there!"

"That's right, but we can't just give up on them," she replied. "They've done so much for us."

Kim scoffed. "Yeah, right."

Maxwell widened her eyes. "Bui went hungry for two weeks so you can eat! But she didn't tell you that, did she?!" She ran her hands through her hair stressfully. "Candreva and Yanes traveled over nights just to find some *seeds* for us to *attempt* to grow!" She shook her head, jaw dropped. "Sterling worked his ass off to get the RV up and running again——and you're sittin' here trying to tell me they haven't done a *thing?*"

She looked at Watkins in disbelief.

"Back me up here?!"

Watkins sighed, turning around to Kim. "Listen, Eliza, Kiara's right. The group has risked their lives going out there to look for García. The least we can do is do the same for them."

"We *have* to find them." Maxwell gripped the steering wheel tighter.

She wasn't going to give up on us. The world has shrunken down compared to what it used to be. It was smaller now—lonelier now, but she's been used to that long before the outbreak started.

Kiara has always been stubborn, hard-headed, and I will always believe that is the best thing about her. The eldest child always had it worse. That's how it was when it came to her family, my family, Sergeant's family, Johnson's family... it was almost like, our parents did everything wrong with us to do everything right with our younger siblings... and boy, did that fuck a few of us up.

Kiara loved her mom. She loved her more than anything, even when it never felt like she was there. She was always off working night shifts and sleeping for the next during the day, so it was up to Kiara to take care of her five siblings *and* manage high school.

She was like every other teenager, out and about. But then she grew up. I remember seeing the *teen* drain from her eyes, smoking with her in the front seat of her car in the school's parking lot. She was growing up; transitioning from life as a careless teenager to a well-rounded adult in the real world. That diligence—that perseverance, courage, and the way she held herself together so strongly—that never left her, no matter how hard people tried stripping her of her worth, nothing ever phased her.

She knew there was a matter of time till we reunited again, but she didn't realize that in the meantime, she'd run into someone else.

MARCH 6 / DAY 358 / A WEEK AFTER THE NIGHT WE SCATTERED

We've all been having a hard time keeping track of how many weeks have passed and whatnot. Dates don't matter to us anymore, but it would be nice to know. I mean, I had the scratches above my bedpost to help but you'd have to be absolutely crazy if you think I'm gonna spend the time and effort to count each individual line. (Also, I would often forget to mark a day sometimes—and by sometimes, I mean all the time.)

It's all confusing now, but thanks to Scheuch's odd notebook, we know a few important ones.

We all woke up around Day 153 of the apocalypse and found Jade Street around Day 174. The others traveled to the city the same day I left Jade Street with Scheuch to search for Tyson, so that must've been on Day 187, which means the day I pulled a gun out on Kim would be Day 207. I can't remember if the fight between Watkins and Klein happened that close or not—no, no, because Colón died not long before Conti and Johnson did, so that means nothing much happened during November and December.

So if Watkins and Klein fought not long after Day 207, and after that was nothing but supply runs and searching for García, Colón must've died around *Day 298*. That was the day I died too.

Looking back on it now, I don't think I should've trusted Scheuch with something like this. I mean he *is* pretty calculated and well-coordinated, but he's also... Aaron Scheuch.

I've seen him lick a rock because he thought it would taste like peppermint. I've seen him run into a tree and tell me he was curious as to who was stronger, him or the tree. I've seen him munch on a tomato like it was an apple and pick up a styrofoam squash during a supply run because he thought it was funny that it looked like a penis.

Okay, so, nobody knew how long we've been living like this and how much time had passed in between significant events.

Cool. Good to know.

But after Conti and Johnson, we began to realize how much it *did* matter. Time went by even slower without each other, and there was absolutely no way we could keep track of how many times the sun was setting on us when we were stranded out there.

"What's the date?" Maxwell asked Watkins, smoking a cigarette, leaning against the car as the three of them got their fresh air for the day.

Watkins scoffed, "Fuck do I know?"

"Shit," she shook her head. "We're in the middle of nowhere and fuel's low——not that that matters knowing gasoline's gonna go bad within another year."

Kim was staying away from them, arms still crossed and pouting. Maxwell turned to Watkins.

"Um," his raspy voice replied, leaning over the hood. "Well, we've already checked down *these* two routes—which were overrun—which *means* they must've headed down southeast."

"Alright," she patted down her jeans, "grab the bags. We're traveling on foot."

"Seriously?!" Kim whined.

Maxwell took a deep breath. "Then what do you suggest then, Eliza?"

"That you come live with us for a bit—" a deep, intimate, masculine voice spoke from behind them, "we'll help you find your friends again, Kie."

Maxwell shot her body around, feeling her stomach drop. Hearing a nostalgic voice like that should've given off the same comfort as the sound of a fireplace crackling or foggy autumn rain, but it didn't. Chills rushed down her spine, and suddenly she couldn't think anymore.

"Keigan?"

7 SEPTEMBER. 2021.

"How's it going?" Scheuch asked.

The crickets chirped and the moon shone every night, and every night, I found myself on that porch with him.

"Fine," I replied softly. "Why?"

His fingers intertwined. His elbows rested on his knees.

"You seemed upset earlier," he replied.

I turned and smiled. *"Really?"*

"Yes," he lowered his eyebrows and nodded, "you went quiet before the group went out this morning."

If I wanted him to see me as an equal, I couldn't complain to him about it. I rephrase my words carefully, "I just find it annoying that they still think I'm incapable of handling things. How am I supposed to quote, *gain experience,* if y'all aren't gonna let me go out there and *get* experience?"

He paused, phrasing his words carefully too. "I will say, during times like these, we need our strongest members out there to ensure we have everything we need," he explained. "Sergeant chooses roles based on capability, so him not allowing you to go on supply runs doesn't necessarily mean you're incapable of handling it, it could just mean you work better as a leader back *here*."

My frustration rapidly decreased. "I guess so," I shrugged softly, "they don't listen to me as well as they listen to *you*."

"Speak louder and with more authority."

When you do it, you're intimidating. If I do it, I'm bossy.

"They talk over me," I replied. "One time, Johnson came up and just *ripped* the paper from my hands and took over the whole thing!"

He looked over, sighing and pinching the bridge of his nose, he mumbled, "Well, you don't have to worry about *that* happening anymore."

"Oh—" We let silence pass by. "I still feel like I barely *lead*."

"You were in a leadership position back in school?"

"Well, *yeah*," I replied, "but I was only the *assistant*..."

"*I* got assistant *supply* as a freshman, did you know that?" He turned and smiled softly. "The options were *limited*——the bar was low, considering how new and small our program was—but to get on the command staff within *less* than a year in the program, you had to be willing to take things seriously, which is what you do," he said. "You still have stuff to learn—we *all* do—but you've truly improved a lot since then."

"*Really?!*" I bit back my smile.

"There were *some* negatives," he looked down, tapping his feet, "but like I said, you've gotten bett—" I watched his eyes shift up and look past me. "Klein's knocking at your front door."

I snapped my head to the left. "What?!"

I didn't think he'd have the guts to come back again. I thought it was over this time, but I was wrong.

Something cannot be over if it never even started.

He was there, there at my front door again to *start something*.

"*Oh* shit, he's coming this way." I heard Scheuch say quietly before we both shot up from our spots, scurrying into the pizzeria as quietly as possible. I was giggling at his frantics. He held his finger at his lips, shushing me with widened eyes.

"*Go!*" He pointed at one of the green leather booths before a couple knocks sounded from the door.

He cleared his throat and cracked it open. "What?"

"Hey Aaron, what's up, man?" Klein asked, voice and tone a *bit* more charismatic than usual.

"Nothing," he replied, "why aren't you in bed? It's almost curfew."

"*Relax,* no one's gonna care." Klein pushed his way in, making himself at home at a booth—*the same booth I was hiding behind.*

Scheuch watched him tap his fingers on the granite table surface, observing the place from ceiling to floor slowly. "You two really turned this place around, huh?" he said, looking at all the fake vines along the ceiling's edges and renaissance art paintings along the pepper green walls.

"I don't think it's a good idea for you to be in here."

Klein pursed his lips, "Why?" He lowered his eyebrows, "Are you not—*fond*—of me anymore, *Aaron?*"

Scheuch chuckled, "Ha-Ha—*No,*" he responded, "but I know you and my roommate aren't on the best terms right now, and not gonna lie, I'm too lazy to be cleaning blood off floor tiles right now."

"Mm," Klein nodded, "okay."

"We can talk tomorrow," he said, "now shoo, I want to go to bed."

"You're not even in your pajam—"

"You don't know what my pajamas look like," he blurted out, ushering him out the booth, "now shoo!"

Klein scooched out of the booth with his hands up. "At *eight-thirty,* that's a little early don't you think?"

"I need my beauty sleep, now shoo!"

I clenched my jaw to restrain my laughter.

"Yeah you sure do," he rolled his eyes. "Fine, just let me use the—"

SHIT! I began crawling into the nearest room I saw, and it stupidly happened to be the—

"—bathroom," Klein told Scheuch.

Oh no, this is going to be perceived incredibly wrong. I got up on my feet and hid behind the door.

"O-Okay, but—" I heard Scheuch's voice come closer and closer, "—*wait!*"

"What?" Klein's voice replied. "I can't even take a piss now?"

The door opened and I began scooting closer and closer to the corner. I ran into at least five cobwebs, and it took everything in me not to make a noise. I covered my mouth with my hand.

"You don't want to go in there," Scheuch said quickly. *I could tell just by his tone he was smiling widely.* "Trust me, you don't want to go in there."

I looked down to see Klein's shadow turn.

"*Ooh,*" Klein nodded.

"*Yeah,*" Scheuch blurted out. "I ate something bad earlier."

Toilets stopped working a while ago. I just stood and prayed Klein wouldn't think anything of it. Please, Jake, please be stupider just for tonight.

"OK," he narrowed his eyes—*he definitely knows*—grinning, "Aaron?"

"Yes?"

"You don't happen to have seen Mj around, have you?" he asked slowly.

My heart dropped as Scheuch's voice resumed back to normal. "No, why?"

"No reason." He cocked an eyebrow.

Scheuch cleared his throat. "I would suggest checking *her* place rather than mine," he said, "but I don't recommend carrying on with whatever your intentions are with her."

There was a long pause between them. I found myself pressing my ear against the wood, desperate to listen in.

Klein chuckled, "Are you implying *you* think I shouldn't be talking to her?"

"No, not at all," Scheuch replied casually, intertwining his fingers beneath him. "I meant that she is probably *sleeping* right now, and if you want to see how good of a mood she's in when you wake her up, sure, *be my guest!*"

"And how would you know how *good* her mood would be?"

"Uh-I—" he chuckled a bit, "Maxwell and I pranked her once—wasn't friendly."

"Is she *ever* friendly?" Klein scoffed, attempting to bond with him.

"*Klein*, I don't know," Scheuch patted his shoulder, leaning in. "Nor do I really *care.*"

"*Aaron!*" Watkin's voice called from upstairs.

"That stuff doesn't concern me," he said as I felt myself being able to breathe again. He grabbed Klein's shoulder and began leading him to the door. "Alright, I think it's time for you to go now."

"*Fi—*" **SLAM!**

I stepped out of the bathroom giggling at the look on his face. He had his hands at his hips, head to the ground.

"Thank you," I giggled, sitting myself on top of a table comfortably.

"*Why* are you laughing?" He lifted his head.

"I'm sorry," I laughed harder, "it's kinda funny."

He sighed, stepping over and leaning against the booth beside me. "What's even going on between you guys?"

"*Nothing!* I swear!" I replied. "I genuinely don't know *why* he *wants* to talk to me!"

He looked down, muttering, "Probably to talk about how sadistic he is or something."

I burst out laughing and he quickly covered my mouth, eyes widened. "Sorry, sorry," I giggled at his facial expression, removing his hand gently. "I'm sorry."

"I know it's funny, but you have to keep it down," he replied, lowering his finger from his lips.

"You're not wrong," I calmed down. "You're not."

"Okay," he asked, "then what *happened?*"

When I started talking to Klein again, I prepared for people's attention to immediately shift on us. That was something Klein made clear wasn't in his control.

Everywhere he goes, their eyes linger, so in response, I want him away from me, regardless if it seems like I'm the only place he wants to go to.

But even after all the backlash, I still never expected

Aaron Scheuch

to ask me about him.

A part of me prayed he wouldn't because I knew if he asked, I'd tell.

"He just—" I replied.

"Y-You don't have to tell me if you don't want to."

I want to. I want to so bad because I want to know him and I want him to know and *understand* me, but it's not possible. I know how I am and I know how he is.

"He just stopped talking to me randomly, but I don't really care," I explained. "I don't like how everyone thinks I'm upset. Does it seem like I'm *upset* about this, Aaron?"

He stared at me for a few, shaking his head. "No, not really."

"*Yeah*," I replied with an attitude too. "Do I even need to remind you why or can you just recall back to the time he asked me how *masochistic* I was?"

I don't care about Klein because he goes from trying to talk me into engaging in sexual activities with him, then telling Kim how much my presence makes him want to throw up.

I don't care about Klein because he rambles about how much he likes me but switches from girl to girl, as if he's reminding me my time with him will run up if I don't make the call.

Make *what* call?

Go.

Go to all the girls you can have instead because *I* sure don't want *anything* to do with you. Pressure me into making the call because *yeah*, I'd *definitely* want to *date* Jacob Klein.

I'd rather slit my throat.

Scheuch cracked himself up thinking about something, but when I asked him what it was, he shook his head.

"No, you don't need to remind me," he replied gently, swallowing down his laughter. He sniffled, inhaling sharply, "Anyway, back to the point."

"Yes." I sat up straighter.

RECONCILIATION

"I just wanted to make sure you were alright, considering how you were after *Colón* and *Tyson*... now *Conti*—"

I felt my heart sink as he mentioned their names.

"I'm doing okay," I replied softly.

I feel guilty sometimes, for the wrong reasons.

Someone could feel guilty after a loved one is lost due to something haunting them, something they wish they could've done or said. I feel guilty because I can't feel anything. Nothing.

I've been hurt tremendously—so much that even their deaths don't affect me at all—and I assume that is so because I've been mourning them long before they died.

"I try not to think about them as much," I explained, tilting my head, "because it makes me mad."

He noticed my hands fidgeting in my lap. "Well, other than that, you seem to be doing well regardless," he muttered, looking down at his watch.

"That's how it should be," I turned to him.

"No, I mean—your well-being," he said, looking back up at me. "You don't need them to feel poised."

I narrowed my eyes. *"Poised."*

"Content? Composed? At ease?" He began naming synonyms.

I laughed. "I know what poised means, Aaron," I bit back a smile. "You're saying I seem ... *happier?"*

"Less hostile, more gentle," he explained, sniffling again, "listen, if you *really* want to go on a supply run, I'll arrange a small—not because I think you're incapable, but because Sergeant needs you back here—supply run tomorrow with Sergeant and a couple others. Then, we'll go."

"Okay!" I smiled from ear to ear. "Thank you!"

He nodded, inhaling slowly. "Now if you excuse me, I value my sleep *incredibly* much," he said. "Good night."

I sighed, hopping off the table. "Sweet dreams!"

"I don't dream."

I turned. "Bruh, it's a—*Bruh,* it's just a saying."

"Why would I want my dreams to be sweet?" He asked as I reached for the door handle.

"Fine, then go have a nightmare," I opened the door, "goodnight, Aaron."

8 SEPTEMBER. 2021.

I only think about it so much because of the potential. I think about it because I thought there was a *chance*, a *possibility*.

I knew from the start I wasn't going to be able to take anything Klein said seriously, especially when he was in a mood... and not *that* type of mood.

We were in the back of the pizzeria organizing food crates. There was a glassless window, allowing us to see the large dining area from the kitchen. Klein and I were behind the counters. Maxwell and Watkins were on the other side.

"Scheuch, do you think it would be a better idea to sort crates for each house?" Maxwell called.

Scheuch peeped out of the back part of the kitchen, looking around for her. "Wait, what?"

We all turned to him suspiciously.

I gagged at the rancid stench. "What's that smell?"

"I farte—"

"No you didn't."

"It's rabbit ..." he answered as I immediately made my way around him. "*Don't...* look—"

I regretted my choice immediately, gagging at the sight of the decapitated animal. "Oh—I'm gonna be sick," I covered my face. "What *is* that?"

He remained at a neutral stance, hands in his jean pockets. "What do you *mean*, what is that?"

I hesitate. "I-Is that *dinner?*"

"No, it's a souvenir."

"Actually?"

"No, Bui," Scheuch rubbed his forehead. "*Yes,* it's dinner."

"Oh *Aaron*," Maxwell sighed, chuckling. "Okay, so, I'm thinkin' we give every house a crate of food so they don't have to walk all the way to Klein's or the RV to get a snack if they're hungry after curfew."

"Why would they be hungry after curfew?"

"Maybe someone could just crave a midnight snack?"

"If someone ends their entire day hungry, that's their own fault," he replied.

"Aaron, you're tellin' me you've *never* had a midnight craving before?" Watkins asked curiously. "Wait, so, what happens when you wake up in the middle of the night?"

"I deal with it?" he replied.

Maxwell snickered softly, "Well, I think it's also a good idea 'cause roamers have been showing up a lot lately and it's less risky to keep some food at our places."

"Okay," he agreed, "I'm okay with that—" he began walking back to the back part of the kitchen, looking down at his watch before pointing at her, "—just make sure—all crates are even—and keep in mind of cadets like Bui, who live alone—and be considerate of foods they like and dislike."

"Oh wait, that means we gotta rearrange a few of these," Watkins said, setting down at least three crates on the table to reorganize.

"Okay, thanks," Maxwell told Scheuch, turning to Watkins. "Yeah, it'll be easy. Give me the um—" she snapped her fingers, "—the marmalade—to go with my crackers."

"Gotchu."

"*Watkins, I swear* if you give me that can of rancid *mushroom soup* again, I'm gonna *chuck* it *right* at your head!" Scheuch shouted from the kitchen as I burst out cackling.

Watkins laughed loudly as he stood back up, placing another can of mushroom soup in his crate, which made me laugh even harder. "C'mon Kiara, let's go deliver these."

"Okay," she replied, looking over at me. "You coming?"

"Yeah, just let me finish these last couple crates real quick," I began speeding up, but as soon as they left the front doors, Klein began laughing.

I gulped uncomfortably. "Why are you laughing?"

"I'm just thinkin' about how Scheuch told us about the rabbit," he chuckled, grinning from ear to ear. "Wanna know what *I* want as a souvenir?"

You better not say me.

"Not really," I replied, *sarcastically.*

"Oh *c'mon babeesss.*"

I turned to him in horror and he just laughed at me. I narrowed my eyes, seeing it on his face that he genuinely thought this was turning me on. Does it look like I'm switched on? Can you see it in my face? It's certainly arousing *you!*

"Don't ever call me that again." *I think I might puke.*

"My bad," he bends down, leaning himself against the counter. "But I'm just asking."

"You're just asking *what?*"

"Y'know, what we were talking about last night?" he watched his own fingers tap on the marble countertop.

I dissociate every time he speaks to me.

"I don't remember," I said.

RECONCILIATION

"Yes, you do," he grinned, "I'm quite memorable."

"I genuinely don't remember," I replied, monotone, "seriously, I got a lot on my plate right now."

He rolled his eyes playfully, "Anyway, so, how masochistic are you? Are you *capable* of being with a sadistic *fuck* like me?"

I stood there like an idiot.

...

"What?"

"*Klein!*" The bells clung together loudly. We both looked over and saw it was Sergeant, calling from the front door. "Can I borrow you real quick?"

"Yes, sir," he replied, looking back down at me, grinning as wide as ever. "Left you speechless, huh?" he snickered.

He stepped out right as Scheuch walked back in, and by how casual his demeanor was, I assumed he didn't hear any of that.

"Aaron?" I asked, breaking the silence.

He looked up at me, confused at my frightened tone.

"What does masochistic mean?" I asked tensely.

He widened his eyes before looking away from me and down at the peach-colored floor tiles. "Um, that's when, um, you like *pain,* but um—" I listened, ignoring the subtle pink that rose to his cheeks. "But—pain but like—"

We both stood there looking stupid.

"Go look it up in my dictionary upstairs," he said.

"Why?" I asked.

"Just do it."

"But I don't feel like walking all the way upstairs!"

"Then too bad," he smiled widely.

I made a face at him and he copied it, mocking me.

"Why are you asking me this?" he asked.

"No reason," I tip-toed around the answer.

He narrowed his eyes. "You and Klein—?"

"Hell no, I don't like him," I scoffed. "I could never like anyone in the program."

"What do you mean?" he asked as he began unloading another bag, sorting cans.

"I don't think anyone in the program could like me back eith—"

"Don't say that when you know there's always *possibilities.*"

... What?????

What do you mean by that? Wait, backtrack!

We remained standing in our places silently. He chuckled under his breath. "Did *Klein* ask you that?"

"Yea," I nodded, laughing at the way his head snapped towards me, eyes lit up. "What the *hell* does it *mean?*"

He nearly knocked his own glasses off, cracking up. "Have you given him an answer yet?"

"Wha—*Aaron*, I still don't fully understand what it mea-"

"Can you be stupid?" he said, smiling eagerly.

"*What?!*"

"Think stupid!" he said. "*Please* just give him the stupidest responses to throw him off guard."

"Like *what?*"

He scratched the back of his head. "Ask him what the point slope formula is."

I snickered, "Okay."

KLEIN: ...

ME: I wish I could travel back in time and kidnap someone and bring them back here to see what they would do.

KLEIN: What????

ME: Like—imagine an ancient Egyptian pharaoh reacting to a potato chip or something. Think about how many things could send a pilgrim into cardiac arrest.

— — —

"Mj?" My shoulders shook. "Mj, c'mon, you have to leave in twenty minutes."

I jerked up, seeing Maxwell's worried face.

"Aaron sent me to get you."

"*Shit!*" I turned over, tossing around the shitty alarm clock on my nightstand. "The batteries!" I rubbed my face. "I just had a dream—about something—that happened months ago—and I—"

He wanted all of us to gather out to the truck by the crack of dawn. I didn't know why I was so eager to go. I just knew I liked the idea of having something to *do*.

"Don't you already have everything ready?" She bent down and looked at the bag I packed the night prior. She then smiled at Coco, the tabby cat I've adopted, who was walking by peacefully. "You'll be fine. Go change. It seems like you have that covered already." She pointed at the clothes I've hung up on my door.

I jumped out of bed and found myself out on the street with them ten minutes later. My teeth brushed, my hair braided, I walked up with a smile on my face.

Until I wasn't smiling anymore.

Yanes was packing up the trunk with Scheuch alongside him, thinking. He turned to me with his hand still on his chin.

"Bui, this supply run will be just an easy, quick in-and-out, okay?" He explained to me. "Sergeant wants us back to keep everyone aligned and for you to set up the—um-" He turned to Sergeant. "What do you want her to do?"

"The night duty sheets?" I asked.

"Y-*Yeah*," Scheuch nodded. "That sounds about right."

"I said I'm fine doing it?" Yanes turned in his spot. "I can stay up and keep watch?"

"You've fallen asleep twice in a row now, Yanes," Scheuch replied. "Plus I think it'd be more efficient if we had it assigned."

"Like—you and Candreva could have Tuesdays and Thursdays——and Bailey and Watkins could have Mondays and Wednesdays," I suggested, "and so on."

Yanes nodded, looking back up at Scheuch.

"Alright, are we ready to go?"

"Yeah, we're just waiting on Klein."

"Alright," I sighed, clutching onto my bag.

"Listen Mj, this is *serious* shit," he said, eyeing me. "I'm gonna need you to actually focus up and not be chasing butterflies or whatever you do out there."

...

Are you serious?

"I've literally been out in the fields with you just fine," I said calmly—more confusedly. All I know is, I didn't have an attitude.

I know I didn't.

I know I didn't because I was in front of Aaron.

"Where's this coming from?" I asked.

"Yeah, you were, but you weren't focused," he explained. "You just kept talking about personal issues with other people in the progra—"

"Wha—Bru—You literally asked???" I was in disbelief.

I calmed down the second I realized how quick I got mad.

It was a matter of seconds.

"I think we should all be focusing on *ourselves*, but also be on the lookout for each other just in case," Scheuch said, making his way to the backseat. "Just like how it works in sports, we should be working more as a *team*. There's no need for this."

I immediately felt my temper shift as I smiled. I scooched myself to the middle seat, eager as a little child.

Until I watched Klein scooch in beside me, *still smirking*.

"Hey," he whispered.

Sergeant hopped in the driver's seat and began driving once everyone got situated, and since I was stuck in the middle seat I couldn't gaze out the window without feeling like I was staring at one of them. Klein tried to spark up conversation the entire time, and not with just me. He (now) knew I wasn't that much of a morning person.

Sergeant and Yanes didn't know. They were having their own conversation with Scheuch chiming in every once and a while, but Klein's comments were so long and aggravating to the point where even he could hear them.

I hoped that he did.

I swear this shit is NOT REAL!

"What are you doing?" I rolled my eyes, judging him by the way he was rummaging through his bags.

"Gotta eat breakfast." He pulled out a granola bar.

"I hope you choke," I turned forward, feeling my grin wipe off my face within seconds hearing him reply,

"The only one here that's going to be choking is *you*."

I turned to Scheuch wide-eyed. He looked down at me, and our eyes began communicating.

Please tell me you heard that, I pleaded.

I did, he replied, which I counted as permission to turn back around and say something.

"Oh c'mon, you walked right into that one," Klein chuckled quietly.

"Bruh can you stop," I asked, "you sound really stupid."

The entire car went silent. Sergeant looked at me weirdly through the rearview mirror.

Klein clicked his tongue, lifting his palms up and looking back out the window. "My bad, Mj. My bad."

And this time, instead of making a weird face at him, *another* mean comment, or anything I would do that felt natural to me, I just glanced over at Aaron, and he looked at me the same.

"Bruh," I muttered, leaning in towards him as he lowered his chin to my ear.

"Wanna know what he needs?" he whispered.

"What?" I whispered back, turning my face to look up at him softly. I snickered harder at the look he had on his face. *"What?"*

"He needs a good cheese steak."

We discreetly held in our laughter, exchanging amused glances and stifled giggles. For some reason, that was just something that made the situation ten times better than how it could've gone—and for some reason, after that,

I hoped Klein would never stop talking.

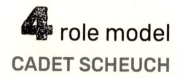 role model
CADET SCHEUCH

There's a cold chunk of ice blurring the emotion behind those eyes.

There's *something* about him.

Colón always had a weird thing about her. I've denied it up to the day she died. She was always spot-on about her thoughts about people. Whenever somebody gave her a bad feeling, she'd tell me, and I wouldn't believe her.

I wouldn't believe her because I knew the things she once said about me, and she couldn't be any more wrong.

But those people, the people she constantly warned and lectured me about, always ended up snaking me in the future.

But she never said anything about Aaron Scheuch, besides the fact he came off as a little intimidating for her and—

"Mj, you got five dollars?" she once asked.

"No," I lied. "Why do you need five dollars?"

"Why don't you have five bucks on you?"

"I'm broke," I lied again, looking around the school lobby, seeing Scheuch over at one of the tables. "Go ask Aaron."

"Oh shit, you right," she nodded, turning around. "Oh naw—bro's picking at his big toe—" she backed up.

"Bruh," I forced myself to look away, "I swear when I first met him, he held himself together so well!"

She turned and stared at me, pointing to the side of her head. "Grill, you done lost more than just your eyesight."

"Okay well, we know looks don't matter to me," I shrugged.

"Yeah, clearly."

"Just hear me out," I placed my palms together. "Hear me out, trust," I said as she made a face at me. "You literally said it yourself, intelligence is what makes guys attractive."

"No, you said that."

"No..." I paused, "*you* said that."

"No?" She shook her head. "*you* said that!"

"I swear *you* did!" I said. "We've both said that numerous times!"

"No, it's just you, baby girl."

"Whatever," I scoffed. "I'd rather spend time with a guy that would mansplain the elements on a periodic table than a bum that smokes so much, he forgets his own name."

She cackled, tapping my shoulder and pointing at him. I hesitated from looking over, but when I did, I saw him sneezing so hard, he knocked his glasses off his face.

"You'd rather be with THAT?"

"I never said anything about 'being-with', María, I'm just saying the fact he's so smart makes stuff like—" We looked over again. His neck was painfully hunched over his papers. His mechanical pencil gripped in his left hand as he repeatedly tapped his forehead with his right wrist joint. "—*that*—easier for him to get away with." I looked back at her to make myself feel less creepy for staring at a guy that's just trying to do his Physics homework. "You ever wonder why I always freak out about being stupid all the time?"

"You don't need to freak out," she replied. "You *are* stupid."

"Yeah, that's why we get along so much, don't we?" I snapped back as she gasped dramatically. "Listen, you could have the perkiest boobs, the roundest ass, the prettiest smile—but if you're dumb, you're nothing but a fuckin' bimbo."

"Yeah, but if you're super smart, wouldn't that just threaten the guy rather than attract them?"

That's the smartest thing I've EVER heard her say.

"Every bitch you meet will ditch yo' ass once they realize you won't fulfill their needs," she said, taking out her vuse and taking a hit. She exhaled the smoke and turned to me, "regardless if you memorize all them $y = mx + b$ shit."

She offered me the vuse and I shook my head.

"Okay well, you know I'm not the type of person that'd do things like that just to make a guy stay." I rolled my eyes. "If their precious needs need to be fulfilled that bad, then they can go fuck themselves."

She grinned, reading the worried look on my face.

"Do you think he's like that?" I asked.

"Why do *you* care?"

"I wouldn't want to be friends with someone like that either?"

She nodded in agreement. "Hm, I don't know. Probably not."

I sighed in relief. "Okay, that's good. I don't think *he*—" We both turned to him again, but turned back once he looked up and made eye contact with me.

Don't laugh. Don't laugh. Don't laugh.

"Oh-" She froze.

I covered my mouth, restraining my laughter.

"Bless you!" she repulsively said.

I looked over at him nervously, watching his eyebrows lower.

"What?" he replied.

"I said, bless you!" she repeated.

"I sneezed fifteen minutes ago?"

"Ah! Delayed reaction," she shrugged as I completely lost it, giggling into her shoulder like a little kid.

It wasn't that funny.

She taught me how to listen to my gut, and my gut always told me there was some type of *feeling* there when it came to Aaron Scheuch. I just never knew what it was, so I never knew how to shake it. I just knew the more I knew I needed to stay away, the more I found myself wanting to get closer.

You would think I learned my lesson after the first fifteen-sum disasters I've willingly traumatized myself with—but I swear every time it's different.

My project on Sterling was put on pause. I knew he just needed someone to be honest with him, so I did it in hopes of fixing him; but Scheuch doesn't need my kind of fixing. If anything, he can bend me back into shape if he wanted to, but he *doesn't* want to. Why? ~~Why? Why? Why?~~

That's what I think when I look at him, I think,

~~I know he's been bit and I'm going to figure out how~~

I am going to figure this boy out.

I thought it would be easy considering how I notice every little thing—sometimes too much.

Let me reword this before I start sounding more 'restraining-order-weird' instead of just 'jrotc-kid-weird'.

There were only two things A-A-Ron Scheuch was afraid of:

an English essay and female interaction.

RECONCILIATION

His nose twitches like a bunny rabbit, and he scrunches it when he speaks to keep his glasses from falling. He doesn't blink as much. The rare times he would, he'd remind me of an emoji when he smiles. He never color-coded his folders in school like how I did, but he didn't have a single one labeled, *organize later*, like how Jonah Adkins did. They were all blue, a sad shade of blue. He was ruthlessly vague— —vaguely ruthless on every other Tuesday, and he was only funny when he wasn't trying.

It was difficult, but I vividly remember joining the program in hopes of finding new friends. Friends that won't degrade me and ruin me. Friends that won't isolate me and hurt me. Friends I could actually learn from instead of constantly worrying about.

Friends.

~~God, I just want people to like me.~~
~~I don't want to be an angry person anymore.~~
~~I've changed.~~

People like Aaron Scheuch don't care about jack shit.

I feel like if he had to sit alone at lunch, he wouldn't even notice. I feel like if people in the hallways judged him as he walked past, he would mindlessly judge them back. I feel like if his best friend treated him like shit, he'd toss him out and go buy a new one. I want to be like that. ~~I used to be like that.~~

I've missed the way I was longer than I could remember.

That's why I don't like thinking about life before the crash, ~~but I do~~. I think about how I made it my mission to be on talking-terms with everyone in the program, and after scoring Conti, Maxwell, and Watkins, I decided going at it in a strategic way would be the smartest option. Aaron Scheuch was Class Commander. Befriending him connects me to all the others easily.

~~He was so cool. I really wanted to be friends with him!~~

At the time, I thought it was a good idea. I felt hopeless and didn't know what to do. I couldn't just live anti-social, guarded, and awkward forever? ~~I don't want to end up alone.~~

The only problem was: that guy was stone cold.

He was so, *so* cold, and I should've seen that as a warning, yet I blinded myself with the possibility that there could be something in him begging to defrost.

I began to think I needed to get to him to figure him out.

I don't know how to form a platonic relationship with a boy just as much as I don't know romantically. I just assumed the guy friends I had only liked me because I looked obscenely familiar to them and the guy friends I've managed to befriend, like Bailey, Johnson, and Candreva for example, all treat me like a sibling.

And one thing I do not want out of this? To be treated like a sibling by somebody like SCHEUCH.

It makes me attach to people easily.

And one thing I did not want to happen? For me to attach to somebody like SCHEUCH.

DAY 351 / THE NIGHT WE SCATTERED

Candreva and Sully drove off alone, leaving Sgt. Rogers and Yanes in the other car to do the same. Scheuch insisted on me staying with Klein instead of waiting on Bailey, so he ended up stranded from all of us that night.

With only the supplies around his waist, he searched the dark woods.

I always shut up when our group brings exercising up. I'm not sure why since I have nothing to be ashamed of.

Yanes and Johnson were always known for their strength. They were always seen working out. Lifting. Pull-ups. Push-ups. Curl-ups. They were built and defined—spent the majority of their time sweaty and sore. And then there were cadets like Sully, Maxwell, and I—where I don't know exactly what they do with their overall fitness, but we're all around the same level.

Sully could beat me in a race, though. She can run a mile about a minute faster than I can.

I could only run miles if I'm properly hydrated to prevent side stitches, but that's difficult for me to do nowadays. Sometimes I stay in my bedroom for so long, I forget to eat and drink. I forget to take care of myself overall. It's nothing like me.

But the reason I bring this up is because Aaron Scheuch is the most fit of us all, whether anyone wants to admit it or not.

He might not be like Klein, Sterling, or Watkins—not even close. Just by looking at him, I don't think he could kick a soccer ball or swing a hockey stick to save his life, let alone catch a damn football sprinting down a field on a sunny day.

But he can run. Fast. And however long you might think he can run for, double it, and guess again.

And the most important thing was that he wasn't scrawny. He's skinny, but not to the point where it looked like a gust of wind could make him tumble over. He was around Klein's size—a bit less muscle and more *toned*. Defined. *Defined* is the word that basically sums up the fact he has all aspects. He was so defined you could see the way his cheekbones sculpted his face, and each bone and vein in his hands, and the ~~bite marks trailing the~~ collarbones beneath his shirt and—

~~no wonder why he might have a bit of an ego problem.~~

yet he was still humble.

He was the most fit out of all of us because no matter how fast a distance runner can run or how heavy a bodybuilder could lift, his mind had more endurance and strength than all of it combined.

He dashed past the roamers approaching him, then hid himself behind a tree to slip his flashlight between his teeth and readjust his pants. He muttered frustratedly as he patted himself down to find his knife, "Why the *hell* did I let myself wear jeans?"

He leaned his head back and rested against the bark, breathing in through his nose and out through his mouth quietly, hearing the roamers groan around him. He scoffed and chuckled to himself, accepting that he was back in the dark, searching for someone he couldn't care less for.

"Bailey," he shook his head before heading off again. "Bui, this better be worth it."

It was not worth it.

Every day I wish I didn't waste so much time running after him. I wish because every time I think about it, I think that maybe, just maybe, things wouldn't have worked out the way they did if I found him first.

I could sit here and say 'what-if' over a hundred times, but what happened, happened. It's not like I can't handle things by myself out there—it's just—after being separated from Klein, Candreva, and Sully, and losing track of time after ~~two-three weeks~~ ~~two-three days?~~ two-three hours?

Things got pretty lonely out there.

Now I can confidently say I'm not the type of person to be scared of being alone, but in the middle of nowhere surrounded by things that wanted nothing but to consume me had me finding difficulty in keeping my composure. Regardless of that, I still pushed through and I *did*.

I knew freaking out would only make things worse.

~~I knew freaking out would prove the others right.~~

"Bui, I'm telling you, you're GONNA start crying out there." Johnson's voice repeated. "You're not going to be able to handle it. You're not ready."

"Yeah, maybe you should wait a little longer," Yanes's voice said more gently. "Maybe gain some more experience."

I have just as much experience as they do.

Last time I checked, we woke up from the same plane crash.

"It's going to be very scary out there," Conti's voice echoed judgefully. "Are you sure?"

Yes. Yes, I'm sure. I literally like this stuff, y'all!

I like the adrenaline. I like coming home with bruised knees, dirt under my nails, and blood bleeding from my bottom lip. Why does no one understand that?!

WHY! DO! THEY! ONLY! SEE! KLEIN! WHEN! THEY! THINK! OF! ME! I'M! SO! MUCH! MORE! THAN! JUST! A! BOY!

I successfully maintained my composure, and so did Scheuch.

I don't know anything relevant about him. I don't think anyone does. I think he makes sure it stays that way.

I don't know about his family the way I knew about Maxwell's. I don't know if he's close with his siblings or if he leans more towards his mother or father. I don't know if he prefers cats or dogs——I actually am afraid to ask him his opinion on animals. The only thing I remember is a picture of a baby goat he sent me around the time we first met.

It was adorable!

He wiped his nose as he kneeled down, picking up a can of tomato soup Bailey must've dropped. He flashed his light, finding the footsteps he left in the mud.

The sky was gray now—gray full of dark clouds, but no birds flew by them like they used to.

He had been searching all night.

I don't know anything. I only notice the little things. I never knew what could make him nearly break until that day we left to go find Tyson. But it certainly wasn't this.

The leaves rustled as his head shot up. His eyes narrowed in an instant as he scanned his area.

"Bailey?"

He listened to the wind whisper through the trees and shut his eyes.

"Bailey, this isn't funny."

He listened again. Nothing.

"Bailey, I'm not in the mood for a round of hide and seek right now," he said. "Where are you?"

Nothing. Just wind.

Now Scheuch was different from Conti whenever the topic of García would come up. He just chose not to say anything, considering how worked up Conti was about it.

But I knew he knew there was absolutely no use going out there looking for him. He saw it as a waste of time. He didn't think García was a big asset to the group. He didn't contribute much. As a matter of fact, I don't think he ever noticed him until he went missing.

But now that it is someone I truly dear, I try not to stress over the fact he's out there in danger for the sake of *my* sanity.

Because he's *not*.

I know after a couple weeks, his priority will shift back to himself.

MARCH 24 2021 / DAY 376

Scheuch was still out in the woods with nothing. Nothing.

Absolutely nothing.

His sense of hearing seemed to begin to play tricks on him.

He swung around, holding his gun up firmly the second he heard rustled footsteps, but it wasn't Bailey. It was a random guy in red plaid. He had a gray beard and a winter hat on.

"Hey, hey, *easy*—" the man immediately held up his hands, widened at the sight of him. "I'm sure I can help you, kid. You look unwell."

"I am aware of how I look." He glared at him.

Blood dripped from his lips, running down his chin and neck. Baggy eyes due to lack of sleep. Skin blue and pale. Not only did he match the smell, he would've fit in with a group of roamers identically.

"That's not my biggest concern right now." He gripped the gun tighter, trying not to eye the half-eaten can of food in the pocket of the man's bag.

He was hungry.

He was *incredibly* hungry.

The man understood and slowly reached for it. He even provided a clean fork. His eyes held sorrow for Scheuch, not fear. He could tell just by looking at him that this wasn't his first time doing this.

"You don't have to kill me for it," he said gently, watching Scheuch's breathing stop. "All you need to do is ask. Not *everyone* out here's out to get cha'. We're just tryna get by these days, y'know?"

Scheuch nodded and grabbed the can from him gently. "T-Thank you," he choked, watching him walk away before nearly gagging from consuming the food too fast. "Shit—" he coughed. "*Oh* shit."

He turned around again, eyes narrowed as if he heard ~~something~~ someone in the distance, but before he could drop the can and head towards it, something stopped him.

I vividly remember feeling so accomplished over the fact I could even track him down in the first place. I was so close.

But we were on opposite sides of a river, and he couldn't hear me call out his name.

I like to think he did have interest in finding any of us again. I like to think he'd stop in his tracks and turn to the side 'cause he thought he heard me calling. But I'm sure he never did.

I'm sure he just focused on what was important. I'm always so fascinated on how a person could do that. How could a person set aside all their quirks, their differences, their feelings, and state of mind, and just do. How does he shut himself off without budging his performance?

It's something I always wanted to learn how to do.

I know I saw his head subtly turn as I called, but yet again, I don't know if he heard *me*. I only watched him pace away, each step having a purpose.

4 SEPTEMBER. 2022.

September 4, 2022.
[untitled]

~~You're super sweet and a great friend, Mj. People around you truly appreciate you. I think life's just keeping you so busy that you don't see it. -Avery <3~~

I hold onto a guy dear to me, but if I'm aware I am too young to know what any of this even means, why do I hold on so tightly? Why when my entire world has shattered into things I used to only see on screens and read in fantasy fictions, I only think of what things would be like if he were here with me?
I think about those who aren't with me all the time. I know I do. I think about that one time Jasmine Giménez held my shoulders and asked me "How long have you been playing?"
Blue socks up to my knees. Shin guards and cleats.
"Oh, I just started," I replied.
She nodded. "You need to keep your head up—make quick but *precise* decisions."
I nodded back. "Okay!"
She smiled. "You kick with impulse. I understand the game is quick and there's a *lot* of pressure, but sometimes you really have to stop and think about what you're going to do. What you do affects the game." She let go of my shoulders and I shivered under the autumn breeze.
"It will come with experience, but right now, Mj, keep your head up."
Every time I think of autumn I think of her, and I wonder how she's doing now. I wonder if she's still alive.

"You never told me you played soccer?" I heard Conti's voice on my side.

I would've flinched, but her voice was calm. I sat with my knees propped up in the driver's seat, in the middle of the empty street.

My hallucinations have gotten worse after the first night with Klein, so it would make sense if they'd get better after we stop talking. But they didn't.

They have grown from just Michelle and Mj. I've seen María. I've seen Kay occasionally. I started seeing Johnson almost immediately after he passed, but tonight, tonight was the first time I've seen Conti.

Seeing her felt so weird though.

I expected to be sad when she died, and of course I *was* in the moment. We were *all* scared—watching the horror in her and Johnson's eyes as the roamer's teeth pierced into their flesh. And of course, I spent the next two months in the woods on the edge of death, so I didn't get the proper chance to grieve.

But the more I lived with it, the more I began to realize I didn't need one.

"You never asked," I replied, looking away from her and back down to the journal in my lap.

> I was 14, and I felt like I knew everything. I was 15, and I felt like I should've known better. I was 16, letting go of all of the stupid things.
> But I turned 18 at midnight today, and I feel like I know nothing.
> Nothing at all.
>
> Amanda never told me Tyson loved me, it was Tyson that invited me in, not her, and it was *me* that let this go too far.
> I was sitting on that kitchen stool, observing her behavior. I listened to her speak to me coldly, looking at me as if she knew something I didn't.
> I was only scared of her because just by looking at her, I knew she'd be a nightmare mother-in-law to someone one day; and I knew no matter how hard I tried to get her son to change, that woman he chooses to marry someday will never be me.
> Yet I mourn him like a widow would. I care for him like a wife would.
> But I shouldn't.
>
> Because after today, I think I'm done pretending that conversation was real.

10 intelligence is only for the gentleman

I think about the car ride back to Jade Street after Tyson's death a lot. What I didn't expect was for *him* to put much thought into it too. I think it was because that was the first time he ever killed a human being.

SEPTEMBER 16 2020 / WHAT REALLY HAPPENED
"Something's *wrong* wit' her," Colón worried after finding me upstairs in our room, shoving food and clothes into my duffle bag.

The others packed up the truck behind Sgt. Rogers as he rubbed his chin. "Well, where is she *now?*"

"I don't know!" she shrugged, beginning to panic.

"OK," he nodded. "Find Scheuch. Ask *him*."

"Who's that?"

He paused. "*Aaron Scheuch?*" he repeated. "Hold on, you're telling me you went through the *entire* school year without knowing who your Class Commander was?"

She didn't show up to school for half the year, what do you expect?

He sighed, rolling his eyes. "Nerdy blonde guy."

"There's multipl–"

"The tall one."

"Everything alright?" Maxwell overheard, peeping her head out the window from the front seat.

"Oooh! *A-A-ron!*" Colón laughed.

"I hope so," Sgt. Rogers turned around, answering her. "We'll figure it out."

— — —

I intended on going to the gun shop to tell Sterling I was leaving. I felt like I owed it to him. I stood there with my bag over my shoulder, my shoelaces tied tight, my navy sweatshirt hood over my head, the same sour look on my face.

Sgt. Rogers was right about Scheuch ~~knowing~~ figuring out. A part of me was hoping I'd run into him. *He* was the one ~~preventing me from leaving~~ I needed to knock some sense into me.

I've been alone for most of my life. I've been used to not having anyone to go to. But what I've noticed these past couple of weeks, all I've just been asking myself is, *"Since when do I care what people think of me?"*

Sterling was in there with us too, of course. He was the one I needed to talk to. "I'm going out," I said to him as he swept the tiled floors behind the glass cases.

"With who?" he asked.

"What? No—I meant I'm heading out of here," I replied as I watched Scheuch look up from the notepad and pen beneath him. His assertive eyes ~~effortlessly~~ drilling into me as he wiped his nose. He instantly inserted himself into the conversation.

"Did *Sergeant* tell you to go somewhere?" he asked.

"AARONN!!!!!!!" Kim's voice whined from upstairs. *"AARON!"*

Silence, deafening silence, although, oddly enough, the only head that turned up to the ceiling was Sterling's. Scheuch looked at me, dropped his pen and crossed his arms slowly. I looked at him, feeling unexpected chills run up my spine and shake me into realization.

He. Knows.

"*I NEED YOUR HELP!!!*" Her voice strained.

"I'LL–"

"Wait, where are you even *planning* on going?" Sterling asked.

Scheuch lowered his head back down, answering for me. "She's *not GOING* anywhere."

"You can't *make* me do anything!" I scoffed.

~~I wasn't going to let anything stop me from leaving those doors.~~ He *knew*.

"*I* can't," he shrugged, tilting his head in a way that may or may not have triggered my fight or flight, "but I *can* at least tell you it's a *STUPID* idea!"

I remained silent before looking over at Sterling. "I'm leaving."

"You're *leaving??*"

"I'm heading back to Central PA—" I explained, "back *home.*"

He paused with his sweeping and looked over at Scheuch's clenched jaw. "You're right, that does sound like a stupid idea."

Scheuch covered his face with his hands and exhaled loudly.

"I'll come back." I made an effort.

He looked up, running his hands down his face. "That's if you don't get yourself killed."

"Why leave in the first place?" Sterling asked curiously.

"I need to revisit a few ~~people~~ places," I responded.

"You don't know if they're even *alive,* Bui!" *He reads me like a book.*

"I don't *belong* here, Scheuch!" I felt myself crumble. "I *don't!* You see the way these people *look* at me!?"

He exhaled again. "And that makes you want to *leave* and find people who *do* look at you a certain way?"

"Why do you even care?" I scoffed.

There are 3 versions of me.

People have many things to say about Michelle Bui, but ~~I don't really pay attention to it much anymore~~ I miss her more than anything. Michelle passed away a long time ago, and ~~anyone with a functioning brain could easily fathom the rule stating, you don't disturb the dead~~ I shouldn't have killed her.

People have things to say about *Mj Bui* too, ~~and the last time I checked, she's pretty well-liked with a relatively good reputation.~~ Last time I checked, she was excited for this Chicago trip to be over so she could ~~tell her sort-of boyfriend all about it~~ go home and see if her ~~boyfriend~~ [insert label] is still mad at her. Last time I checked, she was ~~crazy~~ —*I'm not crazy*— ~~psychotic~~ —*I'm not psychotic, I was just fifteen*—but at least the idiot boys she constantly had around her weren't stupid enough to try to hurt the heart she could barely hold together.

But now, where I am, people only see me as Cadet Bui.

I'm still trying to figure out who she is.

Maybe I don't want ~~to be Cadet Bui~~ change.

He paused, gulping before nodding in agreement and stepped aside, implying that I *was* allowed to leave now. But ~~him doing that made me curious~~ I felt a sense of disappointment quickly drown me.

"Why *do* you even care?" I repeated, ~~eyebrows lowered~~ desperately.

"AARON!"

"Your timing is horrible," he replied instead. He pushed up his glasses. "I don't think it's a good idea for you to leave," he explained, monotone—maybe with a hint of ~~sarcasm~~ sass. "It'd be *unfortunate*, but you're free to leave *whenever*. If you *think* you can survive out there on your own, then go ahead."

"Ok?" ~~I noticed his tone, grasping that he was basically saying I was useful to the group.~~ I needed him to ~~admit that~~ reassure me, but Sterling interrupted him before he could explain further.

"What if you don't make it back?" he asked worriedly. "Wait, are you even *coming* back?? *I* don't want you to leave?"

"What happens if you get bit? Hm?" Scheuch made a point.

"I *won't*." ~~I rolled my eyes~~ I tried not to smile while in my head I was thinking ... almost ... there.

"Yeah, sure," Sterling scoffed before sweeping again.

I scoffed, mocking him back before stepping towards the exit. Scheuch's hand suddenly held out in front of me and I abruptly stopped.

"*Please* ... do *not* ... *leave* ... actually," he changed his mind. "It'd be a big loss."

"Give me one good reason why I shouldn't leave," I said.

"Well for one, you've got one *hell* of a hand," Sterling smiled.

Scheuch and I both turned to him. "*What?!*"

"You're a good shot," he said. "No seriously, some people here *cannot* hold a gun to save their *life*—" he looked down, mumbling, "and we expect 'em to even aim and *shoot!*"

"Cadet Bui, I really think you should just *think* about this."

I was being stubborn. ~~I was surprised~~ to see if he'd put up with it.

BEYOND THE LIVING

I sighed, breaking. "You don't understand—" I sighed shakily, seeing how the look on his face changed.

"Then enlighten me."

"I need to find—"

"Find *who?*" he asked confusingly before taking a deep breath. "Okay. How about we make a *compromise?*"

I sighed again, dropping my shoulders. "What?"

He nudged me back a few steps with an open palm and stepped back directly in front of me. He leaned to his side, resting his hand upon the glass display case beside him and adjusted his glasses in a way that made me ask myself questions I never thought I'd ask. "You *bring* another cadet with you."

"Who?" I immediately asked.

He and I both paused and all I could think was, *please be you, there's no way in hell I'll go with Klein.*

"*I'll* go with you?" *Shut up Sterling!*

I watched Scheuch shrivel in his spot and tried not to laugh.

"No," he shook his head vigorously. "No—no—HELL—NO ... you're gonna have her *die* out there!"

"AARON!" Her voice upstairs called again. Her voice even cracked a bit, and it took me everything not to crack anything even close to a smirk.

Sterling stood frowning as I watched Scheuch remain there silently. I felt the anticipation uncomfortably crawl up my spine. It was as uncomfortable as a bug making its way across my skin. I don't like it.

I. Never. Let. Myself. Break.

"Fine, *I'll* go," he muttered frustratingly, turning around. "I'll go."

"Bu—Aaron, what about Kim?" Sterling said as he opened the door.

He peered over, stone-faced. "Oh well."

And before I knew it, I went from battling with myself internally to nearly tripping over my own feet, trotting out the gun shop and to our left, heading down the sidewalk quietly. I watched him walk in front of me, shaking his head.

"This better be worth it, Bui," he said, stopping and turning around, pointing his index finger at my endearing smile. He sighed despairingly before biting back a faint smile. "This *better* be worth it."

"It will," I replied. "I'll find him."

Suddenly, all the contentment was drained from his face. His subtle smile instantly faded. His eyes turned from softened to laser-focused—almost like how Colón's mother's eyes get before she's about to lecture her.

"Find *him?*" He raised his eyebrows.

I gulped, finding the courage to speak his name.

"Tyson."

His eyebrows raised even higher. "Tyson *Estright.*"

I inhaled a shaky breath. "Yes."

He put his hands together. "You're traveling miles—going back *home*—to find a *boy* from our *high school?*"

Despite his tone, I actually really like Scheuch's voice. ~~I like how he manages to make me sound dumb without being sassy or flat-out rude.~~ I like his voice so I listen to him. I listen to him and actually learn something.

He makes me sound stupid. He makes me sound so, so stupid, there's no other way I can put it that can make it sound better.

Aaron Scheuch *was* occasionally sassy and he *was* in fact, flat-out rude, but that was my favorite thing about him. Hearing him talk would clear my head the quickest, no *Hey, I'm here's* or *It's gonna be okay's* bullshit. He just... *humbles* me.

"Okay, in *my* defense," I replied confidently, "I'm also going back for my house—grab a few things—maybe see if—"

~~Maybe I should listen to him.~~ *Please listen to him. He could seriously knock some sense into me.* ~~He can fix what they broke.~~

"Tyson Estright?" he repeated, making sure this was making just as much sense to him as it was to me. "*My height ... freckles ... short brown hair ...*"

I nodded, feeling that gut-wrenching feeling form in my chest as I began to remember what he looks like ~~and how his voice used to sound and how he looked when he smiled and how he sounded when he laughed.~~

"He ran track," Scheuch continued, "I *think* he ran cross country with me."

In another world, they'd be best friends.

For some reason, I'm confident someone like Aaron would love someone like Tyson. Not sure if Tyson would love him back, though.

Before going into his own little world, he blinked a couple times as he saw me nod. He lowered his chin, ~~his voice remaining monotone.~~ "Are you *kidding* me right now?"

I stammered. "L- Look, I—"

I internally begged him to refuse to let me go, but he didn't. Even *he* knew that was my decision to make, and I knew I *needed* to do this.

I watched him shut his eyes. "Do you really think you're going to find him?"

"I—I don't know, Aaron, staring at the broken flower pots placed along the porch.

...

...

I looked up and flinched as I saw him glare down at me.

"Oh, sorry—*Scheuch*," I corrected myself.

"*Cadet*," he emphasized, cracking a short smile before looking back up, heading up the stone steps.

"*Cadet* Scheuch," I gave him attitude before he stepped into the pizzeria, hearing the discolored golden bells jingle above him. He came out with a bag and a couple more essentials minutes later.

"Do you *really* think you're going to find him?" he asked again.

He has no idea how much this boy means to me. ~~I don't even know myself.~~ I know he means *too much*.

"Do you think I should do this?" I began doubting, not even realizing how much ~~weakness~~ I was showing.

"C'mon," he muttered.

I tossed him the keys as I entered the passenger's side. We ended up driving for hours. He had me hold the map, but to be honest, I wasn't that good at reading it.

~~Just talk to him. Just talk to him.~~

I thought that maybe, if I spend time figuring him out, I can find out what it is about him that makes me *want* to.

I am a well put together person. I *am* a well put together person. I get self-conscious around people I know who are better than me, but not in a jealous or resentful way. I start to close up because I know how *I* can get.

~~If you'd just get to know him, maybe you could learn from him.~~ I can't do it. ~~He's going to look at me differently. He's not going to want anything to do with me.~~ I push good things away.

I sat in the cushioned seat silently, holding my breath. ~~It's not awkward. It's not awkward.~~

"Do you like listening to music?" I broke the silence.

"Sometimes."

Silence passed again.

"Wanna play some right now?"

"Sure, I don't care."

He clicked open the middle compartment as we drove, searching around blindly before holding up a couple disks.

"Do you know how to put these in?"

~~No.~~

"Yeah," I lied, taking them from him and taking them out of the case. I tried to figure it out, but it chose not to cooperate with me. Muttering, I struggled, "It's not—"

He took his eyes off the road. "You have to—"

"No wait, I think I got it!"

I sat back in my seat proudly, looking up at him as we drove around a fallen tree.

"Ooohhh Aaahhh—" the speakers sung, *"It's—been——a tad bit long time—I LOOK-"*

Suddenly it was silent again. I looked over and saw the disk extracting and his hand reaching out for the one in mine. I handed it to him curiously.

He snatched them, rolled down the window, and tossed them.

"Oh-" I broke into soft laughter, which somehow managed to crack a *tiny* smile on him.

~~Just talk to him. Let him warm up to you.~~

"You didn't like the music?" I chuckled.

He scoffed lightly. "I'd rather not torment my ears with that."

I giggled, reciting the lyrics to the song just to mess with him. He looked over at me, narrowing his eyes.

His voice wasn't the only thing that stayed the same. Sometimes it was his face too. He never smiled, so I relied on his eyes. They were green—a gentle mix between forest and olive green. His pupils were often dilated, talking to me, but I got to look closer this time, and honestly, I couldn't tell what he was thinking. I just know at that moment he thought I was funny.

~~He thinks I'm funny. He thinks I'm funny.~~

But there was a blockage.

A wall that prevented me from figuring out if there was any thought behind those eyes or a bunch of secrets I ~~didn't~~ want to figure out. A wall that something had caused to be built.

"That was a disgrace to all music," he said as I giggled harder. He turned and looked forward before I could see him smile.

~~Just talk to him.~~ I prefer being alone. ~~Ask him questions.~~ I don't get attached to people anymore. ~~Be his friend.~~ He and I don't make sense as friends. ~~If you'd just open up, it'd be easier to carry conversations with him.~~ He won't understand. ~~He can change things. He can change ME.~~

I don't need nobody.

I calmed my breathing, watching the horrors out the window beside me. The more I thought about it, the more I kept having to convince myself I was being rational. I kept having this fear that I would be thrown out involuntarily, isolated, and alone in a world like this. I tell myself I don't need the group. I tell myself I can handle things on my own, and truthfully I could.

But I don't want to *have* to.

I want to *want* to.

The group does not need me. I don't have any special attributes that separate me from others.

I'm a good runner, but there are runners who are faster. I'm good with first aid, but there are people who bandage better. I'm good at scavenging, but there are people with better eyes than me. I'm quick and smart, but there are people who are quicker and smarter. I'm a good shot, but there are people with better aim.

They don't need me.

So I need to get them to *want* me.

10 ¼ ~~feelin' peachy~~ closure

Aaron Scheuch has always been incredibly vague. That's just who he was.

I would have to repeat a question in my head over and over and over again before actually asking it in fear of stuttering or it not making any sense.

He's not going to judge you, I tell myself. *He's nice and understanding.*

"Aaron, can I ask you a question?"

"You just did."

I rolled my eyes as he snickered, hands gripping the wheel.

"Do you think people you hang out with can influence your behavior?" I asked, looking over at him.

"In some cases."

I hold my breath.

...

One. Two. Three. Four. Five. Six. Seven. Eight. Nine. Ten. Silence.

...

Uno. Dos. Tres. Cuatro. Cinco. Sies. Siete. Ocho. Nueve. Diez.

"Why do you ask?"

I exhale. "People always told me to stop hanging around María or I'd end up like her."

"And did you?"

"No, not completely," I shook my head. "I always thought that if that statement was true, maybe there was a chance *I* could influence her."

"It's different," he rubbed his nose, glancing up at the rearview mirror, watching the roamers turn their heads as we passed.

"How so?" *I knew exactly how it was different.*

"It's easier for her to influence *you* because people like *you* would give in to—such activities—to—and I'm just saying this as an example—"

"Yeah."

"—to 'fit-in'——feel *accepted*—" he explained, "now if you'd want to influence *her*, it'd be rather difficult. She would have to have the *desire* to change. You see what I mean?"

"Yes."

"But I say I see the understanding behind both because—strong-minded people like you don't give into those things easily."

He thinks I'm strong-minded!

I tried to hide the fact that I was trying to figure out what was so fascinating about him. Why was *he* the one making me doubt rather than someone like Klein or Sterling, who actively tried to change my mind.

I don't let people know me.

But people like him, I want to know.

We passed the wrecked cars, the piles upon piles of dead bodies, yet we talked like things were normal. Like everything was normal.

I saw the maggots and trails of dried blood staining the pavements as I listened to him speak.

~~Sometimes I would catch myself asking questions I already knew just to hear him talk.~~

"Did you do any other events?"

"No," he replied. "I suck at throwing and jumping. Coach told me he was going to put me in the *blah blah blah*—though—to work on my—*blah blah blah*—"

~~What am I doing? What am I doing? What am I doing?~~

~~If I find Tyson, I'll have to leave Scheuch behind and Conti and Maxwell and Watkins and María and—~~

Maybe he'll fit in well with the group.

Sometimes I catch myself being somebody that announces every thought they have aloud, but being around him didn't make it seem so bad. He always had some knowledge behind everything and I liked that.

Eventually I ran out of questions to ask and didn't feel like pointing out the horrors from outside, so I let us sit in silence. To me, it wasn't so awkward now.

"Don't you hate it when someone asks you a question that is so stupid, it makes you violent?"

He turned to me silently. *Is he concerned—or is he agreeing—or is he implying that—wait, he's smiling!*

"OK," I bit back a smile, "in my defense—"

"No—" he chuckled, "no, there's no *defense* to that!"

"*Listen!*" I laughed.

"What was the question you asked me earlier?" he asked, looking from the rearview mirror to me. "Hm?" he raised his eyebrows. "Why do British people lose their accents singing?"

I shrugged. "It's Bri-ish."

He paused. "*What?*"

"You gotta say Bri-ish like Bri-ish," I said, looking at his narrowed eyes. "Bri-ish people don't enunciate the 'T' sound."

"Alright," he exhaled a short laugh, "and what else did you ask me? You asked me if I knew Amish people didn't only speak English."

"I seriously didn't know that."

"Do you need me to give you more examples?"

From Mathematics... to Track & Field... to Pilgrims... to the difference between Christianity and Catholicism to Soccer positions I still can't keep track of... to the plot of Alice and Wonderland, we finally got to the point where it was time to get serious.

"Where do you live?" he asked tensely.

Our hometown was wrecked. Gone. ~~Gone. Gone. Gone.~~

"Go down to Adam's playground—" I replied, "—turn left and head over the bridge. I live further up the hills."

"Street name?"

"Aurora Avenue," I quickly replied.

"Which number?"

"Huh?" I looked over at him quickly.

"Which house *number?*"

I remained silent, letting him see the hesitation on my face. He understood and looked away, hands gripped on the steering wheel, foot on the gas.

I let myself dissociate. We drove down the familiar streets in silence. I listened to him breathe. He turned to me again and asked, "How are we going to find him?"

"Bui?" ... *"Bui!"*

I remained at the front door of my house, staring at the empty walls silently. He was in my cabinets. He checked the pantry. He made his way upstairs for me and found my bedroom left exactly the way it was.

"Where would Tyson be, Bui? I need you to think!" His voice echoed from upstairs. I heard him rummaging through my closet with no second thought.

"We can check his house," I replied. "Maybe look for some clues."

I spend a lot of time wishing I never walked through that door. I spend a lot of time wishing I wasn't given another reason to let go.

I found my footsteps getting faster; my breathing getting heavier. Maybe, just maybe, if I treat it as if it was just ripping off a band-aid, it would hurt less.

"Bui, be careful!"

I barged through the door, immediately turning away from the foul smell.

He's here. He's dead.

More dead than he's been to me for years.

It was nothing more than simple déjà vu. The relief that trickled down my spine was always temporary; the amount of times we ran back to each other after things went bad.

I always seem to know when it's really the last time. I know it when I feel more comfortable saying my last goodbye.

As you grow up, the band-aid isn't so hard to peel off anymore. You rip it off and let the wound heal.

In the middle of the tilted picture frames, misplaced chairs, and empty cabinets, Tyson stood, malnourished and fragile.

~~Mj is dead. Mj is dead. Mj is dead.~~

~~I have to let her go too. I have to let her go too.~~

I stood still with that familiar, invasive pit in my stomach, watching him turn around, glaring with cloudy eyes. I stood there for what felt like days, feeling my knees slowly weaken.

I touch my throat, feeling it tighten. I run my hand from my lips to the side of my face, feeling my jaw wire itself shut. I couldn't bring myself to make a single sound.

I just stood, watching him stagger himself back and forth in the same place his mom made me realize ~~maybe we do have a chance~~ she hated me.

~~She hated me. She hated me. She hated me.~~

I inhaled a shaky breath as my vision grew foggy and lifted up my right hand, running it across my face before smacking the doorframe beside me as hard as I could.

His head shot up. His eyes widened. His nostrils flared. He revealed his yellow, rotting teeth beneath his lips and growled before lunging directly towards me. I inhale again but instead through my mouth, watching him increase his speed.

I guess this was the moment Scheuch realized I wasn't going to move unless he made me.

He grabbed my shoulder tightly, shoving me out the way. He took his steps forward, colliding against him. I watched him reach down to the sheath at his waist as they pushed and shoved. Eventually, Tyson's body went from firmly against the wall to lifelessly on its side, bleeding out on the hardwood floors.

The hunger in his eyes faded. His eyelids fluttered shut. The blade that pierced deep into his skull was pulled out, smeared onto Scheuch's denim jeans, and back into its sheath.

I ~~rushed~~ walked towards him ~~sobbing, holding him tightly,~~ silently, picking up one of his hands, feeling his cold touch. I don't think I was physically capable of hearing anything around me.

"I'm going to clear out each room and find something worth grabbing," Scheuch sighed before pushing himself up.

I was ~~crying so roughly,~~ sitting so still, I bet it scared him—because I wasn't sitting there on my knees, weeping gently like those sentimental movie scenes. ~~I cried with everything I had.~~ I sat and stared in silence.

~~I couldn't even look at him~~ I looked at him coldly, and every second that passed, it just reminded me of how much I *wish* ~~I listened to him.~~ I could just cry and mourn like a normal person would, but things are different for me. I always wish I could just feel bad and forgive like a normal person would, but things are different for me. It's always different for me that it scares me.

I sat and pushed. I sat and pushed and pushed and pushed but I couldn't bring myself to cry.

I needed to cry. I desperately *wanted* to cry, but it was like I couldn't anymore. I couldn't cry for him because I've already cried enough. If anything, I *wanted* to cry for *me*.

He was the only person that could still convince me I was a good person, but as I looked at the blue veins that ran up and down his arms and flimsy body, I realized I was looking at the only reason why I would even doubt something like that.

Putting all our ~~silly~~ *degrading* arguments aside—all our ~~ups and downs~~ high *highs* and low *lows*, I ~~didn't have that~~ had many regrets.

I stayed with ~~him, being grateful for having~~ somebody who ~~willing to put up with my bullshit and sit me down in my place if he had to~~ took advantage of the love I have for him when what I should've done was listen when ~~he~~ they told me, ~~"If you'd do anything for me, move on for me then."~~ "Soon it'll be too late to know when you need to leave."

But now I ~~can't~~ can.

Because when he died, ~~it felt like a part of me died with him~~ I was finally given the permission to grieve the part he took from me. The part I knew was still alive, but she didn't belong to me anymore.

I lifted up Tyson's wrist, adjusting his palm and fingers against my right cheek. ~~Just like he used to. Just like he used to. Just like he used to.~~

I laughed to myself as I felt his touch and imitated, mocking his voice, "I'm sorry Mj," I whispered softly. "You didn't deserve that. I care about you a lot, you know that."

I inhaled sharply, quickly wiping away the tears ~~I cried for me~~ aggressively.

"Thank you, Tyson," I replied, in my normal voice, opening my eyes; looking away from him and up at the ceiling. "That means a lot."

I slammed the door shut after reentering the passenger seat and held my emotions tightly in the palm of my hand. I listened as Scheuch put my bag in the backseat for me and started up the engine. I stared directly forward as Scheuch removed my weapons from their holders, keeping them stashed away somewhere I couldn't see and reach.

"Are you *okay?*" he then said, hands on the steering wheel.

"Yeah." I removed my jacket to allow myself to get situated. "I'm a little hungry," I replied, casually.

I reached behind me to grab the nearest can of food I packed. He opened it for me before starting our drive back home.

~~It's okay now. It's okay now. It's okay now.~~

This was something I knew would keep me up at night and guilt me when I woke up in the morning. This was something I knew would always follow me wherever I go. Now even though the pain might not seem significant at the moment, I knew it was never going to get easier, I was just going to get better at dealing with it.

About an hour of silence later, he stopped the car, glanced around outside, and sighed.

"What are you doing?" I broke the silence—my voice up two octaves. I cleared my throat.

He shook his head and turned off the engine. "We are going to have to spend the night here and begin driving early tomorrow. We're not going to be able to make it back before the sun sets."

"Okay," I smiled lightly.

"You can take the back," he said as I nodded, climbing to the backseats.

I folded up my jacket to use as a pillow as Scheuch moved to the passenger seat, leaning it back.

"Bui."

I turned to him, eyes widened as he took off his glasses.

Damn!

He noticed the worry on my face and said, "We should be safe as long as we don't make any noise."

"Okay," I choke up, studying the face he hid under those lenses.

He ignored it—or I assume just took it as a compliment.

"Do you snore?" he asked.

"No, I don't think so," I replied.

He raised his eyebrows. "You don't *know?*"

I shook my head nervously.

He looked me directly in the eyes, tone crystal clear. "If you start snoring, I'll strangle you in your sleep."

"I—okay."

We laid ourselves down, but I wasn't ready to fall asleep just yet. I looked to my side, watching him stare forward, watching the sky turn orange.

"Scheuch," I broke the silence again.

"Yes?" he replied.

I enjoyed listening to how passionate he'd get talking about the things he liked.

"What's the difference between Calculus, Statistics, Algebra, and Physics?" I asked him.

"Errr—" he mumbled. "That Physics was a science credit?"

"And what's the point of taking AP US History if we're just going to learn the same Pilgrim-this, Pilgrim-that story?"

It's all irrelevant to us now, but *God,* he had me hypnotized.

But before I knew it, the silence he gave me wasn't due to an incoming sassy remark or a pause to let him think, he was just asleep; head to the side, eyelids gently shut.

I turned to the other side, biting back the smile I had on my face before letting it quiver away. I scrunched up, burying my face into my hands to finally

Let

Myself

Cry.

10 ½ who are we gonna tell? the police?

I was woken up to the sound of the door opening and two hands gripping tightly around my ankles. My body dragged across the leather seats as I restrained myself from squealing, making *any* noise.

"Aaron...?" I scanned my surroundings. "Ow!" I winced softly as my head hit the bottom edge of the car. I look over at him sleeping soundly. "Aaron!"

The roamers often come out at night. It's colder.

Standing in the middle of the wrecked highway full of abandoned, rusted cars and roamers staggering by, was a masked man with a gun to my head. I was out of the vehicle, back against the rough pavement beneath us. He leaned in close, so close that I could tell you what he ate for dinner that night, and chuckled softly.

"I'm guessing I don't need to tell you what'll happen if you make a noise, sweetheart," he whispered.

We'll call him Person A.

"The hell?" I muttered as I looked to my left, seeing another man looking into the passenger's seat.

We'll call him Person B.

Person A and B were basically wearing the same thing. It was some sort of uniform with a warrior symbol near the collar, but to be honest I wasn't paying close attention to any of that. I was too focused on Scheuch. I could hear him replying to Person B nonchalantly.

"Quoi?" Person B then smashed his gloved fist into the glass, grabbing Scheuch by the collar as at least five to seven roamers turned in our direction. "Do you think I'm fuckin' with you?" His French accent seeped through. *"Lève-toi!"*

"Look at me," Person A hovering over me said gently—unsettlingly, creepily, spine-chillingly gently. "Don't worry about him. This will be quick."

I didn't listen and just continued looking over at him, holding my breath. I exhaled stressfully, squirming harder as I saw the gun in Person B's hand.

"What did I just say?" I heard Person A getting more aggressive. "Turn and look at *me*. Now."

I turned, stone-faced. "Bruh, I'm trying!" I replied, raising my eyebrows. "You're kinda all up in my face, man."

I don't handle situations like these well.

I can't take myself seriously.

But I think this was one of those rare moments where I was actually a *little* frightened. I wasn't sure what was going to happen. I wasn't sure of what their intentions were, and I wasn't sure if *he* was going to be safe.

"What's the point of wearing the masks?" I stalled. "You guys look stupid."

"We wear 'em to hide our *stupid* identités!" Person B responded.

"Who are we gonna describe your descriptions to?" I scoffed. "The police?"

Scheuch chuckled under his breath.

Person B rolled his eyes. "You two look too clean to be living alone in some—*shitty* car!"

He had the gun up to Scheuch's face, ready to blow a hole through his head if he were to try and do anything stupid. Scheuch was completely still, blank—coming off as mindless and oblivious, but I prayed and prayed he thought of something because I didn't have my weapons on me and I assumed he didn't either.

"Where are you guys heading?" Person B asked. "Do we have a community we don't know about?"

"Got food? *Water?*" Person A interrogated me. "Roofs?"

"And why would that concern the two of you?" Scheuch asked, drum-roll please, monotone.

Person B's eyes remained on Scheuch, unwavering. I saw Person A's smile through his mask.

"I suppose we would have to earn that information, am I right?" He leaned in closer, his other hand now on my waist.

I scrunched up in disgust, but remained calm considering the firearm against my neck.

"How about I make you happy for a few minutes, and then you'll owe me one, yeah?"

"Stop—Yo chill," I choked up the lump in my throat, feeling his hand slide down to my butt. "Bro—stop!"

"She's sixteen." Even Scheuch's tone budged a bit.

"Years *old?*" Person A's eyebrows shot up. "*Damn* girl!"

"Sérieusement mec ?" Person B cringed, gun still up and aimed.

"*Oui*, elle a seize ans !" Scheuch nodded.

He gasped softly. "Hein? Tu parles français?"

"Hey, you can't blame me man," Person A on top of me grinned, lifting my hips up. I felt his hand squeeze me and his breathing getting heavier. He came closer. "It's been a long time since I've seen a woman. A man has needs, y'know?"

"I'm not a woman," I spat, resisting his touch.

My breathing steady, my voice cold. I obviously wasn't pleased but I wouldn't say I felt vulnerable as I was being violated either. It was like he was taking advantage of a dead body, because my mind was somewhere else.

It was still on that kitchen floor.

~~Scheuch, please do something. I'm not okay.~~

"I'm *not* a fucking woman, I'm just a girl!" My voice trembled. I grew frustrated. *"Stop!"*

"How many people?" Person B interrogated, looking at the disturbance on Scheuch's face.

"Stop!" I kept muttering, angry. *"Stop!* No!"

No. No. No. This cannot happen. This is disgusting.

"What?" Scheuch let out.

Still. Fucking. Monotone.

"The community you are living in," Person B replied. "Tell me how many, and I will get him to stop."

I'm fine. I'm fine. I'm fine.

I can handle it. I can handle it. I can handle it.

I'm not vulnerable right now. I'm not vulnerable right now.

I'm just a *tad* bit weirded out.

"How many goodies you got?" Person A whispered in my ear, hand still on my body. "Hm?"

"Get your fucking hands off me and I'll tell you!"

"Aw," he scoffed. "You're bluffing."

I remove his hands from my thighs, preventing them from unbuttoning my jeans. It was difficult, but I managed. His weight on me felt suffocating, but I'd rather be squished than rat out information.

"She's a tough one," Person A lifted up his head. "Feisty."

"Get off of me," I demanded.

"You got guns, sweetheart?" he asked. "Ammo?"

I held back the tears in my eyes and inhaled sharply, lifting myself up so close, my nose could touch his. "I got one bullet just for you."

He chuckled, which made me realize my anger rather amused him more than anything. But I wasn't going to say anything.

I wasn't going to say anything.

No matter how hard he was going to push, I knew between me and Scheuch, it was going to be *him* that would spill. I would be able to handle how degrading this was, but I wouldn't be able to handle the burden of putting the others in danger, no matter how angry I could be with any of them.

So I rely on Scheuch.

"*Where* is it?" Person A began demanding. "My buddy and I haven't eaten properly in days. We only have food that'll last us a week or two!"

"How the *fuck* is that *my* problem?!"

He smacked me across the face, leaving my face red and jaw clenched, feeling my dignity wanting to wither away, but I held onto my self-worth tighter than anything.

"I didn't want it to come to this." I felt his fingertips trailing closer and closer to the button and zipper on my jeans. I gasped.

Person B urged Scheuch as if he were on our side for even just a second. They began communicating in French.

"Combien ?"

"Dix-huit," Scheuch replied calmly. "Un homme adulte. Dix lycéens. Sept lycéennes."

"Ouah," he replied. "Est-ce sûr?"

"Euh—assez."

He tilted his head. *"Assez ?* Il faut être plus précis que ça."

Scheuch took a deep breath, composed. "Parfois, quelques dizaines de—*zombies* franchissent les barrières, mais nous avons suffisamment de—*cadets* pour garder les toits chaque nuit."

"Stop!" I kept saying. "Stop!" Stop. Stop. Stop. Stop. Stop.

"Cadets ?" Person B's eyebrows raised. "Comme à l'armée ?"

"Adolescents du JROTC." Scheuch spat out. "Maintenant, éloignez-le d'elle."

Person B cocked an eyebrow before repositioning his gun, shooting Person A ruthlessly. My hand covered my quick gasp as his body weight dropped on me; blood spurting onto my skin and clothes. I pushed him off and covered my face, catching my breath softly.

Holy shit. Holy shit. Holy shit.

"Trời ơi!" I gasped, looking over at them.

"We just revealed our location to every zombie within a two-mile radius, so I will make this easy," Person B spoke slowly, accent seeping through. "Tell me more about where you live, and I'll let you guys go—and you guys can go back and tell your *cadets,*" he mocked, "to start packing."

Scheuch stared at him blankly, eyebrows slowly lowering, jaw slowly tightening. Suddenly, the wall that hid everything about him in his eyes thickened. Suddenly I didn't recognize the teenage boy who runs into trees by accident; the boy who would play hangman using only elements on the periodic table. Suddenly I knew the boy ~~I thought so highly of~~ that fascinated me so much, was someone I needed to stay away from.

But deep down, I don't want to. Deep down, I know in moments like these, I need him.

Scheuch reached out his hand, grabbing the gun from Person B swiftly. He held it up, smacking the side of his head as hard as he could.

I didn't expect him to be strong, quick with hand-to-hand combat. He was still awkward, a bit stiff, but his choices were quick and cleverly made. Soon he had Person B on the ground beneath him. Person B, who was bigger and stronger than him, was pinned and helpless, squirming to regain control.

The gun was knocked from his hands and kicked away. Person B's mask was torn off, revealing his identity. He wasn't a day past twenty-four.

Scheuch managed to get a firm hold on him after they spent moments tossing and turning. I've watched plenty of fights in my lifetime, yet I still flinched at every punch I heard him swing.

He reached his hands up to his neck, choking him tightly, all while keeping a chilling glare in his eyes. He didn't blink once. He didn't make a single sound.

Person B's hands gripped on his wrists as he gasped for air. That only made Scheuch's grip grow tighter. He then tried to smack him. That only made Scheuch's stare colder. He reached out to his sides for anything to grab, anything to hold and bash into the side of Scheuch's head, but it was over. He lost.

Scheuch reached his right hand down to his waist, removing his knife from its sheath, watching Person B's eyes grow in fear before slicing open his throat.

When he stood back up, he was normal again; blinking and breathing. He was the regular Aaron Scheuch, though instead of being covered in mud, it was the blood of the man he just killed.

I was still on the ground, knees propped up, hands on my face. For a second, I was just frozen, processing what had just happened. I couldn't cry yet. I couldn't throw up either, despite how much blood was on the both of us. It was so quiet, I could hear him catch his breath behind me. I could hear him step over and get on a knee, urging me up.

"D-Don't touch me," I immediately said, sitting myself up.

It wasn't dramatic. It wasn't dramatic. It wasn't dramatic.

It wasn't traumatic in a way where I couldn't stop feeling the same hands on me, no, because that part I handled fine. It was the fact I lost control of the only thing I had left nowadays.

And God, I hated that.

I hated that. I hated that.

I hated him.

And suddenly I was hysterically laughing as I gently laid my forehead onto my knees, sighing in relief and amusement. "Oh my God, Scheuch."

He readjusted himself, allowing him to sit up with his elbows on his knees beside me.

I softened my laugh, feeling my back shrivel up and tremble. "Dude—I—I'm—"

He stared into the trees. He stared as those walls thickened and thickened while mine were slowly wrecking apart. He glanced over at me, eyebrows lowered. "Bui."

"I—" I inhaled shakily.

"Lift up your head."

I do as he says and turn to look over at him. I'm not sure why I still felt the need to restrain myself from him. He just saved my life. *Again.*

"Are you hurt?" he asked coldly.

"I'm fine," I lied, steadying my breath. "I'm *fine*—it's just——we've been fighting roamers for so long, I forgot what other kind of dickheads were out there with us."

"We need to leave before the roamers find us."

I nodded, gulping.

He blinked slowly and said, "It's not safe out here anymore."

"It never was."

10 ¾ want a bite?

The rest of the night was a blur. I only remember watching him silently pick out glass shards from his face with tweezers before asking him if I could come up to the front seat to sleep next to him. It took me a lot of courage to ask that, and he knew it.

He turned around worriedly. "How—would you—*fit-*?"

"I meant in the seat beside you, Aaron," I chuckled, seeing it click in his head.

"*Ooh*," he nodded, taking a blanket and brushing off the shards on the seat before laying it down for me.

I climbed over. "Thanks," I shivered, feeling the cold air coming from the open window beside me.

"Are you *sure* you're not hurt?" he persisted. "No *cuts*—anything at all?"

I shook my head. "No, I'm fine. Thank you," I smiled, watching him clean up and start up the engine.

We drove in silence for a few minutes, processing what had just happened. I curled up every time I remembered whose blood was on my face. He winced every time he bent his fingers wrong.

"Do you want me to bandage your knuckles up a bit?" I broke the silence. "You hurt them pretty badly."

"Um—they should be fine."

"*Aaron*, you're *bleeding.*"

He glanced at them and sighed, reaching down, grabbing the kit. I readjusted myself in my seat, gently bandaging his right hand, just like the way he taught me.

There was something significant about the air that night. It was clear; *crisp*. Every breath I took felt like chills rushing down my spine, electricity rushing through my veins; like it wasn't real. I saw the blood and gashes on his face and finally broke a bit. He looked over at me hesitantly once he heard me cry.

I wiped my tears immediately and sniffled. "Allergies. I'm just allergic. Totally."

He faintly smiled. "Gotcha."

I took a shaky breath.

It was just the thought. The sight of the blood dripping down his fingers only made me think about it more. It had me looking at him, wondering, *how could someone be so strong but so fragile?*

He drove blank-faced, looking back over at me every two or three seconds, as if he couldn't keep his eyes on the road. I was done with his hand now and curled up, facing him.

"Are you French?" I asked.

He looked over at me, blinking. "No."

I widened my eyes, smiling. "So *what*—you're just—*casually* fluent?" I turned away, muttering under my breath, "Damn, what can't you do at this point?"

"What?" He made a face.

"Nothin'–"

I woke up a few hours later, feeling a thin black jacket covering me. I readjusted myself, moving my hair out of the way. It was morning now and he was still driving us home.

He looked at me and I smiled faintly. "Morning."

"Morning," he replied back.

I inhaled. "Is there anything I can do to help when we get back?"

"Um," he thought aloud, looking at me again. "I'll let you know when I think of something."

I couldn't shut up. It was like suddenly, I loved talking in the mornings. I looked over, hesitating, "Hey Scheuch?"

"Hm?"

"Did you really mean it—" I fidgeted with the zipper on my jacket, "—when you said it'd be a big loss for us if I left?"

He took a few seconds to reply. "In a way, yes," he answered, pausing again, "but I mostly said it to convince you to stay on base."

"Oh," I replied softly, letting the silence pass by. We didn't rest well at all. I'm not sure if he even went back to sleep.

"What's wrong?" he asked.

"*Nothing's* wrong," I replied, smiling widely. "Why would you think anything's wrong?"

"You were being *quiet*." He raised his eyebrows. "It's *worrying*."

"Oh—okay," I rubbed my forehead. "Can you be honest to me about something?"

"Sure."

"Do you think I'm just as useless as Kim makes me seem like?" I waited impatiently for his response.

"Do *you* agree with what she says about you?" he asked.

"No," I replied.

He nodded, remaining silent.

I sighed frustratedly, remembering the things we've both seen, the things we've been through and the things she's said and people agreed with. I always had the reflex to constantly guard, defend, and stand up for myself. That's all I knew.

If I would just let my guard down and talk to him, maybe he'll do the same.

"I know it might seem like I don't know what I'm doing, and maybe I don't," I said, "but I know I'm doing a *damn* good job." I inhaled sharply. "Over the past couple months, we've seen our friends—friends who were stronger, faster, SMARTER than me—drop like flies——and it's unfortunate, it really is, but I'm not sitting here due to luck, Scheuch."

"Mj, I don't think any less of you." *He called me by my first name.* "If you're asking me what I personally think, then no, I don't think you're useless. I personally think *everyone* has a use for something."

He grunted softly as he felt blood dripping out his nose. We've all been getting those so often, we don't even react to it anymore.

"If you're feeling doubt, try to remember you can't control how others perceive things," he said, grabbing the tissue I quickly handed him. "If you are secure with how you feel about yourself, you wouldn't feel the need to make sure others feel the same."

I shoved down that lump that formed in my throat once again. "But don't you ever worry others will judge you?" I began chuckling. "Like that one time you bit that flower off its stem in front of Kiara and she started yelling at you to spit it out." I watched him squint to remember the moment I was talking about. "Like—you don't ever think the person beside you might think, *This dude's WEIRD, man.*"

He smiled. "I like to think of it as a game," he explained. "If a person were to find me weird, I'd find a way to make them think I was *weirder*—just to amuse myself." He raised his eyebrows, turning and looking over at me. "So, just for an example, if I was eating that flower and a person beside me were to judge, I'd give the flower stem to them and ask them if they want a bite."

I giggled as he turned forward again. "Was that flower good?"

"Could've used a bit of salt."

The feeling I felt during that car ride home was unexplainable. I wasn't relieved enough to be able to lift myself up and fly away, but I wasn't heavy enough to stay stuck to the ground. I knew it was a matter of time until I start missing Tyson again, until I begin reminiscing about the moments where it felt like all that pain was worth it.

But I didn't feel that way at the moment.

I stood up there with my body out the sunroof and leaned my head back, allowing myself to breathe. My heart felt unchained. For the first time in a long time, it wasn't tied down to anyone or anything but *me*. I didn't know what that sensation was, I just knew suddenly, the wind that blew against my skin didn't feel so much like a burden anymore.

To prevent the others from seeing us come back to Jade Street like this, I had to sneak him in through my bar. We were crammed up in the downstairs bathroom with no source of light other than the shitty cobwebbed lantern flickering above us.

There was something about this moment that stuck out to me. We were silent, looking at our reflections. He leaned over the sink, picking out a glass shard he must've missed before picking up a rag, wetting it with a water bottle.

I stood and watched him rub the blood splattered across his forehead in the mirror before looking down at me. He handed me the cloth gently, and something about the look he had in his eyes made my walls immediately thaw; the walls made of thick ice I've built to stay away from people, away from people who affect me how he does. They were gone now, melted.

"Aaron, can you do me a favor, please?" I asked gently, grabbing the rag from him.

"Hm."

"Don't tell anyone what happened."

He broke eye contact with me, looking down at the rusted sink. "Wasn't planning to."

"Wasn't planning to do *what?*" Colón's voice asked firmly.

5 no, *you* go sleep
CADET BAILEY

I remember when I first met Scheuch and Bailey. I met them around the same time, for similar reasons and circumstances.

I've mentioned I grew close to Bailey after he helped me memorize the General Orders. That moment was significant because of the way he did it.

He had a wooden meter stick and a stopwatch. He gave me five minutes to look over the eleven orders, and then he took the book from me and asked, "What's your first order of the sentry?"

I would stare back at him nervously. "Uh... T-To take—charge—of this—" *What's the word? What's the word?*

I'd watch him imitate the word I'm missing as if we were playing a game of charades. Sometimes I would purposely mess up on a few just to watch him act them out. It was funny, and it was nice having company.

"To take charge of this post and all government property in view," I replied.

He scoffed, shaking his head. "Say it with some *confidence!*"

"To take charge of this post and all government property in view!" I did not change my tone.

"Okay, what's the sixth?"

"BRUH!"

I would spin around in the swivel chair in Sgt. Roger's office, watching him pace back and forth with the meter stick. He'd either pretend it was a rifle and start shooting at the walls—*or me*—or he'd start marching with it or pretend it was a katana.

When he helped me with the phonetic alphabet, it was even funnier. He was sitting on a desk in front of me.

"A."

"Alpha," I replied uncomfortably.

His blue eyes glared at me, *glared*. "B."

"Bravo."

"C." He smiled as he watched me think.

"Charlie," I replied.

"L."

"L?!" I raised my eyebrows. "Hmmm ... Lime?"

He smacked his forehead. "No, we'll come back to that one later." He looked down at the paper. "S."

"S?!"

"It's the—uh—" He thought. "It's the desert!"

"Sienna?" I shrugged.

He sighed, smiling. "The *desert?! SIENNA!?*"

Scheuch looked up from his spot. "Bailey, the desert you are talking about is called the *Sahara* desert," he corrected with a smug grin on his face. "You're confusing her with a clue that is incorrect."

"Shut up, Aaron."

Whenever I would ask him for help on schoolwork, it was different. He'd look at the English assignment and laugh. "I suck at English!" He'd stare at the math problems and pat my back, "Ahh, this is easy. You got this, kid."

RECONCILIATION

"If it's easy, why can't you explain it to me?"

He stood there, smiling at me blankly. Candreva would walk by and look at it too. "Yeah, that's a problem for Scheuch."

When it comes to math, I genuinely wasn't *that* bad. Mrs. Khanna, the teacher who changed it all for me, also taught Scheuch's pre-calc class.

For me to pick up on math, I'd have to *really* focus, but it's mostly all on the teacher. In this case, Mrs. Khanna was scary, in my opinion. She was quick and strict, and over time, I told myself I thought I had grown on her, but that probably wasn't the case.

She was just a good teacher, and I was a quick learner.

So whenever I would miss a class due to a personal issue, I'd sit behind the homework assignment baffled.

"I need her to explain this to me in order for me to understand," I told Candreva, "but I can't wait because if I go up to her next period, she'll count the assignment as late and I'll lose points."

"Ah, who cares if you lose a couple points or two."

"*I* care," I shrugged.

"Of course you do."

I turned around, finding Scheuch with his nose stuck in a textbook. He looked up at me and raised his eyebrows. "Are you doing anything important right now?" I asked nervously.

"No."

"Can you explain this to me please?"

He nodded, taking out a piece of scrap paper, a pencil, and his calculator—almost *excitedly*. He looked at the worksheet and within seconds he began explaining what I needed to do, and the truth is, I got it about twenty seconds in.

"For this one, you have to multiply the fraction by its reciprocal to—*blah blah blah—*" he explained, pushing up his glasses with his knuckles, "—*blah blah blah*—Do you get how I got to this point?"

I knew what to do from this point on. I may not be a math prodigy, but I'm not brain-dead.

"No," I lied. "What's a reciprocal?"

"A reciprocal is the inverse of a value or a number."

It was the same fraction but flipped upside down. Dammit, Aaron, just say it's upside down!

"So in this case, the fraction ⅔ would become—3-over—2," He wrote it down to show me. "See, it's the same, but flipped upside down." He held up his hand and began gesturing it, flipping the peace sign he had made back and forth.

I had to stop myself from laughing.

"You get it now?" he asked.

"Yes," I broke into a chuckle.

"So what's the reciprocal of 5?"

I narrowed my eyes at him. "⅕."

MARCH 24 2021 / DAY 376

To think the two most socially awkward cadets in our program hate each other shouldn't be that surprising. I don't know if they actually hate each other. I only remember Scheuch's *horrifyingly* indiscreet dirty looks, eye rolls, occasional comments, and most importantly, the time I asked him and got a scoff for a reply. "No."

Bailey doesn't make it clear he dislikes you. He doesn't talk to enough people to have some to dislike. I mean, he would joke about it sometimes. He once said he hated me too, but he hugs me when I cry and talks to me when no one else cares to.

Scheuch is different. I used to convince myself he was more on the gentleman's side, and that if he were to not like somebody, he would simply *and awkwardly* avoid them, but I was wrong. Scheuch doesn't speak his mind, but his face would tell you enough, his actions would show you enough. Scheuch was not rude in a petty or instigative way. He was just brutal. He was so *carefully* brutal to the point where if you never realized he didn't like you, that was nobody else's fault but yours.

So, naturally, if Bailey were to let it be known to you, it would hurt less than having Scheuch make you realize.

A big similarity I notice between them is how long they take to respond when spoken to.

Bailey is usually quiet. Whenever he *does* talk, people usually don't pay attention, and whenever people talk to him, *he* doesn't pay attention. He usually just stands there and looks at the floor until you awkwardly walk away. Scheuch is almost the same, but he doesn't often use that pause to think of a response. He's usually quick and clever with his responses. I'm jealous of him. He actually pauses as a chance to let you evaluate what you had just said to him (before he can call you stupid).

They're similar in many ways, which was why it was such a shock to me that they didn't like each other.

"*Jesus,*" Bailey's eyes widened at the sight of him. "Don't you look fresh?"

I knew how to loosen up and joke sometimes. It's just who *I* was; but ever since this never-ending nightmare has started, I never knew how it was so easy for people like Bailey to maintain a sarcastic, playful manner with the others. How could you joke in a time and place like this?

Maybe I'm just too used to setting away all my bullshit for JROTC. Maybe I spend so much time convincing myself of explanations and solutions to everything, I'm forgetting the parts of me that freak out and make impulsive decisions.

That should be good, right?

No.

It's not.

I want to feel like myself again.

Scheuch turned around, backing up in a way where he wasn't as thrilled to find him as he thought he would be. He saw it as a task to finish rather than a mission to reunite with a companion—and you can tell by knowing Scheuch never smiled or sighed in relief or even hugged him. He just jumped a little, wide-eyed.

"You look *horrible!*"

Bailey backed up from him, gripping his knife tighter.

"Bail—"

"Oh!" He realized, dropping his shoulders disappointedly. "You're still alive."

Scheuch narrowed his eyes. "Why *wouldn't* I be?"

You missed the joke, Aaron. It was a joke!

Bailey grinned, pointing up to his lips. "You got a lil' some'—"

Scheuch slowly licked his lips, lifting his hand to smear the blood off his face, nodding.

"Did you eat a *roamer?!*" His eyes lit up.

"*What?*"

"Wait—*What* are you doing out here?" He threw questions. "Did they finally get sick of you and kick you out?!"

"*No,* Bailey, I was sent—to search—for *you.*"

"Oh," he dropped his shoulders again, smiling wide. "And why would you do that?!" he asked as if it was unbelievable.

Scheuch chuckled, looking up from the ground. "Because, Bailey," he shook his head, "you are the *light* of my life!"

At least now he knew all those restless days and nights he spent had some sort of productive outcome. He accomplished nothing new other than eating an animal raw out of pure desperation—or perhaps *some* curiosity.

Now their next task was to make it back to Jade Street—*alive.*

But the problem was, they both had no clue where they were—meaning Bailey's map was useless at that point.

"What happened?" Bailey asked as they walked through the woods. "Did the others make it back?"

Scheuch shook his head. "No."

"Okay."

Bailey's responses were also often vague—and his voice often remained monotone as well unless he was talking about hurdles, swimming, or World Wars. So you could probably imagine how their conversations went through this period.

Super productive.

"Did Aj make it?" Bailey asked.

"*Mj Bui*," Scheuch corrected. "We should be referring to each other by our last names, Bailey. You know better than that."

Silence passed as they passed trees. Bailey still had a faint smile on his face.

He was always approachable, at least from my perspective. People always thought he was weird. People also thought he would treat me horribly. Klein once warned me about his opinion on Japan, like that would have anything to do with me.

"*Klein, I'm not Japanese.*"

"*You think Bailey knows the difference?*"

I scoffed. "*YOU clearly don't.*"

Bailey had energy that would make you naturally want to avoid him, which I won't deny. I stopped pushing conversations with him after a while and just let him come up to me, and by come up, I mean stomp.

He'd stomp his feet—his blue eyes glaring into mine. "Do hurdles, kid!"

I cringed. "Nah ... I fell and rolled across the turf like a tumbleweed my seventh-grade year ... *NEVER* again!"

Bailey is the type of person you can only talk to when *he* wants to talk. You can easily tell when he does and when he doesn't. When he doesn't, he stares forward with his hands in his pockets. He listens to what you have to say and just stands there. It took me a while to realize he was doing that on purpose. I always thought he just needed extra time to process what I was saying.

When he *does* feel like talking to you, he'll smile *faintly* and have a subtle light in his eye. That was my queue, basically. I only get those every once and a while, so I have to say what I want to say quickly.

"Does Bui know I'm okay?" Bailey asked as they walked under the cloudy sky. A couple seconds of silence passed before he asked concernedly, "Did she not make it?"

Scheuch kicked away leaves and sighed. "I'm not sure."

"You're not *sure*." His tone shifted. "The fuck happened?"

"Are you asking me *before* or *after* we got ambushed?" Scheuch replied, subtly snarky. "Cause I'm assuming you didn't do much either time."

"*After.*"

Scheuch exhaled calmly. "Bui made it back to the highway. Johnson and Conti——did not."

Bailey nodded subtly, lacking empathy, acting as if he predicted that.

"We got split up," Scheuch explained, leading him past the river and more northwest—*farther away from where I was.* "Candreva and Sully drove off. I couldn't see Sergeant and Yanes past the roamers—and I told Bui to stay with Klein, but she didn't listen to me."

"That's a shocker."

"*What's* a shocker?"

"One, that she didn't listen to you," Bailey chuckled as they passed by trees and bushes, "and two, how you thought she would want to stay back with Klein."

Scheuch stopped walking and turned around, looking back at Bailey's faint smile. "I thought her—and—Klein——were talking again?" His eyebrows lowered.

~~Aaron Scheuch debriefing what he calls 'girl-talk' is gotta be the funniest thing ever!~~

Bailey let out a laugh, a *genuine, authentic, pure* laugh. No explanation, just a laugh.

To properly picture a conversation between these two, just picture two guys actively trying to mansplain things to each other as if the other was clueless.

It's hilarious.

Scheuch shrugged after he began to realize how long he had paused. "Has she said anything to you about it?"

"Nope," Bailey replied, "she doesn't need to. You do realize Bui's not an idiot, right?"

Scheuch scoffed.

"She's certainly not dumb enough to get herself *killed?*" He made a point. "What makes you think she's dumb enough to allow herself to get played by a guy like *Klein?*"

"Because she's not specialized in everything," Scheuch replied, rolling his eyes before turning around and moving again. "Nobody is."

Bailey shook his head, mumbling, "Nobody but *you*, of course."

Scheuch grinned, replying. "Thank you!"

Now *Bailey* was the one rolling his eyes. He stopped smiling. "Scheuch, I dare you to jump over a few hurdles without face-planting and *then* come back to me."

"Bailey, I dare you to *run* the thirty-two hundred," he replied smugly. "Since you might be having trouble comprehending that, I would like to emphasize *run*, not *walk, run.*"

"Ahhh, it's just running?"

"Yet you couldn't do it."

Bailey scoffed. His smile was back now. For an odd reason, he seemed to enjoy getting on Scheuch's last nerve.

"You run fast in a circle eight times, so *what?*" he shrugged. "How about somethin' that actually requires neurons."

"Is that why you placed fourth pole vaulting?"

He let out another laugh. "Do I have a personal fan here?"

Scheuch rolled his eyes so aggressively they nearly got stuck.

"And I did *not* do such a thing, Scheuch!" Bailey chuckled, patting his shoulder as they walked.

"I am already aware of the things you do not do, Bailey."

This went on for hours.

Hours.

HOURS!

Soon it was getting dark again, so dark that it'd simply be too dangerous for them to continue. The fire was lit. The tent Bailey had retrieved from scavenging was half-done being set up.

"You have to connect that piece wit—"

Bailey ignored him, confident that his way was right. He then glared up. "Why am I even setting this up? I should be making *you* do this!"

"And *why* would I set up a tent for you?" Scheuch asked.

"Because I said so," Bailey replied with a smile as Scheuch—you guessed it—rolled his eyes and stepped over.

"What?" he asked. "If you're going to comment on it so much, you might as well just build it yourself."

"Maybe if you'd set it up right, I wouldn't need to make so many comments."

Bailey tilted his head, placing his hand behind his ear. "I'm sorry, what was that?"

Scheuch scoffed. When he was done, he sat back down on the log in front of the warm fire, elbows on his knees.

For a second, it seemed like they were about to get along and have a deep, engaging conversation due to Scheuch's frustrated, yet relieved face and Bailey's sudden silence. But that moment only lasted about three seconds.

Three seconds after Bailey did the impossible.

The hunger in Scheuch's stomach felt as if it was invading—like something unbelonging was consuming him from the inside, but he ignored it and told himself this was just another way of emphasizing he was extremely hungry.

"Bailey, do you still have all the food we left with you?" he asked.

Bailey sat there silent with the same faint smile, looking into the fire.

Scheuch glared at him. "Don't tell me you ate it all."

"Nope," he shook his head. "It doesn't seem like *you* need it anyway."

Scheuch lowered his eyebrows. "Are you calling me *fat?*"

"You know exactly what I'm talking about," His grin grew bigger. He lifted his chin. "How'd that animal you mauled taste?"

Scheuch gulped, settling back down. "Needed a bit of salt."

He chuckled. "Did you even *cook* it?"

"With what?" Scheuch replied, "With the portable stove and pan I carry around with me?"

He lost his grin, looking at the blank look on Scheuch's face.

~~He hadn't seen Scheuch this bloody in a *long* time.~~

"Alright, if you're going to be like this all night, we might as well just be quiet," he scoffed.

"Be like *what?*"

"Cold," he replied.

Scheuch intertwined his fingers tightly. "That's hilarious coming from *you.*"

"Erm, *actually!*" he held his pointer finger up, mocking him.

"Bailey, I don't do that!"

"I am *quiet* and *awkward*, not cold," he corrected—for the first time ever he doesn't sound so damn anti-social. "I *joke* about being cold, heartless, and *psychotic*—but—*you're* just psychotic."

"Okay, sure."

Bailey shook his head, a part of him knowing it was no use.

The more you peel layers off of Scheuch, the more he seems to clone to protect himself. He's like an infinite onion. Specifically, a PURPLE onion. 'Red' onions are *purple!*

He's purple and *not* white because purple onions are more ONION!!! and white onions are like *onion!*

I tried explaining it to him once, (the difference in their enunciation, not the fact he reminded me of an onion), and all he did was look at me weirdly and reply blankly, "Red onions earned their name because their purplish skins have been historically used to make red dyes."

"Bailey," Scheuch said, "if you would just shift your priorities, it'd be easier to stand being around you."

"My priority right now *is* you, Aaron," he replied. "I've grown a sense of responsibility for you since Shel—"

Scheuch abruptly stopped him, eyes shut. "Don't."

He sighed. "*Fine.* Fine!" He looked away, shaking his head. He then looked back at him, tone completely shifted. "You can keep acting like that," he said. "You can keep hiding in that *damn* indestructible *shell* you've built, but I'll still remember what you did."

Scheuch froze, holding all of it—all the pain and the memories and the bullshit. He held it in his throat and did everything he could to prevent himself from puking.

"It's been like—what—like four years?" Bailey shrugged. "When you were in eighth and I was a sophomore, right?" He chuckled a bit. "Back when you had that *shaggy-ass* haircut."

Scheuch rolled his eyes.

He sighed again. "I'm telling you, it's time to let it go."

Scheuch's hands were now tightened together. His feet were buried in the dirt. His eyes glaring at him as he replied, "My behavior didn't affect anyone around me."

"Oh, but it *did*," Bailey said, "and it *will* once you start disappointing the ones who look up to you."

He shook his head. "Bailey..."

"I should be *mad* at you—I should be mad that the numerous times you *knew* you needed me by your side, you pushed me away!"

"Bailey, enou—"

"But I know it's in fact, *not* me, and it's *you*," Bailey explained. "I've given you enough time, Aaron. You need to stop punishing yourself over something that wasn't even your fault!"

"Quinn, *enough.*"

Bailey's first name is Quinn. I would've never guessed that.

Scheuch wiped his face, regaining his composure. "Go get some good rest," he said. "I'll stay up—keep watch."

Bailey smiled—eyes shining brighter than the moon itself. "No, *you* go sleep. *I'll* stay up."

Scheuch turned in his spot, narrowing his eyes. "No, *you* go sleep."

"No, *you* go sleep."

"No, *you* go sleep."

"No, *you* go sleep."

                                                                            "No, *you* go sleep."

"No, *you* go sleep."

                                                                            "No, *you* go sleep."

                             "No, *you* go sleep!"

20 SEPTEMBER. 2021.

I try to write in my journal as much as I can. There's nothing much I can do these days anyway.

I also realize I should stop talking like this before it starts to become my only personality trait. So here is *one* positive thing I like about this group: I like how we have a system for nearly everything.

I used to always stir things up and do things I never expected myself to do just for the thrill of it. I've now grown into a sense of discipline. For some reason, I just like doing everything in one way, every day.

Laundry is a group thing and only happens in bulk every fourteen days. We take care of undergarments on our own, because if we didn't, that'd be gross.

Every week, we all meet up with lists of things we want the cadets who *are* going to the monthly supply run to scavenge for.

But it has to be serious, of course.

"No, Bailey," Scheuch rolled his eyes. "Why would we need that?"

But as I was walking to the pizzeria, I stumbled across Kim's journal, and *Klein's* journal, and *Scheuch's* and *Maxwell's* journal.

We all had journals.

All for different reasons.

I didn't mean to look through her stuff, and in no way was I looking for my name in her writing. It just caught my eye because for some reason, I thought it could give me a possible explanation as to *why* she acts like...

that.

He's so cute—blah blah blah—he's so—

BEYOND THE LIVING

"What the fuck?" I flinched as she caught me. She stepped over and ripped the journal out of my hands. "Why are you reading that? It's mine!"

"I—I'm sorry. I was looking for mine."

"So you thought that gave you permission to go through mine?" she scoffed.

"Dawg, we have the same journal." (As in the same brand and color, not that we're both boy-crazy.)

I know just as much about Kim as she does about me, which is basically nothing. I know her dad was Korean, and her mom was some suburban white lady who worked for—*what was it*—the state?

I don't know. I just knew despite all the jokes about us being the only two Asians in the program and *not* being best friends weren't funny. We had nothing in common.

"You have a crush on Aaron?" I snickered. "I thought you liked Klein."

She shivered. "*Hell* no," she shook her head. "He tried to get me to go hiking in the woods the other day with him."

"What? *Alone?*" I chuckled.

"*Yeah,*" she nodded.

For a second it felt like we could really bond, but I saw through it. I saw through *her* and her deceiving tactics.

We paused for a moment, just looking at each other.

"So Aaron, huh?" I smiled faintly, holding in my laugh as I recited lines from her pages, teasing her, *"He's so breath-taking, I literally melt inside when he looks at me."*

~~I wonder how she would react to his secret.~~

She covered her face, blushing. "Oh—like the entire girl's tennis team our freshman year didn't think like that either!"

RECONCILIATION

"*Girls look, he's about to run by!*" They'd stare in awe mid-practice. "*Isn't he SO hot?*"

"*That's* fangirling—this is some serial killer shit, bro!" I laughed as I began making my way towards the door. "Does *he* know you have polaroids of him?"

She hesitated. "No."

"Hm, interesting," I nodded. "Why don't you just make a move on him?"

"Can't," she replied. "He's not wired like that—not anymore."

"Damn, that sucks," *I want to know. I want to know it all.* "I won't tell him—y'know—about the pictures." *Yes, I am.* "It's not my business to tell him, but I still think *you* should."

"Thanks," she smiled. "Where are you going? We should hang out sometime—despite how our relationship has been."

Do not tell her you're going to the pizzeria. Also, HELL no!

"I—I got some chores to do later, but I'll see if I can."

Her obsession with Aaron Scheuch wasn't the only thing I remembered from her journal. Of course, the rest of it was kinda depressing.

> Every time I close my eyes and try to forget the world we once lived in, I remember how we left it. I remember the protests, the rallies, the riots. I remember everyone ranting about how we needed to save our planet before it was too late. I remember Avery advocating for it and always asking me why it seemed like I didn't care.
> I did care, I guess I just knew it was too late because my mom told me everything.

That was one example of how we are drastically different. I think about life before the outbreak all the time, but I don't think about *that*. I don't think about that because I know despite our efforts, what is happening right now is the process of our population's extinction. There's nothing we can do.

There's nothing. No cure, no hope.

That's what happens when you take advantage of things you think you want instead of valuing things you know you need.

"Let me show you something," Scheuch said to me.

I followed him curiously into a separate room—a room full of shelves stacked with textbooks and newspapers plastered on the walls. There was a huge bulletin board hung on the right with thumbtacks pinned and sticky notes written so frantic that I could easily tell it was his handwriting.

"Don't tell anyone, but Watkins and I have—" he explained.

"*HUH!*" Watkins shouted from the bedroom once he heard his name.

"I'm following *my* thought process, doesn't matter if you did or not!" he yelled, snickering as he turned back to me. "Anyways, what I meant to say—he and I have been trying to figure out how it all started."

"I can see that," I replied, reading all the connected information they've organized together. I turned. "Is that why he's always in here and you're always out to find more—"

He nodded, smiling.

"So, you guys are trying to research for a cure?"

He shook his head quickly, "No."

He began pointing at several news articles, explaining his reasonings vigorously. I tried my best to keep up.

"We don't have enough technology available to *research* a cure, let alone make one," he responded. "We're trying to pinpoint an exact time people began turning—more specifically *why*." He turned to me, looking me in the eyes. "I don't buy Philip's story one bit."

"One thing most researchers needed to consider is the fact these roamers—are practically *perpetual motion machines—*" he went on, "they break the laws of thermodynamics!"

What's thermodynamics...?

What is a perpetual motion machine...?

"What's this?" My fingers trailed against the pictures of deer.

"Oh—that's CWD," he responded. "Chronic Wasting Disease is the *closest* explanation we've found to what we've seen out there."

"It says here that this disease affects deer—elk—*moose—*"

"*Yes,*" he pointed at me. "There were no *reported* cases of *humans* attracting CWD, but get this, when these animals get the disease, it affects their spinal cord, tissue, and *eyes.* There are *neurological and behavioral changes, loss of body condition* too—as if their *brain* is *rotting away!"*

He explained this all with a humongous smile on his face. I knew it was serious, so I tried not to smile back, regardless of how contagious it was.

"That would explain why they only die when we strike the brain," I responded, fascinated. "But how could this disease make roamers feel the need to get violent towards *us?* Does CWD spread through bite marks?"

"It can through saliva and blood, yes," he said, hand on his chin. "We're trying to figure that other one out."

"I see," I responded. "Now if you guys are right, how could a virus as rare as this cause such a global outbreak? And what explains the blindness?"

He looked at me quickly, narrowing his eyes. "When you die, your corneas cloud up."

"Oh!" I nodded, pretending I knew what a cornea was.

"A cornea is the transparent layer forming the front of the eye." He read my face.

I giggled softly. "Okay, wait, so if the roamers are blind, would it make sense for their sense of hearing to heighten?" I asked, skimming through his books.

"I suppose so."

"But when deer attract CWD, it says here that their ears become droopy," I read aloud. "Could that mean anything?"

"I don't know," he replied. "I'll look into that later," he said, looking over what he had put together with Watkins proudly. *"Anyway,* what do you need?"

"Oh," I replied, shrugging, "I was going to show you something too over in my room, but it's not as close to cool as what you just showed me."

I wanted to show Aaron my room today, but not for the reason everyone might think. I watched him step in, wandering curiously.

"Sick!" He pointed at the cups and palettes on the floor in the corner. "Are those the paints I gave you?"

"Yeah," I smiled eagerly, "I can't thank you enough. That's all I've been doing these days."

"It was Maxwell's idea." He cleared his throat, "and you've mentioned—you like—*painting*—so–"

I like how he notices and remembers the little things, like I do. And I like how he's so random, it makes me feel like I can be more like myself around him.

RECONCILIATION

~~He's been keeping a secret from us for years.~~

As much as I could stand and fangirl *too* in that moment, I was more distracted observing the way the look in his eyes was changing, looking at the paint strokes of various colors along my walls.

"Do you think it looks cool?" I asked nervously, breaking the silence. "Or do you think the green is too much?"

He looked back down at me. "I think you should paint things however you want to paint them," he replied. "Do *you* think the green is too much?"

"A little," I shrugged. "Looks a lil' neon-ish."

He smiled, looking back at the wall, narrowing his eyes as he picked up the nearest bottle of paint, opening it. "Why are you showing me this?"

He squeezed out a drop onto his finger and began smearing it across his cheek spontaneously.

I giggled. "Um-I haven't—really—talked to the others in a long time."

He blinked slowly, looking over at me, holding out his finger.

"AYE!" I snatched his wrist.

He chuckled, getting some on me. "But you talk to *me*."

I froze with blue paint on my nose, not even realizing it.

I talk to no one, but Aaron. ~~I talk to no one, but *Tyson*.~~

It's how it's always been. ~~It's happening again.~~

"Why is that?" he asked.

"Because you're the only one who wouldn't care," I replied, plopping down onto my bed—which wasn't really a *bed* and was more just piled blankets, pillows, and cushions on the hardwood floor.

"Yeah I can see that," he tilted his head, "I would say it might be harder for the others to understand what you're going through."

"My family and friends weren't the only ones who died, Aaron," I replied. "A lot of us had loving parents, *siblings*, loved ones we haven't seen alive in a *very* long time. I just happen to have seen them—in *that*—state—" I said. "It was *real*. It was *in front of me*. They can't just *expect* me to be strong enough to push *through that!*"

"What if I say... they're not expecting you to, they just know you can?" he replied calmly.

"Well I'm doing a pretty decent job with the tasks I've been given, right?"

He nodded. "Yes."

"Then I don't know," I replied.

I don't know why it suddenly hurts so bad. I was fine when it happened. I was fine just months ago.

I don't know why I'm suddenly so violent, so hateful—like everything I've been trying to accomplish suddenly lost its value. I don't know why I feel nothing towards no one; why I feel so angry now and not when I was actually going through it with them. I always told everyone it was *okay*.

It was never okay. It was *never* okay to me.

I just wanted them to stay.

"You don't know what?" he asked, looking at the way I sunk into my pillow. He went and sat on the floor, next to my legs. "Is it *Colón?*"

People in my life that are dead never apologized to me, so I live on. I live on wondering what would happen if they ever did, but then again I know there wouldn't be that much of a difference.

I just like the idea of them feeling sorry for making me feel this way, but that isn't possible. People like that don't *ever* feel sorry, they only do for themselves. People like that take a piece of me when they leave. I walk around with a pit in my stomach and push people away because I don't have anything left of myself to give them.

I haven't felt like myself in a long time, which is weird, because I remember being exactly like this—so sad and so angry.

So, so angry.

I guess I just grew out of it, so it feels weird now that I'm back.

I don't want to be back.

It doesn't feel good anymore.

"I guess I just miss her," I said, immediately feeling my throat close up.

Miss what? Miss *what*, Mj?

Miss how she ridiculed you in public? Miss the things she'd post on the internet about you? Miss the way she'd hang out with the same girls you've never spoken a word to, yet they want to quote 'rock-your-shit' because apparently you were 'talking smack' on them? Miss the way she'd use things against you? Miss the way she'd yell at you and make *you* apologize? What were you apologizing for, *Michelle?* The misunderstandings *she* had?

I shouldn't miss *shit*.

I miss the time I wasted trying to change her.

That's what I miss.

"And I guess I'm just mad at the group right now for acting hypocritical," I explained, hiding the sudden break in my tone. "They might listen to what I say now, and think I'm someone who knows what she is doing—" *No they don't.* "But they don't *like* me," ~~I began crying.~~ I said calmly, as if I didn't care. "They don't like me. I know they don't, and that's fine," I shrugged. "All they did was stick their noses in my business 'cause they were so *concerned* that I went back to Jake. How the hell are you gonna ask me questions about that shit like I'm your friend, then turn around and act like *I'm* the only one causing problems around here?"

He sighed as Coco trotted over, making herself comfortable. He awkwardly petted her. "I will say, the reason why they could be hesitant towards you is because—well, to be fair," he smiled, "you *did* draw a gun on Kim in front of them."

My jaw dropped. "You—"

"*I* understand there was context behind it," he said, yawning. "So does *Sully* and Bailey, so does Maxwell and Watkins, and see? We don't treat you that way."

"No one feels resentment towards Klein and Watkins for starting a cat-fight and getting Terry and the Adkins brothers killed?"

He raised his eyebrows, nodding.

"I'm so *sick* of them," I scoffed. "I'm not gonna spend my time around a bunch of people who have—some sort of *vendetta* against me—I *swear!* All they do is just pick apart what I do!"

"That's not—what vendetta—originally—means."

I made a face and looked over, seeing that he had fallen asleep with his head resting on my couch cushions and Coco in his lap. I glanced at my clock, realizing that I had accidentally kept him over past curfew.

"You're such a nerd," I chuckled softly, taking his glasses off for him and turning over, facing the wall.

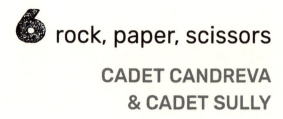 rock, paper, scissors
CADET CANDREVA & CADET SULLY

If I'm gonna be honest, I don't know how I survived out there alone, *mentally*, I mean. I don't really like talking about it. I don't like remembering how I had to spend nights out there in the woods, injured, cold, and hungry; scared to death. I don't like remembering how I spent nights with a knife in my hand because I was too scared to fall asleep.

I remember waking up after collapsing. My hand reached up to my head as it pounded, feeling the blood stain my fingertips. I came across a lot of things before finding Bailey and Scheuch. I've found tents, *trailers,* even some sheds and cabins. I've looted anything I think could be useful, even with the possibility of never seeing any of them again.

I guess a part of me had faith, even with the fear and exhaustion. I knew standing there on the hardwood floors of the cabins after rummaging through the desk drawers, I could just cry for a bit, but I couldn't. I knew going out there and *trying,* seeing them again—will make it all worth it.

Right? What's the point of trying to survive if you have nothing to survive for?

But after a certain point of time, my body couldn't keep up with my mind, and I gave in. I dropped to the ground, hand on my stomach. I rested myself against a tree, head against the rough bark. I breathed heavily, desperate as I scoured through my bag for *anything.* Water. Food. A damn piece of chewing gum.

My socks worn out with holes, my shoes caused blisters to form on my feet (ew), my braided hair unkempt, and my *body*. My lungs, my heart, my stomach.

I couldn't take it anymore. My eyes couldn't keep themselves open. My panting couldn't get any harder. My skin couldn't get any greener. *I couldn't take it.*

God, I fought so hard.

I fought to stay strong until the dead trees in front of me were the last thing I saw.

DAY 351 / THE NIGHT WE SCATTERED

Candreva stomped on the brakes, nearly launching the two of them forward. The high beams nearly blinded Klein. The two watched in shock, seeing the state of his condition. They hadn't seen him this bloody since he cat-fought with Watkins.

Candreva rolled down the window, sticking his head out. "What are you waiting for? *Get in!*"

Sully stuck her head out too, asking, "Where's Bui?!"

Klein winced, still shielding his eyes. "I lost her."

"You *lost* her?!"

Candreva sighed and continued to urge him to get in, but Klein refused.

"Bro, just get *in!*" Sully sighed.

"I can't," Klein began shifting away from the vehicle. "I *have* to go find her. Meet back up at Jade Street!"

"No—Jake——No!"

"Bruh."

Candreva pressed the gas pedal again, driving away. Sully gazed out the window, seeing the roamers turn as they passed.

"I'm sure he will be fine, Mary," he broke the silence.

"I hope so," she sighed. "I'm worried about Bui too."

I left Klein to go after Scheuch, and in response he followed me instead of sticking with them. He never ended up finding me, so just from that, you can picture how bad this situation was. Our group was split up in all sorts of directions in a world that was decaying.

It took us months to find each other again.

We're lucky it didn't take longer.

"I don't understand why he would run after her," Sully sat with her hands in her lap.

"Because he's a fucking idiot, that's why."

"Oh-" she raised her eyebrows.

Candreva scoffed. "He went and ran after someone who ran away for a *reason*."

"Brody, we can't just assu-"

"If Bui wanted to get away, she *would*," he explained. "She's smart, we know that."

"So she stayed *back* to go after Scheuch..." Sully gasped quietly.

"Yep, so they can go *search* for Bailey," he shook his head, clenching his jaw. "We lost *more* people tonight 'cause we went to look for *one*."

"It was the right thing to do!"

"But was it a *smart* thing to do?" He shrugged, driving through the dark. "I swear, I don't know how Sergeant listened to Conti on this one."

Sully shook her head. "Brody."

"Now Klein's missing—chasing after Bui," he scoffed. "And we have no clue where Sergeant went with Yanes—and we have no idea where *the hell* that herd came from—"

"Brody, think about that day we went to the city—" Sully said, watching him take a deep breath. "You backed me up when I tried to convince them there was *hope* and there's gotta be some sort of *other* possibility!"

"I also said we should really look around and focus on what we need to focus on, Mary," he replied. "Yes, there *could* be a possibility that García's still out there, but we've been searching for weeks, possibly a month or two!"

"I guess you're right," she frowned, turning out to the window again. A few minutes passed before she looked over again, "So, what are we gonna do?"

"Meet back at Jade Street first?" He shrugged. "Then I'm assuming we're going out again to look for all of them."

"So you think they could still be alive."

"I think Sergeant won't be able to maintain his state of mind leaving Bui and Scheuch out there," he explained, driving around a fallen tree slowly. "They might not be the biggest and strongest of our group—but they don't break when shit starts tumblin' down."

Sully nodded in agreement. "Yeah, we need people like that because they react the quickest to situations."

"No, Scheuch does, remaining *composure* too," he said, wiping the blood running down his nose. "*Bui*? She's still getting better and better at it ... with experience, y'know? It'd be way easier for her if they'd just leave her alone—but—"

"She'll pull through."

He nodded. "Yeah, and once she does, *that'd* be the thing that'd make them strong."

Candreva has always been very kind to me. I met him at our district's halloween parade, 2019. He was in a brown denim jacket, dirty blue jeans, and a mask of a mass murderer from a classic horror movie. For some reason, I can never remember which one.

I was wrong about him being the second-biggest redneck I knew. (He got offended when I told him that.)

He was one of the very few cadets that never lost the true versions of themselves in the apocalypse. He never completely switched to survival mode. He only did when he was with Sully to protect her.

He was a huge horror fanatic. It showed through the clothes he would wear and the keychains that would rattle on his bags. All the cartoon-like icons in his notebooks would be drawn by no one other than him. The only things in his camera roll used to be homework answers sent from Yanes, audio clips that would eventually be produced into a remix, mini-movies he directed, and violent memes to giggle at with Bailey.

I guarantee you, if it were possible, Candreva would still be lounging on a cushioned couch next to Bailey, Yanes, and Johnson, playing mobile shooting games with everything going on.

I never thought of him the same as I would others. Never once has he commented snide remarks talking about me. Never once have I seen a judgeful look in his eye talking to me. I saw him as a person who squinted when he smiled, placed his hands on his hips or his arms crossed over his chest when he listened to you speak.

I remember when I first met Sully too.

I don't know if she knows this, but I always knew she existed. I always saw her running distance during track season, but I never mustered up the courage to talk to her. What was I supposed to say?

ME: Hey, good run!
MARY: Uhhhhhhhhh ... who *are* you?

I thought she'd reply something like that to me, but knowing her now, she would never.

But back then, I always thought she was just a pretty girl who would never talk to me; a girl who would find me annoying and weird. So it took me about four months to start talking to her, and even now I still hesitate on initiating conversations first.

I've always restrained myself from talking to her about boys, but sometimes out of all girls in the program, she would be the one that would understand the most. So why don't I?

I've always viewed her as an independent, strong-minded person. She was perfect, but not in a beachy, blue-eyed blonde, popular girl way. She was perfect 'cause she was irrelevant enough to not be drama-oriented, but relevant *just* enough where she had a small group of friends, *nice* friends. She was perfect because she maintained top-notch grades also while being athletic and musically talented. She was perfect because her clothes always fit her right and she never had to wear makeup to be pretty.

She was in the top five in her class. She went to states for both Cross Country and Band.

Of course, I'd think she'd be mean.

But she wasn't.

She was always so nice to me, and sometimes I would question why. I find myself relating to her often. I can't blame her if she feels shy. I'd be scared approaching me too.

The first time I talked to her was when we were helping out at this bingo event for families to gain community service hours. We were sitting on opposite sides of a table counting raffle tickets, gossiping, or probably *attempting* to.

I restrained myself from doing so because I was afraid she'd think I was drama-oriented; and I assumed she restrained from doing so because she didn't want me to be uncomfortable.

"What happened?" She tilted her head, quickly interrupting herself. "You don't have to tell me if you don't want to."

"It's okay," I chuckled nervously. "We can just talk about something else."

"Yeah."

I surprisingly don't gossip often, at least not *badly*. Girls often accuse me of *talking shit,* of course, but I don't think I am half the time. It's not shit-talking if I'm saying it directly to you, bitch!

RANDO: Do we have a problem, girly?

ME: Yeah, my problem is how you can't keep your fucking legs closed.

I used to talk to Colón about boys, but I stopped after I turned fourteen and realized the more I did, the more she'd yell at me. With Sully things were less aggressive. With Sully, all the hair-pulling catfights, dirty looks, and backhanded compliments disappear. With Sully, I am just a *teenage girl.*

"Yeah, I think Kiara's nice too," Sully smiled. "She's a little wild."

"Oh no, I love her," I replied.

"So wait, why are you so nervous talking to Aaron?" She raised her eyebrows.

I tried playing it off. "Who wouldn't?" I chuckled.

"I don't know," she shrugged as a group of cheerleaders walked past us, giggling. "Probably them?"

I snickered to hide the fact my cheeks were red. widened my eyes, my cheeks turning red. "Is it really that obvious?" She laughed as I covered my face, shrugging. "It's not like—it's not a weird thing I promise—it's like—"

"No, yeah, I barely talk to him. He's a little *weird*," She chuckled nervously.

"It's just—" I hesitated, "I've never seen a boy that age so sure of themselves."

"He's arrogant," she shrugged.

"Really?" I gasped. "I never thought of him like that."

"Yeah," she giggled. "Brody calls him *Arrogant Aaron.*"

I view Sully and Scheuch similarly, only Sully was a girl and less... *strange*, so of course it was easier to approach her. She was warm and he was cold, so it was safe to say the more I talked to her, the more it made sense that she, out of all the gorgeous girls in our program, got the genuine, romantic, long-term relationship with a guy like Brody Candreva.

That was why it always felt like she would never understand.

That was why I always felt the urge to tell her about my problems with Tyson or the bullshit with Klein and tell her she was so lucky to have someone like Candreva, but I'm glad I never did.

Because you can't base things off of assumptions, I should know this.

Just because someone is a good person, doesn't mean they're a good significant other.

Candreva drove quietly, trying not to eye the forests on his left. He worked to steady his breathing and push away the fact he just watched one of his best friends get eaten alive in front of him.

"I'm sorry," Sully sighed, fidgeting in her lap. "Now I got you worrying too."

"No, Mary, it's alright, just—" He removed his hand from his mouth, wiping blood onto his jeans. "I think Bui shouldn't have gone after him—" He shook his head. "It was *stupid*."

Sully turned to him, narrowing her eyes concernedly. "Brody, what are you saying?"

"She shouldn't have gone," he shrugged, "and for *Scheuch*? Jesus, I wish she could've just *thought* for a second at that moment!"

He paused and looked over at Sully's face.

"What?" He read her face then scoffed. "You can't tell me you trust him."

She crumbled. "Well, *yeah*, I guess I *do*," she replied. "He's nice to me."

"He's nice to you," he scoffed again. *"Arrogant Aaron?"*

"He calms me down when I get anxious," she shrugged, chuckling a little at the nickname.

Scheuch was a good liar. That was a gift that came along with his stoneface and monotone voice.

He would spend his time lying to Sully over little things like telling her there was still candy left from the food stash but give her *his* chocolate in hopes she wouldn't catch on. He would spend his time lying to her about the amount of ammo we had when we were running low, making sure her weapons were loaded, even if it meant going out with zero bullets in his chamber. ~~He lied to her when she asked him if he apologized to me yet. He lied to her about getting bit.~~

Candreva widened his eyes, looking forward again.

"What?" she asked, trying to stay calm, but thinking about this particular situation would've riled her up rather than calm her.

But she's been wanting to say this for a while now.

"It would be *you* if you'd stop hanging around the guys all the time?" she said.

He turned to her, hitting the brakes. "So in response, you spend all your time being comforted by Aaron?"

"No," she scoffed. "He's just Aaron. He comforts *everybody.*"

He paused then nodded in agreement. "True. True."

"That's not the point, Brody," she sighed. "I'm sorry, I should've worded it better. I'm just saying it would be nice if you'd just spend more time with me."

"I can't just spend time with you *all* the time?"

"Well, I'm not asking you to do that?" She shook her head, taking a deep breath. "Y'know what, nevermind."

"No, *what*, Mary?" he asked softly. "Tell me what's wrong."

She wiped her nose and sniffled. "I just feel stupid asking you for something you should already be giving me."

"I need to be spending time with *everyone*, Mary," he replied, "not just you. We don't know when our last day with each other is—I still have stuff to tell *Johnson* and *see?*"

She shook her head, blinking away the tears. "That doesn't make any sense, Brody. You say you need to spend more time with *everyone* because of that, but if that's the case then why haven't things changed with *us?*"

"What are you talking about?"

She sniffled. "You haven't changed at all since before the crash. I thought that maybe—with *everything* going on, maybe it would mend everything that happened between us and we'd be closer, but it hasn't. So tell me, Brody. Tell me why—even when the entire world has ended and we should all be brought together during times like these, you're still distant from me!"

Candreva slowly turned forward, hands gripping the wheels. Sully cupped her face in her hands, crying softly. He took a deep, steadying breath before driving again, letting Sully calm down.

After a couple of minutes he turned and looked at her, sighing. "I'm sorry. Why didn't you say anything sooner?"

"Because I heard—what you said—" She sniffled, running her hands down her face, wiping the tears on her jeans. She turned and looked at him with softened eyes, "—when you told Yanes you were planning on breaking up with me, but since the plane crashed and now—we're living like *this*, you decided to stay with me," she explained. "But you haven't changed at all."

25 SEPTEMBER. 2021.

For so long, I refused to talk about it because I knew I'd break down into tears immediately; and yet I've cried in front of him before. Those weren't my *best* moments, so I'd like it better if he had a different view on me.

I've mentioned many times that I was scared to approach, but I think it's safe to say there were many moments we've had since then that have sort of—*secured*—our friendship.

But I think this night was the night that changed everything. *This* particular night, not the night after I found Tyson, the night after María died, the night we reunited, or the countless nights we've spent on the porch.

Tonight.

I knew something was wrong the second I stepped back into *my* door. I knew my stomach turning wasn't a good sign.

Yet I prayed.

I prayed everything would be okay because I knew I wouldn't be able to handle it if I lost him too.

I've shown him my paintings, he's shown me his bulletin board. I've laughed in front of him; I've cried and I've yelled and I've argued in front of him. ~~I've seen him kill. He's seen me kill.~~

Yet we barely know anything about each other. Regardless of everything we've been through, and all the time we've spent, I still have yet to figure him out.

He's read my journal. Yes, he's read it. Almost *all* of it.

I've read over his sticky notes and articles he's put together. I even tried to decipher his old notebooks from school, but I guess Calculus isn't for me.

I want to say I don't know but I do. I know exactly why things changed after tonight.

"May I ask, why *do* you expect the worst out of people?" He fidgeted with an irish pennant from his shirt, looking back over at me. "I assume something happened."

I took a deep breath, looking at him with trust as the evening breeze brushed against our skin.

"I honestly don't know where it exactly started," I responded. "Kinda like a *build-up*, almost."

"Hm."

Sometimes I feel guilty. He remembers the little things I wrote, deciphering codes even I've forgotten I put for my future self, but if you were to ask me something small and specific about his bulletin board, I wouldn't be able to tell you.

I know it's rude to admit, but I can't help it. Sometimes when he tells me about a new clue he found, it just goes through one ear and out the other. I'm too busy looking at him. His eyes. His smile.

~~The eyes and smile of a liar.~~

"María and I have been best friends since I can remember," I explained, "and I say that because I literally *can't* remember anything in my childhood."

Kim might make me come off as 'boy-obsessed' because the first person I thought of when everyone was panicking for their loved ones was *Tyson,* a boy who only loved me *sometimes*; but what she doesn't realize is that when everyone was crying, calling their parents frantically and grieving the potential loss of their loved ones, I didn't have anyone to grieve.

I didn't have anyone because I've been grieving them for a long time now. I don't talk about my parents or what I have endured growing up. I don't need people looking at me any differently than they already do. I don't talk about my parents or what I have endured as a child because it's the one topic that brings me to tears faster than anything.

"But I watched María grow worse, she tried hiding it from me until I began doing similar stuff too—*drinking and popping pills*," I took a shaky breath under the moonlight. "I know it doesn't sound like me, but that's the part you guys don't see. I know how she is, because I was so close to being *just like her.*"

I used to be

just

like her.

She was tougher, of course she was tougher. A couple years in juvie will do that to you. Her schemes began to escalate so much that every police officer at the local police station knew her name, but that was the difference between us two.

I was smart enough to not get caught. I was smart enough to play my cards right and get myself out.

If I was strong enough to turn a corner and change, *she* is too. If anything, I wouldn't be as persistent and stubborn without her influence. So why *couldn't* she.

Just *why* couldn't she?

She used to protect me. She used to love me.

~~Why did she stop? Why did she stop? Why did she stop? Why did she stop? Why did she stop? Why did she stop? Why did she stop? Why did she stop? Why did she stop? Why did she stop?~~

"I know you might think it's stupid, but my break up with Kay took a big toll on me too," I said. "God, I was *just* fourteen. I don't understand how I had the strength to push through that."

What happened came straight out of a situation college students would be dealing with, young adults would be dealing with, early marriages would be dealing with—*not* fourteen year olds.

I should've been playing with damn dolls.

He never hit me.

He never hit me, but he ridiculed me in front of our friends. He never hit me, but *he* got mad when I found out there were other girls and *I* had to apologize. He never hit me, but he threatened to after I found him on a dating app. He never hit me, but he called me a whore and accused me of sleeping with other guys. He never hit me, but he flirted with my own best friends. He never hit me, but he personally had something against María since she was the only one who would protect me during those times.

He never hit me.

Until he did.

"Did you hit him back?" Aaron asked casually.

I chuckled. "You know it."

I sniffled, breathing in the night air.

"Who else knows about this?" he asked.

I shrugged. "*Cameron*, of course. Kiara—Bailey—and I think I told Jonah a while back."

Adkins and I were closer than everyone thought. I just never talked about him much.

What I never noticed was how our groups were mostly separated into what sports we did, which would explain why Schuech and Sully were so tight-knit. Cross Country runners, man.

I was looped in with Bailey. I was glad I was. We were known as the swimmers, which in my opinion, as someone who both swam and ran long distance, swimming is far more impressive. But due to being looped in with swimmers, I was *also* looped in with Terry.

Man 'til this day, I don't know what the hell her problem was! And I know I'm not crazy! Sasha Klarke even said Terry just dislikes anyone who's better than her.

I inhaled. "I think after that, I swore I'd never be caught in a vulnerable situation like that again. That's why I'm so defensive."

I see the worst in people because I rather be right than be shocked that I never expected that out of them. I see the worst in people because I'd rather be right than be disappointed. I see the worst in people because I tend to paint a new picture of them once they show me their true colors.

And I'm tired of having to let people go. I'm tired of grieving.

But it's hard when I live in a world where that is absolutely everywhere, so I've grown numb to it.

"I've had—sort of—*similar* experiences," he said after a moment of silence.

"Really?" I turned. "Like with a *girl?*"

He nodded. "But *no* not—not like that—um—I shouldn't have said similar, no—"

"Yeah," I chuckled, crossing my arms. "She play tennis?"

"*Yes...?*" He looked at me weirdly. "How did you kno—"

"Lucky guess."

"Um," he gulped, itching the side of his head. "I just——This happened years ago, probably around the same time you and Kay were——she was in *your* grade—"

"Oh really?" I replied. "Were you two—*dating?*"

He seemed disturbed at the thought of her. "No—*Yes*, I don't think she——um—my point is, things ended pretty bad and it's been years and I still think about her."

"In a sense where—"

"No," he replied, "but in a sense where I wish I could go back and do things differently. I'm saying this—in hopes it'd make you feel better——because if Kay—that was his name right?"

"Yeah, short for Kaden."

"If—Kaden was still alive right now, he would feel sorry," he said. "*Trust* me, he would feel sorry. Someone would have to be extremely miserable to enforce that on someone else."

I smiled, looking at him. "How bad?" I asked.

"W-What?"

"How bad did things end with that girl?"

He widened his eyes. "Pretty bad."

I chuckled jokingly, "What? Did you eat her?"

His entire face dropped—like his soul had just been sucked from his body. It was uncanny. Terrifying. I never understood something so fast.

Silence passed. I sat there processing it, processing it hard. The boy I've been spending so much time with is a murderer, a cannibal, and I don't know what is more terrifying: the fact he was sitting there like it was no big deal, or the fact that *I* was.

I thought and I thought. I recalled back to every memory and every morbid joke he made and everything that happened when I was thirteen and fourteen in our hometown just to figure out any possibility as to how the hell he would've gotten away with something like that.

The silence between us felt like adhesive gluing broken shards of glass together. We broke for a reason, but what broke us had inevitably bonded us back together while we knew we didn't want to. *He* didn't want to. A part of me will still protect him no matter what, and that was where the problem was stemming.

"Aaron, when did you get those bite marks?" I asked chillingly, looking over at him like it didn't bother me at all.

He looked back at me the same, replying nonchalantly. "I got them on a solo run a couple months ago."

I narrowed my eyes. "And... nothing?"

"They bled for a couple days," he explained, looking down and fidgeting with his t-shirt. "I didn't have any symptoms so I figured there was no use for taking antibiotics."

"You're immune to the virus," I gasped softly.

He nodded. "Mj," he said, like it hurt him, "I'm telling you this in confidence."

"Yeah, I understand."

"I know this could be frightening to you, but—"

"No, yeah, Aaron, I'm not telling *anyone*."

He sighed. I sighed too, looking forward.

"Do you think-" I asked nervously, "-that you're immune due to consuming human flesh *before* the outbreak hit?" I glanced back over at him. His eyes indicated that I was closer and closer to getting fully caught up now. Now I just needed to know who.

"Which girl was it?" I asked, remaining casual, watching him hesitate. "It's okay, I don't need to know." *I want to know. I want to understand.*

He looked normal now—at least I think he did.

He took a deep breath, preparing himself as if he hadn't said her name aloud in a *long* time.

"Shelly Cuvillier."

October 4. 2021.
[untitled]

I think Aaron had a bad day today. I asked him if he wanted to talk but he said no. Just a straight and quick, "No," so I gave him space and left him alone. Maybe he'll open up later.

October 19. 2021.
[untitled]

I don't know why he's been acting so cold. He's suddenly extremely monotone again. I asked to go on this month's supply run, and he was quick to tell me the seats were filled up, which would be understandable if I didn't see him ask Sully to come along for this month. I shouldn't take it personally. Maybe Sully was just the better option for this month. It's fine.
He wasn't in the mood to talk tonight either, and I could tell without even needing to ask him, so I just went directly to bed tonight. It was disappointing because I just wanted to tell him about a dream I had.
I don't know if something's wrong. There's something about the look in his eye, y'know? That—*spark*—is gone! But it's whatever, if he continues to act like this for another week, I'll ask him what's wrong.

November 6. 2021.
[untitled]

He's been really weird. He asked me a question today but when I gave him a longer answer than he liked, he cut me off and said he "didn't need any feedback."
He's been giving me short, *cold* answers. It seems like he's been really trying to avoid me, but I honestly think I'm just being paranoid. I didn't do anything for him to act this way. Maybe he just felt like doing something else today, I understand.
If he continues to act like this for another week, I'll ask him what's wrong.
~~If he continues to act like this for another week, I'll ask him what's wrong.~~
~~If he continues to act like this for another week, I'll ask him what's wrong.~~

November 13. 2021.
[untitled]

~~If he continues to act like this for another week, I'll ask him what's wrong.~~
~~If he continues to act like this for another week, I'll ask him what's wrong.~~
~~If he continues to act like this for another week, I'll ask him what's wrong.~~
~~If he continues to act like this for another week, I'll ask him what's wrong.~~
~~If he continues to act like this for another week, I'll ask him what's wrong.~~

~~If he continues to act like this for another week, I'll ask him what's wrong.~~
~~If he continues to act like this for another week, I'll ask him what's wrong.~~
~~If he continues to act like this for another week, I'll ask him what's wrong.~~
~~If he continues to act like this for another week, I'll ask him what's wrong.~~
~~If he continues to act like this for another week, I'll ask him what's wrong.~~
~~If he continues to act like this for another week, I'll ask him what's wrong.~~
~~If he continues to act like this for another week, I'll ask him what's wrong.~~
~~If he continues to act like this for another week, I'll ask him what's wrong.~~

7 [untitled]
CADET KIM

I don't feel like talking about her.

19 NOVEMBER. 2021.

I stormed out of my room, each step down the staircase causing my stomach to turn.

~~Just ask him. Just ask him.~~

I shouldn't have.

I should've just let him think I was too stupid to see it.

I steadied my breath as I approached his door, stepping onto the same porch we've spent nights on for the past three months. Raising my fist to knock, I swallowed the lump in my throat. Watkins answered.

"Hey," he dabbed me up, "what's up?"

"I need to talk to Aaron." My voice broke.

"What's wrong?" He lowered his eyebrows. "Did something happen?"

Yes. Something happened. Something *changed*. "No, I just need to ask him something," I replied softly, hand on my stomach.

"Okay," he nodded, *reeking of alcohol and cigarettes.* "Aaron!"

Silence.

"Aaron!"

Nothing.

Then Watkins turned back to me, relieving me by suggesting, "He could be sleeping."

I narrow my eyes. "What *time* is it?"

"Like eight-thirty?" He shrugged as I took a deep breath. "I'll tell him you came by, okay?"

"Okay."

"But *hey,* is everything okay?" he asked.

I let out a shaky breath. "Things should be."

He told me to come back the next day an hour before curfew, but I didn't. I actually planned on spending the night painting in hopes of calming down. It didn't help.

Nothing but the sound of his voice telling me I'm wrong was going to help, and I knew that. I just didn't want to admit it.

With a paintbrush in my hand, I painted. I painted vast landscapes of scenes of what our lives could've been. I painted tall, strong trees with wind through their leaves and waterfalls with water so clear, you can see it travel through the rocks at the bottom. I painted soft, green grass you can lay upon and sunbathe; and animals, animals roaming free.

I painted *everything*
to remind us of what we *did*.

"You know you have to." Mj's voice spoke beside me.

They were back. They came back as if they never left.

I gulped. "I know," I replied softly.

I heard a sniffle from the opposite direction so I turned. It was Michelle rubbing her nose. She looked as if she had been crying.

"Why are you so sad?" I asked.

She shook her head. "I'm not."

I scoffed. "Even I lie to *myself*, damn."

Her cherry drop earrings dangled, "I just—I don't know."

"*She's* the romantic one," Mj explained, turning to me, "she's probably just scared he's gonna react how they usually do."

Would it be stupid to tell her she's leaning on wet paint right now?

Is she aware her existence only exists in my mind?

Mj hopped to her feet, turning to see what I had come up with. She then widened her eyes and arched her back.

"*Awww man,*" she groaned, "I got paint all over my shirt, man!"

I chuckled softly. "It's alright."

"No, it's not! This shit's white!"

I dipped my paintbrush into the paintcup and stood up, hesitating.

She narrowed her eyes on me. "Wha—Why are you looking at me like that?"

I stood with my hand reaching out, hesitating.

"Uh, *hello?*" she scoffed at me. "Y'know, it's kinda weird to stare at your own boobs."

"I'm not looking at your boobs, *asshole!*" I scoffed back. "I just wanted to—" I attempted to grab her shoulder and turn her around to see how bad the paint was, but the second I touched her, she was gone. They both were.

Despite them being technically a part of *me,* I prefer it without their presence. I've let go of these parts of myself for a reason. I need space to grow.

All my hallucinations stopped when I started spending more time with him, but now Mj and Michelle are back.

That must mean something.

Taking a deep breath, I storm down the stairs and pace out the front door. I breathe in and breathe out. I do it slowly. I do it quickly. I found a way to bring myself to do it because I knew if I didn't do it right then and there, I never will.

It was always, *maybe he's just having a bad day, I'll give him another week.* It was always, *if this continues on for another week, I'll ask if I did something.* It was always, *he's just like that, why do I have to take everything so personally?*

I don't care about this stuff. I *don't.*

I *really* don't care.

I usually don't care if a person likes me, or if a person is mad at me, or if my relationship has been tarnished—because most of the time, they do dislike me, I'm more mad at them than they are at me, and the relationship that I always grip on to was done before it even began.

Nothing I have ever has that much value to it because I know it will leave. Nothing I do will ever seem worth it to me, because how could I be excited for the days full of sunshine and rainbows when I know thunderstorms will shower me again. I'm just not wired like that, so the fact that I did care this time, even for the slightest bit, must've *meant* something.

I knocked on his door and held my breath until he answered. It was him this time, I made sure of that.

"Can I talk to you about something?" I asked nervously. "It isn't abou-"

"Will it be quick?"

"Yeah—" I patted down my jeans, looking past him and at the leather booths, "can I come in?"

"Ask it out here."

"Oh—um," I looked down, picking at my nails. "I was just gonna ask if we were good and if I did something wrong—"

I watched him look down and swallow down whatever he *was* going to say.

"I was—distancing myself from you due to—" He cleared his throat. "—new feelings that might've developed in the past few months—" He looked back up at me swiftly and I widened my eyes a little. "—I believe this has gone out of proportion and that we should maintain a more *professional* relationship with one another."

"I—I'm sorry, I— I—" I stammered, shaking my head, "—I *don't* know you enough to have—I wasn't trying to get anything out of this, I was just trying to get to know you."

"Well I have no interest in you getting to know me." He looked away again.

I stood there stiff. "Oh."

...

"Is that all?"

No, it's not.

I took a deep breath, remaining calm. "How long have you been feeling this way?" I asked.

"For a while now," he began picking at the chipped white paint on his door frame. *He won't look me in the eye.*

I held in my reaction. "Then why didn't you just act like this to begin with?" I asked, calmly.

"Uh—because it didn't get as annoying?"

...

It didn't get as annoying.

It.

Didn't.

Get.

As.

Annoying.

I inhaled sharply, "What did I do that was so annoying?"

"Nothing."

...

???

I let the silence pass for a bit.

"Is that all?"

I inhaled again. "Wait—so—I'm *confused,* are we cool?" I asked. "Can we just continue on as *friends?*"

He looked up at me, raising his eyebrows, pausing. "No."

I lowered my eyebrows. *Is he ... fucking smiling?*

"I only call a few people friends, it's nothing personal," he responded. "We can carry on as just—*acquaintances.*"

I exhaled.

Don't say it's okay.

Don't say it's okay.

> I'M SO TIRED
> OF TELLING EVERYONE IT'S OKAY
> WHEN IT'S NOT.
> IT'S NOT.
> IT'S NEVER BEEN.

"Okay," I sniffled, shivering from the cold.

He saw the look on my face. He knows.

"I just—I just don't know if that'd be difficult for me."

That's bullshit.

If I can handle a toxic, stoner ex-boyfriend, a sorry excuse for a best friend, parents who can't parent, and a potential drinking problem, I can definitely handle the fact that

Aaron Scheuch does not want anything to do with me.

"Why would that be difficult for you?"

~~"Because I'll never be able to understand
why I let you see me in places
I wouldn't even let María see me in."~~

~~"Because I'll never be able to understand
why it seems like you're sweet
to every other female here
but me—"~~

~~"Because I can't stand the fact
you are now another way
to remind me
I am not enough."~~

~~I'm not even enough to be friends with.
Are you serious?~~

I inhaled sharply again. "Because I can't carry on thinking—" I shook my head, "even after—everything we've been through," I felt my voice break. "—you never *cared?*"

He sighed. "Look,"

Prepare for it.

~~Tell me you take it back. Tell me you understand.~~

"I don't care about you, I cared *for* you," he responded.

"What?" I crossed my arms.

"You were the one—*one* of the only ones that had it in you," he explained. "Everyone else was *freaking out*—crying——trying to call their moms and dads. *You?* You were *silent,* and that's how I knew you could remain content, despite all the *speculations* of *cures* and the '*roamers are still human*' B.S."

"I didn't *have* anyone to call," I replied, looking at the look on his face. I scoffed softly. "It's all about survival to you, isn't it?"

He gripped the door tighter, the moonlight reflecting on his glasses. He stood there looking how he usually looks, looking me straight in the eyes; but when I looked closer this time, I realized there wasn't any *wall* covering or barricading or blurring *anything*.

This was just who he was.

And suddenly, all those times I've thought so highly of him, those times thought of going to him for advice and/or comfort, those moments I've cherished so much, were gone. My entire image of him was ripped into pieces within a matter of seconds and I stood there pretending it wasn't completely heart-shattering.

"I truly don't care about you or *anything* you have going on," he said. "No part of me wants to be involved with you, and seeming as the temporary feelings you feel right now are *not* related to our daily tasks, I don't care. Don't show up on this porch trying to talk to me again, and don't nag any of the others about anything related to me."

I stood there with a blank look on my face, looking almost insensitive—as if I didn't register a thing. I awkwardly hopped down the steps, hearing him shut the door behind me. I walked back to my bar quietly, feeling his echoing words begin to consume me. I breathed in, wiping my nose, feeling the heat rise up my spine. I ignored the tears rapidly streaming down my face as I stormed back inside because I knew he had shut the door by now and had made his way upstairs—upstairs to perhaps go to sleep or stay up and study or to do whatever weird nerd type-shit he does—with no thought of me.

~~Please think about me. Please think about what you just said.~~
I shut my door.

"Dude, you just embarrassed yourself HARDCORE!" Mj scoffed beside me.

I burst into tears. Her face changed. "Aw, *Michelle*," she said.

"Don't fucking call me that."

I stormed up the stairs, knocking the paint bottles and palettes and cups off my shelves. Mj watched in horror as I destroyed everything.

"Mj, *stop!*" she yelled.

I flopped onto my bed, sobbing—so loud that Sully and Candreva could probably hear me from the opposite side of the road from their RV.

"It's okay, Mj," she held me. "It's okay, he's just some dumb-ass guy. It's *okay*."

"It's not," I whimpered, feeling her wipe my hair out my face. *I swear this was the most surrealist thing ever.* "He thinks I'm a bad person. I know he does."

"Then he can go hit himself in the head and try again," she scoffed. "Plus, you shouldn't care what he thinks of you. So *what if* he can pull a bunch of calculations out from his ass?"

"Mj, *you* thought he was cool too."

"Yeah," she sighed. "I really did, didn't I?" She chuckled, looking down at me. "But it's fine. I don't care."

I didn't expect myself to be that upset to be honest, but I surely knew *why* I was. I was never the type of person that'd rely on someone for comfort, but there was just *something* about him, something so ineffable that I ended up feeling comfort anyway; a type of comfort so rare due to the *lack* of cheesy romance and lust.

I believe stuff like that comes naturally to a person, but I've never found myself in a situation where it didn't matter, where it wasn't everything.

Never once did I think the one thing I admired about him would be the same thing that'd make me hate him.

8 [untitled]

~~JAKE~~ CADET KLEIN

I don't really feel like talking about him either.

BEYOND THE LIVING

23 NOVEMBER. 2021.

Maxwell found Scheuch on the peach-tiled floor against what used to be the pizzeria's freezer. He was sitting rather quietly, resting his forehead gently against his knees, surrounded by the pots and pans she assumed he had knocked over.

His fingers nervously tapped his watch. "If you've come here to lecture me—"

"I'm not going to lecture you, bud," she sighed, hand on her hip as she looked at him. "You didn't do anything wrong. I think—I think she just looked up to you a little too much."

He nodded gently, gulping.

"I'm going to go get Sergeant, is that okay?"

"Yeah," he replied.

Sergeant came in a few minutes later. Scheuch hadn't moved.

"What's going on?" he asked.

Scheuch fidgeted with his shoelace, staring into blank space. "I saw her," he replied.

"You saw *who?*" Sergeant listened to the deafening silence. "Wait, hold on, you mean *physically* or—" he searched for the right word, "*imaginatively...?*"

Scheuch didn't respond, but after a couple of seconds, Sergeant didn't need him to.

"Who did you see?" he asked. "Your mother?"

Scheuch shook his head.

"Hm," he nodded, stepping over to the backpacks laid upon the countertops. He rummaged through and took out a couple cans of sodas. "Want one?"

"I'm not that big of a fan of soda."

"Okay," he nodded again, stepping over as he clicked it open, taking a sip. "Aw, this tastes disgusting!"

He crouched down, sitting against the kitchen island to face him. He crossed his ankles, sighing as he looked at him.

"Kiara said you'd be in here," he said, tapping his finger against the aluminum. "I'm totally okay with just sitting here with you. We don't need to talk."

The autumn leaves broke off its stems. The wind blew them against the windows, occasionally making their way in through the cracks. The sun was out today. It hadn't been for a while, so the group was outside enjoying it. Everyone but Scheuch and I, and Sergeant knew why.

"My dad always wanted me to do everything myself—" Scheuch broke the silence, "—and my mom? Pfft. She was the complete opposite," he ran his fingers through his hair, "she kept trying to do everything *for* me—"

He looked up, resting his head against the brick walls, gulping, "—to make up for all the things she didn't do," he explained. "It wasn't *her* fault that she was sick."

"What was she sick with?"

"Everything. Everything you can imagine."

Sergeant paused, looking at him as his respect for him shot up three-hundred levels. "Is *this* why you're such a smartass?"

Scheuch chuckled softly. Sergeant began laughing.

"Am I right?" His smile was as wide as ever. "'Cause you mentioned you weren't interested in becoming—um—a paramedic."

"*Hell,* no."

"No interest in Pre-Med, at all?"

"I mean, I like Physics?"

Sergeant nodded. "So you took care of her."

"Yeah," he spoke softly, wiping his nose. "I would pick up shifts with Quinn and our dad occasionally—but—it was always just me at home, them working nights to pay off all the—bills."

... *Hold on, wait, they're brothers?!*

"One time Quinn and I were on this um—this camping trip," he began explaining hesitantly. "My—*Shelly*, she—"

"Hold on, who's *Shelly*?"

Scheuch paused, glancing down. "My-My ex."

"*You* had a girlfriend?" Sergeant raised his eyebrows.

"Yeah—this was-um—this was right after her cheer-"

"Hold on, *you* had a *girlfriend* who was a *cheerleader*." He smiled widely, shaking his head as he looked up to the ceiling. "Man, that's cliche."

Scheuch smiled faintly. "That trip went wrong. I don't like to think about it often, but I keep seeing her." He quickly blinked away the tears. "Shelly got hurt hiking one of the trails. We were in the middle of nowhere. We didn't know what to do, so she bled out."

Sergeant's face dropped, watching Scheuch rub his hands down his face, desperately trying to rid his mind of the memory, but he couldn't. No matter how many times he could make himself throw up, he couldn't stomach it.

"We were out there for weeks before we could get help," Scheuch explained. "Bailey—Bailey never ate much, but I—"

He had to.

Sergeant nodded, leaning closer to him. "Look me in the eye, Scheuch."

He did as he was told.

"I need you to pull yourself together," he ordered firmly. "Those hallucinations——they-they *can* get to you. I know they can, but you're somethin' else, Scheuch. I've never met anyone quite like you."

Scheuch nodded, smiling.

Sergeant leaned back. "Bui told me what happened," he took a sip of the expired soda.

"How's she been?"

"Same as you?" Sergeant shrugged, "Locked in your homes, staring at the walls."

"I know I said things I probably shouldn't have said," he admitted. "Or I—I know *now* that—that might've not been the best way to word things."

"What do you plan on doing?"

"I-I know I need to apologize," he sniffled, wiping his nose. "I just don't know *how*. She seems a little too *childish*."

"Childish?"

"Not in a sense that—she's immature," he quickly corrected. "She's too—casual about everything—and she's too *animated*. I don't think I—I can be the type of person that can get along with her."

"Yeah, she doesn't *understand* that," Sergeant sighed. "Scheuch, when it comes to Bui, it's good to let her loosen up around people who let her be a kid. She found that sense of safety with you."

"She *did*?"

"I watched you slowly bring the light back in her eyes?" Sergeant shrugged. "She spent *years* being a parent to her friends. Think about what that looks like to you, Scheuch? *Children* raising

RECONCILIATION

children." He inhaled, shrugging again. "So I *agree* with her, I think we should all try and—continue on with this as if everything was normal. It's not good to be in complete *survival mode* all the time."

"I don't believe that's setting an example," Scheuch replied worriedly. "I feel like if we aren't as functional and *professional* as to how—we were in the program—"

"Scheuch, I hate to break it to you," Sergeant sighed, looking at him with empathy, "but the world has *ended*. We are *allowed* to be vulnerable with one another!"

We're not a JROTC program anymore. This is life for us now. You can let the ranks and regulations go.

Those words hit him like bullets.

He sat there, suddenly uncertain. "But then, what would my purpose be?"

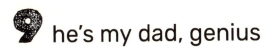 he's my dad, genius

SERGEANT ROGERS & CADET YANES

I understand a big part of the reason why the other cadets treat me the way they do is because they think Sergeant favors me over everyone else, but that's simply not true. If anything, I think he favors *himself* out of everyone else.

Sgt. Rogers holds himself together like the strongest super glue on the market. Sure, occasionally he breaks a *little* bit, but that's only because he's missing his partner-in-crime, his wife who was also in the military with him, which is understandable.

Sgt. Rogers speaks confidently and with a purpose. He can debate with you over a bottle cap and still win. He reads situations and he always knows what exactly to say.

So when he told me I was similar to him, I didn't know what he was talking about.

I don't hold myself together as well as he does, but to be fair he is a grown man and I'm a teenage girl, so that's *pretty* understandable. But putting those factors aside, I don't see myself as composed as he is in twenty years because I don't hold myself together like glue. I feel like I kinda wrap myself in layers of *really, really* sticky duct tape and start panicking once I let someone rip off a strip. I don't break apart when I lose ones I feel I think I need, as much as people might say I would. In reality, I break when they *are* with me because it gives me something to lose. It shifts my priorities in directions I don't want them to be in. It gives me a reason. And most importantly, I don't speak the same way he does. I force myself to be quiet unless I've been given a task that requires the ability to speak that way—which is why I would never debate over bottle caps or tell people what they want to hear after reading situations. I wouldn't because it wouldn't be my problem.

If it's not my problem, why the hell would I care?

Sergeant is the type of person that can walk into a room full of new people and adapt quickly. I am not. I just happen to be very open expressing *my* problems to him and he just so happens to have advice that resonates. It's that simple.

There's no *favoritism* here.

Yet Kim had a lot of things to say, and so did Terry. And so did a hell of a lot of cadets in the program. Well guess what, morons? A good chunk out of the huge chunk of them are *dead!*

So sitting around debriefing and whining and complaining about it will do... drum roll please...

Nothing.

Sometimes I can tell when he thinks I'm progressing. He just looks at me with a disappointed look on his face, because he's told me time and time again what he knows I *could* be. He just doesn't know how to get it out.

I say I don't know either, but I do.

I know exactly how to handle situations and how to keep my composure, and I know that from the thousand therapy sessions he's given me.

Now *I* just gotta want to.

DAY 351 / THE NIGHT WE SCATTERED

When he and Yanes were driving away from the crowd that night, it wasn't difficult for them to figure out where everyone else was.

"Did you see Klein go with Sully and Candreva?" Sergeant asked as he drove, and Yanes would answer from the backseat, *No, he ran off after Bui,* as he looked out from behind him in hopes to see at least *something.*

"*Bui's* not with them either?!" Sergeant tried not to stress. "What was she doing?"

"I saw her run after Scheuch," Yanes wiped the blood and guts off his face.

"Oh dear *Lord,*" Sergeant stomped on the petal, getting away from the crowd.

"Sir, you do realize we are going the opposite way Sully and Candreva are going, right?"

"I'm driving us back to Jade Street," he responded. "I don't know what those two are doing, but as long as they're not doing anything excruciatingly *stupid,* it doesn't matter to me."

"Then what *does* concern you?"

"Where the hell all those roamers came from," he sighed, looking over at him. "I don't think Scheuch was kidding about the temperature getting to those motherfuckers. They're heading more and more towards us."

They arrived back at early sunrise. The sky was dull and cloudy. The air was cold and foggy. The street was quiet, and the barriers we've built were demolished. Far away, the staggered roamers went about their own business.

The buildings looked exactly as we had first found them, which alarmed the two. Several windows were shattered or left open. The doors were broken off their hinges, and those that weren't were swaying sadly with the wind. They stepped out of the vehicle and immediately jogged up to Scheuch and Watkin's pizzeria, but found nothing. They ran across the street and entered the gun shop—nothing either.

My bar was empty. The RV was empty.

There was only one message written in roamer blood over the wall where Candreva usually spray-painted his cartoons.

WENT TO LOOK FOR OTHERS. MEET BACK HERE. - CAM.

Sergeant couldn't stomach the idea of leaving the rest of us out there alone, Candreva was right. We were always going to feel like a responsibility to him, regardless if the state of the world gives him a way out.

So the two spent the next two weeks searching the perimeters, occasionally heading back to the street to restock supplies. Sergeant knew what he was doing. Yanes knew how to be rational during times like these.

I don't think I've ever seen Yanes be anything but at peace. He has the strengths, yet he's as gentle to me as a lion to its cub. He was always really nice—and he was one of the only ones who never gave me direct shit about Klein. He already wasn't that fond of him, and I knew that once he eventually found out what he did to me, it pretty much sealed the deal.

I never brought myself to get close with him, though, even after our conversation in the woods when we searched for García. He was always either hanging out with Candreva, working out with Johnson, or teasing Conti. He was doing his own thing and I was doing mine—mine as in playing soccer with Jonah Atkins on the streets or showing Scheuch what I painted or having another therapy session with Sgt. Rogers or taking care of Colón or telling Watkins or Maxwell about the latest, *what the hell is this bitch's problem? story* because I wasn't allowed to go on many supply runs before Conti and Johnson's death unless someone older was *chaperoning.*

Sergeant and Yanes spent days camping out in the woods, even when they knew it was dangerous. It's safe to say they were the happiest pair of all of those who were stranded after that night, unless I would consider myself the most content.

I just spent the entire time talking to myself.

Literally.

Michelle and Mj were all I got.

Sgt. Rogers spends most of his time laughing, that one thing I know for a fact we have in common. And Yanes was pretty funny, and I like to think he found me funny too, even when most of our racially motivated jokes never made sense.

"I'm not Chinese," I would say.

"And I'm not Mexican," he would reply.

So the two spent the weeks searching, and after a while it started to feel like it was no use. The woods were quiet, eerily quiet. So quiet where it began to feel like the voices they heard through the bushes were just in their heads. There were no signs. Nothing.

Candreva and Sully were living on the road, sleeping in the truck every night. Scheuch and Bailey were still bickering, living in their tent, or *tents* I should say. Maxwell, Watkins, and Kim were out looking for them with the help of her former lover, Keigan. I was in the middle of nowhere, living on my own. And Klein?

I don't know.

He came back a different person. We all did.

"Stop where you are," A voice spoke from behind a tree.

They froze in their tracks, carefully scanning around.

"Drop your weapon," the feminine voice spoke again.

"The hell—" Sgt. Rogers turned back and forth, "—are you *coming* from?"

"Drop your weapon, I'm *serious*."

They both gave in, slowly kneeling, placing their weapons on the ground. When they looked up, at least four people appeared, surrounding them. They all looked the same. All in black. All wearing gas masks.

"Where are you guys heading?" the main woman asked, scoffing at their silence. "You two look too clean to be just living on the road by yourselves. Tell me, where are the rest of you guys."

"*Why?*" Yanes scowled.

"Because we *want* to know how the hell y'all are immu—"

"April!" the one on the right began talking. "April, *stop!*" She commanded as *April* turned in her spot. "April, he's with *me!*"

"What?" She tilted her head. "You *know* him?"

"Yes," she wiped the dirt off her mask, revealing her round blue eyes, "he's my dad, genius."

Sgt. Rogers widened his eyes, looking into the mask carefully. And soon, Yanes watched what once was seriousness in his eyes, turn into a look of faith.

"Dad?" the muffled voice asked.

Zoey Rogers.

We've all heard stories about her.

BEYOND THE LIVING

9 ½ am i immature or just too young?
CADET ROGERS

OCTOBER 26 2019 / SIX MONTHS BEFORE THE OUTBREAK
The first time I cried in front of Sergeant basically sealed our bond for what was left of our school year. I never brought it upon myself to talk to my male teachers, so it was nice having someone to talk to. (I will never trust female staff members after last year).

I'm sure this day was memorable for others too, considering how Yanes also remembered it.

Sergeant was leaning back in his chair, cross armed. I was leaning against a desk, face in my hands.

"What's wrong?" he asked. "Is it Klein?"

"I don't know," I replied, wiping the eyeliner smearing down my face, hesitating.

There were a lot of things wrong at the moment—a lot of things I don't usually talk about because I don't like to hear the sound of my voice breaking.

My parents fought hard last night because my sister left the house without letting them know—and somehow that led to one subject to another. Nothing new. My mom did call me selfish though—when I told her I didn't want to hear about it. I'm a child. I don't want to know about it. I don't *need* to know about it. I don't need to know how much you regret a marriage and wish I wasn't such a burden to you.

I yell at anyone who speaks to me about things I don't want to speak about. I am not *forced* to talk to *anyone*.

It doesn't matter if you're a teacher, and I'm a student.

It doesn't matter if you're a parent, and I'm your child.

It doesn't matter if you're older, and I'm younger.

If I don't want to **FUCKING** talk to you, and you *make* me, don't get **FUCKING** mad you don't get the responses you want.

I am not

the type of person.

that accommodates *anyone*.

María and Jada aren't talking to me. María is still mad at me for not letting go of the forty bucks she said she'd pay me back, and I know that because she yelled at me to get the fuck away from her when I realized she was absolutely baked in the school bathroom stall, so I cannot ask her if she's okay or if she's doing well, but I don't need to ask. She is *not* doing well and she will not be in a long time. I've known that.

I was there ready to hold her hair back just in case she needed to throw up after that party she and Jada went to. I was there when she was too scared to look at the pregnancy test after pregnancy test on the bathroom counter. I was there talking to her soothingly in fear she might be greening out, because we both knew Jada's loud-ass wouldn't do shit? She was on the phone with a guy, ready to leave to hook up with him.

I don't understand. I've dropped everything and I've done everything I could to help her every time she needed me, but I am still *a bitch* and a *bad friend*.

I am a *bad friend*.

But even with everything going on, everything those damn cadets know *could* be going on, *everything about me has to revolve around some boy,* and I hate it because in a sense, it's true. This is how I break away. I fixate on the things I *don't* care about to forget that the most important people in my life are horrible to me.

"*Is it?*" Sgt. Rogers asked again. "He *did* tell me what happened."

I scoffed. "Of course he did."

He paused. "Is—that—a bad thing?"

I rolled my eyes. "Just find it a little odd for him to tell me to not tell anybody but then turn around and—"

"Tell everyone a different story." He finished my sentence with me.

I nodded. "I know it's not that big of a deal, but it just annoys me." *Don't make it sound like it got to you.* ~~It did.~~ "It's an inconvenience, that's what it is," I said. "I don't need random people asking me questions about this shit. I just want to focus on what I need to focus on."

I don't like how my GPA is a 3.8—gotta get it up to a 4.

"Well, *different* doesn't necessarily mean a *bad* thing," Sgt. Rogers explained. "It could just be his perspective."

"Well, he clearly needs a pair of fucking glasses then!"

People like Klein make me *want* to be alone.

How can one tell me, "I think we should break up," when we're not even dating? Oh wait, apparently we *were* when he texted Kiara to stay away from me! Oh wait! I don't know if it's just me—but that shit is fucking weird! We haven't even known each other for a damn month!

How can one tell me, "I don't plan on telling the others what happened, so I'd appreciate it if you wouldn't either—*especially* Kiara," but when I check my phone's notifications it's Avery and Kiara texting me asking me if I'm *okay* and suddenly Elizabeth Kim sitting up a little straighter, smiling my way like

she

wants

to

get

HIT!

How can one tell *me,* "I don't like flings," but tell *Kim,* "I think I might have a fling with her," but then tell *Avery Conti,* "I don't think this might work in the *long*-long run," like we're getting married or something—like *calm... down...*

We just met, dude.

How can one tell me, "Don't tell Kiara what happened," but then turn around and say, "Hey, Kiara, I don't want you to think I'm the bad guy—I'm just having some mental problems right now—*blah blah blah,*" and feel the embarrassment when she replies, "I don't care?" because by some *miracle,* people like her actually have something to do with their lives. How can one tell me to specifically *not* tell Sergeant in fear of him considering it *fraternization,* but then turn around and tell him how and why we're not *together* anymore. How can one excuse their own actions by telling me, "I'm just going through something mentally right now," like it makes everything okay. It doesn't. I have shit weigh my shoulders, but you don't see me waking up every day to make it somebody else's problem?

How bored can you be?

How bored do you have to be to pull this indecisive bullshit and twist words around, and now people in the program are looking at me like I'm stupid.

Like GO *DO* SOMETHING!

I began crying harder, and he nodded, leaning further back, putting his feet up on the desk.

"I remember when I got my heart broken for the first time," he chuckled as I looked up from my hands slowly.

"It was my junior year of high school," he said. "You know if you take a left here and go out to the plaza, there's a diner out—"

"No," I replied, wiping my face. "I don't go out much."

"By the river?" he asked. "There's a little diner?"

I shook my head.

"Oh, well," he shrugged, "We were in the parking lot. I was about to drive her home, and just as I was opening the door for her, she looked right at me and confessed she kissed a guy at last week's football game."

"Oh—" I covered my mouth. "No *way,* that shit sounds straight out of a movie."

"Under the bleachers," he laughed, shaking his head, "and God, I was *crushed.* I was stuck on it for a while, actually. My girlfriend of what—like two years cheating on me—but," he shook his head. "That's what you get out of dating in high school, Mj."

"So nothing changes."

"Sure, some people mature, some don't," he shrugged, chuckling a bit. "She and that guy went out and ended up getting married——but y'know, she left me a voicemail the night before her wedding, sobbing."

"Holy shit!" My eyes lit up.

"This was a few years back," he quickly added. "She called me—said she wished it was me."

"What did you do?!" I adjusted myself above the desk, crossing my legs.

"Nothing," he replied. "I was already married—Zoey's little sister was on the way. Life happens. She probably just moved on."

"I'm not *heartbroken*, Sergeant," I said, scoffing. "I don't actually care that much."

"Then what is *wrong?*"

There are so many things wrong.

So many.

Too many.

But I don't talk about this shit for a reason.

"I just should've known," I replied. "This isn't the first time, this is just the first time I'm able to detach before it gets worse."

I sighed and rubbed my forehead.

"Seventeen years old and pulling that shit on me, are you serious?!" I scoffed. "Like go fucking do something!" I shook my head, "Cause now people are waltzing up to me, talkin' bout some, *are you okay...?* Like leave me alone!"

"Sorry to disappoint you Mj," he replied, "but him being seventeen years old doesn't mean *shit*."

"I'm *fifteen* and I know not to do somethin' like that!" I scoffed. "I just find it hilarious he always has something dumb to say, like—*Oooh Mj, she's so manipulative! She's so immature!*—Well, if I'm so *immature*, **KLEIN**, here's a *bright* idea!"

DATE SOMEONE YOUR AGE!

"I'm so stupid," I groaned, rubbing my hands down my face. "I should've *known*."

"People make mistakes, Mj. You can just learn from this," he replied. "You're allowed to *hurt*. You're allowed to *feel*. You don't *have* to beat yourself up over every *thing* you could've done better."

But that's all I do.

"I know it's dramatic, but I know how this shit ends," I spiraled. "Pull dumb shit like this on me then boom, it's gonna happen over n' over n' over again—and I know how I am, so I know I'm gonna keep letting it happen."

I took a deep sigh.

"So I'm not going to this time."

He sighed too, looking away for a bit. "Okay, are you good? You let it all out?"

"Yeah,"

"Mj, the thing you need to know is that dating at this age is never that serious and that *high school* is the time where you open up your circle and figure out what you want and don't want in a relationship," he told me. "You're going to meet *so many people* in the next few years."

"They're all the same."

He stopped and sighed. "Listen, Mj," holding his hand out, "you're just *extremely* used to the same people that you don't realize there are better people out there."

If a boy like Jake Klein could turn out to be that way too, then going around trying to find someone who could deceive me better wasn't worth it.

I am not hurt. I am not hurt. I am not hurt. I. Am. Not. Hurt.

Leave me alone.

"People mature differently," he explained, "which is why it does not matter that he's seventeen. Mj, trust me, he'll probably be like this for the rest of his life."

"That's a damn shame."

He chuckled. "And people are invested," he shrugged again, "people like *drama,* so they ask."

"Why can't they just mind their own business?" I scoffed.

"Mj, they're his friends."

That's the dumbest fucking excuse I've ever heard.

"Uhhhhh... that's not an excuse," I felt myself getting angry. "Whenever *my* guy friends have shit going on, I don't go sniffing around all up in their business, the fuck? That's so weird!"

Yeah, my guy friend just had a fall-out with a girl, and instead of actually going to do something with my life, let me go *skippin'* up to her and pester her with some *questions!* Hooray!

Yeah, no.

I scoffed in disbelief. "No girl actually cares that much."

"Not everyone is like you."

My conversations with Sergeant were basically like that from that point on, except when Klein came back again the night on the rooftop. That's when my conversations with *everyone* changed.

Except for *Watkins, Bailey, Maxwell, and Scheuch,* of course.

But it made me sad.

Watkins was always doing his own thing or helping Bailey, and Bailey was always busy building the barriers with the others, and of course, they refused to let me help.

"Just teach me how to do it!" I would say cheerfully.

Candreva would try, but after a while, he told me it'd be easier if I did another task—only those tasks were always already taken.

I don't want them to think I am useless.

I don't want them to think I am useless.

Please, let me do *something*. I feel like I am doing *nothing*.

Maxwell was always on supply runs, supply runs that I wasn't allowed to accompany.

And Scheuch—

...

"So I see you're talking to Klein again," Sgt. Rogers said after calling me into the gun shop a few weeks after that night.

I stood still, not knowing what to say.

"Johnson told me."

"How the—" I muttered. "Whatever."

Sergeant talked to me a lot about Klein, and I know now that he was doing it out of genuine concern for me. (Almost) All of them were, but after a while, it really frustrated me.

I don't need you to tell me to stay away from him. I know.

"I don't care what you do at this point. You guys are teenagers. The world has ended," he began to say. "As long as it doesn't turn out in a way where it'll affect the others, I *seriously* don't care."

"So why am I here?" I asked.

"Because I *do* care," he said. "Mj, you and I both know this will not end well. Look, I've been through this with my daughter."

I sighed.

I don't know why I let him back.

~~I want him to hurt the way I did.~~

I know I have no interest in him whatsoever.

~~I just want to be able to tell him no.~~

I know this could only end in two ways.

~~I want to see the look on his face.~~

The plan could work or it wouldn't.

"Well, I figured since there's no difference in talking to the group whether I am on good terms with him or not," I explained, "I might as well just make up with *him* so I have *someone* to talk to."

Sgt. Roger sighed annoyedly and covered his face with his hands. "What are you talking about?"

"When Jake and I are on bad terms, everyone's awkward," I replied. "I can feel the tension when we're all standing together."

"It's-"

"It's *not* in my head," I said. "Jake gets weird. He like—stands there like—" I posed to demonstrate, crossing my arms smugly, "—and thinks he's too cool to take anything seriously."

High and righteous.

"But now that we *are* talking again, everyone just decides to suddenly be fuckin' weird like—bro," I scoffed. "So it was *okay* for them to hang out with him, but if *I* do it, then it's wrong."

"*They* are friends with him," he replied. "*You* two have history."

~~They're my friends too!~~

"Yeah," I snarked. "History that is not *their* business."

He shook his head. "Mj, why don't you just loosen up, be yourself, and try to get to really *know* them?"

~~I know them.~~

"Like *who?*" I scoffed. "I swear it's impossible with them."

If I talk to Sterling, I'm weird and annoying, and he's fucking Sterling. I can't have one damn conversation with him without him asking me out the week later. If I talk to Maxwell, I'm nosey and bossy. I'm uptight and can't take a joke. Why is it normal for Scheuch to shut every social interaction he has down, but if Maxwell isn't in the mood to be energetic, it must be *that time of the month?* If I talk to Watkins, I'm involved with drugs and alcohol. And so... *freaking...* on.

"It's not *impossible*," he shook his head. "You got along with other kids in your grade well?"

"Okay, well, that's 'cause Adkins was really sweet," I sighed, "but he's not here anymore."

He nodded. "Look, all I'm saying is talking to Klein again is a *terrible* idea. I don't understand how you two haven't moved on."

"I guess I wasn't up to date with how the group felt about him at the moment," I shrugged as I began to start heading out. Curfew was coming.

"Are you *listening* to what I am saying?"

I turned around again and sighed with my hand on the door handle. "Yeah-Yeah," I lied, pausing before laughing at the stern look he had on his face.

DAY 372 / 2 WEEKS AFTER THE NIGHT WE SCATTERED

When Yanes and Sergeant reunited with Zoey, it felt weird. Sergeant was looking at someone who looked like his daughter, but it felt as if he didn't even know her. She was a new person now.

I was friends with Zoey Rogers. She was a grade below me, meaning that when she was in eighth grade, she planned on joining the program when she moved up to high school. That never happened, obviously.

Knowing her and her personality, I knew she would only join the program because of her dad. I knew she wouldn't give a shit about everything else going on. They were identical, except her hair color was slightly darker than his. They were both tall and fit—had the same facial features and laugh. Since she was just like him and I got along with her dad well, it made perfect sense for us to be good friends.

It was nice.

It was relieving to know she had been okay all this time.

"Wha—H-How have you been?" Sergeant was in shock.

He had many questions, but all he could do was stare and notice how her blue eyes still had that same spark it always did and her smile was still just as bright. She and him really *are* the same.

"Good!" she replied before dropping her bags and hugging him tightly, chuckled in relief. "Really good."

He laughed out of relief. *Sergeant doesn't cry.*

"What?" she chuckled back.

"Nothing, you've just grown so much," he replied, rocking her side to side.

"*Zoey.*" April rolled her eyes beneath the mask.

She let go and patted her jeans down. "Sorry, we might have to—head back—" she paused and narrowed her eyes at Yanes.

Yanes looked at her back the same way.

"Who *are* you?" she asked.

"Mickey Yanes?"

She paused again before a puzzled look began to grow on her face. She looked at April and then back at her dad.

"What?" Sgt. Rogers made a face.

"Dad, you might want to come with us."

"You guys just held guns to our heads—" Yanes scoffed.

"Trust me, you're gonna wanna see this," she insisted, picking up her stuff as she began leading both of them through the woods.

Yanes must've been nervous, regardless of the stone face he put on. For Sergeant, however, it must've been extremely relieving for him as they hiked through trees under the cloudy sky.

"Holy shit," Yanes let out.

They were surrounded by large trucks and vans filled with boxes of supplies and people with clipboards sectioning them out. It was an interesting sight, but there was something else that interested both of them more.

Sgt. Rogers began chuckling loudly, shaking his head. "Son of a bitch." He began walking towards us.

We had found each other.

Maxwell, Watkins, and Kim were huddled up by their car with Klein in the backseat of it. Bailey, Scheuch, and I were leaning against the steel guardrails by the highway roads, watching Sergeant walk up to us with a big smile on his face.

We had found each other, but we all looked different.

Yanes glanced around with his eyes softened while Sergeant patted every one of us on the back.

"Glad you made it," he said. "Glad you're safe. We pushed through you guys."

Yanes bit his bottom lip and looked down before looking back up again. The only other person who seemed to notice what was wrong was Scheuch.

"Where's Mary and Brody?"

section 2
éloignement

10 who passed *your* license?

The day I reunited with the group replays in my head just as much as the night we scattered. After I passed out against the tree trunk, I woke up to the sound of Bailey's voice and his gentle hands on my shoulders. "Hey *kid!*" He shook my shoulders. *"Mj—"* He turned, scoffing, "—Aaron, can you hurry up and give the kid some damn *food?* She's damn near *green!*"

My eyes fluttered open. My stomach curled into itself. It was hard to make out their faces. It took me a bit to decide if they were real or not.

"I have—" he held out an opened water bottle, "—this. She's dehydrated, Bailey."

I spent weeks searching for them, but instead, *they* found *me.*

I grabbed it gently, and drank.

"Slowly," he said. "Don't chug."

They tried bringing me to my feet, but I was so weak that I couldn't stand. I rode on Bailey's back until we met back up with Maxwell, Watkins, and Kim, who had the safety kit with them. Scheuch quickly checked my head.

"I'm so glad you're okay," Maxwell sniffled, hugging me softly.

I smiled as Scheuch placed his hand on my chin gently, turning my head to face him.

"Any *headache*—or *pressure?*" He asked as he shined a low-beam flashlight from the outer edge of my eye inward.

I tried not to squint, shaking my head.

"Are you nauseous?" he asked. "*Not* from the scent of blood." *I shook my head again.* "Any *vomiting, balance problems, dizziness,* or *blurry or double vision?*" he asked.

"Noo—?" I flinched as he slammed his palm onto the hood of the car loudly.

"Loud noise," he smiled, nodding proudly. "Are you *bothered* by that?"

"No."

He narrowed his eyes, thinking. "Hm, what is——your— *fourth* order to the sentry?"

To repeat all calls from posts more distant than the guardhouse or quarterdeck than my own.

I lowered my eyebrows. *"What?"*

"Ah," he nodded, "I can see why that could be—a bad question—here—what's——hm—what is your *favorite* color?"

"Um," I replied. "Blue?"

It was not blue.

"What's *my* favorite color?"

I smiled softly. "Purple!"

"Memory is *decent.*" He looked up at Maxwell's confused face and smiled widely. "She *doesn't* have a concussion!"

I think about these moments a lot. I would say I don't know why, but I do know why. I know *exactly* why.

I think of them because I like the torture of reminding myself that for a certain amount of time, he did in fact like me, and I must've done something for him not to.

RECONCILIATION **246**

Although, surprisingly, I *didn't* think of him much on that car ride that night.

That night.

My birthday.

SEPTEMBER 4, 2022

Maxwell took a deep breath as she drove, scanning the roads. She was furious, with the group as a whole, I mean. I've heard numerous stories from her perspective on what she has endured from them, so it made sense that she was mad. She was mad she couldn't protect me from it, no matter how hard she tried.

"Klein, I'm going to need you to either *help* or *be quiet*," she said. "Okay?"

"O-ka—"

She gripped the wheel harder, inhaling again sharply. "I can't *possibly* understand *how* you could let her drive off?"

"She would've run my ass over, Kie," he replied, running his hand down his face, "and if I knew you were gonna spend this entire car ride lecturing me, I would've just let you bring Aaron instead."

"Well, it *would've* been him," she sighed. "Sergeant would've sent the *highest* ranked on the command staff-"

"But *I* am higher than you."

"You are?"

"Yes," he explained. "Conti wrote the order wrong."

XO was higher than SR. ENLISTED. Whatever, to-may-to, to-mah-to. Klein didn't contribute much to his position due to being bitter Scheuch got the one he wanted. Cadet Klein as our Class Commander? Sounds like a nightmare!

"Okay, well, they're not really *happy* with each other right now," she replied snarkily.

Klein paused, looking like he just tasted something sour. "Is *that* why she stormed off?"

"Probably *not*," she replied. "Mj doesn't get mad like that, Jake. There has to be—some sort of *build-up*. This must be an *ongoing* thing."

"Yeah ... she said something like that before leaving," he took a deep breath, looking out the window beside him, "something 'bout—um—the group always being *mean* to her or something."

"Did she *actually* say that or is that just what you *got* from it?"

He rolled his eyes. "She's always complaining about how people treat her. I think people just tune her out at this point."

She quickly swerved, avoiding a lone roamer. Klein shifted to the side, nearly hitting his head. "What the—*hell?*"

"Do you see how that's a *problem?*" she asked, resuming back to a regular speed.

"I see whoever passed your driver's license test was clearly *crazy!*" he scoffed, shaking his head.

"I'm *glad* she's complaining," she replied. "I'm tired of watching her not speak up for herself."

Klein's jaw dropped dramatically. I obviously wasn't there, but I could clearly picture what his face looked like. Klein does this thing with his tongue every time something doesn't go his way. He lowers his eyebrows and sticks his tongue into his cheek, making himself, in my opinion, look incredibly stupid.

"Um—Kiara, remind me if I'm going a little crazy *too* here—but does she *not* already stand up for herself *enough?*" He scoffed. "She literally drew a gun on Kim."

"*That* was a moment—where—"

"Mhm."

"It was an act of anger in—"

"Mhm."

"Not that it excuses it, but she was griev—"

"Mhm."

She looked over at him, glaring directly into his eyes. "It was a *reaction*," she said. "She was *clearly* in a vulnerable position and had a lot of things weighing on her. Mj's tough, Jake, but she was under a *lot* of pressure when Kim was provoking her—"

"*Okay*, Kiara, I don't need a philosophical explanation about everyone I bring up to you."

"Okay," she shook her head disappointedly, driving in silence.

"Fine."

She couldn't even look at him. She couldn't because if she did, she'd be looking at the one person she once saw as a little brother to her. His face was so familiar, yet he was a stranger.

"You're wasting your time," he broke the silence. "Michelle's a total nutcase."

"Why are you calling her Michelle if you never knew her as *Michelle?*" She quickly interrupted.

"I am *telling* you, she is *too* far *gone!*"

"Well, *look around*, Klein!" she replied, "she's basically all you've got left. Do not tell me what you do or do not—"

"Kim's not wrong," he interrupted her. "She is not who you think she is. That bitch is *crazy!*"

"And you know that because of the amount of time you spend with her? Oh wait, you don't," she snarked. "You literally *left* her!"

"Uh, can you *blame* me?" he laughed. "She was *screaming*—fuckin'—seizing in her seat and *hitting* herself before she drove off—" he told her, his voice raising, "—if I didn't back up, her *fist* was gonna come slammin' through the glass. Do you really *think* someone like that deserves any sympathy right now?"

She stomped on the break, fully turning towards him with her index finger up. She was teary-eyed now, lips quivering in fury.

"*Until* you are protecting her from a guy she doesn't have the strength to realize she needs to leave—or helping her cover bruises along her hips and thighs—you do not get to *tell* me——you know—how—she is."

She inhaled sharply.

"You have no *idea*," she spat. "You have no absolute *idea* how much that girl *reminds* me of me and I will do *everything* in my power to protect her since *no one else* will!"

She quickly turned back, catching her breath. She pressed the gas again, carrying on silently.

Klein looked at her with softened eyes. I guess he just didn't know what to say to that. He knew exactly what he was signing up for, liking somebody like me. It shouldn't have been a shock to him that I reacted the way I did when he left the first time, yet he still responded after a few silent seconds, in a soft, pitiful tone,

"I didn't know any of that."

"Of course you didn't," she replied, calmer now. "All you ever care about is yourself?"

"That's not true, Kie."

"Klein, I'm *really* not in the right state of mind for this right now," she said. "I just need you to focus so we can both make sure she's okay—" **BANG!**

She hit the brakes. They both glanced around wide-eyed, specifically behind them.

"What the hell?" Klein muttered.

"*Sh!*"

"Just keep on driving, it's probably nothing."

"Who the hell's out shooting guns at this hour?!" she asked astonishedly, gently pressing the gas pedal.

"It's probably an—emergency thing—"

She drove slowly, cautiously with slight fear in her voice. "W-What?"

"Like—an in-the-moment thing, a close call," he suggested.

"Or it could be *Mj* in *trouble*," she worried.

BANG! BANG! BANG!

"Drive," Klein immediately ordered. *"Drive! Now!"* He reached over, steering the wheel sharply, preventing the two from crashing into another vehicle.

"Does that seem like an emergency thing *now?*" Maxwell scoffed, foot now pressing the pedal, trying to keep calm.

"There's no way that's Mj." He swung around, hand on the back of her seat, squinting into the darkness behind them.

"Of *course,* that's not Mj," she replied, looking over at him. He didn't respond. *"Klein,* Mj wouldn't do that!"

"Sure she wouldn't."

"Klein," she repeated. "Mj *wouldn't—*"

BANG! "Kiara!" **POP!**

"*Shit.*" Maxwell's fingertips trailed across her head, feeling the blood trickle down her face. She looked over, seeing Klein's hand pinch the bridge of his nose. He hissed at the pain.

"What—happened—" Her eyes fluttered open, seeing all the shattered glass on their laps, in their hands, cutting their faces.

"You hit the breaks," he replied.

"W-What?"

"You're *not* supposed to hit the breaks when your tire pops," he replied condescendingly, grunting as he unbuckled his seatbelt.

"I didn't *mean* t—" She turned over wide-eyed, seeing a figure approach their vehicle. Their headlights were broken now. All she could make out were the scuffs on the man's mustard yellow combat boots.

She heard a gun cock, assuming Klein beside her did too.

"Step out of the car slowly," the man ordered. "Now."

"Uh," Maxwell took a deep breath, unbuckling her seat belt to climb out of the upturned vehicle. She winced as the glass shards from the window slashed open her clothes and crawled out to the concrete pavement slowly, feeling sick from being upside down. Her eyes widened when she saw what he was wearing, seeing Klein have to do the same in her peripheral vision.

"*Stand* up," his voice ordered through the gas mask. "Raise your hands to your head. Interlace your fingers."

She did as he told her, watching Klein being forced to do the same in her peripheral. Two other men came out of nowhere and began searching them, patting them down head-to-toe.

Something in the air stung her throat as she attempted to breathe. "We—We don't want trouble," she choked.

The man that stood in front of her remained chillingly still, so still that for a second, she thought he wasn't even going to answer her. All he gave was a harsh, "Did I *ask* you what you wanted?"

For what felt like an eternity, the two of them stood frozen as they were frisked and robbed of their weapons and belongings from the wreck. It's weird using the word *their*, as if they owned them. In circumstances like these, everything belonged to everybody.

At least that was the logic those masked men followed.

It's kinda hard to explain these things knowing in those moments, you try your best to remain composure and observe everything going on. They questioned the men's humanity and their morals, and they did so instinctively as if it was some sort of *procedure* or *protocol* they'd set in their heads. We gained that habit once we realized the things *we* had to do out there.

To think after all this time struggling to fight, none of us would be scared of death anymore—but after facing this, we realized how wrong we were. For all this time, we were fearing the roamers; the unknown; but in reality, those roamers were nothing but victims. All this time, we should've been fearing our *own*.

"Yes, sir, we've found them," one of the men spoke into a two-way radio alongside them, which quickly caught Klein's attention.

"Sir, I can assure you, we are *not* the people you are after," he quickly said, *seriously*. "You're mistaken!" he said, nearly pleading as he watched Maxwell cry when they began zip-tying her wrists together.

"*Quiet!*" Klein winced as he took a blow from the man silencing him. The man lowered his rifle, looking deep into his eyes. "Speak again, and it'll be your pretty friend you have over here," he said as two men quickly draped cloth sacks over their heads, blocking their vision.

No patience. No empathy. Nothing.

Those men ordered the two around like dogs. Kicking and shoving as they shouted—managing to hurt them more than the car crash did with blows to the neck, the back, and the legs. It didn't take long for Klein's nose to start bleeding down to his lips.

They were scared to death; clenching their jaws; keeping their chins high. No matter how tough a person could be, in situations like those, *anyone* would've shat their pants, whether they chose to show or not.

I remember laying on the cold concrete as that *vulgar* man barricaded me to it. I remember the panic, hearing the sound of his belt unbuckling, and I remember watching that *heartless* French man point a gun at ~~my friend's~~ Cadet Scheuch's forehead.

I remember trying to convince myself that I wasn't scared, but I was. I was. I was so, so, scared.

~~I am not built for this anymore. I'm breaking.~~

11 sitting there. alone. restrained.

My fingertips scratched at the grime beneath me. No matter how many times I could've opened my eyes, the only thing I would see, the only thing I would feel, is the black fabric covering my sight. My ankles squirmed. My wrists behind my back did too.

I never thought of myself as someone who was claustrophobic, but in that moment it felt so wrong to try and focus on my breathing.

Sitting there. Alone. Restrained.

Inhale. Exhale. Inhale. Exhale. Inhale. Exhale.

Slower.

Inhale... Exhale... Inhale... Exhale... Inhale... Exhale...

SLOWER.

Inhale......? Ex—

"Hey, darling?" A guy—most likely in his early twenties snatched the sack from my head.

My eyes opened slowly to adjust to the bright light from the lantern above. I began to make out his face. I figured this one was James. He was standing over me with an opened bottle of water.

"Drink it," he lowered the bottle, attempting to tip it in my mouth for me. I've seen enough of these scenes in movies to know not to drink that. They put shit in it. I don't know *what*, but they put shit in it to get you to talk.

"I ain't drinkin' that," I muttered.

"C'mon, I know you're thirsty." *I am—more than I've ever been since the plane crash.* I'm still not drinkin' that.

"Fine." He sighed, bending back up. "You got a couple visitors."

I quickly looked past him, naturally scanning my surroundings. I was in a room, most likely underground by the looks of the leaking pipes from the ceiling, the rusting, unfinished walls, and the floor beneath me staining my jeans.

Floor, there was no floor? This was straight-up dirt!

I watched nervously as two men shoved Klein and Maxwell into the room in the same condition I was in. Maxwell was so tired she collapsed to her knees before she could even get to me. They snatched the sacks off, letting them acknowledge their surroundings. I think this was the first time Maxwell wasn't relieved to see me.

They were forced to sit against the back wall beside me silently until further notice, which allowed Maxwell to tell me what happened. At first, I was too tired to listen, but something she said caught my attention. It didn't take long for me to connect the dots, but I wanted to be sure I wasn't crazy.

Too bad I am not on speaking terms with him to confirm.

Many men entered and exited the room. They all looked the same: malnourished, exhausted, mindless. None of them looked like they could be the leader. There were very few women. That was the first thing I noticed. A person could easily tell just by looking at the way the men acted once they saw me and Maxwell.

One man approached us, speaking into his walkie-talkie.

"I got three of them here," he said, bending down to one knee, looking at me so closely that I could smell his coffee breath. "I think this Asian's the one that killed *Benny*."

I think this Asian's the one that killed Benny. Well *shit!*

"She's got a few tattoos—" he pulled down my shirt from the collar, "—a nice pair of koi fish——she's got a star behind her ear," he looked at the dangling cross on my left ear, "nice earrings too."

"I don't care, moron," the other line replied. "Tell me if she's dangerous! How do we know her people ain't comin' to go look for her right now?"

"It wouldn't be much of a concern if you guys do your damn job right?" He got up, looking down at Maxwell now. "Hey, her friend's here too."

"The stupid one?"

He paused. *"What?"*

"The Latina—" the other line replied, "—the one that laughs like a *damn* hyena!"

"No," he shook his head, squinting at her, "the firefighter," he turned heading back towards the door. "Rodney might know her."

"R-Rodney?" Her head shot up. She began inching towards him with pleading eyes. "Rodney *Daffodil?*"

He turned around. "She *does* know him." He spoke about her in a way she's never been spoken to before, at least not for a very long time. Kiara Maxwell was well-liked and well-respected, and anyone who didn't clearly had something wrong with them. That's how I always saw it——but he dehumanized her, looking at her like she was a beat up dog on the side of the street, like a homeless person begging for spare change.

"Please." This was the first time I ever saw her tolerate this type of behavior. "Just let me talk to him. *Please.*"

I looked over to Klein, feeling my shoulders immediately tense—like he, out of everything going on in that moment, was the one to trigger my fight or flight. I don't know what I expected looking over at him as if we could communicate through our eyes. I look at him and I see someone I don't know. He just blinked once, almost mechanically, and somehow I knew that meant the group was going to resent me for this. I know they are.

I just don't care.

The man scoffed and exited the room. Maxwell lowered her head to the floor in defeat.

"Who knows you two were out there looking for me?" I asked calmly.

Maxwell groaned, her stomach throbbing from the dozen punches. "I think—"

"No one that would notice," I figured. "Great. Good to know."

"You shouldn't have gone off," Klein sighed.

My head snapped towards him. "You shouldn't have *followed* me."

"Wasn't *my* idea," he rolled his eyes, looking away.

"Then whose was it?"

He didn't answer. I quickly looked over at Maxwell. She was still groaning. "Who?" I urged her.

"Bailey wouldn't stop bugging Sche—"

The door bursts open again, having the three of us sit back up attentively. I inhaled sharply, holding my breath.

RECONCILIATION   **258**

The man had a sharp square jaw, was about as tall as Klein, and had the same grandpa-lookin' glasses Sterling used to wear. He bent over, narrowing his eyes at Maxwell, then me, then Klein.

"*Holy* shit, is that *you*, Jake?" he scoffed. He pursed his lips, looking at the way Klein glared back at him. "You look a lot less stupid without all that gel you used to put in your hair, pfft," he teased him. "Looked like you came *straight* out of 2012."

I held in my laugh.

"And *you*," he looked at me, eyes exploring my tattoos and the tired look on my face, "I don't know you."

"You graduated before she came to the—"

"Shh, I wasn't talking to you," he spoke tenderly. He used his finger to lift my chin and I pushed him away. "You're a pretty one, aren't you."

"Rodney, just tell your men they've got the wrong guys," I muttered.

"Hm?" The way he said it was chilling.

"Tell them—they've got the wrong guys—" I glared at him.

"But we *do* have the right guys, we *do*," he taunted. "We saw you kill—our Benny—with our own eyes."

I remained nonchalant. I still have trouble taking situations like this seriously. It's like the feeling in me just shuts off.

"That wasn't me."

"So there just happens to be a five-foot-ish Asian out there with the same tattoos and earrings as you?"

"Yep," I sneered. "You've been mistaken. We're just trying to mind our own. We mean no harm to your people."

"Funny saying that knowing everyone in this room has shot a couple dozen or two."

"Those people weren't *people*."

He attempted to run his fingers through my hair and I nudged them away, which changed his demeanor completely. He stood back up, unbuckling his belt.

Maxwell exhaled frightenedly. "C'mon Rodney, you *know* us. We went to school together. We were all just *kids* at some point," she pleaded. "Don't *do* this to us!"

That's when we all realized he wasn't in here due to her simply requesting it. He was in here for procedure.

"Are you guys familiar with a ... *Morgan Rogers?*"

"Not at all." I didn't hesitate, subtly tapping Maxwell's shoe with my toe to reassure her—keep us on the right page.

Rodney's face tightened. "This isn't going to work if you're going to lie."

I scrunch my nose at him as a way to show my arrogance.

"Fine," he whipped his belt at Klein's face. "What about now?"

I scoffed. "I'm sorry, Morgan *who?*"

Maxwell and I flinched, hearing Klein get whipped again. I couldn't bring myself to look at him (I'll laugh) and see the, *are you serious?* look on his face.

"You." He pointed his index finger at me, more at the navy leather wrapped around my upper body. He took out a small knife and cut the zip-tie holding my wrists together. He motioned and I understood immediately.

"No."

"Take it off." I flinched as he struck Klein again. He glared at me silently as Maxwell and Klein watched someone they used to know turn into the exact person they thought he would be.

"Fine!" He threw his belt to the ground, pulling his gun from the holster at his thigh. He aimed it right at my forehead.

"You want me to strip?" I tilted my head. "How desperate are you for me to reveal my adolescence?"

He repositioned his gun, shooting the wall directly beside my head. I shut my eyes slowly, fighting to keep my lips from trembling. I opened my eyes to see his face watching the single tear drift down from my eye, like candle wax.

"Don't get cocky now." He quickly grabbed my throat, pinning me against the wall. I was sitting tensed now with my face adjusted so that I had to look him in the eye.

He had brown eyes; brown eyes that once cried for his mother because he got hurt while playing football in the backyard of his home with his father; brown eyes that are now glaring into mine with no compassion, no sense of humanity, nothing. He had nothing but a clenched jaw and lustful desire.

"Thanks to nutjob over here, she has revealed our age gap," he grinned wider, grazing his thumb against my lips softly, attempting to slide it inside.

Do it, I hope you do, I thought at that moment, *I'll bite it off!*

Don't fuckin' play wit' me.

"And if I'm doing the math right—" He moved his thumb from my lips and to the side of my face, caressing my cheek, "—that makes you *eighteen.*"

"Rodney," Maxwell cried softly from behind me—her voice portraying pure horror, "just tell us what you want from us."

"I want her to take her damn jacket off, it's that damn simple!" He began getting aggressive again; his hand gripping the gun tighter. "C'mon darling, it's *hot* in here!"

It's freezing cold.

He trailed the gun from beneath my chin to the silver zipper trailing down my torso. I did what I was told, feeling as though my dignity was being stripped off of me.

He stared me down. "The shirt."

I inhaled—my arms shivering. "No."

He huffed and kicked me in the face, enough to knock me out. I groaned softly as my head hit the metal pipe behind me, but I brought all the strength I had in me to lift my head back up, opening my eyes gently.

"Now," he demanded.

"Just do it, Mj," Maxwell mumbled beside me as I stared straight at the floor between his worn-out boots, ignoring the grin on his face.

He looked at both Klein and Maxwell's mortified faces. "You guys too," he ordered.

They obeyed, only slower. My eyes remained closed hearing them wince and hiss from the pain of taking their sleeves off, but yet we refused to just sit with our heads low in shame. We held our chins high, listening to him interrogate us.

"Alright, let's cut the bullshit." He had his fun, picking back up his belt from the ground. "Now I know—*you* know—*I know*—you *know* a Morgan Rogers."

I snickered softly. "You know *what?*"

WHIP!

"Dammit, Mj!" Klein scowled at me.

"Okay," Maxwell replied back annoyedly, "what do we know about Sgt. Rogers that concerns you?"

Rodney smiled, satisfied, "Because my men and I are—in *great desire*—of his whereabouts."

"Dawg, so you just expect me to be driving around during the middle of the night in the middle of nowhere and just telepathically know where my Sergeant is?" I scoffed.

WHIP!

"It's true!"

WHIP!

"Jesus, Mj, do you ever shut the hell up?!" Klein got frustrated with me, which made me turn to him with no compassion.

"Don't use—the Lord's name—in vain, buddy," I replied back, with sass. He could hear the grin in my voice.

I don't care if I die here. Nothing Jake Klein can do will make me gain an ounce of sympathy or respect for him.

"She's right," Rodney sprinkled, looking at my necklace. "She knows her facts."

"Alright, get on with it!" Maxwell rolled her eyes.

"Wh—What do you mean, *get on with it,* Kiara?" he scoffed. "I'm waiting on *you!*"

"She's not wrong," she replied. "*She* stormed off from the group and *we* went after her. How could we *possibly* know his whereabouts?"

"Better question," Klein interfered, "*why* do you want to know his whereabouts?"

"He has some—*unfinished business*—with us," he replied.

We all sat in silence. Now I knew that Klein and Maxwell weren't as fond of Sergeant as I was and that they preferred Sgt. Greene much better, but even they knew Sergeant wouldn't go behind our backs and do things that could potentially put us on the line like this. He wouldn't. He's not like that.

"And what makes you think we're going to tell you—even *if* we knew?" Klein followed up, and I tilted my head, agreeing.

Rodney could strip us bare and slowly shoot us one by one, but we'd rather die than throw Sergeant under the bus like that, not after everything he's done for us. Not only did he go out of his way to make our year fun with a military ball, parades, festive potlucks for the holidays, and field trips—but ever since we wound up in this mess, he's been leading the way. We're not just going to betray him like that. That's not who we are.

"Look, we can do this the easy way or the hard way."

"Is that supposed to shit my pants?" I scoffed.

WHIP! Only it was to me this time, so hard that it left a red mark across my collarbone. I sat smiling as it stung.

"Where's your Sergeant?" he persisted. *"Where?"*

We all remained silent, settled with our decision not to speak. I eyed the two from the side. They weren't going to budge, I knew they weren't. We were ready for each and every blow and whip coming for us, but nothing could've prepared *me* for what Rodney was going to do next.

He turned, whistling. Two other men entered the room rapidly. One grabbed Maxwell and threw her over his shoulder like she was as light as a feather. The other yanked Klein from his spot and shoved him through the door. I clenched my teeth to refrain from giggling at how dumb he looked trying to balance with his ankles tied.

Rodney snapped his fingers in front of my eyes, regaining my full attention. He then picked me up by the waist and placed me down on a metal fold-up chair he had dragged over using his foot. I was forced to stay still as he retied my wrists. He then dragged over a chair for himself.

"I've been doing my homework on you," he said, which startled me a bit. I just wish at the time I knew why.

I was looking at someone who seemed to know everything about me, but I knew nearly everything about him too. But tonight was the first night we ever met. Weird, right?

Mj would've loved meeting him. Unfortunately, I am not her anymore. I've been in a three-year debate on whether I should bring her back or get rid of her for good.

He sat down, intertwining his fingers. "You're a tough nut to crack, aren't you?"

I squinted at him, gulping.

"Looks like it," he broke eye contact, admiring me. "How'd you get those?" He was referring to the scars on my hands.

I held my chin high. "Threw too many punches. Got too rough."

"Hm," he smiled, tilting his head, pointing at his left eyebrow to point out the scar on mine. "And that one?"

"Took a few punches myself," I replied.

He nodded, grinning. "You think you can take anything, can you?"

"I like to think so."

He cocked an eyebrow. "You can't."

"You wanna bet?" I grinned, inhaling sharply.

"Well," he rubbed his hands down his thighs, "I'm not the one tied up right now, am I?"

He bent over a bit, looking me in the eye. "C'mon, you're only making this harder on yourself." He inhaled, looking at the blank look on my face. "You're gonna break, Mj. *I'm* going to break you."

"I don't break."

"*Everyone* breaks."

"Not me," I shook my head. "Not my people. *We* don't."

He didn't blink. I didn't either.

"You will," he said, breaking into a chuckle. "I know what type of person you are."

"You don't know jack shit," I spat. "Do you get off on this, Rodney? Knowing we all had lives of our own?" I scrunch my nose in slight pain, feeling the blood trickle down my upper lip. "How does that make you feel?"

"I could ask you the same question about—my dear friend Benny."

"That lunatic deserved it."

"*You* deserve it," he quickly said. I scoffed. He shook his head. "You deserved everything life threw at you, and you know it."

He maintained eye contact with me, speaking clearly.

"You think overcoming a few hardships earns you respect? That just 'cause you had it hard and you've *changed* now makes you all *noble?*" He leaned in closer, speaking through gritted teeth. "You—are worth—nothing."

I stared back at him blankly. He slapped me. Hard. And I turned back to him with nothing to say.

"You are nothing but an unworthy whore, and cheating through life, hittin' boys you know wouldn't hit yo' ass back doesn't earn you *shit!*" He spat in my face.

"You don't know—nothin'—" My voice trembled.

RECONCILIATION 266

"You don't have no damn life, Mj," he said. "You have no family. No friends sober enough to appreciate you. Tell me, Mj, name one friend that would take a bullet for you. Name me *one*."

I looked down from his face, staring at my thighs.

"You can sit here and act tough all you want, bitch," he said, "but I know you live in fear. It drowns you."

"I ain't afraid of you," I whispered, shutting my eyes.

"Really, 'cause I haven't heard that snarky attitude come out of you since."

"I'm not wasting my energy on you."

"Or maybe you're just too scared to admit you're scared of people leavin' you," he chuckled, leaning in closer, so close that I could feel his breath against my ear, "which—in my opinion, is the most pathetic—of all them *pussy fears* y'all come up wit'-"

11 ½ you like my pet?

We were all back in the same room now. A couple days had passed. We were all interrogated the same way. None of us revealed Sergeant's location.

We kept track of the days by paying attention to the two men who would enter the room at 0500 every morning to pour buckets of ice water over us. It would dampen our jeans and take a whole day to dry considering how cold it was down there.

Rodney was in front of us again, glaring. "Where's Sgt. Rogers?" he asked. We were too tired to respond. "Where did you last see him?" he asked.

"I don't remember," I lied.

"Liar," he kicked me in my face, nearly knocking my front tooth out. *Oh, I would've been PISSED.*

"I don't know," I replied, rubbing my chest gently. "Like the other fifty times I've told you guys already. I don't *know!*"

He kneeled down and punched me in the stomach.

"*HEY!*" Maxwell yelled.

He turned swiftly, pointing a finger at her angrily. "*Where?!*"

"We don't *know*, Rodney!" She snapped, clenching her jaw shut the second she saw the gun leave from his holster again.

He stood up angrily and shot Klein twice. One at his lower abdomen, the other near his shoulder. He sat and groaned violently.

"I don't know!" I shouted, panicking. "I don't know! I don't know! What the hell am I supposed to do? What am I supposed to say? I don't fucking *KNOW!*"

I was screaming now, screaming so loud that the floors above us could've heard me like I was screaming directly into their ear, only they wouldn't do anything. They *couldn't* do anything.

He could hit me as much as he wanted. It saves me the trouble of hitting myself.

He backed up, eating up my reaction to this. I quickly realized my anger only made him happier.

"Very well then." He readjusted his glasses calmly. He exited the room as if nothing happened, and I broke down crying.

Maxwell tried to hold me, but she was too weak to wrap her arms around me. She was crying too, only softer and more of a *'frustrated'* cry. In a weird way, we couldn't bring ourselves to be scared or sorrowful over this situation. We only felt one thing, one thing that enraged every bad thing we kept deep down inside us.

I felt it in my veins. I felt it rushing up and down my spine, overflowing my head. I tried to calm myself, but it got to the point where I began to shut down. It got to the point where I began to think this was it.

This was my ending.

I wasn't sad or scared that I was going to die.

All I felt was the one thing people have always criticized me for; the one thing that has always held me back. My damn anger. My fuckin' weakness.

I wiped the tears off my face aggressively, heavily sniffling. "Untie me."

"W-What?"

"My ankles," I persisted, adjusting myself as quickly as I could. "Pull. I don't care if you hurt me, just get these off!"

I sat with my palms supporting me, using all the strength I could pull together to yank my ankles apart from one another. I exhaled a breath of relief hearing the sound of it snapping. She quickly moved so I could do the same for her.

By the time we got to Klein, we began to panic, hearing two pairs of footsteps coming from down the hall. One heavy, one staggered. I had taken my pants off to let him use to apply pressure on his wounds. It didn't take long for us to realize he didn't just make us strip for his own pleasure, he did it to prepare.

"Klein, you're gonna have to at least *try*," Maxwell scoffed, attempting to snap the zip-tie off of him. "Dammit, it's too tight!" She turned to me helplessly. "Bui, *you* try! Your fingers are smaller!"

I turned my head from the door and scoffed, scooching over to attempt. We soon realized we were too late.

Rodney was coming back in, only with a roamer on a leash. Before he could pass through the door frame, Klein turned himself around and aggressively began kicking the wall, wedging his feet on each side of the metal pipe, forcing the zip-tie to burst.

We all spun back into place, squishing our feet together to keep the illusion. We couldn't hear Rodney's words over the roamer's moaning. It was after the blood from Klein's broken nose, which was too fragile for him to try to wipe away.

"LAST CHANCE! WHERE IS HE?" He waved the roamer around, but it wasn't just *some* roamer. It was dressed in armor head-to-toe, armor with sharp spikes that would slash us apart if it were to just run into us. Knives were tied onto its wrists. Razor blades were pierced into its face. He waved it around as if the roamer wasn't someone who was once one of us; someone with a mom and dad, and brothers and sisters, and a loved one that probably had to watch them turn. There he was, just waving it around like a puppet, a feral dog on its restraints, a ticking time bomb. "You like my pet?" he taunted.

Okay, maybe it did shit my pants a little bit.

"Let's see how much he likes you!" He grinned as he released the roamer, quickly backing up and out of the way.

"Move," Klein whispered. We all scooted out of its way, attempting to stay silent at first.

Rodney scoffed and took out his gun, shooting shots at the pipes behind us, revealing our presence. The roamer turned around angrily, quickly reaching out for us.

We only had a certain amount of time to think, but it didn't seem hard. There was only one of them and three of us.

"Here!" Maxwell picked up the cardboard boxes lying around the room. "If we put enough weight on it to keep it in place, we can find something to—" She quickly dodged, watching it run into the wall behind her.

"Kill it, we *know!*" Klein quickly replied, picking up the heavy box with his good arm as I watched him and the roamer lunge toward each other.

I dodged as the roamer slammed against the pipes, groaning as it made its way towards me. The roamer was large, nearly abnormally large. I didn't stand a chance, I'll humbly admit, so I resorted to knocking down stacks of crates and pushing carts in its path in hopes it would slow it down.

I panted, out of breath, wincing each time my feet hit the ground—the glass shards piercing my skin. I didn't want to risk taking my eyes off of it, but using my arms to keep me aware of my surroundings wasn't enough. It backed me into a corner until Maxwell came out of nowhere, using a box as a shield, using all her strength to push it back into the wall.

She screamed as one of the spikes slashed into her arm, deep enough to have the blood gush down to her hands. I immediately hurled, looking away from something I thought I was over. I wasn't.

"Klein! Klein!" She yelled out in pain. "*JAKE!* Get the wrench!"

I fell face first attempting to go and grab it for him. The gunshot wounds were weakening him. He could barely keep himself upright.

He was on the floor, heavily breathing. My body scraped against the broken glass and rusted nails scattered around and barely managed to reach for the wrench in front of me. I coughed up blood as I propped myself up, shriveling in pain, but as I staggered over to the roamer trying to strike its head, its arm swung and tore the flesh at the side of my thigh.

I winced out in pain as it pushed the both of us back, tripping over *me* and landing right near Klein.

It bit him. Klein got bit. We watched it in horror before finally killing it, only we were a couple seconds too behind.

12 station 45

"Shit," I muttered, looking at the bite marks alongside his arm and neck. Maxwell and I just sat on our knees, speechless. It said a lot about our character how we couldn't even bring ourselves to say we were sorry.

I knew I should've said it, even if it wouldn't have helped anything. I knew I should've said it, knowing it was right, but I couldn't do it. Like how my body was from the start of *'us'* again, it wouldn't let me.

I collapsed onto my side, the side that wasn't sliced open, and wiped the sweat from my face. Maxwell propped her knees up, scrunching up into a ball.

"What are we gonna do?" I asked, staring up at the open ceiling. Scoffing, I shook my head, "What *can* we do?"

"They'll notice we've been gone for longer than usual," Maxwell replied. "I trust that they'll come and look for us."

"And what if we're dead by the time they get here?" I asked, my voice breaking. "Kiara, *you're* cut into pieces, *I'm* sliced open, *Klein's* bit—and who knows what Rodney has next for us?"

"What did Sergeant do to make these men so *mad*?" She attempted to lift her head and failed.

"I don't think he *did* do anything," I replied. "It probably has something to do with how I killed Benny."

"That was *years* ago." Her voice muffled through her arms. "And if they saw that you killed him, they would've seen him hold Sterling at knife-point and realize it was something you *had* to do."

"Or they could've realized how we could potentially be a *danger* to *their* group."

"We could all just agree to leave each other alone?" Maxwell rubbed her hands through her hair. "Keep out of their territory and they keep out of ours."

Klein shook his head. "It doesn't really work like that anymore, Kiara."

"*Shit!*" I began to feel dizzy from the blood loss. I fought to keep my conscience. I looked up at Maxwell. "Dude, we need to find a way to get our asses out of here before our wounds get infected!"

"What?" It was happening to her too.

"If we leave these *cuts* unattended, we could get infected!" I rubbed my forehead to contain the dizziness. "*Shit!*"

It didn't take long for us to realize Rodney wasn't going to come back any time soon. We had nothing to do but wait.

We moved Klein into a better position, just to make things more comfortable for him, but we had to use Maxwell's belt to restrain him for when he turns.

It made me sad how numb I was to grief now. He was dying right in front of me, and I had no strength left to cry. I look at him and I see someone I don't recognize. He is not the same guy with callouses on his fingertips with a romantic spark to his voice. I was naturally drawn *away* from him, I needed to accept that. Because despite how he did sometimes smell like onions, he peeled like one. (A white one, not red.)

Behind his dazzling, sharp green eyes and charming, alluring grin, was nothing but *one* desire. One desire not only from me, but from girls *like* me, girls like Maxwell, Conti, Terry, and even Kim.

He didn't like me, he just wanted *somebody*, and that was fine. But to the group, it wasn't fine the second *I* just wanted somebody too.

It would be wrong to say I was just bored. It would be wrong to say I just wanted revenge. But it would also be wrong to say I don't regret it because then I'd be lying. I do regret it, for many reasons: the fact I wasted my time and should've known it wouldn't heal my pain any faster, and the fact I could've gone a good three months without having my room have his clothes on the floor and smell like his cologne.

QUICK DISCLAIMER: I do not partake in such activities. I am JUST famous for stealing people's clothes. Every time he would happen to be *sleeping over...* he'd be on the floor, with *no* blanket, and *no* pillow. I kick in my sleep.

I do regret it. I regret it every time I look him in the eye. I regret it so deeply because I knew I had to anticipate the feeling of losing him again.

"Do you hear that?" Maxwell started rummaging through the boxes.

"Hear what?" I replied, scooting over carefully.

"That—*damn* song—" she said, dumping out boxes.

It was a song—most likely from the 1940s. It had been playing on a loop, which I assume was intended to make us feel unsettled.

She held out a small radio, trying to switch it off. Only it began speaking.

"He—*Hello*—" We made out. "I don't—k-know if anyone can hear this right now, but this is Lindsey from Station 45 by the East Coast."

"Don't reply," I quickly said.

"If you are stranded or in need in *any* way," Lindsey's voice spoke through the radio, "we are accepting refugees. We are located in New Jersey—in Brigantine. We have cures, if you can believe it. *Vaccines*—for those who are bit and have yet to turn."

"*Vaccines?*" I gasped.

"I knew it," Maxwell sighed, finding it in herself to smile.

"*Please*," Lindsey's voice muffled, "if *anyone* is listening. Please find us. If we all come together, we can get through this."

Maxwell looked up at me sharply. I gave her a reassuring nod.

She held onto the button. "Hello?" She hesitantly spoke. "Hello? Lindsey?"

Nothing.

"Shit," I sighed, taking the radio from her shaky hands, changing the channel. I held it up to my lips slowly.

"This is Cadet Bui," I said, pausing. "I've been abducted by a group associated with Rodney Daffodil. Klein and Maxwell are with me—but Klein is bit. He's been shot at too. His wounds are fatal," I hiccupped. "And Maxwell and I are severely hurt."

I took a deep breath, trying to keep my tone calm.

"I know you guys may not be happy with me right now," I said shakily, "but please, for the sake of Kiara's life, please come find us. She doesn't deserve to die on behalf of my mistakes."

"It's not your fault," she shook her head. "You didn't storm off knowing this was going to happen." She lowered her head, looking me in the eyes. "You hear me? It's *not* your fault! They don't have any reason to be angry with you."

She looked at the look I had on my face.

"Aaron's *not* going to get mad. He's too *content* to be mad," she explained. "If he *were* the type, he would've been furious the day you left with him for Tyson and had him—"

I nodded as she stopped herself.

"Aaron-" she sighed. "Mj, I genuinely think—he has so much *pressure* on him all the time—to be *good;* to call the *shots.*" She shook her head. "I guess he kinda—*freaked out*—under the pressure. I'm sure he didn't mean to hurt you."

"I thought he'd be smart enough not to say somethin' like that to me."

"He *is* smart, just not *that* type of smart," she sighed. "Give it time. It'll all work out—"

"Who the hell cares about him?" Klein scoffed. "Fuck him for what he did to you."

My head snapped toward him. "Dawg, you don't even know what happened."

"I'm more of a *catch* compared to him," he grinned softly.

It completely baffled me how he can be shot and bit and too tired to hold himself upright, but can still speak to me in that *bitch-ass* seductive tone like it's going to *do* anything to me!

I looked over at Maxwell to make sure I was listening to this right. She looked at me the same.

"What the hell-" Maxwell covered her face with her hands.

"So *what* if he can speak a little French—*I* can speak French too," he weakly leaned closer, *still* grinning. "Il ne se soucie pas de toi comme moi."

I physically felt the disgust in my body. I literally felt my stomach turn itself inside out, my joints scrape against one another, and my entire back warm up in the most excruciating way. Not having your feelings reciprocate is one thing, but this, this was straight up rejection. Physical. Rejection. Like your body throwing up a pill you forced yourself to swallow.

I looked over at Maxwell with the most horrified look on my face. "The hell did this bitch just say to me?"

"I don't know?" she shrugged. "I took Spanish in school."

I sighed, "Yo también."

"Je te donnerais le monde si tu me le permets," Klein said confidently. I crushed him.

"Dawg, he certainly doesn't speak French like *that?*" I scoffed. "Man, why can't you talk about Physics or something?!"

That silenced him for a good bit. I sat there trying to feel bad.

"Kiara," he suddenly muttered. He had a vicious cold sweat, now. He was so pale, we could see his veins. "Kiara, I'm sorry for everything."

He owes her more of an apology than me. I don't know their situation. ~~I should be getting an apology too!~~ He owes her more of an apology than me. I don't know their situation. ~~I should be getting an apology too!~~ He owes her more of an apology than me. I don't know their situation. ~~I should be getting an apology too!~~

I've been unable to really *look* at him for a long time. If eye contact for even just a second irks me, how can I look this man in the face and have anything to say? How can he look at the person I am and have anything to say? After everything we've been through, the good and bad, I don't understand. Knowing how I am, how did we just get up and go on with our lives like nothing happened?

RECONCILIATION

How was I able to get up in the morning without that hollow feeling in my chest? How was I able to go along with my day, knowing how it felt to kiss him? How is he able to go about his day knowing he left me? Did he ever think about me? He must've, considering all the shit he talked afterward. I've gathered enough experience to at least know that's a sign of a boy's ego breaking, but how did I do it?

I didn't care.

I *don't* care.

I can't bring an ounce or a nerve in my body to feel a thing for this man, because I knew. I knew the second I realized he never held my hand unless I asked, or when I realized he didn't know the sidewalk rule, or when I would be at his house and he'd immediately think I was talking about alcohol when I asked him for a drink.

But I don't want to admit that even for a second I might've believed him when *some* of his actions indicated that he had changed. But what is better?

Having the group think I'm so vulnerable and easy that Jake Klein can easily toss me around or that I'm so petty, I'm willing to go back just to get back at him for hurting me.

What is better?

Forever being stuck as the girl associated with Jake Klein and have girls you thought you could be friends with hate you, or be stuck over the possibility that

if I never talked to him, maybe Kim would've never bothered me, maybe Conti and I would actually get to be best friends, maybe María and I would've never fallen out, maybe Aaron wouldn't have lost his respect for me

BANG! BANG!

We all flinched in our places, but were too weak to get up and see. Klein grabbed my wrist tightly and looked me in the eye.

"Mj, I care about you so much," he muttered.

I didn't look at his teary eyes. I looked at the sweat running down his forehead.

His voice broke. "I'm sorry I was such an asshole."

I clenched my jaw. "Then why'd you leave?" I asked coldly.

"I wasn't in—"

"*The best mental state, we know,*" Maxwell and I synchronized, which made me laugh hysterically.

"I know you. I used to be you," I spat. "You don't like *me*, you like the chase—and typically a person like that would eventually get sick of crashing down every time they *fuck* shit up, but as you can see, you don't have the luxury of *time* anymore. You will never get the chance to grow the hell up, and that's on nobody but you."

He could walk around acting like there was really nothing that wrong with me, so the reason he left was just that I was *too crazy*, but I could say the same thing. I could say he was perfect. He was tall. He had a good-looking face—a *killer* physique—and the fact that he played guitar—WOW—that really ... *really* made me drool.

Can you picture the look on my face right now?

I'm drooling.

He could have nine out of the ten things I needed in a guy, but eventually, it all came down to

his personality.

RECONCILIATION

13 getaway

Scheuch and Bailey crouched on the outskirts of the facility. Fingers interlacing with the wired fence, they watched for ways to get inside, get to *us*.

"Why did I go with you?" Scheuch asked himself.

"Come through here," Bailey said, slipping through a small opening.

"You sure you can fit?" He chuckled softly. *"OW!"*

"Don't be a jackass," Bailey lowered his leg from kicking Scheuch in the kneecap. He climbed through, immediately checking his surroundings. "You see a way in?"

"Yeah," Scheuch patted away the dirt on his thighs. "Follow me." They quickly scurried to one of the small entrances from the side; the emergency door with the low-quality light engulfed in cobwebs. He jammed on the door handle. "Hm."

"Move," Bailey scoffed. "This is how real men do it."

He lifted his elbow and slammed down the handle. He winced and tried again, then again, then again. He eyed Scheuch from the side. "Don't start."

"I didn't say *anything*," Scheuch raised his eyebrows, grinning.

Bailey glared at him. "I don't know why you're taking your sweet ol' time. Bui could be dead."

I don't care? That doesn't pertain to me, I would expect him to say.

He didn't say anything. He just backed up from the door, pulling his gun out its holster silently. He raised his left hand, aiming right at the door. **BANG!**

They hurried in, eyes jolting around, reading every sign that labeled every hallway. Scheuch always said he never thought.

I don't think, he says, but I never believe him.

I don't think anyone in a moment like that could have thought of something like this.

He grabbed the closest man walking by them, shoving him into the nearest supply closet. Bailey read his mind, pulling out his gun and aiming it at the man's forehead.

The man squirmed and panicked, shoving Scheuch back. He shoved him into the wooden bookshelves, holding him in place with an arm. The man stared back terrified, seeing Scheuch hold his index finger up to his lips.

"Take off your uniform."

"W-What?" he gasped.

"Take it *off?*" Scheuch lowered his eyebrows. "What? Do you need *help?*"

He arrogantly began tearing his clothes off and then his own, changing into the man's uniform. When he was done, they found another for Bailey.

"Can I shoot them?" he asked before leaving.

Scheuch looked at him then to the two men tied up on the ground. "*No,* you can't shoot them!" he scoffed. "Let's go!"

They both slid out of the closet, blending in. They remained calm walking through the hallways peeking through each of the rooms and listening in to conversations. Their steps gradually grew quicker; their thoughts gradually grew more frantic.

"Psst, hey!" Bailey grabbed Scheuch's shoulder, stopping him mid-step. They looked over to the room beside them, listening in carefully.

"I'm going back downstairs again in a few."

"What's the wait?"

"I need her to regenerate her energy. She's gonna need it for later."

"HEY!" They both flinched as a man yelled from down the hallway. "IT'S THEM!"

"Oh shit!" Scheuch nudged Bailey forward as they both ran down the hallway, knocking bookshelves down and pulling nearby people in the way.

"There!" Bailey pointed to the staircase leading down to the basement.

They rushed down frantically, sealing the door behind them. Their shoes picked up dirt from the floor as they paced down the hallway, looking into each chamber vigorously.

BANG! BANG! The muffled gunshots fired as they caught their breath, wiping the sweat dripping down their faces.

They stopped in horror when they found us.

"Holy shit," Bailey gasped as Scheuch immediately stripped off his jacket, covering me. He didn't take another second to think before rushing over to us.

He cupped Maxwell's face. "Kie! Kie!" He tapped her face repeatedly.

"Oh thank God, you're here," she fluttered her eyes open, wrapping his jacket around her. "Quinn, they were going to kill us."

"What did they do to you?" He gasped softly, looking at the blood trickling down her arms.

"Bui," Scheuch's voice repeated. I could hear it in his voice. "Bui-" He looked down, seeing the large cut gushing blood down my leg and onto the ground. "Are you able to walk?"

I shook my head. He stared back at me blankly.

"Aaron!" Bailey called, wrapping Maxwell's arm around his shoulder. "C'mon, we need to go!"

He looked past me and to Klein, who had turned by now. He was growling, squirming in his restraints to get to my leg. I reached up to his face weakly, turning him towards me. I think this was one of the first times I saw him scared. It wasn't a good look on him. It made *me* scared.

He didn't respond. He just looked at me before gently scooping me up into his arms, trying his best not to tear the wound any further. I held on gently, too dizzy to hold my head up on my own. He never laid his eyes off of Klein. I think, like me, he couldn't bring himself to put him down; but we couldn't just leave him there.

"Quinn," he said softly, turning. I hissed as he tugged on my leg the wrong way. "Sorry," he whispered in my ear.

Bailey was already assisting Maxwell out the door with his gun in his other hand. The pounding on the door down the hallway only became louder.

BANG! BANG!

"Can you—"

"Yeah," Bailey sighed, holding his gun up calmly.

I looked away when he did it. I closed my eyes when I felt us leaving the room.

"We can't go out that door." I heard Scheuch's voice close to my ear. He lifted me up a bit to adjust his arms, holding me tighter.

"There should be one over here," Maxwell began pointing around. Scheuch followed them through the commotion.

"Aaron?" Sterling's voice stopped him in his tracks.

"SCHEUCH, GET DOWN!" I yelled as he ducked, speeding through the hallways with his legs bent, dodging the gunshots.

"The hell is he doing here?!" he mumbled.

"I don't know," I replied as we burst through the exit doors.

"Brody! Meet us around the back!" Bailey yelled as he stopped, picking up Maxwell off her feet, running straight to the opening gates.

The gunshots fired. I tucked my head like it would do any good. Turning as we ran, I pulled the pistol from the holster at Scheuch's thigh and shot back one-handed.

"Fuck!" I wasn't trained enough for one-handed shooting. Dammit, Brody.

Scheuch swung us around and placed me inside the second Yanes opened the car door. Fast, but gentle. He hopped in right after, kicking the car door shut.

"KLEIN?" Candreva yelled through the mayhem.

"He didn't make it," Scheuch shook his head. *"Go!"*

He stomped on the gas, getting us out of there. Bailey was digging through bags to find water, and any sort of *food*. Maxwell was green, malnourished and dehydrated.

"GET DOWN!" Yanes called from the passenger seat. The four of us ducked as rapid gunshots fired, shattering the rear window into a million pieces.

Bailey and Scheuch hauled out rifles from beneath them swiftly, shooting them back from the back seats. Maxwell and I bent our upper bodies down, covering our ears.

"MICKEY!" Candreva yelled.

"*LEFT!* BRODY!" He yelled back. "LEFT! OFF THAT EXIT!"

Scheuch stopped, watching the car following us drive off the road. He took a deep sigh, feeling the adrenaline fade.

He turned back to me. "Tell me what happened."

"C'mon, Aaron, you need to give them some time to process," Yanes quickly interfered sympathetically.

"Time will alter her memory," he quickly replied. "Now Bui," he held onto my shoulders. *"Tell me*—what——did they want from you? *Look* at me!"

He cupped my face, forcing me to look at him. *"What!"*

I burst into tears softly, leaning into his shoulder without trying to. "They're mad I killed Benny," I hiccuped, "and they want to know where Sergeant is."

Scheuch widened his eyes and glared up at Maxwell.

"Keep your pants on," she scoffed, "we told them we didn't know."

"My pants *are* on," he replied smugly, smiling as I cried. He awkwardly patted my head, which made me laugh a little. For some reason, I was grateful. I thought he'd push me away.

"It would make sense for you three to not know his whereabouts," he explained.

"The same way it makes sense why *you're* the one getting me out of that shithole and not somebody *else?*" I snarked.

"Yes," he replied, completely missing my point. "Watkins and Sully are on an emergency supply run, and Sgt. Rogers is missing."

14 spare me, aaron!

I watched his head fall in disappointment, palms resting on the cold steel counter. My leg had stopped bleeding now, and luckily for me, Sully had found more tubed ointments. She came in and set them down. I prayed she would stay, but she didn't. She only asked a few questions pertaining to Scheuch, and then left.

"Dang, Aaron, why not have her lay on a bed or something?" she chuckled to loosen the air.

"I'm not getting blood on my bed." He quickly tied it up again.

She raised her eyebrows, looking at me. "Do you want me to get you a pillow, Mj?"

"Yes, please," I winced, readjusting my leg on the kitchen island countertop, where pizzas used to be made.

Sully came back moments later with a pillow. Once I thanked her and watched her leave, I turned and asked Scheuch what was wrong. He turned around with a blank look on his face. "You need stitches," he replied, "but I don't have access to lidocaine."

"So?"

"So," he stepped closer, taking a deep breath, "it's gonna hurt like a bitch."

I sat silent awkwardly as he got all the supplies ready, having me lay over on my side. "Have you ever done stitches?" I asked nervously, flinching as I felt him cleaning the wound.

"Mhm."

"Okay, just asking," I yawned. He had made me take a melatonin pill in hopes I'd be in a deeper sleep so that he'd be able to operate efficiently. As he could clearly see, I was still awake.

He randomly stopped and just stood there looking at me.

I turned, wide-eyed. "What?" I asked.

"N-Nothing—I was just—wondering—" He looked up at the dangling pots and pans above us, "—what if I just——knock you out?"

"Do that and I'll hurt you."

He leaned in closer, smiling softly. "No, you wouldn't," he shook his head, whispering, "you'd be knocked out."

I rolled my eyes and turned back to my side mumbling, "I hate you," hearing him chuckle softly.

It was nice hearing him laugh again.

I laid uncomfortably in my spot, jolting every time it hurt a little more than I could pretend it didn't. He would stop and ask me if I needed a break, and I'd tell him no—and he'd continue instead of deciding for me like how the others probably would, despite how hard he could see my hand grip the pillow.

"Where'd you learn?" I asked to break the silence, my voice content.

"What?" he stitched as I winced silently, biting my lip.

"How'd you learn how to stitch wounds?"

"Practiced."

His responses never stopped being cold, so I left it alone. Silence passed for a couple minutes before he spoke again.

"So," he cleared his throat, "are you going to tell me why you left?"

I felt myself tense up. My first initial thought being, *"If he doesn't care about me, why does he feel the need to ask?"*

"If this is about the last supply run, I don't know what else to tell you," he sighed.

"*Spare me,* Aaron!" I turned and scoffed. I knew exactly what he was talking about. "My world doesn't *revolve* around you!"

"Are you trying to convince *me* that or yourself?"

My face dropped. "Mày mất dạy hả?"

"W—What?"

"Nothing."

"Why are you such a dick?!" I could've spat. *"Why do you always feel compelled to act insufferable the moment you wake up every morning?"* I could've replied, but I didn't.

But I didn't choose to say nothing this time.

I didn't say anything because I simply couldn't. If it was Klein or Kim or anybody else, I would, but it was Aaron. A part of me still had respect for him.

I looked away and let him continue. He wiped his nose with his shoulder, sniffling. "You're gonna want to sit up and watch this."

"What?" I turned back confusedly.

"I want you to learn how to stitch too," he said.

"And why would you want that?" I copied his way of speaking. It completely flew over his head.

"Because it is protocol," he replied coldly. "You don't know for sure I will be here tomorrow." He looked down, showing me. "For deep ones, hold both sides of the wound with your less dominant hand."

"I thought you were left handed."

He paused. "I practiced till I was dominant in both," he explained.

"What? On yourself?" I gasped.

"Anyway, back to the point," he cleared his throat, "hold both sides with one hand and stitch with the other, starting from the middle." He showed me again gently. "As the stitches hold the edges together, the wound will ultimately become inflamed, which is *completely* normal. That just means *new* cells are repairing the tissue," he rambled. "Afterwards—conn—connective tissues and collagens will create skin. *Then*, blood vessels will form to *nourish* these developing tissues, filling in the area."

"How about you go teach Mary instead?" I muttered, rolling my eyes.

He paused. "Bui," he said. "You're being—"

"What?" I asked. "Immature?"

He set down his tools and stepped back, leaning against the counter, facing me. He took off his glasses, stress-cleaning them.

"*No.*" He shook his head. "Just——I'm just getting really frustrated here. You're not giving me anything."

I scoffed. "*I'm* not giving you anything?"

He looked at me defeatedly.

I scoffed again, looking away. "If Sergeant saw us right now, he'd literally just lock us in a room with *our* wrists tied until we worked things out."

He gave me a stern look.

"What?" I chuckled. "Too soon?"

"I already told you everything is resolved on my end," he said. "I don't understand why we aren't moving on from this?"

"Because I can't lay here on a kitchen island like I don't *care* about your absence watching you stitch me back up!"

He paused. I hate how he always seems to be thinking about the right thing to say, and still manages to say the worst thing possible.

"I can't be *absent* if I wasn't *present* to begin with."

~~That's bullshit. There's no way that wasn't real.~~

"Yeah, that's the *fucking* problem!" I snapped, rubbing my forehead after seeing his reaction. "I'm sorry," I slipped out. "I'm sorry, I shouldn't have said that. I'm just tired from—all the others telling me I need to *relax* and shit." I sniffled roughly, wiping the tears coming down my face. "Does it look like I can relax, Aaron?"

He shrugged. "I don't know. You seemed pretty comfortable a couple minutes ago?"

I wasn't. I felt like I was suffocating. I can't even look at him.

Scheuch and I have been like this since he left. I thought through time I'd be over it, but in reality, I never truly left that porch. Minutes and hours, days and nights, weeks and months, and *years* pass, and I'm still standing on that porch. I'm still seventeen, and silent. There's no use in not paying attention to it if I know the feeling is always going to be there. That's one of the reasons why I'm so angry. I am angry that I stood there pretending nothing was wrong when I've never felt so upset over something so small. I am angry I've let him manipulate and deceive me into believing he is someone he's not. I am angry that I've adapted to a system where he can talk to me whenever *he* feels like, but I can't talk to *him* unless he feels like talking to *me*.

I'm so angry to the point where I'm not.

One second, his demeanor becomes so unwelcome that I'd have better luck having a conversation with Kim. He talks to me like he looks down on me. He makes me feel like an idiot for ever respecting him. Then the next second, he inserts himself in the conversations I have with Sully and answers the questions I'm asking *her*. I never get it. As someone who keeps to himself and doesn't like talking, why are you talking to me with a bright smile on your face when I am turned towards Mary, making eye contact with Mary, her name is in the question I'm asking, and you aren't even in the conversation! As someone who wants nothing to do with me, why are you talking to me more *now* compared to when we *were* friends? ~~Are you sorry? Do you take back the things you said?~~ Because I'm sitting here thinking the way you looked at me means more.

It *means* something more!

There's more than hurt in those eyes that once showed nothing! I *mean* something! ~~I mean nothing. If I ever meant something in the first place, he wouldn't have made me feel this way.~~

But the second I start thinking he might change his mind, I'm back to asking myself if I did something wrong. I'm back to feeling like no matter what I do and how much I try to let this go, every time I'm near him, I'm just so angry. I'm hurt.

It's me this time, not him. I will admit it.

It's me this time 'cause instead of asking myself when did it go wrong, I'm asking myself why I was so stupid that I couldn't see that it was. Why was I so optimistic that I kept denying it?

So I *don't* feel a slight strike of anger burn in my chest every time I see him treat ~~somebody~~ her how ~~I'm begging~~ I want him to treat *me*. So I don't feel a rush of confusion every time he brushes me off with one-word responses and stares blankly at the jokes I know for sure he'd chuckle at if it came out of ~~someone else's~~ her mouth. So I don't feel a graze of sadness ache in the heart every time someone mentions *anything* in the slightest about mathematics and cross country, or how my vocabulary has drastically changed, and how I was so diligent when it came to anything NJROTC-related; and for what? For our beloved, well-respected Class Commander to gain an ounce of respect for me?

I don't feel anything. It doesn't bother me that it seems like he is everywhere I go. It doesn't bother me that if he ever told me he was sorry and took back the words he said, and told me he'd change, I wouldn't see through him, I'd believe it for my own sake.

Why should I be jealous? Why should I? How could I blame him if I have everything to blame myself?

It's on me. I'm angry for convincing myself he was perfect, and now that I see that he's not, I have everything to blame. I can't sit here and have my inner fifteen-year-old-self say, "Yeah, fuck you for not owning up and being responsible and not caring about me n' shit!"

Because it would be my own fault for thinking he ever would.

I know better than to fight for a man's approval like it means anything to me. He's not my problem, so why do I care that he's gone?

"Why do you think these people want to know where Sergeant is?" he asked.

I shook my head. "I don't know," I replied defeatedly. "Better yet, how the hell do they know I killed Benny? And does them knowing imply they know we live here?"

He nodded. "Yeah, they definitely know we live here." He began rummaging through the cabinets, turning back around, setting a couple travel-size petroleum jelly packets and bandages on the counter. "Wash around the wound with warm water, apply a thin layer of *this*," he held up the packets, "if you feel the need to. We're a little short on dressings right now, but if you need to change out into a new one, I'll get one for you," he quickly mumbled all the instructions.

"Okay," I replied softly.

"Make sure the bandages are non-stick," he said, tearing open one of the packets, applying the ointment for me gently.

I steady my breath. "What are we going to do?" I stressed. "Does this mean there are many connected groups out there we don't know about? They outnumber us!"

"I don't know." He sighed, moving my leg. He looked up at me. "Did you see—the warrior on Rodney's jacket?" he asked.

I felt relieved for some reason, hearing that. I cherish every moment I have with him where it doesn't seem like he's making me feel like I'm crazy.

"Those men were part of this group weren't they?" I connected the dots.

"I don't see why they wouldn't be," I heard his voice shifting again, and I didn't know why.

I took a deep breath. "Then should we come clean? They're *going* to have questions."

He didn't answer, he just stared at me. "Do you want to?"

"I think we should," I replied.

"Then that's what we'll do."

"But wait—" I watched him stop. "Don't tell them about Sterling."

14 ⅓ warrior

"I don't understand how you can keep something like that from us," Candreva lectured me.

Scheuch ordered an emergency group meeting to discuss what had just happened, but we also took it upon ourselves to tell them what really happened that day I went back for Tyson.

Candreva was pacing back and forth with his hand at his chin. "Do you understand how much danger our group could be in right now?"

"Those guys died on the road," I defended.

"Right, so now you've killed three of their men," Kim rubbed her hands through her hair. "That only gives them more reasons to come after us!"

That's the most useful thing I've ever heard her say!

"She's right!" Candreva followed. "What if someone saw you two killing them? What if *they* followed you and *Arrogant Aaron* over here," he muttered through his teeth, "*home* and found out where we lived?"

I tried not to giggle as Scheuch replied nonchalantly. "I can see that as a possibility," he said. "Although, spending our time 'what-if-ing' through this situation isn't going to benefit anyone."

I appreciate the back-up, but I'd appreciate an apology more.

"Brody," I explained, "if they saw that I killed Benny, they would've already been aware of our location."

"Oh, shit, I guess you're right," he nodded, hands on his hips. "It's still concerning you never told us. Think about it! How do you expect the group to trust you if you can't even tell us about something like this?"

~~"I don't have to tell you guys anything I don't want to," I replied.~~ That would've been the worst possible thing to say.

"I didn't think it would matter," I replied calmly. "Think about it, you guys go out on runs every month and *you* don't come home and tell us how many people you've killed?"

"That's 'cause we don't *see* anyone on our runs to *kill!*" He slapped his forehead. "Mj, this *puts* us in jeopardy!"

"That's enough," Scheuch shut it down. "Debating this doesn't help anybody."

"Can we please focus on where the hell Sergeant is?" Maxwell asked. She was sitting next to Watkins, who was sitting slouched next to Yanes. We were all in a circle basically. Our group has gotten so much smaller.

"The last time we saw him was right before Sully and Watkins went out," Scheuch answered.

"Hold on," I said. "If Sully and Watkins were out for supplies—and you, Bailey, Candreva, and Yanes were at the facility to get Maxwell and I, what the hell were *you* doing?" I turned to Kim.

"I—I was told to stay back here—"

"Right, but what were you doing?" I asked again. "You didn't see Sergeant at *all?*"

"Um—u-um..."

I waited patiently. I *somehow* waited patiently. Until I didn't.

"Um—u-um... *what?!*" I asked. "You were told to stay back and be on the lookout, now did you actually do that or were you too busy writing love notes?"

"Bui, c'mon," Scheuch got between us. *Oh, he knows.*

"She's not wrong," Yanes said in the most respectful way possible. "Kim, if you were paying more attention, we might actually know where Sergeant could be right now."

I looked over and let out a huge groan. "Annndddd *here* comes the waterworks!" I said the second I saw the tears.

I look over at Scheuch. He was rolling his eyes.

"This is exactly what I was talking about. How are we supposed to *trust* you?" Kim asked. "Brody is right. You shouldn't have kept something like that from us!"

"Trust," I scoffed, taking a look around the group, "Brody, Mickey, you two aren't *that* hung up over this, right?"

Candreva and Yanes shook their heads. "I don't care?" Yanes shrugged. "There's nothing we can do now?"

"Kiara?" I asked. "Cameron?" They shook their heads too, so I turned over. "Quinn?"

"I'm with you, kid."

I looked at Sully. She sighed, "I don't see how knowing Aaron and Mj killed two guys on a run helps us at all—"

"So in conclusion, nobody here has a damn problem but *you,*" I scoffed, looking at Kim's scrunched up face.

"*Hey—*" Scheuch eyed me hard as the group continued discussing. "Tone it down," he mouthed sternly.

I do agree—*to an extent*—I keep taking things out of proportion, but judging by his face, he understands that I have just been held hostage by a group of maniacs, so it makes sense that I am not the friendliest at the moment.

"Okay, but how do we know for sure those two guys from the highway figure into *these* guys from the facility?" Candreva asked.

"The warriors on their jackets," I replied.

"The *warriors?*" Watkins asked.

"The symbols on their jackets! I *know* what I saw!"

"Okay," Candreva nodded, "but so what if they just happen to have the same symbol on their clothes? That has no sense of confirmation. We don't have time for conspiracy theories right now, Mj?"

"It's not—a *damn*—conspiracy theory!" I tried my best not to sound mad. Candreva would never mean it in a mean way, (I think). "I think the fact they keep asking us similar questions like *how are we immune to the toxic air*—and telling us *specifically* to pack our bags and leave—the fact that they *have* masks—and those *symbols* on their uniforms is enough confirmation for us!"

"Hey, notice how all these—let's call them *warriors*—" Bailey said, almost immediately looking at the look Scheuch had on his face. I had a confused face too. Bailey almost never talks during meetings like these.

"They're a step ahead of us," he said, crossing his arms.

"And why do you think that?" Scheuch asked.

Bailey held out his hand and pointed at me. "I mean think about it, if these warriors are so angry that Bui killed Benny, how did they happen to know where she was that night on the highway?"

"And if they were there on behalf of Benny's death, wouldn't they say something?" Maxwell asked.

"That could be true," I glanced up at Scheuch, "they *did* tell us to go home and pack. That could've meant something."

"Or it could be a total coincidence, I don't see how this pertains to us," he said.

"How would the warriors have known to go after Bui the night she left then?" Bailey asked. "And how'd they know to go after Maxwell and Klein too?"

"No—yeah," Watkins sighed. "I agree with Bailey. There's no way that was a coincidence."

"Yeah, he's right. It *was* weird," I explained quietly. Scheuch was looking down at me firmly. "Rodney put me in a room and started interrogating me as if he knew me. *I'm gonna figure you out, Mj,*" I mocked him. "He sounded stupid as hell."

"I think we both know how he could've possibly known you," Scheuch muttered under his breath, looking back up again.

I took a deep breath, ignoring his tone and how he was wrong. Sterling doesn't know me like that to tell Rodney that information kind of about me.

"What the hell does that mean—does that mean there could be a possible *mole* among us?" Candreva waved his hands around stressfully as the group tensely stared at one another.

"What? Why would any of us do that?" Kim asked.

"That's an *excellent* question," Scheuch replied.

I held in my chuckle.

"I don't know, *I* can certainly believe it? Someone listening in here and reporting back to *them?*" Candreva shrugged, looking at the blank look on Scheuch's face.

He sighed. "What would any of us *gain* from doing that?"

"Aaron, why are you being so adamant about this?"

The room went silent again. Scheuch glanced at all of the looks on our faces. "What's that supposed to mean?" he replied defensively. "Are you implying you think *I* am the mole?"

"I don't know, you've been pretty distant from us lately," Yanes rubbed the back of his head.

"Statistically speaking, it wouldn't make sense for *me* to turn out to be the mole when our buddies, Bailey and Watkins over here are *also*—from your perspective—*distant* from the group," he said smugly. "So by your logic, does that suggest that we're *all* moles?"

"Pfft, Bailey and Watkins barely go outside the barriers," Candreva scoffed. "However, you're always somewhere in some place *we* don't know!"

Scheuch glared at him in disbelief. We all studied the look on his face, maybe I even considered the possibility of him being the mole—which would explain a lot. But I knew he wouldn't. I stood there ignoring that feeling in my chest, praying he wouldn't.

I glanced over to Bailey, who was looking at him the same.

"I-I don't think Aaron's out there doing anything *bad?*" Sully said. "Wouldn't him coming home with bags of food for us be enough proof he's not doing anything fishy?"

"Oh! So you're defending *him* now?" Candreva scoffed. "We don't know where and *how* he could've got that?"

"I can have my own opinions, Brody," she quickly sighed.

"C'mon, Brody, Aaron would never do that," Watkins defended.

Maxwell followed up too. "He's a bit of an oddball sometimes, but he wouldn't go out of his way to *hurt* us?"

"Well there's ought-a be *some* explanation to how these warriors track us?"

"Ought-a?" Sully chuckled.

"Hung around Sterling too much," he muttered. "Man, I *miss* messing with that kid."

I rolled my eyes at the nonsense. "I'm more distant from you guys than Scheuch, does that mean I'm a mole too?" I defended him.

Candreva crossed his arms, tilting his head. "Yeah, but you're always persistent on wanting to help out."

"Which would, in a case where I am the mole," I began speaking slowly to make sure I made sense, "would help disguise my role——as a mole—" *Ooh, it rhymes!* "—more distinctively."

"You're not helping your case here," he sighed. "Are you trying to defend Scheuch or make yourself sound suspicious?"

"What I'm—*trying to say*—is us ambushing each other won't help us at all!" I explained. They all stared at me silently, which implied they didn't understand. I took a deep breath, "I feel like the warriors almost *want* this from us, y'know? They want us to go against each other when we should be bonded."

"I——agree with Bui—" Scheuch said as he looked at his watch. He exhaled slowly. "It's late, you guys," he said. "Tomorrow morning, I want everyone gathering more information on these people—and I want a group out for more supplies. We are running low on everything." He looked at me and asked if I wanted to add anything. I shook my head. He turned back again, looking at Candreva, "And it's best if we disregard this idea of a *mole*. You said it yourself, we don't have time for conspiracy theories right now."

There was an awfully long pause between them. For a second it looked like we were going to have another Klein-and-Watkins moment, but knowing them, they would *never*. It'd sure be entertaining, but it wouldn't be rational in a time like this.

"Hol—Hold on," Yanes looked at me. I glanced over at him hoping he'd say something useful. He did. "Where were warrior symbols located on their jackets?"

"Top left—on the chest—" I replied.

"I think Sergeant and I came across a group like them too," Yanes explained. "They were the ones that led us back to the highway before heading off."

"Holy shit!" Maxwell gasped. "*That group?* So Keigan's in on this too?! They've been around us this whole time!"

"Oh for Pete's sake, why didn't you say something about that *sooner?!*" Candreva smacked his forehead. "Mickey, you got me over here accusing poor *Arrogant Aaron* over here!"

He stepped over to him, placing his hand firmly on Scheuch's shoulder. "I'm sorry, man."

"You're good," Scheuch replied, feeling the weight shake off his shoulders, "and can you stop calling me that?"

"Nope." Candreva chuckled before swiftly yanking him into a chokehold, giving him a noogie as if we were in a movie.

"Stop it!" Scheuch swatted at him. "Brody! *Stop* it!"

Candreva swung him back and forth laughing, purposely crooking his glasses.

"*Stop it!!!*"

14 2/3 just marry her!

I don't think anyone can understand how much it hurts to have someone value you as a cadet but not as a person. To him, I am a valuable asset, but if I were just a girl he knew, he'd treat me like ███████████████.

I'm not being dramatic if this is truly how it feels like.

"Bui, Maxwell, you two can stay here for tonight if you wish," Scheuch said as everyone began piling out the front door, rubbing the top of his head awkwardly. "Watkins and I will be here to help out. There's Tylenol in the left cabinet you can take——for the pain."

"Thanks," Maxwell mumbled as she began making her way up the stairs. Watkins followed.

I didn't hesitate this time. "Aaron, I need to talk to you."

He turned.

The way he reacts to me is drastically different from all the other boys I've dealt with throughout the years. I'm used to the nonchalant, tough scoffs; the stubborn and condescending demeanors. Acts that make me feel like I'm crazy and dramatic and *'I'm just making a big deal out of nothing'*. And then, I've had guys who make me oddly *grateful* for their patronizing behaviors. I've had guys who taunt me simply because my anger turns them on. I'd rather *not* have that, to be honest here. Boys like that make me wish I was just a kid.

But the look on Aaron's face doesn't match either of those descriptions, in the least insulting way possible, he reacts exactly how a girl would; how *I* would. He has a sense of hurt in his eyes——as if what I said crushed him, even just for a little bit. A look of shock maybe. Surprise. But then again, his behavior proves my perception of him is wrong, *so* wrong.

If you are so hurt, Aaron——if what I'm saying is really going through to you, why aren't you saying anything? And if you don't care, at all, and I truly mean nothing to you, why are we *here*?

"What is the issue?" I watch his demeanor solidify.

Dammit, he's just like them.

He's just like them. He's just like them. He's just like them. He's just like them. He's just like them. He's just like them. He's just like them. He's just like them. He's just like them. He's just like them. He's just like them. He's just like them. He's just like them. He's just like them. He's just like them. He's just like them.

"You said you wanted to talk about it," I leaned back against a booth, "let's talk about it."

"About what?"

"The last supply run?" I crossed my arms. "Where you had me following you around like a lost puppy?"

"That was—my bad," he looked down, fidgeting with the edge of his black t-shirt. "My bad. I should've elaborated."

Since when does Aaron Scheuch say *my bad*?

We both went silent for a bit. I saw the look on his face.

"Can you quit that?" I scoffed. His eyes turn, then shift back. "Stop acting like I want to *fucking* marry *you!*"

~~"I don't know if you hit your head when you fuckin' woke up this morning," I scolded, "but I'ma need you to pull out that stick you have up your ass before I shove my fist so far down your throat, it'll make your fucking jaw lock!"~~

I could never say that to him.

I wouldn't be able to stand the look on his face.

He's so important, but not because he impacted my life or anything. (I stopped being so violent and angry.) He's important because for the first time in my life, I was actually thinking about the things I said to people. For the first time in my life, I paid attention to how my actions could possibly impact other people.

"I am still not caught up with what the issue is," he replied, *nonchalantly*. He wasn't looking at me anymore.

I contain my anger. "The issue is *you*."

"And what about me?"

I am not going to stand here and beg for someone's kindness. I am not going to stand here and let someone see how easy it is to be able to get to me. I am not going to stand here and let a boy dictate the way I feel, but he does it so easily that I have to make sure *it doesn't break my heart.*

"I'm not gonna stand here and beg you to be *fuckin'* nice to me," I scoffed. "You've known me long enough to know that's not something I'd do."

I felt my voice growing louder—his eyes growing softer. "I'm not *begging* for your damn *love* like this is some corny movie—or for us to lock arms, *skippin' around* like best *fuckin'* friends, Aaron? I just want you to stop treating me like a damn dog, is that so hard to fucking *ask?*" I blinked away the tears. "You can share umbrellas in the *pouring* rain, and *hold* doors, and have *full grown*

RECONCILIATION

conversations with *Sully,* but you can't even be *decent* enough to not *leave* me outside in the *fucking* cold?!"

I stood out in the cold our last supply run; my hair wet from racing Bailey in the water previously. I stood out in the cold our last supply run and he couldn't even bring himself to *look at me,* to *say a damn word to me,* but he could leave me out there. Just standing there.

"*I just don't like talking,*" he'd say, but that's bullshit. His entire tenth grade Biology Honors class can testify against that. "*The loudness—and the chattiness—*"

I lowered my eyebrows, stepping closer to him, coming down to nearly a whisper, "I don't want to hear how it wasn't *registered*—in your head—or how it—*wasn't personal*—because that's *bullshit!*" I wiped my tears, sniffling. "That's bullshit because I know you would've *never* done that to Mary, and it has me here wondering what is *so* wrong with me that you have to *treat* me like that!"

~~Everything is wrong with me. I don't cover my mouth when I laugh too loud. I don't control what I say and I talk too much. The clothes I like to wear aren't modest enough, and it reflects on how people view me. Of course a good man like that would never want anything to do with me.~~

Tell me what am I supposed to do with myself? What am I supposed to do with this? How am I supposed to look at myself in the mirror and believe all the delusions I convince myself? Because if someone so simple as Aaron Scheuch can't even like me, then who would? If someone so kind as Avery Conti couldn't be a good friend to me, then I must be a bad person. If the only people I can call friends are people like María Colón, I'm screwed!

So tell me, what am I supposed to do with myself?

There are so many things more important than wanting someone to just *fucking* like you, but I can't bear it.

Please tell me.

Tell me why I've gone all my teenage years not caring what a boy could think of me, but when it comes to you, it changes everything. Why is it when Kay left me for those girls who weren't worth as half of me, and when I wasn't good enough for Tyson to admit he liked me, and when Jake made it clear he loved Avery more and showed me I wasn't anything more to him than just a good time, I felt nothing—nothing other than, "It's not *my* fault they don't feel that way towards me? Whatever! My world isn't going to end just because of some guy." But when *Aaron Scheuch* tells me,

"I'm going to tell you right now, I'll never treat you the same as I treat Mary. That's not going to happen—*blah blah blah*—I've known Mary for much longer—*blah blah blah*——I *like* her—*blah blah*—we've worked together, I've taken classes with her—*blah blah*—"

all I can hear is, "~~MARY IS BETTER THAN YOU! MARY IS BETTER THAN YOU! MARY IS BETTER THAN YOU!~~"

rather than just, "*Blah blah*——I ran cross country with her——I've been with—*known*—her for five years now——I. Like. Mary."

<u>*"I'm not going to treat someone*</u>
<u>*I like*</u>
<u>*the same way I treat someone*</u>
<u>*I **don't** like."*</u>

RECONCILIATION

I stood there, and instead of feeling any anger, for the first time in my life, I had to pretend something someone said didn't hurt me. For the first time in my life, I stopped and thought, *Damn*.

"Make sense?" He added the cherry on top.

I forced myself to look him in the eye. My voice breaking, I ask, "You don't like me?"

"No."

I watch him—give that girl *everything*—I wanted.

He didn't even hesitate, and I had to just stand there pretending it didn't feel like he just clawed his way into my body and ripped my heart out from my chest. The silence was so loud, we could hear the crickets chirping from outside.

"Okay," I replied nonchalantly.

Not one nerve in my face twitched. Not one tear formed in my eye. Nothing. I just stood there and took it.

Maybe the silence was a good thing. If I got any angrier; if we argued any louder, we wouldn't have heard the rustling outside beneath the window.

"Did you hear that?" I asked concernedly.

We both looked at the window beside us, eyes widening to the sight of someone frantically running away. We carefully approached the window, crouching a bit, looking to see who it was. We know it definitely wasn't one of ours, but if it wasn't, who was it?

"Watch out!" He covered me as we both ducked the moment a brick came flying through the glass. My heart jumped, watching it tumble across the floor. I watch him steady his breath and step over to it, picking it up to see the words carved on the back of it.

THIS ISN'T OVER.

"Well ain't that corny," I scoffed, looking at it too.

He sighed as he entered the kitchen and came out with a broom and dustpan. "Anything else?" he asked as he swept.

"What do you mean *anything else?*" I scoffed softly.

"Anything else you want from me?"

I want you to talk to me like it doesn't feel like a chore. I want you to smile when you talk to me instead of making me stand there feeling stupid. I want you to give me *more* than just terse responses so I don't feel like I'm doing something wrong. I want you to laugh at my jokes how you used to, and have that look in your eye you had when you looked at me.

I want you to give me that feeling I crave, so I don't have to spend the rest of my life searching for it in someone else.

I don't know what to tell you, he says, *that's just the way I am.*

But if I said that to excuse all the things I would've done, *I* would be in the wrong. I would lose all my friends and all the respect I've earned, I wouldn't have been included in the drill team, I would've lost my chances for a promotion or possibly lose my position on the command staff, and I would eventually be driven out of the program. But why the hell would I want to willingly stay somewhere knowing it makes me feel like shit? If these people embody this logic then maybe I *don't* want to be fucking friends with them. Maybe I'd rather be alone.

All this bullshit—just to be able to print an acronym on my college resume. This wasn't worth it.

He stood there looking at the look I had on my face with a dustpan full of shards of glass. "Would you like me to leave?"

"Yeah," I whispered, sniffling. "Just go."

"Okay, if you need anything, just let me know," he said softly.

15 love and revenge

I always thought dog food was extremely inhumane. I don't often find myself feeling as much empathy as I used to, so I figured I couldn't let go of this thought for a reason.

I sat on the wooden stool in the gun shop's basement, looking at the boy in the cage silently. I could finally make out his facial features now that his bruises were healed. He was sitting up against the wall, feet gently swaying side to side.

He glanced up at me. "I already told you guys I don't know anything," he said.

Candreva and Yanes never told me what they ended up doing to that boy. They only told Scheuch, who told *me* I didn't need to worry. I was shocked that he survived the raids and the months following the night we scattered.

His soft, sweet voice revealed so much about his character that I felt I could understand him completely.

"I'm not here to hurt you," I replied. "Not if you give me any reason to."

I approached the cage slowly, giving him an opened can of macaroni and cheese. He looked at it curiously before reaching his hand out through the bars, grabbing it from me. I even gave him a plastic spoon.

"I wasn't sure what you liked," I said.

"This is good." He was smiling, scooping up each bite. "Thank you."

I lowered my eyebrows. "What's your name?"

"Seth."

"Okay, Seth, what *do* you like?"

He looked up at me, still smiling softly. I examined the scars all over his face. "Something sweet."

I nodded, returning back to the stool.

"Why are you doing this?" he asked; mouth full of macaroni.

"Well, I figure since I did something nice for you—"

"You want me to talk." He finished my sentence, nodding to himself. "I don't *know* anything!" He began growing frustrated. "I swear, you guys picked the worst guy to kidnap!"

"Why do you say that?" Scheuch asked.

He was down here with me too, leaning on a table on my left.

Seth gulped, remaining silent. It didn't take long for me to pick up that he couldn't trust us, let alone anyone else in our group. I couldn't blame him. Scheuch and I weren't always the most pleasant to look at. Often labeled as the rigid ones of the group, we were told we distinguished ourselves from Bailey and Watkins by, according to a remark I cannot remember from whom, being sassier. Sassier! *Seriously?*

I guess we just had that look. The look of worn, torn clothes, blood-stained knuckles, clenched jaws, and hardened eyes. I've been so desensitized to what he and I have had to do, I often forget how terrified I would be if I ever crossed us.

My tone and voice quickly melts that character of mine, Scheuch's doesn't.

"He's scared." I turned to him. "Scheuch, tell him a fun fact."

He narrowed his eyes. "How would that make him feel better?"

I hesitated. "They made *me* feel better?" I replied softly, quickly looking back at Seth.

"Your brain blocks out the feeling of your organs moving around in your body," Scheuch's voice eerily spoke as my head snapped back over at him.

"What the *hell's* the matter with you?!" I spat, as if at one point I wasn't terrified that he was a future serial killer in the making. ~~I'd much rather him murder me then break my heart.~~

Scheuch snickered, making me laugh a little too. I quickly stopped and turned back to Seth.

"Your liver can regenerate itself, even if you get two-thirds of it removed," Scheuch said. "How fun of a fact is that?"

"Super fun," Seth replied with his eyes widened.

"Aaron, I think if you were a bird, you'd be a Cuckoo," I giggled.

"Great, now can you *speak?*"

How condescending... I sighed, watching Seth look down and take a deep breath. "I don't belong to that group."

He watched the both of us quickly melt back into our strict demeanors. Scheuch tilted his head. "Then *why* were you there?"

"I was stranded from mine," he explained. "The guys from the city took me in 'cause I was so hurt. I was planning on staying there 'till my brother came back for me."

"Damn." I shook my head. *We really kidnapped the worst guy.*

"Who's your brother and who's he with?" Scheuch asked.

"Elijah," Seth answered, "and he's with all our friends. We all used to work together."

"How many?"

"Ten including me."

"You guys armed?" I asked.

"Of course we are."

"*How* armed?"

"Armed enough," he sniffled as I noticed he was more focused on the food now. He then looked up, wiping the cheese around his lips. "Why do you guys call each other by your last names?"

I hesitated. "I don't know. We *were* at a place where it was required to do so, now I guess—" I watched Scheuch stand up and begin walking upstairs, "—it's just engraved in our heads now."

"Oh," Seth nodded, as I rolled my eyes at him. "yeah, I know a few people that had to do that."

I turned back to him. "Seth, do you remember anyone in the city wearing jackets with warriors on them?"

"Uhh..."

I heard Scheuch stop walking abruptly and turn back around. He approached me from behind and glared at him.

"I-I don't remember," Seth shook his head. "It was a while ago—and—your friend gave me a pretty *good* beating."

"Dammit, Bailey," I scoffed, removing the hand at my hip, rubbing my forehead. "Alright," I yawned, "we can—"

"What do you and your friends wear?" Scheuch asked sternly.

Seth looked up confusedly. *"Clothes?"*

"What *type* of clothes?"

"Mostly our—guard shirts?" he answered nervously. "I don't know. We just wore what we salvaged from our homes?"

"Guard—shirts—?" Scheuch looked over at me.

"Are you guys lifeguards?" I asked.

Seth nodded softly.

"O-Okay," I nodded back as Scheuch began walking back upstairs. I leaned in closer, grasping the cold railing. "Don't worry, I'll talk to him about letting you out."

He scoffed. "How do you know I'm not gonna kill all of you?"

I lowered my eyebrows.

"These four walls are the only things I've seen for the past year and a half," he chuckled. "How do you know I haven't gone *rogue* yet?"

"Man, do you want to get out or not?" I scoffed, hopping back up the stairs.

Scheuch stopped me before I could leave without saying goodbye to him.

"Bui, can you note down we need more ammo for the next run?" He asked. *He would have noted that himself.*

"Yeah," I replied nonchalantly.

"Thanks."

"No problem."

"Motherfucker, I'll *give* him something to dislike!" Mj popped out of nowhere, angry as ever. She scolded me as if her heart was aching for the sake of both of us.

"It's not worth it, Mj."

"Are you *kidding* me?" she shouted, pausing once she saw the look on my face. "Bui, I think this *left—left—left-right—left* bullshit gave you brain damage or somethin'—"

"I think we're just expecting too much from them."

"You have been *nothing* but *respectful* and *nice* and a damn *suck-up* to all these motherfuckers—" she said, "—please, just take a moment to reflect on this. Look at everything you've done for them and look at what the *hell* you get back!"

I groaned and began moping up the stairs.

She followed me, agitating me. "Open your *eyes, Mj!*" She pleaded. "You have been nothing but *cooperative* and *competent* and *listening* and *adjusting* to make *others* feel better, and *this—THIS* is what you get back. They don't appreciate a *thing* you do! They just keep picking you apart—like what? Like *they're* flawless?"

"Maybe they're just—"

"Nah, you're doin' it again," she said. "Stop making excuses for their actions. That's why you *keep* getting hurt."

I stopped and took a deep breath. She stepped closer to me, lifting her hand to fix my hair a bit.

"You're giving me too much credit," I replied softly, watching her wipe her face. "It's not that big of a deal."

"If it wasn't that big of a deal, you wouldn't be feeling this way," she said, looking me dead in the eyes. "If it *truly* wasn't that big of a deal, you would be talking to Michelle right now."

She stepped closer to me, holding my shoulders. "Don't tell me these people just want the best for you. Name me *one* damn person?" she asked. "Aaron? A guy who openly admits he doesn't give a flying *fuck* about you? Or Jake? A guy who just wanted you to *suck* him? Or! Or! *Avery!!!* A girl who hangs out with the same people she tells you to stay away from!" She pitched her voice up, mocking her. "Hey, you wanna hang out? *No, sorry! I'm busy! I'm busy!*" She mimicked, "Now tell me, who do you see her with on Insta?"

She laughed. You can tell just by looking at the two of us who really cared and who didn't.

"You need to stand up. Have some *damn* self-respect," she said, chuckling a bit out of frustration. "Do you have *any* idea what *I* would've done?"

When Tyson died, I could've been bedridden. I could've drank myself to sleep every night until my liver gave out. I literally live in a bar!

But I didn't.

When Kim taunted me by the creek, I could've shot her. When Kim made those comments and made those pouty-ass faces towards me, I could've wallowed up into a big ol' miserable ball and cry big ol' miserable tears and moan big ol' miserable complaints and just sit and soak up all my miserableness exactly how a miserable person like her would.

But I didn't.

Instead, I (attempted) to make amends two weeks after I had that dream about shooting her to prove I was capable of being the bigger person. The group didn't know. She never took accountability and apologized for anything. That's fine. It was fair to assume out of the two of us, I would be the one that'd apologize and not mean it.

"You could've been so much worse," Mj said. "You *should've* been much worse," she scoffed, subtly wiping the tears now streaming down her face. I let her cry because she was crying for the both of us. I had no strength left to cry.

"You should've told *every* boy in this program mansplaining common knowledge to you won't grow their dicks any longer," she cried, "and you should've told every girl in this program pampering Klein won't make him want them any more, and—"

"But can't you see how bad it is to be so angry?" I asked her.

"Oh, *shut up,* you sound like Michelle."

"No, Mj, *you* don't understand!" I covered my face, sighing.

"Then fuckin' *enlighten* me!"

"You don't get it. I can see *why* he wouldn't want anything to do with me, Mj!" I sobbed.

I expected her to say something to contradict me, but instead she helped me prove my own point, which made me feel worse.

"Girl, it wouldn't make any sense for him to anyway," she sighed, looking at me. "Look at *me* and then look at him."

Silver hoop earrings. Tattoos. Chain cross necklace. Navy tank top. Denim shorts. RBF. Bloodshot eyes. Scarred knuckles. Eyebrow slit.

Crooked glasses. Mismatched neon socks. Muddy white sneakers. Lack of social skills. Blue jeans with a calculator in the back pocket.

"What are you saying?" I asked confusedly.

"I'm *saying,* he's an awkward bookworm and you intimidate the shit out of people!" she scoffed.

"You realize I've drastically changed since—you—right?"

"Sure." She rolled her eyes. "You were on a steady pathway to some bougie university to major in *How Big of a Pain in the Ass Can I be Tomorrow?* So tell me, why would you go and bend over backwards for a guy who'd probably snort pencil shavings?"

I chuckled softly. "He *would* do that."

"And if you can see why he wouldn't want anything to do with you, then why didn't you *see* it when Klein left you?"

"Because when Klein stopped being nice to me, he stopped being nice to *everyone*—"

"No, let me tell you why," she interrupted me. "You didn't give a shit when he left because you never had respect for him in the first place. His presence never had any significance to you, so neither did his absence. The problem is you put too much value on a person like Scheuch and now you're disappointed that he didn't meet your standards. It's not *his* fault you idolized him? So lemme ask you this: who the hell *is* he to you, Bui? What has he done for you that allows him to impact your life *this* much?!"

"Alright, Mj, *enough*," Michelle spawned. "Yelling at her isn't going to make her feel any better."

"It sure makes *me* feel better?" She scoffed. "How could someone be so stupid!?"

"Just—go upstairs and paint or something," Michelle rolled her eyes. "*I'll* talk to her."

Mj scoffed and turned back to me. "I can't even look at you. You've become such a people pleaser, it hurts me."

"Better than punching my *fists* through doors every time I get pushed over the edge?" I replied. "Being angry and reacting like that is bad for our soul and you know it!"

"Well being sad just lets 'em know how easy it is to break ya!"

"How about you two just learn how to let it go?" Michelle sighed from behind the bar counter. "Accept that it happened and live the rest of your life in peace. Life's too short to wonder about things you don't need answers to."

"See?" Mj held her hand out. "Doing *that* will just make them hurt you over and over again."

"They can only hurt you if you let them," Michelle put her hand on her hip. "You should be protecting your peace. Letting go and moving on."

"*I* think… that if he dislikes you *this much* after everything you've done for him, you should—"

"No," I shook my head at Mj, already knowing where this was going. "No. Hurting him back won't heal me any faster."

"How does he get to just—*move on*—with his life after leaving you in *shambles* like this?!"

"For someone to feel the need to make a person feel this way must feel the same to do so," I said. "He's hurt, so he hurt me."

"Aw," Michelle sympathized. "Why's he hurt?"

I looked at her judgefully. "Fuck do I know?"

"Damn," Mj sighed. "Okay, I'm tired." She turned to Michelle. "All you now."

Michelle turned as she watched Mj storm up the stairs, then turned back to me. She had more light in her eyes. She was more content, compared to Mj and I.

"You keep carrying around this burden along with you," she said. "You keep reminding yourself that you're a bitter, violent, irrational person—and that you're a hypocrite—and that you're forever meant to be alone and difficult to get along with."

She sighed and shook her head, looking at the person I've become. I am not as strong as I think I am. If I was strong, I would've never let these people mold me into the shape they wanted me in.

"But don't you ever just think maybe—just *maybe*—" she said, "you were *just* fifteen years old?"

She took it upon herself to walk away, and I suddenly felt the weight of two hundred pounds drop from my shoulders.

I don't like talking to them. I like being me. I like being neutral and nonchalant—like a damn teenage boy—so nothing can hurt me. I liked the idea of laughing over immature things and not caring about a thing in the world—because talking to Mj and Michelle only make me realize that

    all Michelle wants is love and all Mj wants is revenge.

 vacay

"Why are we down here and not upstairs?" Maxwell asked as we piled into the basement of the gunshop. She looked over at Seth in his cage. "Holy shit, he's still *here?!*"

Bailey chuckled in his spot. "Tough kid."

"How'd he survive the *raids* and—"

"Maybe 'cause he was down *here* and not outside?" Candreva replied as he walked by.

"I mean how did he not *starve* to death!" she rolled her eyes, pulling a stool over, sitting herself down.

Scheuch came pacing in last, fidgeting with his knuckles. He looked over at Maxwell swiftly, pointing at her with his index fingers, "Um—we're down here because—" He sniffled and adjusted his glasses, quickly realizing his nose was bleeding.

"Here," Sully quickly gave him a tissue.

We've been prone to nosebleeds for so long now, it's practical for us to carry around packs of tissues.

"Thanks," he carelessly shoved it up his nose, continuing as if nothing happened. "Bui and I have reason to believe we're being watched. There is *no* mole," He slyly glanced over at Candreva. "Our conversations are *constantly* listened to, that's why they seem to know everything about us." He looked over at me. "We found out when—um—Bui and I were *talking* last night and we heard rustling out our window."

"Just rustling?" Bailey asked.

"They left a present?" Scheuch turned around, picking up the brick that they threw.

"*Shit,*" Yanes sighed. "Were you and Bui talking about anything important? Anything they can use against us?"

I watched him look down at the floor, rubbing the back of his head. "Um—" I stared him down, "not that I know of."

"Okay so, we're down here to be sure they can't hear anything," Candreva nodded, glancing over at Seth in his cage, "but what about him?"

"He's fine," Scheuch disregarded him. "Bui, you wanna start with the radio stuff?" he mumbled.

"Sure," I scooched myself onto a stool.

We had grouped ourselves into a large circle, or what we used to call it, an East Cumberland circle, known as a circle shaped like a warped watermelon or a squashed square. It varies.

"Maxwell and I overheard a woman speaking on the radio when we were down there," I explained. "Her name was Lindsey—said she was stationed somewhere in Brigantine."

"W-Where's Brigantine?" Candreva asked, hand on his chin.

"Brigantine is a beach located in Atlantic County, New Jersey," Scheuch answered.

He made a subtle face and replied, "Thanks."

"We didn't reply to her," Maxwell continued explaining, "but we heard her say they were accepting refugees. They have cures—*vaccines*—for those who have been bit."

"How can we be sure if they're telling the truth?" Candreva asked.

"Do we have a *choice?*" she replied. "We're being *hunted* by the warriors here. Our best option is to leave, so we might as well go to *someplace* worthwhile!"

"Yeah, Aaron, weren't you talking about heading south that one time?" Watkins looked up.

"Jersey is West," Kim muttered.

"*No*, Kim, New Jersey is East," Scheuch shook his head, thinking. He was leaning against one of the tables next to him and Candreva. "Yes—" he paused, "—at the time, I thought it'd be logical because then our base wouldn't be located *right* where all these herds are migrating."

"What changed your mind?" Maxwell asked.

"The night we scattered?" he shrugged, crossing his feet below him. "Figured it'd be best to settle back down here before moving again. At first, it made logical sense to head towards the coast. Carcasses can't swim."

People started shouting out questions and debating with one another. We've never gotten better at group discussions, no matter how many group bonding activities Sgt. Rogers encouraged us to do. Only what was left of the command staff remained quiet, which at the time, said a lot.

"What about the one that killed María?" My question silenced the room.

He glanced at me, sighing. "That's what made me change my mind."

"Wouldn't going someplace warmer be better?" Watkins asked. "The roamers could decompose faster."

"The mosquitos," I replied. "They'll most likely carry the disease—get us infected."

"*Bug spray* is a thing," Kim snarked.

"Hey—" Seth weakly stood up in his cage before I could respond, dragging himself over to the corner. He gripped the metal poles with his pale, freckled hands. "If you guys move, what's going to happen to me?"

I sighed, looking back over at Scheuch.

"We'll—" he looked down, fidgeting with his hands, "—figure that out at a different time."

Seth scoffed softly, quickly looking at me. "We'll figure it out," I reassured him. "We're not just going to leave you here."

He gulped desperately. I wasn't sure why he was stressing so much. We were *going* to let him come with us. There wasn't any other option, no other option Sully, Maxwell, and I wouldn't be okay with.

"Gentlemen, can we get back on track here?" Maxwell asked. "New Jersey——are we going or not?"

"We *are* on track, Kiara?" Candreva sighed frantically. "This is a serious debate. We're not standing 'round here plannin' a damn girl's trip!"

"Brody, there are ways to get your point across without being rude," Scheuch crossed his arms.

"Yeah, you wouldn't know," I scoffed under my breath.

"I'm worried if the air and water near the coast is safe or not?" Candreva turned a bit, holding his hand out, snapping his fingers. "Uhh—"

Scheuch cleared his throat. "With the circumstances we have, a beach is not ideally the safest place to settle down by," he explained. "Areas with natural barriers like mountains or dense forests would be perfect to get away from the radiation, but we'd be closer to the roamers depending on which area we pick."

"Do we have *time* to be searchin' around for forest?" Maxwell asked concernedly. "Do we have the fuel?"

"Why bother taking the radiation into consideration if we're immune?" Candreva asked. *"Man,* you're like a walking textbook!"

"For our crops?" he rolled his eyes, smiling a little. "Also, thanks."

Candreva looked back at him with a straight face. "That wasn't a compliment."

He looked down, nodding. "Well, if you haven't *noticed,*" he slid his hands into his pockets, leaning back against the steel table, crossing his legs beneath him, "we're a pretty isolated group here."

The group went quiet for a bit. He looked at Bailey, who was leaning against the cage with his arms crossed. He inhaled slowly.

"He's right. We've looted every gas station, pharmacy, and convenience store in the area," he explained. "There are no supermarkets or warehouses nearby that *aren't* overrun *or* burnt down."

"We can handle a group of roamers or two, can we?" Yanes asked, looking over at me.

"We don't have the ammunition," I answered.

"We can't survive off of the food we have," Sully shook her head. "I mean look at all of us, we're all malnourished!"

"I mean, the vitamins I found should help a little with that, right?" Kim asked.

"Alright, let's steer back on track here," Scheuch pinched the bridge of his nose firmly. "The reason why radiation-talk pertains to us is because of our buddy, Seth, over here." The group turned towards him. Scheuch removed his hand from his face and sniffled, "My concern is how do we test if he's immune to the air without killing him?"

I watched as they all remained silent, lost in thought. Kim was the first to suggest something, but it was so stupid that I can't even remember it. However, it did spark an idea for me.

I swiftly turned around, looking at Seth closely. "Wait!" I exclaimed. "Have you had any hallucinations at all?"

"What do you mean?" he replied softly. "From being locked up for this long?"

"Bad question," I nodded. "Okay, how about any *nosebleeds?*"

He nodded. "A few. My brother would get them too."

"What does that have to do with anything?" Candreva asked.

"Think about it," I turned around smiling. "It's something we've all had in common since the crash! We can take that chance, can we?"

"How are you so enthusiastic about this?" Yanes asked me. "We're being hunted here."

He said it like it was my fault we were, although I'm sure he didn't mean to. I know he knows that whether I let Benny kill Sterling or not, the warriors would still be upset because we took over their street and ruined their chamber of roamers.

"Are you sure you're able to do this, Mj?" Yanes asked concernedly. "Don't you need time to grieve Klein?"

I made a face, looking over at Maxwell then back at him. "No?"

They all looked at me like they didn't believe me, which pissed me off. Yanes narrowed his eyes on me. "Then why are you still wearing his clothes?"

I looked down at the thin, maroon t-shirt I've tied up to fit me better. I scrunch my face up, "What? His *clothes* didn't do anything to me?"

This meeting went on for another fifteen-some-minutes, and it still went nowhere. The decision was still up for debate. I know Maxwell, Watkins, and Bailey are definitely adamant about going; and Candreva's just a natural worrier, always reading between the lines. I know Kim said something about how *this might not be the best way to approach this, and that we should probably try to reason with them maturely*—like *yes, girl!* In the current society we live in, *yes!* That's the *best* possible decision we can make!

Jeez, and I thought *I* was dumb.

When the meeting ended, I walked out with Sully, who asked me how I was doing. ~~I've been avoiding her how I used to avoid Conti.~~ I looked over at her, replying with a rather simple reply, and as expected, she didn't believe me. We were walking the opposite way of Scheuch and Watkins.

"Why can't you realize she just wants somebody to talk to?" Watkins looked down at the pavement as he walked.

"What?" Scheuch replied.

"I don't think she's interested in anything else?"

"I'm not sure—if—I'm the best *alternative*," Scheuch replied. "Why can't she just talk to her friends? Wouldn't it be easier to do all this—*girl-talk*—if it's with actual girls?"

"Yeah, but she tells me the girls here only talked to her to entertain themselves, and she doesn't like it," Watkins replied. "She wants to prove she's more than that, y'know?"

"Then *you* talk to her."

Watkins sighed annoyedly, "You're missing my point here."

"That is?"

"She enjoyed talking to *you*. I wanted *you* to care."

"*Then* she's in bad luck here," Scheuch shrugged nonchalantly, causing Watkins to sigh in defeat.

"You remind me so much of my brother."

Scheuch quickly changed the subject. "Hey, how's it going with um—" he wiped his nose, sniffling, "Avery—and all that?"

Watkins looked away, watching Sully and I enter my bar from across the street. "I'm over her," he looked back at Scheuch, watching him raise his eyebrows. "Completely," he sniffled, looking down at his sneakers under the stormy sky. "It hurt me a lot when she stopped talking to me, but honestly that was all I needed," he explained. "I needed her to hurt me to get past her."

"Do—Do you think it's good to feel this way after she—"

"I've done a lot to make up for what I did and I understand I hurt her really badly—but she hurt me too," he explained. "But it's all in the past now, and that's where I'm leaving it."

Scheuch nodded. "I'm glad—" he said, "*that*—you're doing better."

Scheuch wasn't wrong. It *was* a better idea to talk to someone other than him. It wasn't easier, though.

"What do you think about Scheuch wanting to go to New Jersey?" Sully asked as I made my way around the counter, grabbing a water bottle.

"I'm honestly down," I replied, opening it. "I'm sick of living off canned fruit and stale chips—and lemme tell you, these warriors aren't messin' around!" I sighed. "We have no idea how much they truly outnumber us, and we don't *have* the ammunition."

"I was hoping someone could talk to him more about it," she replied. "I'm wondering how we're going to pack up and leave without the warriors seeing us, and a lot of us aren't comfortable leaving without Sergeant."

"I'm sure he'll listen to *you?*" I muttered, shrugging.

"Hey! What's *that* supposed to mean?"

~~Just looking at her makes my heart break.~~

"He didn't tell you?" I asked.

"N-No-?"

"How much do you know?"

"I know—that things are *tense* and people can tell something happened?"

"Great," I forced a smile on my face. "Good to know."

I sat myself down on my bed beside her, looking at the wall.

"How long?"

"Um," she rubbed her forehead. "I mean, back in school he used to tell me he thought it was weird you kept asking him for help on homework that was easy."

I snickered softly. "He saw through that, huh?"

"Yeah, I always figured you were way smarter than you present yourself to be," she replied, turning to me. "Why do you do that?"

"Do what?"

"Why do you let people think you're less intelligent if intelligence is so important to you?" she asked.

"Because I've lost the ability to determine if someone's a good person or not," I replied. "A part of me sees the worst in them, and the other part of me sees their potential disguised as their *good*. Making myself come off as naive will let people think they can walk all over me, and the second they do, I go." I sighed. "It's better than sitting here wonderin' what I did wrong."

I *am* sitting here wondering what I did wrong.

I never saw anything in him. I only saw possibilities, possibilities *he* promised.

"It was different with him," I quickly said, my voice breaking a little. "I just liked hearing him talk."

She sat there, hesitating. "Do-Do you like——*love* him?"

I widened my eyes. *"What?"*

"Like—are you like—in—*love* with *him?"*

I stared back at her. "Nah," I choked. "I mean, I love him how I love *you?"* I shrugged. "If that's what you're asking."

"Ah, nevermind." She smiled softly. "I hope you guys resolve it soon. I like it better when we're all getting along!" she sighed. "I think he just got nervous and thought you really liked him or something. He's not really good at that kind of stuff."

I narrowed my eyes, looking over at her. "What—"

~~Is it really that obvious?!~~ *I didn't want him to think that.*

"He's *smart*, Mj," she chuckled awkwardly. "He sees the way you look at him."

I melted into my hands, scoffing. "Who the hell acts like that when they think someone likes them?!"

"Well, would you want to date him?"

"I-don't—*know?!*" I exclaimed, so vibrant that I had to quickly correct myself. I thought it was rude for me to say that. I'm sure any girl would be lucky to date Aaron Scheuch.

That girl is not me.

"Again, he's not good at that stuff. *Look* at him."

~~Look at what happened to Shelly.~~

It didn't take us long to switch subjects because I know boy-talk doesn't really interest her. Boy-talk has never really interested me either.

"*Oh! My boyfriend, this. My boyfriend, that!*"

Shut up!

But we've been there for each other lately. She's been spending the night here with me since she and Candreva broke up.

Because truth be told, I've actually been close with Sully for a while—not just since our conversation today or the one around the fire the night I left. I got close to her the night Aaron left. She heard me crying from my room and went to check on me with Maxwell.

But I don't acknowledge it.

I refuse to admire her the same way I used to admire Conti due to the fear of our relationships turning out the same way, and I'm left feeling betrayed. I refuse to acknowledge how good of a friend she is, how loyal she is, and how quick she is to drop anything for me. I refuse to think of the numerous times she let me cry in her arms, and *she* cared. *She* cared when nobody did, and I can't even look at her because the first thought that comes into my head isn't, "Oh, that's my best friend, Mary."

The first thing I think of is, "Aaron likes her more than me."

Every compliment she gives me feels like a bullet to my chest. Every hug she gives me suffocates me in guilt that I feel this way in the first place. Every time I look at her I just pick her apart, then pick myself apart, and I wonder why can't I just be her?

~~Why can't I be her?~~ What is wrong with me?

Johnson was right.

There is something seriously wrong with me.

"The hell's that?" I quickly shot up from my spot, looking out the window. It was dark and thundering outside now, so seeing a white light flashing from the barriers was rather alarming.

Sully squinted beside me, looking at the silhouette roughly climbing over the barriers. I didn't think twice before snatching the pistol from my nightstand and storming downstairs. She followed after me doing the same.

With my gun held up firmly, we quickly but cautiously approached the silhouette, the silhouette who we thought was the one warrior reporting back to all of them. The rain made it hard to see.

"DON'T SHOOT!" The feminine voice frantically spoke through the mask. "DON'T!"

She flung off her mask, breathing in the poisonous air as the rain above dampened her wavy, light brown hair.

"Zoey?" I lowered my gun, my eyes darting to the warrior symbol on her uniform.

"Can we go inside first? I think it's raining," she said jokingly.

(If you haven't caught on, it was pouring rain.)

We brought her inside, and despite how much we trusted her, we still searched her head to toe for any listening devices. I sat her down after giving her a change of clothes.

"You're immune to the air!" I exclaimed curiously.

She nodded.

"How?" I asked.

"I don't know," she replied. "I always kept it a secret from Gideon-"

"Who's Gideon?" Sully asked.

"Our leader," she sighed nervously. Sully noticed and gave her water. "They're obsessed with finding immunity to the air."

My head snapped to Sully. "That's—why-"

"My dad—I mean—*Sergeant*," she began explaining quickly. "He went back to find me after realizing my people kidnapped your people, but they took him!" She sniffled. "They think that since he was enlisted or somethin', he knows something they don't."

"Shit, and it wouldn't help his case considering he's immune too," I rubbed my hands down my face. "Fuck!"

Our heads darted towards the door creaking open. It was Scheuch. He took a glance at Zoey and didn't think twice.

"Pack bags," he said, looking at all the scattered items in my room; my room that once was cleaned spotless. "We don't have time to goof off. Leave unimportant things behind."

We stared back at him like he was speaking a different language, but he didn't care. He was sleep-deprived, malnourished, and grumpy.

"We leave first thing in the morning," he ordered. "0400."

Judging by his demeanor, we could tell how much the others were arguing with him on this.

"And I don't care what you guys have to say about it," he spat sternly, "we're going."

17 hey, texan

"Did you just say Station 45?" Zoey gasped, her eyes wide. "No! No! It's a trap! Don't *go!*"

She rushed up the aisle, looking at the terrified looks on both Maxwell and Watkins' faces, hands on each of their seats.

"What do you mean?" Maxwell asked.

"It's a trap they set up!" She snatched the walkie from the dashboard, pushing the button vigorously. "Hello? Mj!"

I only heard static from my end.

I wish I would've paid attention.

I was too busy bitchin' with Scheuch in the front seat.

SEPTEMBER 11 2022 / FIVE HOURS EARLIER

"The seating is assigned," I announced to the group, looking up to only see a couple of them really listening, but I didn't like it when Scheuch had to tell them to *fall in.*

Seeing the group in formation, standing at the position of attention, is the ~~corniest fuckin' thing ever.~~

No wonder why people back in school bullied us.

"Why would seats matter at this point?" Kim asked.

I watched them all mope and yawn under the chilly moonlight from being woken up so early, and I tried not to let my frustration take hold of me. Cadets like Kim, cadets like *them,* don't understand the urgency of this situation. We are hunted. We are targeted. There are no resources or any other rational solution. What were we supposed to do? File a restraining order?

"It'd be a horrible idea to group the strongest cadets together," I explained nonchalantly. "What would happen if Scheuch, Yanes, Candreva, Bailey, and Watkins were all in one car, and something were to happen to us in the other?"

~~You're being too chatty.~~

"So we always rely on the boys, that's what you're saying." She twisted my words.

"I don't see a reason not to. This isn't about who has what genital and who doesn't, Kim!" My voice angered. I quickly took a deep breath. "Most of these *warriors* and roamers are twice the size and height as me, so *yes,* forgive me for feeling safer if someone a little bigger than me is around to assist!" I quickly leaned to my side, sighing with one hand on my forehead and the other on my hip.

Maxwell stepped in, gently grabbing the note from my hand. She cleared her throat and read. "Kim, you're going in the RV with me," she looked up. "Watkins, looks like *you're* driving this time."

She paused to let them haul in more luggage.

"Hey, Quinn, you got Coco, right?" I whispered.

"Yep, she's in her cage in the RV," he nodded.

"Alright, thank you," I smiled as Maxwell sniffled, wiping the blood from her nose.

"Candreva, Scheuch, and Bui?" she chuckled, muttering through her teeth. "*That* sounds like a fun car ride!"

"Carry on with it, Kiara," Kim rolled her eyes.

"Which car?" Scheuch asked calmly.

"Yanes, Bailey, Sully—and, *Seth,* right?" she announced, looking up to see Seth nodding. "You four are in the black one."

"Got it," Yanes nodded as he caught the keys being tossed towards him.

"Where—Who am I going with?" ~~Zoey~~ Rogers asked.

"RV," Maxwell motioned her hands, welcoming her in. "Let's go, everyone. Chop, chop!"

"Maxwell," Scheuch repeated calmly. "Which car is it?"

"Red," she replied, hopping in. "The one with the shattered window."

Damn.

Scheuch and I agreed that it would be smarter to go one vehicle at a time. It'd be rather suspicious to just up and leave all at once. Doing so could potentially prompt whoever was watching us to report back to Gideon, so we decided on hour-and-a-half intervals.

"Mj, can I go with you?" Sully whispered. "I don't want to be the only girl in my car."

I looked past her shoulder, seeing Yanes and Bailey enter the black car with Seth. I could tell by the way they were play-fighting that they were taking this as an opportunity to get to know Seth better, and perhaps *apologize,* but Sully was too calm for them. She liked the quiet.

"Yeah, that's fine," I replied, "but remember that Brody's in this car."

"Oh *yeah...*" she thought, "well, he did say after the move, he wanted to like—try to make amends and sort things out? Maybe this could be a—little *baby step!*"

I blinked blankly. "Alright. C'mon, our car leaves first."

I sat with my knees propped up, clenching my jaw. Sully and Candreva were in the back, getting cozy with blankets and pillows. It was going to be a long car ride, for sure. I didn't bring anything but Tyson's clothes and a plush he once bought to win me back. I left everything else behind.

Even my paints. Even my journal.

Scheuch entered the front seat, looking up at Sully and Candreva through the rearview mirror blankly. He looked over at me before starting up the vehicle.

"There is some water in the trunk," he said, gulping quietly. "Let me know if you want me to stop and get you any."

I scratched my head, looking at myself in the side-view mirror. I quickly looked back at him. "Me?"

"I was talking to Sully, but that pertains to you too."

~~Oh, I thought you couldn't be as nice to me as you are to her!~~

I quickly tightened up, subtly embarrassed. We continued on with the rest of the car ride silent. I managed the car sickness with the help of the air blowing against my face, so thanks, Person B, for doing that, I guess.

He would rather sit in silence. That's fine. ~~He could've just told me that. I watch Mary start conversations with him every day.~~ I'm pretty used to doing that. I used to do it all the time with Tyson.

The RV left last with Watkins driving and Maxwell beside him, handling directions with Kim and Zoey in the back. I imagine that car ride to be just as awkward as this one, but honestly, I'd rather listen to the way Scheuch talks to Sully than Kim complain about how bored she is.

"Hey Aaron," Candreva snickered.

We were on hour three. I was, in fact, thirsty and nauseous. I was breathing heavily, turning damn near green, but I refused to ask him to stop.

Why?

"Mary, are you sure you don't want me to stop?"

"No, it's fine."

That's why.

"Hey *Aaron!*"

I didn't have to turn my head and look to know he was rolling his eyes. Candreva snickered so hard, he snorted. "Did you hear—that—Oxygen and Potassium went on a date?"

"OK."

"Oh."

The car became deathly silent. I wouldn't have minded it, but Sully tapped me lightly on the shoulder. "Please say something," she whispered.

I shrugged, mumbling. "I don't know?"

"Ooh, I know another one," Candreva jumped up. "Aaron, what do you do when you lose an electron?"

...

"You have to keep an ion it!"

Scheuch turned silently, still driving down the clustered highway, and stared at him. Sully leaned closer to him, smiling widely. "I see a smirk," she giggled, turning to Candreva. "Do you see a smirk?"

I crumpled the paper map in my hands, realizing now that I lied. I'd much rather be in any other space than confined here.

"Do *you* get it, Mj?" she chuckled softly.

RECONCILIATION

I nodded silently. They both stopped and soaked in the awkwardness.

"A car ride with Arrogant Aaron and Miserable Michelle," Candreva shook his head disappointedly, sitting back in his seat. "Ain't this fun."

"Don't call me that," Scheuch and I both scoffed, turning around and glaring back at him.

I chuckled a bit at the way our tones matched as I turned forward, shaking my head.

"*What* was that Michelle?"

"Don't fucking call me Michelle," I snapped at him again, nauseous. "I'm not in the mood right now."

"Brody, stop," Sully sighed.

"Sorry, not the time?" Candreva nodded. "Here's some water."

"There are better ways of addressing things, Bui," Scheuch said as I grabbed the bottle from him. "There is no need to speak with a hostile attitude, let alone use profanity."

"*My bad,* Aaron." I sipped.

He snapped his head towards me, so fast that it nearly made me flinch and spill the water all over myself. "*Who?*"

I turned to him, eyes widened. "You?"

"*What* did you just call me?"

I held in my laugh. "My bad, *Scheuch.*"

"Oh *here* we go," Candreva sighed quietly behind us.

"Sorry, the circumstances of this situation right now might restrict my ability to be *fucking* friendly, *Scheuch,*" I sneered, although most of my words cut out due to the *speed bumps* we drove over—or at least I *wanted* them to be speed bumps. They were dead roamers.

"I don't care how bad a situation can be, as a responsible cadet, you should discipline yourself enough to not *lash out* at those around you!" he snapped back.

"Yeah, you would know a lot about that," I scoffed, "and I don't know *who* you're talking to like that, but I know it ain't me!"

"Guys, pleas—" Sully gasped softly.

"Just let them resolve it," Candreva replied.

"No—I hate it when they fight!"

I immediately burst out laughing, and then into tears.

"Resolve?!" I laughed, then laughed even harder, and harder, until my face was in my hands and Sully was looking at me with softened eyes.

"I don't understand what it is that you want of me," Scheuch gripped the steering wheel tighter, glaring over at me. "I can't change the way I am."

"I'm not asking you to," I cried softly. "God, that's the *last* thing I want you to do."

I heard him sigh. "Tell me what you need me to do so we can drop this and move on."

I felt a punch to my stomach. "I know what I want," I gulped, "I just can't ask that from you."

"And that is?"

I'M. SORRY. Two words. *I'm sorry.*

I want you to *want* to.

I want you to look me in the eyes and tell me you understand how you've hurt me and that you *apologize* 'cause I *know* you do and I *know* you want to. I *know* by the way you've been looking at me lately that *you know* what you did, and *you know* how much I miss you, and *you know* you wish you said things differently, *so why aren't you saying it?*

God, I just want you to tell me it was all a misunderstanding.

But I refuse to pour my heart out just to give you another opportunity to rub it in my face that you don't care about me.

I should probably leave it alone, leave *you* alone. It is selfish of me to ask so much out of you. If I refuse to accommodate any of the others, what makes myself in the equation any different? Why should *you* accommodate my heartache? It's not *your* fault you feel the way you feel about me? It's not your fault I can't change?

So why are we here? Why do you act like a part of you still cares, and why am I letting it hold such a tight grip on me?

I never let boys humble me, *never*.

What the hell did you do to me... *Fuck!*

Scheuch began driving off the road. I felt the air against my face as he stomped on the gas. I picked up the walkie as we flew, communicating with Yanes and Bailey.

"What is it?" Sully bent herself around, looking out the rear window. "Aaron, what did you *see?!*"

"They found us," he swerved through the trees, making me have to grip onto the middle compartment to hold on.

BANG!

We all flinched. Scheuch swerved to the left, and then to the right, rocking the four of us back and forth.

"SCHEUCH, WATCH OUT!" I yelled as Scheuch quickly swerved out of the black vehicle's way—a black car that we know for a fact was not Yanes and Bailey's—and crashed into a tree.

I lifted my head sorely. My fingers traced along the blood running from my nose.

"Are you okay?" Candreva worried behind me.

"Yeah, I'm fine," Sully wiggled out from his arms, barely bruised from being shielded by him. I grunted as I felt Scheuch turn to me.

"Pinch your nose to stop the bleeding," he said calmly. "Pinching puts pressure on the blood vessels and helps stop the blood flow."

"I think it's a little *broken*, jackass!" I snapped as he reached over, turning my face toward him gently. I thawed immediately, sniffling shakily as he examined my nose, looking at the swelling and the subtle crookedness.

He shook his head. "I'm sorry" he stammered, "—guys," he quickly turned towards the two in the back, letting go of my face. "I—I should've looked."

"The hell were you speeding from anyway? For Pete's sake, you could've killed one of us!" He rubbed the back of his neck, muttering under his breath. "Guess I gotta hotwire another car now."

"Get down!" We ducked as gunshots began firing through the rear window, covering our heads with our hands as glass shards showered us. We lay there still, even minutes after it stopped.

Scheuch sniffled roughly, squirming out of his position and out of the car.

"Stay close. Stay quiet. Don't be stupid," he ordered quietly as he pulled out his handgun, feet sticking to the mud beneath him.

I prepared to do the same, stepping out of the car quietly to scout for the warriors. They were everywhere, coming from all directions.

"Shoot at anything that moves," Scheuch ordered. "I know the fog kinda fucks you up but—" He shot, listening for the distant *plop*.

I haven't had a good night's sleep since getting abducted. I sleep clutched onto my plush. If it's a bad night, a pillow. I wake up in the middle of the night with clammy hands, a cold sweat, and heavy breathing, essentially waking Sully up too. My night terrors had gotten worse, so bad that some nights I'd refuse to go to sleep in fear of attracting roamers with the sound of my screaming.

I was scared those few days. I was so, so scared.

A state so vulnerable that I had no possible idea what they were going to do to me. That was scary to me. I was scared for my life.

But after today, it's safe to say I felt a greater fear than that.

I was scared for his.

I was scared, watching a warrior swing Scheuch around, throwing him onto the ground, but before I could do anything, a female warrior yanked me by my hair.

"Drop it." I recognized her voice. This was the same one that took me that night.

I instinctively swung at her, pistol still in hand, hitting her good in the head, nearly knocking her gas mask off. She grunted as we tumbled onto the ground, rolling back and forth. More warriors appeared. Soon, they had us all on the ground, throwing punches like it would've done anything.

I was on top of mine. I've knocked her mask off by now, allowing me to finally see her face-to-face.

She was my age, possibly younger. It was weird to think that in another world, we would be sharing homework answers, but in this one, I was reaching for the knife in my sheath to stab her; because if I didn't, she would.

"No—NO!" She grunted frantically, grabbing my wrist.

I stared blankly through her eyes of terror, freezing once I felt the muzzle of a rifle tap against the back of my head. I exhaled slowly, feeling her squirm below me.

"Do *not* shoot her!" I immediately heard Rodney's voice order. "Gideon specifically wants *her* alive!"

I dropped the knife in my hand shakily, feeling the girl loosen her grip. *She doesn't want to do this any more than I do.*

"You hear me?" Rodney ordered. He was shouting orders to all of them now. "None of these bastards will be killed today, warriors!"

The girl rolled me over on my back, punching me in the face twice. I groaned, rubbing my throbbing jaw softly. Rodney then stepped over, grabbed me by my collar, dragged me across the muddy ground like a rag doll, and threw me into the circle with the rest of them. I pulled up my jeans and wiped the blood from my nose as we were all ordered to sit on our knees and remain in the spot where we were placed. It didn't take long for them to reveal their objective by dragging Sgt Rogers out to us the same way, placing him in front of us.

"There is a clear difference between you people—and —*our*—people," a tall, slim, caucasian male began speaking. This was Gideon. We could just tell.

He crouched down, rifle in his hands, smiling at Sully.

"Would you be a dear, and tell me what that is?"

Sully glared up nervously, hands shakily placed in her lap as her weapons were being kicked away. "You guys are wearing masks and we aren't?"

"*Bingo!*" Gideon stood back up, celebrating.

He stepped over to Scheuch next to her, tilting his head a bit.

"You're a very strange-looking individual."

DO. NOT. LAUGH.

Scheuch looked up nonchalantly. "Cool."

Gideon made an appalled face, looking up at his fellow comrades. "Did this bastard just ask me, *who?*"

"I didn't say *who* I said *cool*," he replied.

I clench my jaw. Gideon made a face at me.

"Something funny, bitch?" He sneers as he kicks Scheuch in the jaw, wiping the smirk off my face as I watch him thud onto the ground. He began circling us like a maniac.

"Now it has come to my attention, your group is immune to the radiation that's out here kicking *our* asses," his voice spoke eerily through the mask. "Why is that?"

"Couldn't tell ya," Candreva glared up at him, keeping his breathing steady.

We side-eyed each other, thinking the same thing. *Y'all should've listened to me. We should've listened to you.*

"Funny, that's what your buddy, Sergeant Rogers, over here's been tellin' us too!" Gideon chuckled charmingly. "It's starting to make me wonder if y'all are immune to the ghouls out here too."

I glanced over at Scheuch, who was still lying on his back, groaning softly. I subtly leaned over, pulling down his black t-shirt, covering the bite scars that trailed along his abdomen.

"That's what I'm callin' you from now on, Four-Eyes," Gideon looked over as Scheuch bent back up, rubbing his jaw. "A Ghoul."

"Gotcha," he replied nonchalantly.

I sat still, using my peripherals, tuning out Gideon's bullshit to listen around me. Listen for *anything* around me. Anything.

Anything to escape because I simply refuse to die here, to die like this.

It didn't take me long to realize Bailey, Yanes, and Seth had caught up to us, realizing what was happening.

Gideon sniffled roughly, crouching down in front of me. We read each other's eyes. Mine a fierce, yet blank brown and his, a spine-chilling blue through the lens of his mask. I inhaled slowly, as a way to brag, maybe to distract him from a portion of his warriors leaving the premises to hunt the three. I could hear them hiding behind trees and bushes, strategically shooting and killing a couple at a time with the silencers.

Damn, those silencers are a lifesaver. Glad Watkins found them.

"You can hurt me all you want, but it won't bring Benny back to life," I said.

"Oh honey, I know it won't," he sneered, "and not only did you kill him—but——when I sent out two men from my group about a month later——they didn't come back."

Person A and Person B.

"Know anything about that?" he asked me, tilting his head eerily. "It wasn't till I found them on Route 76. Gunshot wound. Stabbed to death."

I didn't answer. Only stared with hatred, deep deep deep hatred. He nodded, and by the way he did, I knew he was smiling.

"I know hurting you won't do any damage," he swiftly lifted his hand, gripping my face tightly, *right* were my face was throbbing earlier, "but... thanks to some newfound information," he looked over, naturally causing me to do so too, "I strike you as a person who'd care if *we*... hurt *them*."

Sterling stood with a rifle in hand, wearing *their uniform*, looking at us without saying a single word. I looked at him wide-eyed, and so did the rest of them. Betrayal. That was all I felt.

I felt it in my veins, not my heart. I felt anger chill up my spine, taunting me, not anguish hollowing my stomach from the inside out. After all I did for that motherfucker, are you serious?

ARE YOU SERIOUS?

He blinked twice, still staring blankly at me, and then I understood. I understood faster than anybody.

I flinched as the warrior behind me hit Candreva in the head, causing him to fall forward. My body began shriveling. Sully began screaming, watching three of them beat him up on the ground.

"STOP! *STOP* IT!" She screamed as another warrior came up behind Scheuch, shoving him forward and submerging his face into the mud.

Fuck. Fuck. Fuck!

I watch in horror as Scheuch's body squirmed helplessly, the bubbles gurgle rapidly. I clench my fists, lowering my head to my knees, violently shutting my eyes.

Shit. Shit. Shit!

"*OKAY!*" I shouted, thrusting out all the air that was left in my lungs. The warriors stopped, letting Candreva lay there groaning and Scheuch wipe the mud off his face, regaining his breath. I exhaled, crying softly.

"Okay," I lift my head and wipe my nose. I shivered in terror, realizing the reason why they haven't batted much of an eye towards Sully and I, and only hurt the boys. They were saving us for later, later as in when they are done with us here and ready to bring us back to the facility for further questioning.

"Okay what?" Rodney urged. "What *is* it?"

"We aren't lying when we say we don't know why we're immune," I explained, "but when we woke up to the outbreak, we were in a plane crash six months prior."

He paused, looking at me. "Are you fuckin' with me, Mj?"

"No."

"What the *hell* are you saying then?"

"I'm saying we crashed in March and woke up in August," I spat, "and we've been nothin' but *screwed* up since!"

He kicked me in my face and I groaned. I opened my eyes to Scheuch's arm guarding me. I looked at him with softened eyes as he glared up at him with mud smeared down his face.

"It's true!" he said.

"We are *asking you* how the *hell* you are capable of being out in this type of radiation and the best you can give me is some *supernatural* time jump y'all woke up from two years ago?!" Rodney scoffed, turning away muttering. "Dumb Asian bitch!"

"Yeah, *fuck* you too!" I spat out blood as Scheuch cautiously lowered his arm. "If it's making you lose that much sleep, how 'bout you just do the world a big ol' favor and go *kill yourself!*"

Sully screamed as the warrior behind Candreva began hitting him again, nearly fracturing his shoulder. I figured I should shut the hell up now, but I just couldn't help myself.

"And what about the roamers then?" Rodney turned back around, glaring at me and Scheuch. "So what? Does that mean you're immune to the virus too?"

We knew the answer to that one. We just weren't giving it.

"How about instead of interrogating people you *think* know the answers to your problems," I snarked, "you go and bring your little warriors out on a field trip and actually try to figure shit out."

"Don't be a smart-ass—" Rodney came charging at me before Candreva and Sergeant stepped in.

"Okay, STOP!" Candreva insisted, holding out his hand.

I chuckled, licking the blood trickling down from my nose.

Gideon stared at me, amused. He looked up and over at all his followers. "May I have a word with you all?" He turned to Sterling. "You. Karlee. Watch these five."

He stepped away with Rodney, James, and April and a good bit of them to *discuss*. That left us kneeling with Sterling and his girlfriend guarding us, and when I say I've never been so uncomfortable in my life, I mean it.

Karlee smiled through her mask. Even though we couldn't see it, we knew she was. She was swaying side-to-side, finger trailing along the trigger.

"Hey Texan," she said.

He turned.

"Wanna go do some' later?" she asked flirtatiously. "You sure know how to kiss, lemme tell you that."

"Oh, you *gotta* be kidding me," Sergeant muttered.

Scheuch and I eyed each other, and then Sully and I did, and then Sully and Candreva did, and then Sergeant and I did, and then Sergeant and Scheuch did. We were all forced to kneel there, listening to these two knuckleheads flirt like pubescent middle schoolers for the next ten minutes, rambling about hockey and Texas and country music and cowboy hats and more hockey and more Texas and more music and cowboy boots and

I can't do this anymore!!!

"Warriors!" Gideon ordered. "Take these five back to Facility A—send them straight to laboratory for testing," he said, making me immediately turn to Sergeant, seeing the needle scars along his arms.

"We're not immune," I confessed. "There's no use keeping us like lab rats. You're not going to get anything!"

"You're a lying—littl—"

"Alright, what's the *DAMN* point of asking these questions if you're not gonna believe a word I say anyway?" I rolled my eyes.

My body curled up in pain once the warrior behind me kicked me forward, rolling me over and striking me in the stomach. His hand jerked up to my throat, shoving my face into the ground with his muddy fingers in my mouth, choking me.

Sully panicked with tears streaming down her face. "Stop it! You're going to *kill her!*"

"That's *enough!*" Sergeant shouted. *"Stop!"*

"Don't get cocky now," Rodney told the warrior.

I laid there and just took it, how I take everything; hitting at his shoulders, legs squirming beneath me, gagging with the earthy taste soaking into my tongue, but then I realized what advantage I had in that moment that he didn't.

I came straight for his mask, prying it off his head, which immediately loosened his grip. I held it up in the air, watching the terror grow in his eyes. I for sure didn't know how deadly the radiation was out here. It didn't *pertain* to me, but it certainly did to him. At least five warrior's aimed their weapons at me with Gideon ordering them not to shoot.

"Give it back!" The warrior shouted angrily.

I grinned as I threw it to the side, making him go and fetch for it, which gave Scheuch time to turn and reach up, doing the same to the warrior behind him.

I came straight for my gun, grabbing it and shooting the warriors coming for Sully and Scheuch. Then I found myself shooting more, and more, and more, giving Sergeant and Candreva time to do the same. I crawled over to the nearest roamer, picking up their rifle.

"BUI!" Sergeant called as I turned, throwing it to him swiftly.

That's where the chaos began. The warriors quickly scurried around, struggling to find their masks. We quickly scattered out through the woods, shooting at anything coming at us.

"FIND THEM, BOYS!" I heard Gideon's voice call as I hid behind a tree, grasping the two pistols in my hands tightly. I had lost Sully and Candreva by now. I thought I was alone 'till Scheuch came sprinting over, nearly tripping over himself as he hid alongside me behind a tree.

"Bailey's coming in," he said. "Trunk and doors will be open. Once he drives by, jump in. No funny business."

I giggled. "You saying *funny business* is funny," I said, turning over, shooting a couple warriors dead.

"Where's Brody?" he asked.

"I lost him and Mary about twenty meters back," I panted, looking up at him. "Brody got shot—or—*stabbed*—I don't kno-"

Our bodies pressed against the bark roughly. My eyes widened with his palm over my mouth, silencing me. I heard the threatening footsteps too as we eyed each other nervously, communicating through our eyes. For the first time in a long time, I was grateful we were able to do that.

We both turned, shooting rapidly before he turned, pushing me forward. We ran and ran and ran, hopping over fallen trees and crouching behind bushes.

"Shit!" I grunted as I tripped over a tree root, falling onto my knees forcefully. He stopped and looked back, seeing the five—six—possibly seven warriors scouring the woods for us. He rolled me over gently.

"What's wrong? What's wrong?" He asked quietly.

"My ankle," I whimpered.

"Shit," he looked up, looking at the couple of dead roamers laying limp a few feet away from us. He let out a quick exhale, looking back down at me. "Do you trust me?" he asked as he quickly readjusted me, piling me with sticks and leaves. He laid himself beside me before dragging a couple roamers over, laying them on top of us.

"Aw *man*," I groaned quietly in disgust.

"Sh!" He scooched uncomfortably as we laid limp and silent, watching the warriors pass us one by one in our peripherals.

I held my breath, trying not to shake, not even realizing I've subconsciously grasped onto his hand, squeezing it tightly. He squeezed my hand back to tell me when the last warrior passed. He shot up, shoving the roamer's corpse off of him.

"Are you able to run on your ankle?" he asked, pushing the corpse off of me.

I panted, my hand on his arm, "Yeah, it's fine." I pushed myself off the ground, unbalanced with the foot for a second. "C'mon, I saw Sully running that way!"

We found her fighting off three warriors by herself. Once she turned and saw us, she cried. "I lost Brody!" She held onto my shoulders, shaking me. "I don't know what to do. I *have* to go back!"

"We can't—" Scheuch replied as he was scanning around.

"We *have* to!"

"We *can't!*" he scolded, grabbing her.

She screamed his name as he dragged her away, screaming in a certain, excruciating way words can't explain. She squirmed in his arms, fighting to be set free.

I've never seen Sully angry with my own two eyes. That's what made her so terrifying. Everything she did, from the way she spoke and the way she carried herself, was rich with tenderness. She was always calm and content. Her actions were always so soft. She always had a smile on her face and a faint spark in her eyes. That's what made her so nice to look at.

Now imagine her pointing a gun at you. Eyes as cold as mine.

Terrifying.

She shoved Scheuch away the second he put her down. It was a small, rather gentle shove, but it was the intention behind it that counted.

She cried aloud, hitting him. "He's gonna *die!*"

"He will be fine," Scheuch ~~replied firmly~~ spoke in a whisper.

"I have to go back!"

"Mary, just *think*." He grabbed her shoulder and pulled her back. She stood there glaring at him for a bit before storming the other way. He looked at the ground before looking back up at her.

"I—I'll go back for him!" he stammered. "*Mary!*"

She turned around.

"I'll go back," he slipped his gun out his holster before running off again. *I didn't follow him this time.*

I stood quietly, staring at the caterpillar wiggling onto the half-dead leaf on the ground. I felt guilty. I felt guilty that in a situation as pivotal as this, all I could regard back to was myself. I felt guilty that I couldn't even look her in the eye. I couldn't bring myself to say a single word to her.

And it's not her fault.

It's not her fault at all, so why am I taking it out on her?

"Bui," she softly said. "Mj, he would've—"

I slowly turned to her, forcing my eyes open to disguise the tears subtly forming. "I don't care about that," I replied coldly. She saw it in my face that I was lying. "Let's get outta here."

Scheuch stumbled through the trees, dodging the gunshots. He found Candreva lying on the ground against a tree just as April shot at him again, only missing him by a few inches, hitting his backpack again. He dropped to his knees, sliding towards him at the speed of light.

"Here, here," Candreva panted, pointing at the blood bleeding through his jeans on his upper thigh.

"Severed artery," Scheuch muttered to himself, quickly taking off his belt.

"I was wrong about you," Candreva winced, laying his head back on the bark as Scheuch tied a tourniquet a couple inches above the wound. "I—I always thought you were a dork—walkin' around wit' high-ass morals—" he inhaled sharply as Scheuch pulled his gun out his holster, shooting at the warriors coming closer, "—like you were——better than all of us."

Scheuch looked back down at him. "My morals are anything *but* high," he muttered, patting his left thigh twice. "C'mon!"

He grunted, lifting Candreva up and over his shoulders; into a fireman's carry.

I jump into the trunk of the black car, quickly shutting it by clicking the red button above us. Sully and I continued shooting back at the warriors as Yanes drove away.

"Use the rifles!" Bailey was back there with us too, making room for Sergeant and Seth, and soon Candreva and Scheuch.

"That way!" Sergeant guided in the front passenger seat.

"I don't know how to use that?" I panicked, as the car slowed. I turned to see Scheuch toss Candreva into the backseat with him screaming in pain, spurting blood, slamming the door shut.

"Drive!" he ordered, hitting the back of his seat aggressively. "Let's *GO!*"

"This whole *time?*" Bailey widened his eyes.

"Y'all wouldn't teach me!" I shouted as I shot.

"Magazine goes here—" Bailey showed me quickly.

Sully shot as a car followed us, speeding faster and faster.

"Release is here," he said. "Make sure it latches—hold back the—*blah blah*—rod—rounds speed up—*blah blah*—" He handed it to me swiftly to hold up his own.

Sully flinched, ducking down as they shot back at us.

"Squeeze the trigger for rapid fire!" He said as he adjusted himself, aiming right at the driver. "*—NOW!*"

18 5.972×10^{24} kg

No one completely understood why, and I get that. I just know it's not hard to see how much I loved this boy just by listening to the way I talked about him, regardless of if he deserved it or not. Every day I wake up with things to tell him. Every day there's some things I wish I could've done, and things I wish I didn't. Every day I wonder if we made it in another life. Every day, I wonder if we had more time; because a part of me still thinks if we did, I could potentially love him enough so that he'd love me back.

But even with the time we had, my love was never enough.

So I sit and daydream that in another life, we have an apartment in New York and spend nights on the balcony together, looking down at the busy city; and I'm able to look at him without knowing the pain of him dying on me.

I sat on my rooftop under the moonlight with my legs propped up, chin resting on my knees. Tyson was beside me, swinging his feet below him like a kid.

"You plan on getting some sleep?" he asked.

I looked over at him, replying, "I can't."

We were all back at Jade Street, recovering. Sergeant Rogers, Yanes, Bailey, and Watkins were out on the barriers, guarding for the night. Everyone else was settling down, getting ready to rest for the night. I simply couldn't.

This was the first time I've ever hallucinated him. He looked as if he had aged with me this entire time. He was a little taller—less antsy and more mature.

He turned and looked down at me. "Stop looking at me."

"Sorry," I quickly giggled, looking away.

He smiled, lost in thought. "You ever wonder if Aaron has a Mj too?"

"A *what?*" I looked up.

"Like—a girl he talks to all the time—" he shrugged, "a girl he tells everything."

"Are you implying I'm *your* Mj?" I smiled widely. I don't know why I bothered trying to hide the look on my face. He could read me faster than anyone.

"Well did he?"

"Yeah, he did," I responded. "Look."

This was the first time I've ever hallucinated them too.

I could hear it from all the way up there, no matter how hard I tried to ignore it. I stopped looking the second I saw him pick her up by the waist and spin her around like they were in some fuck-ass movie—so much for a non-romantic.

Shelly had a witty laugh. She laughed with her mouth open, lifting up her head and squinting her eyes. She was lively. Of course, she was lively. I went to school with her too. She sat two seats behind me in English. ~~She used to make fun of me.~~

They were sitting on the porch of the pizzeria, close. She was giggling over something only she could understand, but she looked pretty doing it. With silky, olive skin, our school colors tied her long, dyed yet glossy blonde hair up in pigtails. Her ocean blue eyes glistened with a spark undeniably caused by something, *someone* that clearly made her just as happy as she made him.

Aaron was only there sitting and smiling.

She removed her arms from her knees and laid them gently on his shoulder. Resting her chin, looking at him with soft eyes. He looked down shyly, causing her to giggle a bit. She began poking his cheek with her nose.

"Stop," he smiled, looking over at her.

She patted down her cheer uniform, blowing bubbles with her gum. "Guess what?" she said, before rambling about the latest gossip.

He just sat and listened. He sat and listened in ways that proved to me there was no way he could *not know* basic social queues and dynamics, and I knew by sitting there and listening, she was both the reason he learned and the reason he stopped.

I couldn't blame him.

If I broke a heart like that, I'd hate myself too.

"Damn, she's hot," Tyson widened his eyes, looking back over at me, watching me nod and shrug. "Good for him."

"Yeah you right," I chuckled. "Do *you* think you could pull someone like her?"

"Pfft, *hell* no."

"*Even* if she liked you first?"

"Nope." He shook his head, wrapping his arms around me the second he noticed I was shivering a little. "I'd probably *try* and get to know her——end up ruining it somehow."

I rolled my eyes, resting my head on his shoulder. "Oh c'mon, they're like us—just more——gentle, I guess," I laughed softly.

I looked up to see him look back down at me confusedly.

"Didn't he fucking *eat* her?"

"That's why I laughed!"

He shook his head, hearing me giggle into his shoulder.

"He's such a nerd, bro," he sighed, smiling softly.

I never noticed that he did this, but he would always say stuff to intensify my laughter once he's already made me do so.

"He turned to me one practice and just randomly told me the mass of the Earth."

I burst out laughing. *"Really?"*

"Yes," he said. "Do *you* know the mass of the Earth?"

I narrowed my eyes on him. "No?"

"Well, just in case you need to know it someday, it's 5.972×10^{24} kilograms," he mocked in a nasally voice, adding a snort at the end of the sentence. I giggled as a couple seconds passed. He quickly took a deep sigh, rubbing his hands on my arms to keep me warm. "And whatchu mean by, they're just like us?"

"She talks a lot and he listens," I answered.

"A lot of people listen to you talk, Mj," he replied. "You never know when to shut the hell up."

I paused. "Wait really?"

He snorted softly again, rocking me side to side gently. "I'm *jokin'* bruh."

"You just *get* me," I explained, resting my head on his shoulder again.

"You got a heavy-ass head." He interrupted me, resting his onto mine.

"You got a heavy-ass head!" I snorted, taking a deep breath.

"You get me in ways no one else takes the time to—" I continued explaining, "—and I feel like we just *click,* y'know? Just like how *they* do—just a whole lot less fightin'."

"You don't know that," he scoffed softly, pausing.

I suddenly felt my heart sink, afraid that I just accidentally started an argument.

"I really did——try to become—a better person," he said.

I looked up at him confusedly.

"Really?" I beamed. "That's *good!*"

"I did it for *you.*" He told me straight, his words knocking the wind out of me. I sat there in shock, feeling my back warm.

He sighed again, looking away, wiping the lower half of his face with the palm of his hand. "You don't believe me," he said softly. "That's fine, I wouldn't believe me either."

"Um—" I replied slowly. "It's *okay,* Tyson. We both made a lot of mistakes—"

"I know," he nodded, "but I'm still sorry I realized I loved you too late."

I felt my entire body freeze, suddenly remembering all the bad that came with the good. Moments like these are what I hold onto. Moments where it really felt like he could change, like he *would've* changed, but moments like these come with consequences. Going back to him is the same as downing a bottle of liquor anticipating the morning after; sinning then feeling convicted. It heals me temporarily, but God, it tears me apart. *He* tears me apart when it's over because he always knows we always come back for more.

His presence feels like foggy autumn rain
until there's heavy thunder.
His presence feels warm
until it is suffocating.
His presence means so much to me
until it is too much,
and I hate it.

They give me all the reasons why he was terrible for me,
but if he was so bad, why did he make me feel so good?
Why was *he* out of all people able to bring me back to my senses
every time things felt like they were going to shit?
Why was he soothing to me, even when it eventually came down to
him stripping every part of me until he ruined everything.

God, I wanted it to be him.
I wanted it to be him more than anything.

"Why'd you have to die on me?" I began crying.

He looked at me with softened eyes, looking away. "I don't know."

I whispered. "God, I can't let you go."

"Mj—I—I didn't mean to make you cry—"

"I keep thinking that maybe—if I left *sooner*—I could've found you," I sobbed. "I could've found you, and things would be better with you here."

"Listen Mj, you're going to fall in love again someday and completely forget about me," he said. "You deserve better. I'm not a good person."

"You were just *hurting*, Tyson, I was hurting too," I sniffled as he wiped my tears gently. "I don't know how the fuck it feels to fall in love. I just know what I felt with you, that shit felt *real*. It just hurt constantly questioning if you ever loved me back."

He took a deep breath, pulling me in closer, kissing my forehead. "I did."

18 ½ where'd you find that, reddit?

"Yo Bui!" Yanes' voice called from the barriers.

I blinked, and suddenly Tyson Estright, Aaron Scheuch, and Shelly Cuvillier were gone. I looked down to see him looking back up at me, rifle in hands.

"What's up?" I replied, subtly wiping away the tears.

"You plan on doing anything?" he asked.

I paused. "Like—*tonight?*"

"No," Yanes shrugged. "Maybe in a couple days or so."

"No, I ain't got nothin' planned."

"Okay," he nodded, "meet down at the gunshop at 1900."

"O-Okay," I replied, a little confusedly.

We ended up stepping into the gunshop together to meet Scheuch, Bailey, Maxwell, and Sergeant inside.

The sunset had long gone so the moonlight lit through the cracks of the boarded up windows. There were battery-powered lanterns placed around the glass display cases along with the dinosaur figurines Sergeant had collected and decorated. He was leaning over the center one with a pen and notepad beneath him.

I could tell by Yanes' demeanor what this meeting was about.

"They're messing with the wrong fuckin' people," he muttered angrily as we approached them, placing his palm upon the cold glass. "We *gotta* fight back," he paused, looking at all of us. "What? Do you guys not agree?"

"No, we *do*, it's just—" Maxwell thought aloud with her hand on her chin, "—we have to consider how outnumbered we are."

"Lack of ammunition too," Scheuch added.

"Well, we can't just be sitting ducks, waitin' for them to come and *take* us all out!" He raised his hand, rubbing his forehead stressfully.

"We *are* built for this, we *ARE*," Sergeant explained to the five of us encouragingly. "You guys are all physically fit, strong, smart, quick on your feet—" he nodded, "you all just need to *keep in mind* how *crucial* every move you make out there is. One wrong move—
—and shit *will* go down, and we can't afford to lose any more people."

He sighed, looking down at the notepad.

"We need medical supplies—" he read aloud, "—ammunition —*gas* if we can find any that's not expired—"

"Hey, how's Candreva's leg doing?" Maxwell asked. "Do we need anything specific for his injury?"

"Um-" Scheuch wiped his nose, "the artery that is severed is rather small——I am hoping to be able to ligate it—"

They all looked at him cluelessly. Maxwell looked over at me.

"He means he could either staple or cauterize it with heat," I explained calmly. "And what about you, Sergeant? Do you need anything?"

"No, I'm fine, thank you."

"Alright, to treat a severed artery, we need sterile gloves, gauze and dressings—either/or—" Scheuch listed. "Hemostatic agents——gauze impregnated with clotting agents—"

"What's a hemostatic agent?" Maxwell asked curiously.

"It's a substance or material that helps control the bleeding, promoting blood clotting to help stop the flow of blood," I answered her.

Shit, I need to stop. I sound like a nerd.

"She is *correct!*" Scheuch nodded, pointing both index fingers at me, "And the impregnated gauze is a type of dressing that contains substances like clotting proteins or chemicals that *aid* in the clotting process."

She awkwardly smiled back at us.

"In simple terms, they stop the bleeding," I quickly said.

"Alright," Yanes nodded. "Where can we find these?"

"The closest hospital near us is *severely* overrun," Bailey shook his head. "It would be nearly impossible to bring a group in and get out alive."

"Yeah, that sounds like more of a *solo* job," Sergeant nodded. "Someone fast that can get in and out quick."

"Any medical stores nearby?" Yanes asked.

"None off the top of my head," Sergeant sighed. "Map doesn't show anything."

"What are some alternatives?" Maxwell asked. "There *has* to be an easier way to acquire these things!"

"Er—Well I would say moss or even plant leaves could work," Scheuch replied, "but we don't really have——much of those."

"Hey, what about clean cloth?" I asked.

He nudged his head. "That could work."

"Okay," Sergeant jotted down, "gloves, gauze, dressings—what else?"

"Batteries——nails—*bullets*," Bailey named.

"More antibiotics," Scheuch added. *"Food."*

"What haven't we looted yet that could have these?" Yanes thought to himself.

"Are there any schools nearby?" I asked. Yanes looked up and made a face at me. "The *nurse offices*—the *cafeteria*—"

"That's smart!" Maxwell nodded. "Bailey, look for any schools nearby!"

"What about ammunition?" Yanes asked.

"There's a police station near the nearest high school!" She clapped in excitement. "Brilliant!"

"Man, I'm still *so* disappointed the coast thing was all a hoax!" Bailey sighed, shaking his head, smiling. "We could've looted the scuba stores for chainmail suits."

Sergeant looked over confusedly. "What would those do?"

"What's a chainmail suit?" I asked.

"Y'know... the sharkproof ones," Bailey explained. "They could prevent the roamers' teeth from penetrating the skin."

"Would it reduce the *pressure?*" Scheuch asked, rather condescending.

"Ah, a human can't bite that hard."

"But these *aren't* humans, they're *roamers.*"

"Here, *I* say, we get four of us in a car tomorrow morning and drive to the coast just how we planned to!" Bailey smiled widely.

"For *what?!*" Scheuch groaned.

"For the *suits!*" He nodded vigorously. "They'll make us *completely* roamer-proof!"

Scheuch smiled slowly without blinking, which made him look terrifying. "You know what that idea is?" he asked, cutting him off before Bailey could tell him it was amazing, "It's stupid." He scoffed. "Where'd you find that? Reddit?"

"Oh for *Pete's* sake—"

"Aaron!" Sully burst through the door, silencing the room. "Brody's having trouble breathing steady and he's turning blue!"

"What?" he turned around.

"His blood pressure's low and his heartbeat's going *super* fast and his skin's all cold and clammy—" Sully began explaining frantically, "I'm afraid he might be going into hypovolemic shock!"

"What's that mean?" Yanes exclaimed. "Scheuch! What's hypovolemic shock?!"

"It can be caused by excessive bleeding," I responded, watching Scheuch drop his stuff to rush out the door.

"Is he nauseous? Thirsty? Any fatigue?" Scheuch began naming symptoms.

"I—I don't *know!*" Sully panicked.

"Hey, how long can we leave the artery untreated before he's dead?" Sergeant asked him as Scheuch approached the front door.

"Um—correct me if I'm wrong, but—" Scheuch tried to calm himself down. We've never seen him that nervous before. "With the way he's recovering he's got three-to-four hours—"

"Three-to-four *hours?!*" Yanes exclaimed.

"No—he has a day—*at most*," he answered, backing up slowly, "but if we leave this wound untreated for any more hours, it could essentially lead to amputation."

He dashed out the door with Sully. We could hear his voice muffle through the walls, shouting out at Watkins, asking him for his blood type. Yanes turned back around with a frightened look on his face. "Never mind," he said. "We're going tonight."

Yanes and Bailey were in the front. Maxwell and I were in the back. The car right there was silent, only full of worry over Candreva's wellbeing. We reached the school and soon it was Maxwell and I's job to get out and head in. Bailey whistled to get my attention. I turned around to see him look at me worriedly, still wearing that white Hollister jacket.

"We'll be over at the police station," he said. "We'll be back in about—eh—twenty—minutes?"

"Okay," I replied.

"Don't do anything stupid, kid."

We entered through the shattered front door of the school, peeking down the eerie hallways.

"Ain't *this* nostalgic?" I scoffed quietly, listening for any staggered footsteps and moaning.

We began creeping in slowly, scanning every classroom we passed. I flinched as my gun accidently hit a locker, causing an echo to wave down the hallway. We freeze in our spots, hearts dropping to our feet. Nothing. No roamers. Yet we still stay silent.

"Nurse offices are usually placed near the main office," I whispered, walking slowly. My black sneakers stepped cautiously. "Here."

We stepped in, immediately closing the door and scouring through the mini connected rooms. Office, empty. Supply room, empty. Bathroom, empty.

"Hey, go in there and see if there's any tampons left," I said as I began scavenging through the cabinets one by one. I've always been told I'm an excessive looter because I take *everything*, everything I deem valuable.

My backpack open on my side, I toss in pill bottles. Ibuprofen. Tylenol. I found bandages, antiseptic wipes, and adhesive tape.

"Shit! These could last us girls a good six months, Mj!" Maxwell celebrated quietly. "This is amazing!"

I stepped over, opening drawers. Q-tips. Vaseline. Petroleum jelly. Cough drops. Allergy medication. Tweezers. Nail clippers.

Gauze pads!

"Hey, I found a kid's diabetic kit," I said aloud as Maxwell scavenged in the supply room. "You think Sully might need that?"

"Mj, she's not diabetic, I think she has—" she snapped her fingers as she thought, "low iron—some' like that—"

"Oh!" I chuckled. "That is *not* the same thing."

I still put it in my bag anyway.

"Oo—a blood pressure cuff!" Maxwell exclaimed to herself. *"Sweet!"* She turned over. "Hey, do you think she would like any of *this* stuff?"

I turned around as she held up a bunch of medical equipment.

Stethoscope. Otoscope. Reflex hammer. Nebulizer.

"Yeah, go for it," I looked through the shelves, clearing them. "Is that all you found back there?"

"Yep!" She replied, "other than some stale chips and granola bars."

"Take them."

We zipped up our bags and exited the office carefully. We began walking slowly back down the hallway, coming across the cafeteria.

"Wanna test our luck?" I dared, grinning.

She looked back at me. "I mean, if *the nurse office* had that much—"

"Let's go then," I nodded, walking towards the cafeteria, making my way through the tables and into the kitchen.

We didn't find much other than simple spices and condiments. I glance around, "Hey, roamer on your left."

She turned, swiftly striking it with her hatchet.

We opened cabinets, tossing canned goods and packaged snacks into our bags. "Look for any bottled water too," her voice whispered across the room as I smiled, finding the cooking oil.

This was going to be a *very* good supply run.

"Hey, how are you holding up with Klein?" Maxwell asked, pausing a bit. "It's okay if it's a sensitive topic. I know the others don't really leave you alone on it."

I sighed, looking back at her. "I mean, I don't really miss him?" I answered. "One time I was hanging out with him and asked for a drink, right, meaning *water?*" I recalled as I gagged a little, disregarding the rotten food. "His face lit up and he offered me tequila."

"You didn't drink with him, did you?" Her head snapped in concern.

I scoffed, "Hell no," shaking my head, pausing before admitting, "I could never love him."

"Then why did you go back?" she asked.

I felt the vomit rise in my throat. "I don't know."

I wanted to feel something, but my intentions were much more pure than his. I knew him as the hopeless romantic, so I came back to him to revive that part of me. Instead, my poor choice of my actions caused not only him but our entire group to make something out of me I never thought I could be. I never thought I could be so cruel, so vile and unforgiving, filled with so much hatred with little-to-no desire to be better. He ruined that last good part of me, and it's my fault for letting him.

"I could never love him," I repeated. "That boy couldn't make up his damn mind. It wasn't fair to me."

"Damn right," she chuckled, "but does it still *hurt* you though?"

It's been three years. I was fifteen when it happened. He was seventeen. I am eighteen now. He died at twenty.

"Lemme ask you this," she said. "Are you mad at Jake for what he did, or are you mad at him for not being the knight in shining armor you expected to get you out of your—*thing* with Tyson?"

I stopped looting and sat myself up on one of the counters, facing her. She did the same.

"I'm mad knowing that if I never talked to him, there's a possibility that I could still have Aaron in my life right now," I sighed like it doesn't kill me to say it. I shifted the subject. "Have you been hallucinating much?" I asked.

She narrowed her eyes, thinking. "Other than my father, not really."

"I saw Tyson earlier," I confessed. "We had a *whole* conversation—" I shook my head, "—and *man*, did that mess with me." I propped up my knees, hugging myself. "Kie, I thought I was over him but now he's back to being all I think about. I don't know what to do."

"I know," she consoled me. "I think you're just still—*grieving*, just slowly."

"Yeah, I think all the shit with Scheuch toppled it," I added, inhaling sharply, "and hey, speaking of Aaron, I wanna go pick up some stuff for him."

We hopped off the counters and headed down the hallway, straight to the library. I wanted to look for some textbooks to perhaps help him with his research, but Maxwell quickly suggested we go look in the Science classrooms instead to look out for extra flashlights, batteries, and cleaning supplies too.

"Hey—janitor's closet might have some stuff too," I said as we strolled down the hallway quietly. I glanced over at her. She could see it in my face, hear it in my voice.

My voice broke. "Is it bad I'm missing somebody I'm not supposed to be missing?" I asked. "The world has crumbled around me and all I can crave is love."

She scoffed softly, "How could you not?" She took a deep breath, fingers tracing along the flakey posters on the wall. "Mj, you're not going to like what I'm about to tell you," she said, looking at me with a straight face.

I've grown to understand that every time someone says that, they end up telling me exactly what I need to hear—exactly what I've been telling myself for ages.

"In moments like those, you think you're in love," she explained, "but you're not. You just love the sense of safety, the comfort; the things that you've grown to become used to—" she picked up a couple of double AA batteries, "and I know this because girls in these types of situations don't like change. I know because I was once that girl."

We entered the empty science classroom, looking through drawers. I shook my head. "Kie, he didn't hurt me like that," I replied. "If anything he—"

He what, Mj? Comparing him to Kay doesn't excuse his actions.

"He wasn't always like that."

"Mj, you have to realize that in reality, he was breaking your heart as much as he was fixing it—" she explained, "and if things didn't change and you never found the strength to leave him, you would've just ended up *tearing* and *tearing* and *tearing* yourself apart until you had nothing left of yourself." She sniffled, seeing a bit of herself in me as she spoke. "I understand he was important to you, but you were *too young* for that type of commitment."

"He was destroying you, and you know it."

I sighed deeply, not knowing what to say. I don't know what to say because

I know.

I know Tyson died a long time ago—even before I found him stumbling in his kitchen after overdosing.

A part of me knew Maxwell was right, but she doesn't *know*.

Maybe I'm just destined to live the rest of my life in denial. Every time I think about him, I don't ever think about the bad things. I don't *tell* anyone, I don't write about it, so I can understand why she doesn't completely get the effect he has on me—even when she says she does.

She doesn't know that she's basically speaking to a fragment of him, not ME. I died when he died. My mind has just been replaying the memories of him to keep us alive, to keep *me* going.

She doesn't know that he actually listened to me when I begged him to stop pushing me away and learn to communicate.

He did. He made an effort. I knew he wasn't going to change overnight, and I accepted that condition. <u>We just ran out of time!</u>

If he were here with me, if he had been with me, I wouldn't be in as much pain as I am right now. I'd much rather be sad *with* him than be sad *without* him. I'd much rather let him make me cry a million times than fall in love with someone new and let *him* break my heart for a change. How am I just supposed to let it go...? How am I supposed to want to?

"I can't help but think he would've changed," I said, hearing her sigh.

"Mj, you are *not* stupid," she told me sternly. She closed the wooden drawer, looking back up at me with a straight face. "If that boy wanted you, he would've *got* you. If that boy loved you, he would've told you. If he *wanted* to change, he *would've*."

He could've not been ready. I could've been rushing him. I should've just been more patient! ~~He should've treated me better. He shouldn't have spoken to me that way.~~

His rage and distrust and misery was neither directed towards or caused by me, he just didn't know how to fight it; and I didn't know how to let him go.

I still don't know how. The reflection I see staring back at me in the mirror looks like him. The words I speak, the looks I give, the thoughts I think; they all resemble him.

"I know this sounds impossible right now," Maxwell said as she tossed bottles of hand sanitizer in her bag, "but one day, believe it or not, one day you'll meet someone so—*so* much bet—"

BANG!

We flinched as the noise echoed through the hallway, sending chills down our spines.

"Could just be one roamer," she whispered.

"Nah, I think there's a <u>reason why this place is so empty</u>," I stepped towards the door frame, peeking down the hallway.

There were desks piled up, barricading them all. Six dozen. No, at least seven, possibly eight dozen. They were all at the end of the hallway, wandering around aimlessly. I creaked open the door only to have it be blocked by a dead roamer laying on the tiled floors.

I covered my mouth to silence my gasp, grossed out by the maggots and rodents. I did my best not to throw up.

"It's okay, you got it," Maxwell whispered as we tip-toed out, flinching as the double doors on the other end of the hallway pushed in and out. She shone her light onto the handles, looking at the chains that have confined them into a room. The pushing gradually grew violent.

"They can smell you." My voice tensed, looking over at her. "Your nose!"

The doors burst open, causing us to swing our backpacks over our shoulders, dashing down the flickering hallways.

"Go! Go! There's no use shooting!" she said as the roamers on the other end began chasing after us.

Our lights flashed frantically, not knowing where to go. The front entrance was just that way! All of the other exits are blocked off! *Gymnasium,* I read on a sign, slamming my body against the doors and dragging her in.

"Climb onto the bleachers, we can leave through the windows," I panted as we scrambled up, kicking at the roamers beneath our feet. I panicked, feeling her help me pull myself up.

I leaned against the wall, attempting to break the glass. I slammed and I slammed, eyeing Maxwell as she crawled her way up.

"Go!" she yelled. "Go! It's fine!"

"What?!" I panic, immediately crawling over to her to help. She grunted and pushed me. I flew out the window and down the slanted roof, plopping on the ground.

No... No, no, no...

The adrenaline helped cushion my fall, but as I stood there under the dark sky, looking back into the windows, hurt was all I could feel. Panic was all that burned in my chest.

My hands shook, throbbing; my feet danced frantically, not knowing what to do. Tears began to stream. My throat began to close.

"Kiara—" I choked, falling to my knees and gripping my hair.

Deep breaths.

In. Out. In. Out. You've been through this before.

~~*She's all I have.*~~

"HEY!" My heart jolted, looking up swiftly; eyes scanning through the windows. Seeing the girl that has been the sister I never had bang her palm against the glass of a first-story window gave me the biggest smile of relief. I let out a short laugh, letting my heart regain its pace. Her voice spoke through the glass happily, "Are you gonna let me out or what?"

19 promise

"Hey! You got hurt? Go to Scheuch!"

"No, Scheuch's busy! Go to Bui instead!"

"Got hurt? Go to Bui!"

"That cut looks pretty bad, someone find Bui."

"That's gonna get infected. Go to Bui."

I've finally got my purpose.

The medicine cabinet is located in the pizzeria. Whenever I'm not out on a supply run, I'm mostly there treating wounds or sorting pill bottle from pill bottle. Scheuch had taught me everything there was to treating cuts and injuries—but knowing that hurts more than any bruise or tear could. It hurts so bad knowing he doesn't take me seriously when I admire him so much. It's been a year since he left me on that porch, and his absence still weighs on me in ways only He can relieve me.

God, I'm never going to get over it.

"Not with that attitude you won't," I immediately heard Mj's voice scoff. I shook it off.

He walked in earlier today. I started fixating hard into counting how many antibiotics we had left to the point where it began to look obvious.

He stood, watching me silently. "Do we need to look out for more?" he asked.

I refused to look at him, ignoring him.

"Bui," he repeated.

He could've thought I was being incompetent to purposely get at him the same way I would to Klein. He could've thought this was just my way of being petty; that this was just who *I* was.

As corny as it is, I just wanted to hear him say my name.

"What?" I replied robotically, "Look out for what?"

"Antibiotics of any kind," he said.

Well, I don't know, *Aaron*, does it look like we need more fucking antibiotics? It had been about a month since the supply run to the school with Maxwell, but our injuries from the day we left for Station 45 caused us to go through them pretty quickly. It has been a month, and we've seen no sign of the warriors.

"Have we tried cutting them (the pills) up?" I asked.

"No——he (Brody) keeps throwing them up."

"All we have left are bottles of Tylenol and Ibuprofen—" I replied. I expected him to nod and continue on, but he didn't. I looked up a little, still refusing to look at his face.

"Do you want me to look out for anything else?" he asked calmly.

"More cat food for Coco," I listed, sighing, "and sunscreen would be nice."

"What she say?" Yanes asked as he stepped in. "Sunscreen?"

"Yeah."

"Yeah, I doubt it's good to be in all that sunlight without it," he agreed, looking over at Scheuch. "Hey, do you know if the radiation could enhance that?"

"In—In what sense?" Scheuch replied.

Here... comes the science lesson...

Radiation levels could alter the composition of the atmosphere—*blah blah blah*—may result in changes of the ozone layer—*blah blah blah*—Radiation can also generate particles in the atmosphere—such as dust and aerosols—*blah blah blah*—which may scatter sunlight differently—*blah blah blah*—so depending on the concentration of these particles, they could potentially enhance or (hopefully) diminish the sunlight intensity.

"You talk a lot for someone who complains about chattiness," I muttered.

"What was that, Mj?" Yanes asked confusedly.

"Nothing. Bye."

Today was a Wednesday, and I knew that because the group going out was all boys. Scheuch, Yanes, Watkins, but no Bailey—apparently Bailey didn't feel like going—and no Candreva, Scheuch says he needs another week and a half.

But Scheuch says a lot of things.

The closest pharmacy was mostly empty. The windows were shattered and the signs were broken off its hinges, crooked and dangling from the tiled ceilings. Scheuch pulled out the paper note from his pocket.

"Look out for feminine hygiene products—Erm——" he wiped his nose, sniffling, "—Yanes, go check in the food aisles for any canned goods——we also need Penicillin, Clindamycin, and Fluconazole tablets—er—"

"*The hell are those?*" his voice echoed.

"*I—I'll* get them," he said. "Just focus on getting cans of food—*none* that are swollen or have dents or rust on them."

They were out there for about an hour, scavenging around. Yanes later found Scheuch in the beauty aisle, gazing mindlessly in front of the shelves of sunscreen. Scheuch glanced over at him then quickly cleared his throat.

"What—" Yanes narrowed his eyes, looking closer, "Oh, are you looking for one you think she'd like?"

"W-What?"

"Hm..." He picked one up, muttering under his breath, "coconut clear spray?" He thought for a moment before slipping out his walkie, clearing his throat. "Yo Brody!" He waited a couple seconds. "Brody?"

"*Yeah, what's good, dawg,*" Brody's voice transferred.

"Ask Mary what scents Mj likes—"

"*You don't have to-*" Scheuch murmured.

"*What?*" Brody asked.

"Like what does she like sniffin'—" Yanes snickered, "does she like smellin' like a flower or a fruit."

"*Mary, what scents does Mj usually like?*"

"*Umm...*" her voice replied on the other end of the line, "*Fruits? Maybe? I don't know,*" she answered as Yanes picked up the closest one, shaking it.

"There's a mango one?" He shrugged, reading the label under his breath, "recommended by the skin cancer foundation."

"*Yoooo*," Candreva's voice chuckled across the line. He spoke in a tired voice, slurring his words. "Why was there a foundation giving people *skin cancer?*"

Yanes shut his eyes. "Bye, Brody!"

He slipped his walkie back onto his belt, grinning over at Scheuch. "And hey bud, if you're lookin' for scents I'd like too, I prefer lavender," he chuckled. "Meet you out in the car in five!"

Sergeant had called me into the gun shop earlier, telling me to sit down. I did, nervously. The first thing I asked was if I was in trouble. He said I wasn't, but I felt like I was. I knew why I was.

"Scheuch had told me what has been going on," he said, "and—*honestly,* Mj? You two need to drop this bullshit and *move* the hell on. We don't have time for this anymore! Understood?"

"Understood," I responded.

He nodded, looking at the look I had on my face. "When you left the first time, I let it slide 'cause we were *all* newly adjusting to all of this," he explained. "You were mourning, and you wanted to leave and go find Tyson. I *understand,*" he widened his eyes, "but you taking off over something like *this??*" He sighed. "Bui, we've been through the *hardest* two years together. I *need* you here."

I shook my head subtly, feeling my eyes tear up.

"Mj, I *swear* to God—" he cupped his face with his hands, "I've told you time and time again what I see in you—" he pleaded, "—tell me, *tell me* how I can get that out of you again because *that* Mj is who we need right now." He paused. "I need you to be a leader—"

"*Why?*" I asked. "We have Aaron and Kiara."

"*You* have the most experience with the warriors than all of us," he explained. "You—and my daughter, you two know what those motherfuckers are capable of."

I blinked a bit, then nodded, but he didn't buy it.

"Mj, as a *father*——I want to *trust* you," he said. "My daughter is *here* now—here after spending *two* of the most *pivotal* years of her life with those people! You know she's definitely seen some things, and I don't want her going down the wrong path," he pleaded. "I want to trust you to *be* a role model—*show* her the right way—but you've grown so immature and less participative lately and I'm going to *have* to take a lot of responsibilities off of you if this behavior doesn't change. I genuinely *don't* want to *have to do that!*"

I've never heard him talk to me like that before. All I could do was sit there in my puddle of shame.

He took a deep breath, looking at the blank look on my face.

"Is it *him?*" he asked.

I hesitated, "Not just him," I lied.

"These people don't have an ounce of respect for me, and you know it," I said tensely. "They start shit, then tell me to be the bigger person. Regardless of *how* much work I put in, they'll never change the way they see me——"

"Mj, I already told you people talk their shit," he said. "It's a part of life."

"I don't care if they're talking shit, they can talk all they want," I said. "I'm just not going to choose to be in an environment where I'm surrounded by people who constantly make me feel like

I—I have to cut *pieces* of myself *off* to fit into a puzzle I *don't* belong in!"

He sighed. "You *do* belong."

"No, I don't," I replied, "I don't and it hurts me. I tell myself I don't care, but *Kim's* the one they invite to hang out, not me."

"Mj, your *entire* world has fallen to pieces, and you still care about what these people are *saying* about you?"

I gulped, hesitating. "I don't feel safe."

His eyebrows furrowed. "What do you mean?"

"If they don't like me, they won't have my back out there," I replied. "I know I can handle myself on my own, but it hurts seeing everyone bond with each other knowing I will never have that——and it hurts that I have to ask if I'm important enough to them to protect."

Sergeant crossed his arms. "You really think that low of us?" he nodded. "Everyone here should protect each other no matter *what*."

I don't want them to need to, I want them to want to.

He paused a bit. "Do you feel judged?"

I nodded.

"They're not judging you," he answered, taking off his glasses and stress-cleaning them. "They're judging those times *in-between*. Those times *outside* of drill, community service, class, supply runs and daily chores. They judge the times they see you sneak out to go *roamer-hunting*, play soccer on the streets, and go and swim in the creek after curfew, laughing and goofing off with your friends," he paused. "*Those* times are the times they doubt your abilities."

"Don't get me wrong," he quickly said. "I'm not asking you to change anything about yourself, Mj," he explained. "*I* can be an unserious person too——there's just this—*sense* of maturity you have to learn," he explained. "There's a *time* and *place*. You're *allowed* to have fun, you're *allowed* to goof off, just—not when things are serious."

I bit my lip in guilt, thinking. "Have I been doing that?"

"Not—*necessarily*," he shrugged. "You're not goofing off or *messing around*, you're just prioritizing the wrong things and you're letting them consume you." He leaned forward over the glass display case. "The Mj during drill, the Mj that's quick on her feet, the Mj that doesn't *think*, she just *does*——*Bui*—*that's* who we need right now."

I remained silent, wiping the tears streaming down my face.

He paused, taking a deep breath. "It's Aaron, isn't it?"

I exhaled. "I just wanted him to think I was cool."

"Stop doing things for others!" he exclaimed. "For once, choose *you! Stop* trying to love others—*stop* trying to get others to love you—love *yourself*, and *soon* you'll attract the right ones!" He pinched the bridge of his nose, exhaling. "I get that you want to feel wanted, but your problem is that you obsess over how things could be instead of seeing and accepting things the way they are," he said. "You look at the way Aaron treats Mary and wish he could treat you that way, but that's just *not* who he is."

That's not who he is. That's not who he is.

<u>That's not who he is. That's not who he is.</u>

I burst out sobbing. His gaze softened.

"Why couldn't he just be a dick to begin with?!" I cried. "Now all I am is just *stuck* on the person he used to be!"

"People change."

"*He* didn't!" I sniffled. "I am not *asking* him to embody a new personality just to accommodate me!" I covered my face, spiraling. "I don't know what to do! Why would he look at me like that if he knew he felt nothing? God, why would he even *put* that thought in my head if he knew he didn't want it?"

"Mj, he doesn't understand your reaction the same way you don't understand his," Sergeant sighed. "You two are completely different people. You stand in front of him crying, he stands there stone-faced." He looked at me with softened eyes. "He is a boy that sees the world in black and white, he doesn't see the gray parts like you do." He sighed again. "But he's *trying*," he said, "he just doesn't—understand—"

"Really?" I sniffled.

"He cared enough to come and talk to *me?*"

I nodded, flinching as I heard the door behind me open. I quickly wiped the tears off my face, turning around. It was him.

"What's up, Aaron?" Sergeant asked. His voice was upbeat now. "How'd the pharmacy run go?"

"Um—Good," he responded. He was covered in muck with blood splattered across the lenses of his glasses. He gulped, "Yanes only found two things of SPAM, though. That's not even enough to feed two of us."

Sergeant looked down and sighed. "Alright, we'll send a group out tomorrow morning."

"I—I was thinking about going out again by myself?" he said.

"Find dinner?"

"We don't even have *dinner?*"

"We're *extremely* low on food," he repeated. "It's going to be harder to keep up—now that we have an extra mouth to feed."

"*Hey,* she's a nepo-baby!" Sergeant joked. "She can eat all she wants. I'll make you give her *your* food!"

I listened to them consult before following him out. I found him packing a bag in the kitchen of the pizzeria, preparing to head out alone.

I didn't want him to. A feeling in my gut didn't want him to, but what was I supposed to do?

"Are you really going out there alone?" I asked.

"Yes."

"Even with the herds?"

"I'll be fine."

I took a deep breath, suddenly feeling a sense of regret. All the pain that I was just feeling was drained from me and replaced with anger and umbrage, and I really wanted to take back what I said about missing him because why *would* I miss him? Why would I miss *this*?

"Let me come with you," I said, grabbing the closest backpack nearby, emptying it out.

"You don't have to."

"I'm not offering. I'm coming with you," I stated, looking at the way his eyes gazed down to mine. "I'll be out in the car."

We drove in silence. I held the map. The CD player was empty. Only this was a new car, a nice white truck Candreva had taught us how to hotwire.

"Okay, A-A-ron, don't total this one either!" he joked.

Hey! That's MY nickname for him! I would've said. I just stood there silently, amusing myself by watching them glare at each other.

The highway could put you to sleep. The trees surrounding revealed nothing but vast plains. The signs were graffitied on, no use relying on them, and the map told me nothing, just like how it told me nothing last time.

"Hey, look, a water tower!" I pointed.

He glanced and nodded. "Cool."

"Water towers gotta be placed near buildings, right?" I asked. "C'mon, we've been driving for forever. This is the first thing we've seen!"

He sighed and began driving off the road carefully, into the hills of dead grass. I waited eagerly in my seat, trying to see.

The building was mid-sized, windowless, and tin-roofed. There were no paths leading to the side-entrances, only locks chaining the door handles and red illuminated EXIT signs above them. We stood under the cloudy sky, hesitating.

I picked the lock carefully, opening the door as quietly as I could. My jaw dropped as I saw what was inside the spacious warehouse. I heard Scheuch cuss behind me, "Holy *shit!*"

Rows upon rows of identical products were neatly stacked, packaged together in cubes. There were wide selections of consumer products, manufactured on a large scale. These were shipments meant to be sold in department stores, yet here they were, untouched.

I quickly rushed in, tearing a box of chocolate out from the racks. I hadn't eaten in days, eaten anything as close to something as sweet as chocolate, of course. Scheuch smiled faintly, watching me tear into the candy.

I gave him the cookies and cream bar, a bar which I knew he liked, and he nodded, thanking me as he sat down alongside me.

"Dude, we hit the *jackpot!*" I exclaimed quietly. "Aaron, look, there's so much food! Who knows how long this could last us!?"

Boxes of instant coffee. Sugar. Bags of white and brown rice. Dried beans. Dry pasta. Freeze-dried vegetables and fruits. Peanuts. Cashews. Tinned fish. Bagged tea. Cereal. Crackers. Pretzels.

"The fuck is *powdered milk?*" I scoffed, mouth full of chocolate. "Man, this is the best thing I've ever eaten!"

"You haven't had chocolate?" he asked beside me, elbows on his knees.

"I always gave my bars to Sully," I confessed, looking over at him. "She loves them."

He nodded as he stood back up. "I'm gonna go get the truck, okay?"

"Okay," I replied softly, standing up too, grabbing three-four boxes from each cube.

He drove the truck over to the door before we began piling up the trunk. We planned on squishing in as much as we could at the moment, and having Candreva, Yanes, and Watkins come back for the rest later.

I was pretty content. Now that I knew he preferred silence, I began to realize how much I preferred it too. Back and forth and back and forth. Box 1, Box 2, Box 3.

"Heads up, herd coming in," I pointed.

"Just let them pass—"

Our heads snapped as we heard something clatter behind us.

I looked back at him silently.

Did you hear that? My eyes asked.

I did. His replied. *I'll go check it out.*
You finish with the pasta here.

Okie-dokie.
Be careful—

"Hey, back up!" I quietly warned as Scheuch flew to the side, dodging the bullet nearly impaling him. The gunshot echoed through the plains, and my mind immediately turned to the herd among the hills. "*Shit,* they're coming."

He took a deep breath, readjusting himself against the rigid walls before heading in. I quickly started filling up the trunk, box after box. It wasn't until I heard another gunshot and a firearm slide across the floor that I immediately darted inside, making my way around the racks. My sneakers crept softly upon the cold stone. My gun was aimed firmly upward. I found him leaning against the packaged nuts, calming his breath. I looked past him to see his gun lying on the floor.

I nudged him out the way to peek over, seeing a rather old man. Fifty-five, maybe. His hands were shaking, even the one with the gun in it, and his eyes were bloodshot. Wide. Alert.

We looked at each other silently, nodding, *okay, one.. two..*

I quickly swerved to my right, shooting the man's gun out of his hand as Scheuch bolted to the other side to grab his own. I stepped closer, aiming fiercely at him. He sat there, guarding a little room, and by the way he did, made me want to know what was in it.

"Who are ya?!" he asked frantically. "This is *my* warehouse!"

"Oh *c'mon*, you don't need all this food for *yourself?*" Scheuch scoffed behind me.

I shrugged, agreeing. "That's fat as fuck!"

"Get—Get outta here before I shoot 'cha!"

"With *what?*" I scoffed.

"What do you have back there that's so important?" Scheuch asked.

The man stammered. "N-Nothin'-"

"So you don't mind if my pal and I take a few packages or two to go back and feed our companions, do ya?" I mimicked his accent.

I noticed carefully how his eyebrows raised. *"Sure!* As a matter of fact, d-darling. How 'bout I *help* y'all pack some things?"

I smiled smugly. "No need."

"Now I *insist!*"

He slowly stood up with his hands up, stepping closer to me. My hands gripped my gun tighter. I looked at his clothes—looked nothin' like a warrior's uniform. He was wearing a red flannel and cowboy boots. He looked like Sterling.

"Please don't shoot me!" *Dawg, you just shot at us.* "Please!"

I blinked a bit as Scheuch slipped his gun back into his holster, heading back out to the truck to finish up.

"Listen," I said softly. "I promise I won't shoot you."

I'm going to in three seconds.

"I know we may have gotten off on the wrong foot here, but I *promise,* I won't shoot you."

Watch me.

I tried not to glare at him as hard.

You can see the lie in my face.

"Just let us package this up, and you'll never have to see us again," I said slowly, trying to buy Scheuch time. "Our people are starving."

He then reached up swiftly, attempting to grab the pistol from me. I swung on him, hitting him in the head with it. He fell to the ground groaning, instinctively crawling towards his gun. He tripped me by my ankles when I tried to stop him. I fell onto the floor too.

I rolled out of the way as he tried to shoot me. Instead he bent up, right as all the roamers from the herd were reaching us.

"BUI! LET'S GO!"

He then shot,
but it wasn't at me.

7 DECEMBER. 2022.

BEYOND THE LIVING

20 repentance

I've never shot a man in the face so fast. I quickly barged into the room, which was full of nothing but hard liquor, empty cigarette boxes, ashtrays, and a poo-bucket. I gagged as I snatched the metal box by the handle from the ground, heading straight to the door. Anger filled my veins, seeing the warrior symbol embedded on the steel as I squished it into the trunk.

I watch him hunch over, groaning before dashing away from the herd stumbling after him. I burst out the nearest exit, sprinting after him.

Panting as I ran, I shot at every roamer I could. I watched them groan and moan. I watched them stagger with desire.

Scheuch ran with no problem, easily outrunning the roamers long enough for me to shoot some down, but there were still about a dozen. And that was a dozen too much.

My anxiety rose the moment I saw him roll his ankle. He grunted as he fell on his side, rolling down the hill roughly.

Panicking, I skewered as many as I could as I vigorously forced myself through them, watching them crawl and claw the moment they caught up to him. At that moment, I guess I didn't really think about anything. I just stabbed anything coming for me, anything coming near me. The adrenaline blocked out so much, I forgot to breathe. My heart forgot to beat.

I didn't even realize one had finished biting through my upper arm until I slashed my blade into its skull.

I was so frantic that I would've done anything. I would've thrown myself on him to shield him if I had to, but I didn't.

About a dozen corpses laid sprinkled around us like fallen leaves. He laid there on his back with a fractured foot as I knelt there next to him, seeing the amount of bites. My eyes glanced away from the teeth marks on my arm. I had no room to think about that.

"Hey," I tapped his face gently, panting. "Hey, you're immune. You should be *fine!*"

The December breeze brushed against us as my lips began to quiver. My back began to weigh, seeing him like this. I let out a short cry as I laid my forehead down on his chest.

"You should be fine, right?" I whispered in his ear. "It's *okay!*"

He reached up weakly, grabbing my wrist. He then lowered my hand to his lower abdomen, pointing to

the gunshot wound.

"Shit!" I quickly applied pressure on the wound, trying to stay calm. My body swung around, seeing how far the truck was from us. His eyes fluttered open weakly.

"Mj." He reached out, grabbing my shoulder. *"Mj."*

I never viewed Scheuch as the strongest. I always thought it'd be weird to say that, but seeing him so weak that he couldn't reach up and hold me was even weirder.

"I regret—what I said," he choked.

I felt my heart burst into flames. It felt inflated and wanted to pop. Suddenly I wasn't able to think. There was nothing I could do to prevent my eyes from instantly tearing up.

"Don't start talkin' like that," I spat. "Don't fuckin' *throw* that shit at me. I'ma punch you in the fucking throat!"

He chuckled softly as I began crying.

"Do—Do you really mean it?"

"I regret *everything*," his voice broke a little as he confessed. "I-I would like to take it back."

And at that moment, I expected myself to feel relieved, but instead, I felt the weight of his apology collapse onto me. The pain ached my shoulders in ways swimming never could. His words punched my stomach as I looked at him in horror.

"No—" I stammered, "No, no, *no*," I whispered, wiping the grime off his face. "*No!* I was *so* mean to *you!*"

I began hysterically sobbing, moving his hand from my arm to his wound, applying force.

"I take it *all* back," he said softly. I could hear the emotion in his voice for the first time, and that broke me. "I'm *sorry*. I know I hurt you."

I stared back at him in shock, realizing I was no longer seventeen. I was now free from that porch,

but at what cost?

I wiped my tears, shooting up from my spot. I grabbed the keys from his pockets as I dashed back over to the truck as fast as I could. I started it up, driving it over like a maniac, running over all the roamers in my path.

"Get up," I said. *"Get up!"*

Panic, that was all I could feel. Denial, that was the only stage I could prepare for. But nothing, nothing gave me more hope than the smile he gave me did.

RECONCILIATION

"It's going to be okay," I said as I sped us down the highway, foot pressed all the way on the petal. My right hand gripped harder on the wheel to stop the shaking. "We're gonna make it, I promise. I'm *not* letting you die on me!"

"You don't need to keep reminding me, Mj," he replied softly beside me. "I know you to—"

"I'm telling *myself!*" I exclaimed, reaching over to the seat compartments, grabbing a bottle of hand sanitizer frantically.

I flicked open the bottle, rolling my sleeve up. I clenched my jaw, bracing for the excruciating burn from the alcohol hitting the wound.

"You got bit?" He realized, softening his gaze.

"*You* have a chance to make it," I replied coldly, wrapping bandages around it, taking a deep breath. Deep breath. Deep breath. ~~I'm going to be dead in 24 hours.~~

If I got to do it all over again with him knowing what would eventually happen, I wouldn't. This isn't one of those times.

I would do it over and over again a hundred times with Tyson, but not him.

If I got to meet him and look at the soft gaze in his eye when he smiled at me again, I would turn the other way. I'd rather let someone run over my ankles than self-inflict that pain upon myself. Meeting him was one of my biggest regrets. Meeting him was one of my biggest regrets because there were no lessons to learn or morals to grasp by losing him.

I gained nothing, but I lost everything.

"HELP!" I screamed as we arrived back at Jade Street, grabbing everyone's attention. "AARON'S BEEN SHOT!"

Sully and Watkins sprinted over with a stretcher as everyone else began crowding around.

"What happened?!" Sully gasped.

"He's been shot by some idiot off Exit-Um—*fuck!*" I shouted through Bailey's shock and Kim's hysteria.

"Where?!" Yanes asked.

"Head *west* and look for a water tower!" I directed. "There's a whole warehouse full of food there!"

"Got it," he nodded, watching Sully and Watkins reel him away. "He dead?"

"Yes! But that doesn't matter? Aaron's been shot!"

"Okay, just checkin'-" he sighed as I stepped away. "I-I don't know, Mj, he's been chewed up pretty good."

"He's immune," Sergeant and I synchronized, following after them. I began picking up my pace. Bailey did too.

"He's lost too much blood!" Sully exclaimed as I opened the front door to the old clothing store Klein used to live in. Now it was used as a second infirmary.

"One—two——three!" Bailey counted before he and Watkins lifted him up, transporting him over to a twin mattress.

Watkins began cutting his black t-shirt down from the center as I rushed to wet a clean cloth to clean the wound.

"How's he not already infected?!" Watkins panicked, touching his forehead with the back of his hand. "You're not sweating or burning up any fever!"

"He's *immune!*" I tried not to cry as I rummaged around for tweezers, desperately trying to remove any visible debris or foreign objects.

"He's—He's *what?*"

"Guys, he already lost a lot of blood—I-" I looked up to see the three of them looking at me sympathetically, tools lowered, "—we don't need to worry about the bites!"

"Mj..." Sully worried, grabbing my shoulder.

"He's going to be *fine!*" I shouted frantically.

"*Mj!*" Bailey exclaimed too. He took the tools from me gently, setting them down, holding my wrists, forcing me to look him in the eyes. "Deep breath."

I hyperventilated heavily.

"Deep breath," he kept saying.

My vision began to blur. I quickly shook myself out of his hands, storming out the front door just as Maxwell was heading in.

I stood, throwing up over the wooden railing. My hands gripped the chipped white paint violently. Two seconds later, Maxwell came stumbling out too, doing the same.

"He's fucked isn't he?" I whispered, shutting my eyes painfully, wiping the vomit off my lips.

She shook her head beside me. "The bullet hit him in a fatal spot."

"Then take it *out?!*" I shouted.

She sniffled shakily, turning to me and holding my shoulders.

"It had—broken—into little shards," she broke the news gently. "There's nothing we can do."

"*No!*" I shook my head, sobbing. "*No!*"

I shove myself back through the front doors, finding Sully crying in Watkins' arms. Bailey was on the floor against the wall, palms covering his face. I paced over, pleading. "Just tell me what I have to do," I begged. "Just tell me what I have to do, and I'll do it."

He looked back at me and said nothing, but that was his response. *Nothing.*

I began to dissociate.

Soon, it was everyone's last chance to say something to him before he took his final breath. I sat out on the wooden steps, arms on my propped-up knees. Maxwell sat beside me with a cigarette between her fingers, listening to everyone's last words to him. God, it was gut-wrenching. My heart began to hollow, hearing Sergeant's *'I'm proud of you's'* and Kim's sobbing through the walls. It wasn't until Maxwell and I heard Candreva and him communicate through the rooms that we began crying harder—his, *'I really liked poking fun at you's'*, and Bailey's *'I'm really going to miss you, kid'*.

It all felt like a nightmare.

Sergeant came out, snatching the bottle of hard liquor in my hand and pouring it out on the grass. "Bui, it's your turn," he said, wiping his nose as Sully walked out behind him, seating herself between Maxwell and I, "everyone else has gone."

"Can I have one?" ... "Sure." I heard the two whisper behind me as I stepped in, finding Bailey and Yanes in there. My hands trembled as the two of them awkwardly left to give me space. My voice broke in ways I never knew it could. Him leaving reopened wounds I thought healed long ago.

As I pulled over a wooden stool, I realized I wasn't numb to the grief after all, because as he was dying, I was dying too. All of me: Mj, Michelle, Cadet Bui.

I didn't know who I was anymore, and no reflection was ever going to ever give me the same amount of reassurance.

He was still alive. Barely. I was holding onto his hand. He was too weak to hold me back. My lips quivered as I removed his glasses for him, letting him go more comfortably.

I never thought I could both miss and hate him so much until this moment. I would never do it again. I would never want to meet him again—because for the longest time, I forgot what it felt like to smile that wide talking to someone, and it pained me to remember how it felt to stop.

"Aaron," I gulped. "Remember that day you got me contacts?"

He smiled softly. "The department run?"

"Yeah, there was an optical section there, remember?" I chuckled. "You helped me figure out my prescription with all your—*nerd-shit*——I hate how you know everything." I sniffled roughly. "And that was the day I found Coco, too—when you named her after a cereal brand."

I lowered my head to his hand, breaking down. I broke down over how I did everything I could. I did everything I could to save his life, to make up for him saving mine, but like everything else I seem to do,

it was never enough.

He was going to go into shock soon. His breathing was getting shallow. His touch was growing cold. All I could do was watch.

"Yeah, I remember," he replied weakly as I sniffled.

"If I could, Aaron," I whispered. "I would go back and do it right."

I wouldn't go back if it were the same. I don't reread chapters expecting new endings, but if I could,

I'd rewrite ours.

i *know* you didn't pass BioChem

When I thought the group shattered after Conti and Johnson, I didn't even think how hard it'd be without Scheuch. We absolutely collapsed when he left.

I had gone home that night expecting to break out in a cold sweat and for my skin to go pale. I lay there, staring up at the ceiling after giving Coco to Maxwell, expecting not to wake up the next morning. Instead, I woke up that morning just like I did the morning before.

I lay there in his clothes, still, too scared to talk.

Roamers don't talk.

I look in the mirror, seeing my reflection stare back at me *clearly*. I wasn't blind.

I remained dysfunctional for the next month. I spent my days rotting in bed, staring at the hardwood floor as life went on. I spent my days not interacting with anyone, not even Sully. I woke up everyday wishing I didn't, until one morning in early February, I woke from the wind being knocked out of me.

I felt my entire body get yanked from my cushions and dragged roughly down the stairs. I squirmed in panic as they covered a black sack over my head, screaming. Screaming and screaming and screaming.

~~Don't look at my scars. Don't look at my scars.~~

It didn't take me long to realize it wasn't the warriors.

It was my own people.

I felt my body get placed in a chair; my wrists and ankles get tied to the arms of it.

"Okay, is the sack really that necessary?" Yanes' voice whispered. "We're just trying to keep her still, not make her relive that night?"

Candreva's voice responded with, "Yeah, you're right."

The sack was lifted from my head, and I stared back at the two with betrayal.

"So," he waited awkwardly with his hands in his pockets, "aren't you gonna ask why we're restraining you?"

"We're doing it out of good intention," Yanes nodded.

"Yeah, it's for your own good."

"How the *hell* is this for my own good?" My voice broke. My wrists squirmed tightly within its restraints. ~~Did they see them?~~ "*Fuck* you, Brody! I hope your artery starts spurtin' again!"

"They killed Scheuch," Yanes' voice pierced me, "and he was your rock."

"He was her cocaine?!" Candreva exclaimed.

"*No*, Brody," Yanes scoffed, rubbing his forehead.

(For those who don't understand, a street name given to cocaine that has been processed from cocaine hydrochloride to a ready-to-use free base for smoking is called *rock*.) (And for those who need double clarification, no, Aaron Scheuch was not a drug to me.)

"Mj, we both know you're—a bit of a hothead—and Scheuch was always the one to keep you steady—" he muttered, nodding, "—the only one that *could* keep you steady."

Salt on the wound, Yanes. Get on with it!

"Now that he's not with us anymore, we don't think it's a good idea for you to be out there with us," Candreva explained. "Just—in case you feel the need to—*avenge*—on his behalf."

I was thinking *just* that.

"Kim believes it could potentially put us in jeopardy, and honestly we do too," Yanes sighed. "I hope you'll be able to understand."

I glared at them silently, fuming. I asked *relatively* calmly, "Did Sergeant agree to this?" as if it would make me feel better if he did, but I watched as they both stood in silence, which indicated that he wasn't aware of this decision being made.

I jumped up in the seat angrily, with tears in my eyes I growled through my teeth. "Let me speak to Bailey!"

"We can't do that."

"Why?" I tilted my head. If my hand wasn't restrained, I would've smacked the side of my head along with saying, "Cause he wouldn't agree to this, that's why!"

"We can't have you out there thinking irrationally, Mj," Yanes explained. "You have a heavy heart right now, and honestly all it's going to do is get any of us, or even worse, yourself *killed*."

"Fuck you!" I spat, looking away from them. "Get outta my face."

"We're—"

"*GET OUT!*" I screamed as they both stood silently, sighing down at me for a bit before going back upstairs and out the gun shop.

I sat limp for what felt like hours, staring at the same four walls through the railings of the chamber. At least they were decent enough to hang up a clock, I could've told myself, but for Pete's sake they could've at least taken the time to realize there were no batteries and putting a clock up there to help me keep track of time was POINTLESS! THIS WAS POINTLESS!

The basement door creaked open. I tensed up hearing the footsteps creak. And I prayed, man did I pray, I prayed it was anyone *but* her, but thanks to my luck...

It was Kim.

She out of everyone was the one to bring down my lunch for the day, and that enraged me in ways I didn't know I could be. Any possible rational thought, any possible moral or value I held in my soul, was sucked out of my body in an instant.

She opened up the chamber with the keys, setting my meal, being an unlabeled can and a plastic spoon, down at my feet. She bent back up, crossing her arms and sighing.

"What?" I scoffed. "You gon' feed it to me?"

She rolled her eyes and exited the chamber, grabbing a stool and pulling it over. She sat herself down, staring at me.

"You're probably wondering why," she broke the silence, "I would be wondering why too."

She took a deep breath as if it was paining her to do this, like it was a hard decision to do. "But we all know how you are, and honestly, this decision was made for the *better*."

She bent down, picking up the mystery can and prying it open with a knife—*Aaron's* knife. She scooped up a spoonful, leaning closer to me with it. I spat in her face.

She violently shut her eyes, groaning softly in defeat. She set the meal down and wiped her face with her hands.

"Fine," she responded, "since you want to go that route, fine."

"I ain't hungry," I shook my head.

"Okay, Michelle, you can't do stuff like this and expect people not to treat you this way."

I remained silent, glaring up at her.

"Notice how every person you have a good relationship with doesn't actually *know* you," she raised her eyebrows. "Look at Aaron," she shrugged, speaking in a whisper, "once he realized who you really were, he left just like everyone else."

"You don't know *shit*," I muttered.

"He didn't like you because he knew once he did, he wasn't allowed to back out," she stated, shrugging. "He's in it forever."

"Once he goes down, he's never getting back up," her words sliced me. "You're *impossible*—to handle—*Mj*. You're *obsessive—possessive*——you suck people in, and you drain them."

No one wants to be around someone like that, she says.

"Look at how you ruined Jake's life," she said, which ignited that bomb in my head again. "Look at how you've—messed up mine—with this—*narrative*—of yours!"

I scoffed. "I don't say nothin' about you, and you know that."

"Don't lie," she replied. "People tell me what you say about me *all* the time."

"Boo-*fucking*-hoo, what do you want *me* to say to that?" I flared up. "I can't control what other people are saying, *dipshit!* It's not my problem if so-and-so wants to waltz up to you startin' shit?"

I inhaled sharply. This is just what she does. She talks her shit then cries when people confront her on it, and turns around and blames it all on me.

Oh, I only said this about her because I heard her say _____ about me!

GROW UP! GET A HOBBY! LEAVE ME *ALONE*!!!!!!!!!!!!!!!

"Y'know what Kim, I *know* how you are. I know how you *talk*," I responded, "and well, since it seems like you know a *shit ton* about me too, you should know if I were to actually say something, I'd say it directly to your face—"

"And Eliza, I guarantee if it was you going back to him, you'd fall to your knees within *seconds*," I scoffed, "and when he's done with you and leaves you in the dirt, you'd be fucking sobbing."

I sat back in my seat, copying her snarky shrug.

"Sorry I wasn't pathetic enough to fall for that shit. Sorry I wanted to have a *little* fun messing with him," I apologized. "If that—is what makes me *such* a bad person, then fuck it."

I'll be the bad guy in this narrative.

"You didn't have to spin him around in circles," she defended him. I quickly groaned once she did, honestly. It irritated me so much that her actions resemble the amount of self-respect she had for herself, which for clarification, was little-to-none.

"He was complaining about you and Scheuch for weeks."

"Bro, that's not my problem?" I scoffed. "Sorry I'd much rather hang out with someone who'd spend time explaining why monosaccharides form ring structures and the difference between an unsaturated and saturated triglyceride than a guy who'd try to convince me to skip school to hang out with him at his house," I snarked. "What did he want to do at his house, tell me? To play *fucking* monopoly on his living room floor? I'm not naive, bitch!"

She did that thing a lot of women used to do when I infuriated them, they would sit in place and shrivel a little bit, purse their lips before spitting out a not-that-well-thought-out comeback.

"At least I'm not naive enough to pretend I don't know what I'm talking about to make conversation!"

I laughed. "You're right, 'cause you don't have to pretend."

She scoffed.

I cackled even louder.

"Bitch, I *know* you didn't pass BioChem!" I grinned widely. "Come talk to me when your GPA's higher than a *2!*"

Bitches talk their shit, but they're not the one with a 4.0 and a varsity letter for Swimming!

Swim a 75 without getting tired! Yea, that's what I thought!

She slapped me. Hard. Hard enough to remind me that I can beat her down with my words as much as I wanted, but at the end of the day, I will be the one tied up, not her.

"We're *going* to go and fight them," she spoke through gritted teeth, "and whether you like it or not, you will not be participating."

We'll be back in four hours, she said.

If we don't make it back, she said, standing up from the stool, *then you know what happened.*

EPILOGUE

Hey.

                         Hello??? Get me out of these!

It's *me*. I *can't*.

                                       Oh. *Great*.

You doin' okay?

                Does it fucking look like I'm doing okay? Mj?

My bad.

...

What are you planning to do about this?

        I'm planning to punch that bitch in the mouth the second I'm unrestrained, that's what! And *fuck* Mickey and Brody! *For my own good*, my *ass!*

...

Would you still say this if they didn't come home tomorrow?

                    Oh shut up, if Kim died, I'd fucking celebrate.

You don't mean that.

                                                I do.

You don't mean that, Bui.
... I know why *I'm* so angry. Why are *you?*

                    Don't fuck with me. If you know why *you're* angry, you know why *I'm* angry.

...

I—I guess we——we spent so much time thinking we had nothing to lose... we've completely numbed to the words they call us.

I didn't care. *You* started to care.

Oh, don't say it like it's *my* fault! Don't act like you're happy living like this.

I'm getting tired of people calling me crazy, but I don't want someone to hold my damn face and tell me
it's not my fault
and
I do deserve better,
<u>I want to *believe* it.</u>

I think you should start off by letting me go then.

But Mj, you're a part of me.

I'm a ghost who haunts you.
Let me go, Bui.

I—I don't know how to—to *manage*.
I'm either *too angry* or not *angry enough*.

Okay, well, let's start off with this:
Why are you so angry?

I—um—I-

You're angry that you let them.
You're angry that the people who hurt you seem like

they got to live on with their *good 'ol lives* after ruining
the *hell* out of yours.
You're angry wondering how could they do that,
and *you* can't.
I get it.
I get that you feel guilt.
A lot of them are dead now, and you should just *'let 'em rest',*
y'know?

> They didn't let *me* rest? I owe 'em nothing!

Bui,
instead of sitting around and wallowing about it,
you need to realize life goes on.
You need to find your *own* fulfillment,
because if it's truly something that makes you happy,
nothing will *ever* be able to take that away.
...
I *would* tell you to enjoy the little things and look outside,
enjoy the fresh air and *beautiful trees*, but...

> Yeah.

So make your *own*. Make *yourself* happy.
You deserve it.

> I deserve what?

<u>To be forgiven.</u>
Now get your ass up, you got more than just roamers to fight.

CADET BUI:
I wish there was something left for us.
I wish the story could continue.
I wish I could say we made a plan to storm all the headquarters around the world,
and figure out how to clean up the mess we made,
but we didn't.
We didn't because they fell first.

TO BE CONTINUED.

Made in the USA
Middletown, DE
17 March 2024